> ## "I want you, Mr. Calhoun," she said, giving him the full force of her compelling gaze.

His groin tightened as the words echoed in his head. *I want you.* Lord, what he'd give to hear a woman like her saying such words with a more intimate meaning!

"And you'll be handsomely paid, I do assure you—with no backbreaking work."

"No, no backbreaking work," he agreed. "I could live real easy, bein' your bodyguard—and get killed with an easy bullet."

Her face paled. "Yes, there is a risk, as you saw this afternoon. But I don't want to die, either. Perhaps all it will take to discourage this *scoundrel* is the presence of a strong, intelligent man prepared to defend me."

"You don't know me," he told her, locking his gaze to hers. "You don't know anythin' about me, Duchess. Everythin' I've told you could be a lie!"

Dear Reader,

Next month, Harlequin Historicals® turns ten years old! But we have such a terrific lineup this month, we thought we'd start celebrating early. To begin, award-winning author Laurie Grant, who is known for her stirring Medievals and gritty Westerns, returns with a delightful new story, *The Duchess and the Desperado*. Here, a rancher turned fugitive inadvertently becomes a bodyguard to the very visible Duchess of Malvern when her life is threatened during a goodwill tour of the American West. Don't miss it!

In *The Shadowed Heart* by Nina Beaumont, set in eighteenth-century Europe, a beautiful young woman on a quest for vengeance unwittingly falls in love with the man she thinks may have harmed her sister…. Also out for revenge is Jesse Kincaid, of MONTANA MAVERICKS: RETURN TO WHITEHORN fame, when he kidnaps his enemy's mail-order bride in *Wild West Wife* by popular Silhouette® author Susan Mallery.

Rounding out the month is *A Warrior's Honor,* the next Medieval in Margaret Moore's popular WARRIOR SERIES. In this tale a knight is tricked by a fellow nobleman into abducting a beautiful lady, but, guided by honor—and love—seeks to rescue her from his former friend.

Whatever your tastes in reading, you'll be sure to find a romantic journey back to the past between the covers of a Harlequin Historical®.

Sincerely,

Tracy Farrell
Senior Editor

Please address questions and book requests to:
Harlequin Reader Service
U.S.: 3010 Walden Ave., P.O. Box 1325, Buffalo, NY 14269
Canadian: P.O. Box 609, Fort Erie, Ont. L2A 5X3

THE DUCHESS AND THE DESPERADO

Laurie Grant

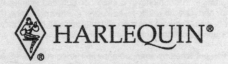

HARLEQUIN®

TORONTO • NEW YORK • LONDON
AMSTERDAM • PARIS • SYDNEY • HAMBURG
STOCKHOLM • ATHENS • TOKYO • MILAN • MADRID
PRAGUE • WARSAW • BUDAPEST • AUCKLAND

To Mary Jo Putney, for teaching me the joys of letters
patent, and, as always, to Michael.

ISBN 0-373-29021-7

THE DUCHESS AND THE DESPERADO

Books by Laurie Grant

Harlequin Historicals

Beloved Deceiver #170
The Raven and the Swan #205
Lord Liar #257
Devil's Dare #300
My Lady Midnight #340
Lawman #367
The Duchess and the Desperado #421

LAURIE GRANT

combines a career as a trauma center emergency room nurse with that of historical romance author; she says living in two worlds keeps her sane. Passionately enthusiastic about the history of both England and Texas, she divides her travel time between these two spots. She is married to her own real-life hero, and has two teenage daughters, two dogs and a cat.

If you would like to write to Laurie, please use the following address: Laurie Grant, P.O. Box 307272, Gahana, OH 43230.

ACKNOWLEDGMENT

I would like to thank the Denver Historical Society for
their invaluable assistance regarding the home of
Territorial Governor McCook and the hotels of the time.

Chapter One

Malvern Hall,
Herefordshire, England,
1872

"I wish you wouldn't go," Sarah heard her sister, Kathryn, mutter as she watched Sarah selecting dresses from her wardrobe and directing the maids in their packing.

Sarah Challoner, Duchess of Malvern, looked over her shoulder at Kathryn and was touched. She thought her younger sibling looked wistful. She smiled. "Going to miss me, are you, Kat?"

Kathryn made a *moue* of disgust. "Don't call me that. Thierry says it isn't dignified." She turned and gazed out the window that looked over the Malvern Hills in all their glory. "And yes, I *am* going to miss you. It sounds as if you'll be gone forever."

"I cannot call you Kat anymore?" Sarah said in mock dismay, struggling to hide her amusement. "But you have been my little sister Kat since you were born! Ah…yes, Tilly, I believe I will take the blue foulard," she said, pointing at a gown the maid held out for consideration.

"But not any longer, if you please," said Kat with stiff

dignity. "I shall be out next year, and Thierry says a nickname is not at all *comme il faut*," she added in an admirable French accent.

Sarah allowed herself to appear impressed. "I see. Well, if Thierry has decreed it, Kathryn it is, then." *Thierry says this, Thierry says that.* She suspected her sister, who at seventeen was barely out of the schoolroom, had a bad case of hero worship for the dashing French count who was secretly Sarah's fiancé. It probably wouldn't be going too far to say she was infatuated with Thierry de Châtellerault.

Ah, well. That's all right. She was just glad that Kathryn liked Thierry. It would be so awkward if her sister hated the man Sarah was going to marry. And it was perfectly normal for young girls to have these infatuations, after all. Sarah could remember a couple of her own—embarrassing, painful things they had been! Once she and Thierry returned from America as man and wife, though, Kathryn—*Kat*, she insisted to herself—would gradually learn to let go of her feelings and concentrate on finding her own special someone.

"Sure you wouldn't like to change your mind and come with me?" Sarah inquired of her sister, who still had her back to her. "Wouldn't you love to see America?"

"No," came the uncompromising reply. "I can't think *I* would enjoy racketing around the States in carriages and on trains, living out of suitcases for months on end! Besides," she said, lowering her voice so that the servants wouldn't hear, "once Thierry joins you in Santa Fe and you get married, I shouldn't like to be the gooseberry."

"Gooseberry?" Sarah repeated, mystified. Kathryn was forever picking up servants' cant.

Kathryn whirled around, her face sullen. "You know, the odd man out. I'd be superfluous."

Sarah suddenly understood. She let go of the gown she was examining and rushed toward her sister. "Nonsense, dear…"

"But of *course* I would," Kat cried. Her face was a study

in disdain, her posture rigid, saying as clearly as if she shouted it that Sarah was not to embrace her. "I can't think of anyone more useless on a honeymoon than one's younger sister."

Sarah stopped short and pushed her glasses back up on her nose. Perhaps she *had* been spending too much time with Thierry, and Kat was feeling left out. The girl's wounded feelings were almost palpable.

"But it isn't as though you'd be *alone* with just us, darling," she said, low-voiced. "Uncle Frederick is coming along, and Donald, and Celia.... Think of all the sights we'd see, going from New York to California to Texas. Just imagine, the Wild West!" If only she could infuse Kat with some of her enthusiasm!

Kat turned her back to Sarah once again. "Yes, but once you join Thierry, I can't imagine anything more boring than spending time with our uncle and your secretary and your dresser while you're off billing and cooing with *him*," Kat said, her voice thick, as if she were fighting tears. "I'm not going, and that's final. I just don't understand *why* you have to go, Sarah."

"If I were a man no one would question it," Sarah observed. "Why should I not get to take a Grand Tour just as if I were a man? I'm duchess in my own right, after all, and I want to do it."

"But men do their Grand Tour in Europe," her sister noted.

Now it was Sarah's turn to make a face. "We went to Paris with Papa, did we not, and on to Italy? The Continent doesn't interest me. No, I want to see *America*—especially the vast open spaces of the West, Kat—ah, Kathryn. It must be so exciting to live there—not like tidy old England, with its manicured lawns and ponds, and quaint little towns several hundred years old. I *need* to see that before I settle down as 'the duchess'—and as Thierry's wife, as wonderful as I know that will be," Sarah said. She willed Kat to face her, but Kat remained rigidly staring out the window. "And besides, it'll give me a little breathing room away from Her Majesty's incessant demand that I marry the boring Duke of Trenton, who'd be my equal in rank. Come, Kathryn, you must agree it's *delicious* to imagine Victoria fuming when I return home married to the Count of Châtellerault instead?"

Kathryn slowly turned to face her, her lips reluctantly curving upward. "Yes…I can just imagine the queen wringing those plump hands. All right, I suppose you will go no matter what *I* say. But tell me—are you going to wear your glasses when you're touring?"

Sarah breathed a sigh of relief that her efforts to mollify Kat had finally succeeded enough that she had turned to teasing. "Hmm…I suppose it depends if it's just us—Uncle Frederick, Donald, Celia and I. You know how vain I am about being seen in my spectacles."

Kat smirked. "I can just imagine—you'll come back and we'll ask what the most impressive sight was and you'll wave your hand and say 'I don't know. It was all just a blur.'"

Sarah didn't mind the sisterly taunt, for she'd always admitted vanity to be her worst failing.

"I'll see you at dinner, Sarah," Kat said, moving toward the door.

"All right, but where are you going in such a hurry?" Sarah asked, picking up the gown she'd discarded only moments ago. It wasn't her favorite, but it would be good for traveling.

"Oh, Thierry said he'd take me riding while you were busy packing," Kat murmured over her shoulder, her hand already on the door. "Since he won't be meeting you in New Mexico right away, he's rather at loose ends, too, you know."

Sarah smiled and bade her sister enjoy herself. It was good

of Thierry to keep Kat occupied, but perhaps she should speak to her fiancé later this evening and warn him that her younger sister had conceived a *tendre* for him. She knew she could count on Thierry to let Kat down easily.

Chapter Two

Denver
Colorado Territory
July 1872

"Oh, Celia, do look," Sarah breathed, gazing out the window as the train wheezed to a stop. She pointed at the distant Rocky Mountains, still snow tipped even though it was midsummer. The sight was enough to make Sarah forget the discomforts of the journey. "Are they not magnificent? Even the Peak District has nothing to compare with them!" She felt the headache that had plagued her all through the jolting, swaying ride slipping away.

"Yes, your grace," her dresser muttered, though she only glanced momentarily at the magnificent mountain range that stood sentinel over Denver. "We've been seein' them for the past two hours." She was nervously watching the motley throng on the station platform from the other side of their luxurious private railway car that had brought them all the way from St. Louis.

"But we can see them so much more clearly now. Just one moment, Celia, and I'll be ready to disembark," Sarah said, folding her spectacles and putting them safely away in her reticule. Not for the world would she have appeared among strangers wearing them. "Carry this, would you please, dear?" she said, handing her servant the reticule. No doubt she'd need her hands free for greeting those who came to welcome her.

The crowd gaped and pointed at the Duchess of Malvern and her entourage as they disembarked from the train at the Kansas Pacific Depot, but to Sarah, minus her spectacles, they were a buzzing blur.

"They're so rude, the way they stare. You'd think they'd never seen a duchess before," her dresser muttered to no one in particular.

Sarah chuckled, saying, "I'm sure they haven't, Celia. This is America, after all. They do not have duchesses here."

"Nor manners, your grace," her dresser retorted as one gawker came even closer and, after blowing his nose noisily on a dirty handkerchief, pointed at the Paris creation on the duchess's head.

"Oh, do stop grumbling, Celia, and take a breath of the fresh, bracing Western air—that should clear out the cobwebs!" Indeed, her own headache was fast diminishing, and she felt almost human again.

"I believe that is Pikes Peak in the distance, your grace," Donald Alconbury, her secretary, murmured in her ear, pointing at the high peak in the distance. "Indeed, the air is very clear here, or we should not be able to see it."

"Ah…beautiful…" she murmured, though of course Donald had forgotten she could not distinguish it from the others without her spectacles.

"I can't imagine where the welcoming committee must be," fretted Lord Halston. "I telegraphed the time of your arrival, and I was promised no less than the mayor and the territorial governor on hand to welcome you to Denver. But perhaps they await us inside the depot," he said, motioning toward the large, two-storied brick building behind them.

"Then go and fetch them, uncle," Sarah said serenely, turning and heading for the rear of the train. "I intend to see Trafalgar properly unloaded."

"But, your grace, your groom will see to that," her dresser fussed. "Come inside, do. Look, there's another of those noisy monsters pulling in, and it'll blow soot all over your clothing!"

The second train's whistle shrieked, splitting the air as it wheezed to a stop a little behind and on a track parallel to the one that had just brought the duchess and her party from St. Louis. Just as Celia had predicted, the locomotive's huge smokestack belched a cloud of smoke.

Sarah paid no heed to the down-drifting particles of soot, however. The train had almost immediately begun disgorging its human contents, and as she passed the open space between one car and another, her attention was caught by a particular passenger who was just stepping down from the other train onto the ground.

With just a few yards between them, she could see him well enough. He was tall and lean and wore a wide-brimmed hat, denim trousers, boots and duster coat. A saddle was slung over one shoulder; he carried a pair of saddlebags in the other hand. His hair was a shade of brown so dark it could pass for black except in bright sunlight, and he needed both a haircut and a shave. He might be handsome once properly groomed—though very different from Thierry, of course— but at present he just looked dangerous, Sarah decided, watching as he narrowed his eyes in the direction of the station house, then started striding toward the rear of the train he had just left.

A sudden wind blew the side of his unbuttoned duster backward, exposing a pistol riding in a holster on his hip. The presence of the pistol confirmed the air of danger he carried with him. A desperado, thought Sarah, remembering the lurid covers of the cheap novels she'd seen on sale not only in

America but in London, too. Perhaps he was an outlaw! But no, surely outlaws did not travel on trains like normal, law-abiding folk. He was probably just an ordinary cowboy, she told herself. Standards of grooming were not the same here as at home. But she was not convinced.

As if aware that he was being watched, however, he paused and looked between the two cars, right at her. Sarah was close enough to see a pair of green eyes studying her from the top of her modish hat to the tips of her buttoned kid boots.

He must have approved of what he saw, for a slow smile spread over his beard-shadowed, lean face and warmed the green of his eyes. He let the band of leather that connected the two saddlebags slide back on his forearm, which enabled him to touch the brim of his hat in a manner of greeting. Then he resumed walking and was lost to her sight.

Sarah felt heat rising up past the pleated edge of her cloak. She'd been looking at him—staring, in fact—and the cowboy had caught her at it and stared right back! Why, his grin had been cheekier than a Cockney beggar's!

She'd been stared at before, especially since coming to the United States, but somehow his bold, direct gaze had affected her differently. For the life of her, though, she could not say why she found his look energizing rather than merely annoying.

In any case, Sarah reminded herself sternly, she must not waste time gaping at the locals. She needed to ensure the safety of her mare. Walking down to the front of the car that she knew held Trafalgar, she was in time to see the door slide back and her groom emerge, bending to extend the wooden ramp down onto the ground.

"Ben! How did she weather the journey?" Sarah called out.

"Well enough, your grace, though she didn't fancy that other train pulling in next to this one," Ben Huddleston, her wiry old groom, informed her. "Been tossin' and plungin' about these last few minutes, she has."

Sarah could hear the thudding of hooves as Trafalgar protested against the boxcar's walls. "Well, bring her out. She'll settle down once she gets out of confinement, I'm certain."

Ben doffed the tweed cap he was never without. "Yes, your grace." He disappeared back into the depths of the boxcar, and Sarah could hear the groom speaking soothingly to the high-spirited thoroughbred, and the mare's snorting, stamping retort.

Sarah smiled. Trafalgar had always been a fractious traveler, and the groom's advice had been to leave the hunter at home in Herefordshire. "The sea voyage alone will shatter her nerves, Duchess, not to mention all the roamin' around that barbarous country. Why not breed her, your grace? By the time you come home, the foal could be weaned and you'll be back chasin' the fox on your mare again."

"Are you more worried about the mare's nerves or yours, Ben?" she had teased him. "I wouldn't think it fair to impose on Trafalgar the very thing I'm trying to escape myself," she had added lightly, and laughed as the implication of her last remark had brought a blush to Ben's cheeks. "Well, it's true. My uncle is pressuring me to marry and so is the queen, but having just reached my majority, I can't imagine why I should settle down meekly and marry whoever the queen thinks suitable for me! I want my favorite mare with me, and so she shall come. She'll do fine, you'll see."

What the Duchess of Malvern wanted, she got, and the tall bay thoroughbred had been brought along. If anyone's nerves had been shattered in the course of the ocean voyage and the "roamin' around" the United States of America, it had been Ben's, not Trafalgar's.

As she waited for her mare, Sarah glanced down the track, but she could no longer see the dangerous-looking American. Too bad, she thought wryly. He had probably never seen such a fine horse as Trafalgar in his life, and she had imagined his eyes widening as he glimpsed her with her handsome hunter. She had been sure he would be impressed.

C'est la guerre, as Thierry would have said. Why did she feel any need to impress such a man, anyway? She was the Duchess of Malvern, and she had the world at her feet. Once she was reunited with her dashing Thierry, she would indeed have everything!

Then, plunging, whinnying and trying to rear, Trafalgar was led down the wooden ramp by Ben, who had blindfolded the horse. Even so, he had his hands full making sure the mare neither careened off the side of the ramp nor did him an injury, and Sarah rushed forward, heedless of the groom's protestations that she'd get her traveling costume dirty.

"I don't know why you bother blindfolding her, Ben," she chided as she whipped the dark cloth from underneath the bay's halter and took the lead rope from her groom. "She's not a whit easier to handle—easy there, girl! Easy... See, you're out of that nasty boxcar and onto solid ground, and I'll see that you rest in a big loose stall tonight with plenty of grain to eat...." It never mattered what she said, only that she kept talking to the skittish thoroughbred.

But this time, even her soothing voice didn't seem to be working its usual magic.

Just then a shot rang out from somewhere in the milling throng on the station platform, a shot that whistled right over Sarah's head and embedded itself in the wood of the boxcar. The mare went wild with terror, rearing and nearly yanking Sarah's arm out of its socket. The screams and shouts of the crowd blended with the frightened whinnying of the thoroughbred as it plunged and kicked. Then, as Sarah struggled to keep hold of the lead rope, another shot rang out, kicking up the dust right in front of the toe of her right boot. The surprise of the second shot made Sarah loosen her grip on the rope—only for a second, but it was enough. Trafalgar gave a mighty toss of her head, yanking the rope out of Sarah's hand, wheeled and went galloping down the tracks, with Ben in hot pursuit.

A weight hit Sarah from behind, knocking her flat a heart-beat before a third shot whistled by her. She heard the wood of the boxcar splinter with the impact of the third bullet. For a fleeting moment she had the ridiculous notion that one of the mountains had somehow moved and fallen on her…and then a voice drawled, "Lady, don't you have the sense to hit the dirt or take cover when you're bein' shot at?" and she realized that it was the dangerous-looking American who had tackled her and knocked her into the dirt, covering her with his body.

Sarah thrashed beneath him, trying to free herself. "How dare you? Get off me, sir!" she demanded. "My mare—I have to catch my mare!" Out of the corner of her eye she could see a blur of movement. People were fleeing the station platform in panicked droves, while others had likewise flat-tened themselves on the ground.

"Forget your mare for the time bein', lady!" he ordered, dragging her to her feet with one hand, holding his drawn pistol with the other. "We're going to take cover until we're certain the shootin's stopped." He pulled her along with him until they had reached the other side of the boxcar.

"Stay there," he said, flattening her against the side of the car with his forearm while he inched around to where he could see the station platform again.

"But I have to see that—"

"*Stay there,*" he ordered over his shoulder. Then, after a silent minute of scanning the crowd, he said, without looking back at her, "Everyone's runnin' to and fro like chickens with their heads cut off. I couldn't see where the shots came from, and now I don't see anyone with a gun." He turned back to her. "Why would anyone want to shoot at you, lady? Who are you?"

She heard Alconbury and Lord Halston calling her, but ignored their cries for the moment. "You think someone was shooting at *me?*" she asked incredulously. "My good man, I hardly think anyone would have a reason to shoot at *me*. I'm but newly arrived in your city, a British subject—" Standing just inches from him, she had no difficulty seeing him clearly, and she saw him raise an eyebrow.

"There's folks that'd argue about my goodness," he drawled, his green eyes mocking. "I *thought* you didn't sound American. So who are you, and what're you doing in Colorado Territory, and why is someone shooting at you?"

She resented his interrogation. "I'm not accustomed to introducing myself to a stranger, sir."

The green eyes narrowed. "I just saved your life, and you want to stand on ceremony?"

She realized he might well be right. "I'm sorry. I'm afraid that being frightened makes me a trifle cross. I spoke more sharply than I intended," Sarah apologized. "I think you did save my life, and I'm very grateful. My secretary will see that you're suitably rewarded, Mr.—"

He hesitated for a moment, then growled, "Morgan Calhoun, and there's no need to be talkin' about any reward. It was just the right thing to do." His expression softened somewhat. "I reckon you're entitled to feel a mite cross at bein' shot at, too. Most females would have had hysterics. Oh, and I'm sorry about dirtyin' your fine clothes, ma'am...."

Sarah managed a tremulous smile. "No apologies are necessary on that score, certainly. I'd rather be a bit soiled and alive than an immaculate corpse."

Morgan Calhoun grinned at that, but still seemed to be waiting for something, and after a moment she realized what it was.

"Oh! How remiss of me! My name is Sarah Challoner," she said, and was about to add her title when Donald Alconbury, Lord Halston and Celia ran panting around the side of the boxcar.

"Your grace! Are you…all right? Were you wounded?" demanded her secretary.

"Who is this ruffian?" Lord Halston asked, pointing at Calhoun. "Unhand the Duchess of Malvern immediately, fellow!"

Morgan Calhoun stared at Sarah. "A duchess? You're a *duchess?*"

She nodded. "The Duchess of Malvern, actually. Yes, Donald, don't worry, I'm quite all right, thanks to Mr. Calhoun, here."

Morgan looked back at Lord Halston, then down at his own hands, one of which still held his drawn pistol; the other held nothing. "I don't reckon I need to 'unhand' what I'm not touchin' at the moment, *fellow,*" he retorted, holstering the pistol. "Who's he?" he asked Sarah, indicating the indignant Lord Halston with a nod of his head.

"Lord Halston, may I present Morgan Calhoun," Sarah said. "Mr. Calhoun, my uncle, Lord Halston. Please stop glaring at Mr. Calhoun, uncle—instead, he deserves our thanks. Had he not thrown me to the ground, that last shot might well have put a period to my existence. And who was shooting at me, anyway?"

Frederick, Lord Halston, muttered something that may have been an apology, then said, "None of these incompetent idiots seems to have a clue who fired the shots, though one woman said they seemed to be coming from one of the upper-story windows in the station, and the train officials went up to check. I think we should make arrangements to leave immediately, your grace. Obviously someone in this barbaric settlement—" he wrinkled his nose as he looked around "—means you harm."

Sarah ignored his suggestion. She pointed down the track,

where her groom led her trembling bay mare. "Oh, good, Ben's caught her. Bravo, Ben!" she called.

"Duchess, I don't know what in thunder you're doin' here, but Lord Whatsis may have a good idea about leavin'," interjected Morgan Calhoun. "Somebody's obviously taken exception to your arrival."

Sarah heard Halston's growl of indignation at the ridiculous name, then she turned back to the American. "Nonsense. We've only just arrived, and I have no intention of getting back on a smelly, noisy, dirty train—or any other form of conveyance. I'm here on a goodwill tour on behalf of Her Majesty the queen, you see, and people are expecting me. Departure today is out of the question."

"But Duchess, someone hasn't got any goodwill for you," Morgan Calhoun noted with maddening persistence. "Surely there's plenty of other cities you could spread that goodwill in."

"Perhaps your rescuer is right, your grace," Donald Alconbury murmured.

"Nonsense, we're made of sterner stuff than that, are we not?" Sarah said. "I have no idea why someone seemed to be shooting at me, unless the person mistook me for someone else? Yes, surely that's it."

She saw Alconbury and Lord Halston exchange a look, as if they knew something more, and was about to challenge them about it when Calhoun spoke up again.

"I don't reckon so, Duchess. You don't look like anyone else in these parts," Calhoun argued, with a meaningful glance at the more humbly dressed women on the station platform.

As she looked in the direction he had nodded, she saw several well-dressed men threading their way through the milling, pointing crowd toward them.

"I believe the welcoming committee's finally caught up with us at last," she murmured.

A tall, thin, worried-looking man with a mustache and a bearded chin, dressed in a frock coat and carrying a stovepipe hat, led the quartet that charged down onto the tracks and threaded their way between the boxcars to reach them.

"The Duchess of Malvern, I presume?" At Sarah's nod, he said, "Your ladyship, I'm terribly sorry to be late, and sorrier still when I was informed of what just befell you. I'm John Harper, the mayor of Denver." There were beads of sweat visible on his balding forehead when he bowed.

Sarah heard Lord Halston clear his throat, and swiftly darted a quelling look at him, guessing he was about to inform the mayor of Denver that a duchess was properly addressed as "your grace," never "your ladyship." Americans had no knowledge of how to address the peerage, and there was nothing to be gained by pompously shaming them in public.

"Mr. Harper, I'm pleased to make your acquaintance," she said, offering her hand. He hesitated, as if he did not know what to do with it, then shook it instead of kissing it. Sarah hid a smile. "It was a rather startling welcome, but I am convinced it was a case of mistaken identity, and so we shall forget it."

She didn't miss Harper's gusty sigh of relief, as if he had feared to be held responsible. "Yes, obviously no one could wish to shoot at *you*, ma'am. It must have been a mistake. But we shall take every precaution for your safety while in our fair city."

Sarah bestowed a deliberately dazzling smile on the mayor, aware that Morgan Calhoun watched her curiously. "I am so pleased to include Denver on my tour of America. Your scenery is magnificent, sir."

Harper beamed, as if the mountain range behind them was due to his own hard work. "Thank you, Duchess," he said, then belatedly remembered to release her hand. "I'm sorry to be a few minutes late in meeting your train. The press of duties, I'm afraid. Governor McCook sends his regrets, too, but of course he will have the opportunity to apologize in person at the reception supper tonight at his residence. I'll be there, too, of course, and you must make me aware of your slightest need. Denver doesn't have a real British duchess visiting every day, you know," he finished enthusiastically.

"I will look forward to it," she said, struggling to look regal rather than amused.

"In the meantime, her grace is tired from the journey, of course," interjected Lord Halston in his officious way. "Has transportation to her hotel been arranged?"

"Of course. Just this way to the carriage, ma'am, and you can tie your horse to the back. She's a high-spirited thing, isn't she? And there's a wagon to follow behind with your luggage and that of your party—"

"Yes, but just one minute, before we leave," she said, and turned back to Morgan Calhoun. "Mr. Calhoun, I'm in your debt. Would you be so kind as to call upon me this afternoon at five for tea? Lord Halston will have your reward ready for you then. Uncle, where is it we are lodging?"

"We have a suite of rooms at the Grand Central Hotel, your grace, but I don't think—" began Lord Halston even as Calhoun was protesting, "There's no need for any reward, Duchess—"

"Well, we can discuss it when you come, can we not?" Sarah interrupted, giving Calhoun her brightest smile. "Please come, Mr. Calhoun, won't you? I'd very much like to thank you properly."

Calhoun's face was a study in indecision. "Well, ma'am, I don't thi—"

"I mustn't keep them waiting longer," she said, nodding toward her party. "At five, then, Mr. Calhoun?" Without waiting to see if he nodded or shook his head, she turned and walked in the direction of the waiting carriage.

Chapter Three

"Why on earth would you encourage such a ruffian, niece?" Lord Halston said, once the carriage conveying Sarah, her secretary, her dresser and himself had pulled away from the station. "Why, for all we know, he could be in league with the sniper."

"What an absurd thing to say, uncle. If that were so, he could have killed me behind the boxcar, couldn't he?"

Sarah frowned, but it didn't discourage Lord Halston. "You heard the man," he said. "He didn't think there was any need for a reward, and I quite agree. He was just doing the decent thing—and rather too enthusiastically, if you ask me. It wasn't at all necessary to throw you to the ground, in my opinion. Your dress will never be the same again. And Sarah," he added, forgetting the presence of her secretary and dresser as he addressed her with the familiarity of a relation, "it's not at all the thing to have such a man calling on you, as if you owed him anything more than the thanks you already gave him...."

Once he began fuming, Uncle Frederick could go on and on like a clockwork toy that refused to wind down. Sarah held up a hand. "Uncle, do stop. I'm getting a headache all over again! And I do not agree—I think saving a life requires much more than a civil thank-you,'' she told him as she gazed out the window at the mostly brick buildings of the young city. She'd read of a fire several years ago that had destroyed much of the town, causing Denverites to use brick when they rebuilt. The streets, however, were still dirt.

"He said he wouldn't take any money," Lord Halston persisted.

"Perhaps we shall persuade him to change his mind, uncle," Sarah said, proud that she sounded serene and unruffled. "But if we do not, we shall at least treat him to an excellent meal. It looks as if it's been a good while since he's had one."

She could not have said why it was so important that she see the American with the drawling voice, mocking green eyes and that air of danger that he carried about him like an all-enveloping cloak, she only knew that it *was* important to her that she see him again, and this time in safe, secure surroundings. She wanted him to see her with the grime of travel bathed away, dressed in one of her prettiest tea gowns—perhaps the dusky rose one.

He might not come, of course—her impulsive invitation had caused Morgan Calhoun to look as startled as one of those wild American mustangs they'd seen running across the plains when the train whistle had startled the herd. He might be intimidated by her obvious wealth and decide he had no clothes fit to wear to take tea with a duchess. Wary, he might figure that the only way to refuse taking money from her was never to see her again. And if he chose not to come, there would be nothing she could do about it. She would never encounter him again.

It shouldn't matter, of course. Thierry would be waiting for her at the prearranged city at the end of her tour, and though her uncle and the rest of her party didn't know it now, she would be returning home a married woman—married to the man of her choice, not the stuffy-but-eligible Duke of Trenton the queen had deemed suitable for her.

What a handsome couple they would make, she and her Thierry, the dashing Comte de Châtellerault. But even Thierry, who had a Gallic tendency to jealousy, could not be upset that she wished to reward a valiant man who had saved her life, could he?

"You don't seem inclined to take your near-assassination very seriously, either," Lord Halston went on in an aggrieved tone. "Good heavens, three *shots* were fired and yet the dreamy-eyed expression on your face would lead one to believe you were picturing a beau!"

His continued ranting, just when she wanted to plan what she would say if Morgan Calhoun did come to tea, made Sarah irritable. "What would you have me do, my lord— weep and wring my handkerchief?" she demanded. "I have said I thought the whole matter a mistake and would forget it, and so I shall. Please have the goodness not to bring up the matter again."

"As your grace wishes," Lord Halston said heavily. "We have arrived, Donald. Please go on in and announce her grace and her party."

"Your grace, Mr....uh...Calhoun has arrived," the somberly dressed woman called from the anteroom, all the while eyeing Morgan suspiciously. After returning her stare with a cool one of his own, he went back to studying the elegant wallpaper and paneling of the anteroom and its paintings of Western mountain scenes. A vase by the door held pink roses that had to have been grown in a hothouse. Compared to the Mountain View Boardinghouse, where he was staying just long enough to gather his provisions before heading up into the mountains, the Grand Central Hotel was a palace. And a duchess was practically a princess, wasn't she? What did that make him—the dragon?

"Show him in, Celia," came the musical, aristocratic voice.

For the hundredth time since he'd seen the duchess ride off in her carriage, Morgan wondered just why he'd obeyed the summons to tea.

He had no intention of taking any money for what he'd done this afternoon. Protecting a helpless woman when there were bullets flying in her direction had been no more or less than the right thing to do, and he would have done the same thing if she'd been homely and dressed in the simplest calico. But telling her his real name, when that name and his likeness were on Wanted posters all over the West, was probably the greatest piece of idiocy he'd committed in the past few years. He should have given his name as Jake Faulkner, or one of the many other aliases he'd used since he'd been on the run.

And coming here simply because she'd asked him to, when he had no intention of taking any reward money from her, was even more stupid. He should be out buying a pack mule and the beans, bacon, salt, flour, sugar and coffee that he'd need to go up into the mountains, not taking tea with a foreign duchess who was so perfectly beautiful she might have been a princess from a fairy tale.

His thoughts made him angry at himself, and so he was edgy and nervous as he followed the woman—what did they call them, ladies-in-waiting?—into the sitting room.

There were more flowers in vases around the room, but he paid little attention to them, for he saw the duchess arising, smiling, from a velvet-upholstered carved-back chair. "Ah, there you are, Mr. Calhoun. It was good of you to come."

She was dressed in a gown that was the same pink as the roses. There was pleated lace in the V-shaped neckline, which matched the lace at her waist. Her golden hair was once again artfully arranged in a coil at the nape of her neck, as it had been before he had knocked her to the ground and disarranged it. But it was her eyes that held his attention, just as when he had first seen her. Then, as now, he was reminded of the vivid blue of a Texas sky on a sunlit spring day.

He caught sight of the grumpy-looking fellow she'd introduced as Lord Halston hovering unhappily behind her chair, looking even more unhappy as his eyes met Morgan's. Morgan saw a disdainful expression creep across Lord Halston's face as he stared at the clean denims and the white shirt Morgan had paid the widow who ran the boardinghouse an extra two bits to press for him. He stared right back until Lord Halston reddened and looked away.

"Hello, Miss—Duchess," he said, feeling more awkward than he ever had in his life. "I'm sorry, I don't know what to call you...and I reckon these aren't goin'-to-tea duds, but I didn't exactly come to Denver prepared to—"

"No apologies are necessary, Mr. Calhoun," the duchess interrupted, extending her hand but not enlightening him as to how to address her. "The pleasure of your company is quite sufficient."

He had the feeling he was supposed to do something with that hand besides shake it. Once he'd seen a European fellow kiss a lady's hand, but he couldn't imagine *he* was supposed to take such a liberty with a duchess. So he just took it in his, savoring its satin-smooth texture. He could just feel the slight tremor in it. So she was nervous, too, he realized. *How much more nervous would she be if she knew I was a wanted man?*

Lord Halston stepped forward as Morgan reluctantly let her hand go. "Her grace has asked me to prepare a reward for your—ahem!—heroic actions this afternoon," he said, looking as if every word pained him.

Morgan saw that he was carrying a small leather pouch that looked as if it were heavily weighted with coins.

"Go ahead, take it," Lord Halston urged, glaring at him. "You'll find it's a substantial amount in gold." His expression told Morgan he hoped he would depart as soon as he'd accepted the bag.

Morgan's eyes cut back to the duchess. "Ma'am, I told you this afternoon I wasn't going to accept any money, and I'm not. You keep your money…though I thank you for offering it," he added belatedly, when his words echoed back too belligerently at him.

Lord Halston appeared relieved, then he and the duchess exchanged a look.

"Are you sure, Mr. Calhoun?" Sarah Challoner inquired in her lovely, well-modulated voice. "Surely you could use it in whatever endeavor you intend to pursue in Colorado Territory?"

Actually, he could—the supplies he had to buy would take most if not all of the money that remained from his last poker winnings—and not taking it was the third stupid thing he'd done today. But he knew he just wouldn't feel right taking money for what he'd done.

"There, you see, uncle? It's just as you said, he won't take it," said the duchess, turning back to her uncle. "So you can now relax. Perhaps you have correspondence to take care of? In that case you must feel free to excuse yourself. Celia will attend me," she said.

Morgan had to admire how neatly she'd gotten rid of the sour old windbag—and against his will, too, he saw with amusement as her uncle struggled to hide his dismay.

"Just as you say, your grace," he said, giving a stiff little bow in her direction. "Mr. Calhoun, I'll bid you good day," he said. The words were civil, the tone hostile.

"Mr. Calhoun, won't you come and sit down?" the duchess said, going over to a low table between two chairs to Morgan's right. He had not even noticed it when he came into the room, for he had been intent on her.

In the center of the table, set on a silver tray, was a great silver teapot, several delicate china cups and a few small plates. Surrounding them lay dishes covered with more food than he'd seen since the war.

"I—I thought you asked me to *tea*, duchess?" he said, certain that he must have misunderstood. "This—this looks like supper to me."

She gave a high, silvery laugh that reminded him of the music of water dancing over stones in a hill country stream. She sat down and indicated he should take the other chair. "Oh, no, Mr. Calhoun, it's merely tea—or high tea, as we should properly call it back home in England—simply something to carry one through until dinner later on. We had some ado to get the hotel cook to make us watercress and cucumber sandwiches, and Celia was only able to get biscuits, jelly and butter rather than scones and crumpets, but I think you'll find the little cakes are quite good. I must confess I nibbled on one while I awaited your arrival."

Her mischievous smile as she admitted the last fact made her suddenly less an aristocrat, more approachable. For a heartbeat he caught a glimpse of what she must have looked like as a young girl. She must have been a handful even then, he decided as he lowered himself carefully into the other chair.

"Shall I pour, your grace?" the female servant inquired, approaching.

"No, Celia, I'll do it, but come and get something to eat. You must be hungry," the duchess said. "Celia, I do not believe you have been properly introduced to Mr. Calhoun. Celia Harris, may I present Mr. Morgan Calhoun? Celia is my dresser," the duchess informed him. "I should be quite lost without her."

The woman's face lost some of its severity. "Thank you, your grace." As the duchess poured a cup of tea, and poured in some cream, Celia came forward and carefully placed a watercress sandwich, a biscuit, a blob of jelly and one of the sugary cakes on her plate. Then, after taking the cup of tea her mistress proffered, she carried her plate and cup over to a chair against the wall and took up a position where it would be easy to keep an eye on Morgan.

Morgan forgot about the servant, hypnotized by the effortless, graceful movements of the duchess's fingers and slender wrists as she poured the steaming tea into the cup without spilling a drop.

"Mr. Calhoun, do you take sugar? Cream?" Her hand, holding a small pair of tongs, was poised over the sugar bowl.

He hadn't tasted tea since courting the banker's daughter when he'd been seventeen. Coffee and whiskey were what he was used to, and the latter only when he had money, and when he was somewhere where he could afford to let his guard down.

"I...I like a lot of sugar, ma'am. No cream." He saw her smile, then watched as she dropped three lumps of sugar into the tea she had poured for him, then handed the cup and saucer to him.

The fragrant aroma of the tea rose around his head, mingled with the scent of roses that seemed to surround her. He took a sip—and promptly burned his tongue. The spoon clattered against the cup and saucer as he hurriedly set the teacup down.

"Oh, I quite forgot to warn you how hot it was," the duchess apologized. "Celia—perhaps a glass of water for Mr. Calhoun?"

Celia's glare as she rose to obey her mistress's request told him she thought him a graceless idiot. He certainly felt like one, but the duchess didn't seem to notice.

"Won't you have something, Mr. Calhoun?" she invited as she put a pair of the impossibly delicate sandwiches on her own plate. "Or perhaps you're not hungry?"

At the moment he would have eaten sawdust if she suggested it. "Yes, ma'am, I am." He picked out a biscuit and gingerly spread some jelly on it, feeling clumsy as he handled the fine china and silverware.

"Well, now—what brings you to Colorado, Mr. Calhoun?"

He stared down at the dark red jelly for what seemed like an eternity. How could he tell her he'd come here to hide out from those who hunted him? How could he make an English noblewoman understand about coming home to Texas after the South had been defeated in the War Between the States, and finding his ranch taken over by some scalawag in the favor of the Federal troops? He'd run the fellow off, of course, but then the whispers had started: *He rode with Mosby's Rangers, you know. He's nothing better than a bandit and a hired killer.* For four years he'd been blamed each time a horse was stolen, each time some cattle were rustled, and though he'd managed to prove his innocence, people began to suspect that where there was smoke, there might be fire. They began to shun him. Finally, three years ago, he'd been falsely accused of holding up the stage that brought the troops' payroll.

Morgan had been pleasantly occupied with a woman that night. But when he'd heard about the robbery, and that he'd been accused of it, he'd known she wasn't the sort of woman who'd disgrace herself by providing him an alibi. Morgan had seen the handwriting on the wall, and he hadn't waited around for a trial. He knew there was no such thing as a fair trial in Federally occupied Texas for a man who'd ridden with Mosby's Rangers.

He'd lit out for New Mexico, and changed his name, and got a job as foreman for a rancher there. That had worked for a while, until someone recognized his face from a Wanted poster in town. He'd headed to Mexico, and stayed till he thought it was safe, then drifted on up to Arizona Territory. He'd taken another name and signed up as wrangler on a ranch. He was there a year until someone recognized him, and he'd had to flee again.

There was to be no starting over for him, it seemed. He hit the trail, living by his wits, surviving on what he could win at cards and occasionally by what he could steal—but only from scoundrels or rich Yankees who could well afford to lose what he took.

He'd been on the run now for three long years, and he was tired of being hunted, his name and likeness on Wanted posters all over the West. He'd decided to go up into the mountains, grow a beard to disguise his features, and prospect. He'd be relatively safe from pursuit in the isolation of the mountains—the mining camps were wild and lawless and the miners had their own shadowy pasts to worry about. Maybe he'd strike it rich and have enough money to hire the best lawyer from the East to go back and clear his name—or maybe he'd just take his money, go down to Mexico and set up a rancho where he could raise horses and live like a king.

"Are you...are you perhaps a rancher, Mr. Calhoun?" the duchess inquired, reminding him that he'd never answered her question.

He felt himself color with embarrassment. "I—I'm sorry, ma'am! I—no, I'm not a rancher. I'm...thinkin' of goin' up into the mountains and minin'."

"Oh! I know nothing about such things, of course, but I thought you had more the look of...of a cowboy," Sarah Challoner told him.

"I was a rancher...before the war," he admitted. "I had a nice spread." A stabbing pain pierced his heart to have to say *had*. *Damn the Yankees and the scalawags who sucked up to them.*

"And where do you come from, Mr. Calhoun?" she continued, her probing gentle. "I'm just learning about all the different accents you have here in this country, but you sound...ah...Southern?"

"Texas, ma'am."

"Yes, I thought so," she said, looking pleased with herself.

He was afraid she'd ask for more detail, and then he'd have to commence lying to her. Somehow he didn't like the idea of telling a lie to this lady whose clear blue eyes studied him so candidly. Perhaps if he distracted her by asking a few questions of his own, it wouldn't be necessary.

"Ma'am, may I ask you a question?"

She looked amused. "Of course, Mr. Calhoun."

"If you're a duchess, are you...I mean, is there...is there a duke?" The question sounded foolish the minute he asked it. "I'm sorry, I guess that's gettin' a little too nosy," he said quickly, after she began to chuckle.

"No, no, not at all, Mr. Calhoun," she said, startling him by leaning forward and laying a hand on his wrist to stop his apology. "Actually, it's quite an intelligent question, for in answering it I am allowed to boast of my own uniqueness. You see, in England a title usually does pass only to a male relative, or falls into abeyance, as it's called, if there isn't one."

She took a breath, and he helped himself to some of the delicate little sandwiches. They were surprisingly delicious, though nothing he'd want to rely upon to keep his stomach from growling on the trail.

"But in the case of the Duchy of Malvern," she went on, "I was quite fortunate in that the original Duke of Malvern, back in the days of Queen Elizabeth, was, for a short time, in the same position as was my own father—a widower with no sons, only daughters, and he didn't like the thought of his brother succeeding to the title. He was able to have the letters patent drawn up so that he could pass the title to his eldest daughter, should there be no direct male issue. But he did remarry, late in life, and sired a son who succeeded him, but the details in the letters patent remained the same, and thus I am the first Duchess of Malvern who is duchess in her own right, and not merely because her husband is a duke. Do you understand?''

He nodded. ''So what you're sayin' is you're one of a kind, ma'am. I guess you could rightly be proud of that.''

She smiled becomingly. ''I *am*, dreadfully so, though it makes for all sorts of difficulties. My peers back at home don't know what to make of me. They think—and Queen Victoria agrees—that the best solution is to have me safely married off.''

''And you don't want to marry?'' he asked, surprised. He thought all women wanted to be wives, even wealthy ladies like this one.

A faint flush of color came and went in her cheeks. So there is someone, he thought, annoyed at himself for finding the idea disappointing.

She waved a hand airily. ''Oh, someday, of course,'' she said. ''But I don't want to wed the Duke of Trenton, the only eligible bachelor whose rank is equal to mine. He's a stuffy fool, and I quite detest him, but he's the man the queen has been pressuring me to wed. It's either that or marry some foreign noble or princeling and have to live somewhere other than England part of the year.''

''And you don't want to do that.''

''No, not really. I love Malvern, my estate, and my horses—and of course there's my younger sister, Kat—Kathryn, who will come out next year. I shouldn't want to be constantly leaving them.''

He hadn't the faintest idea what ''come out'' meant, but he wasn't sure it mattered. ''This uncle of yours,'' he said, nodding toward the closed door Lord Halston had disappeared behind, ''he doesn't mind that you've got the title? He doesn't wish that it'd gone to him?''

She looked amused again, and clapped her hand over her mouth as if to smother a very unduchesslike giggle. ''Oh, actually he does, tremendously, but what can he do?'' she asked in a lowered voice. "He can't change the way the letters patent were written. But he is a marquess, and that's just below me in rank, so he's not *too* deprived." She laughed again. "Mr. Calhoun, I find myself telling you the most shameless things...."

He was just about to promise he wouldn't breathe a word to anyone, thank her for inviting him and begin to take his leave, when he heard the door open from the corridor, and the balding, stoop-shouldered younger man Morgan had seen among the duchess's party at the train station burst into the room.

He was panting and red in the face. "Your grace! Oh, I— I didn't know you were receiving, please pardon me! Th-there was a message left for you—"

"Donald, you're all out of breath!" Sarah Challoner observed. "What is it you're so alarmed about?"

"This, your grace!" he said, handing the duchess a folded piece of paper with her name on the back in bold block letters. "The desk clerk said it had been left for you when he'd stepped away from the desk for a moment, so he didn't see who left it...."

The duchess took the paper, unfolded it, and as she scanned the message, Morgan saw the blood drain from her face. Her hand shook and a moment later she dropped the piece of paper on the thick Turkey carpet.

"Ma'am?"

The duchess was staring straight ahead of her, her eyes wide and unseeing. She looked as if she might pass out in the next moment.

"Ma'am?" Morgan repeated, uncertain as to what to do. His eyes sought Celia, but the servant was already at her mistress's side, bringing a bottle of hartshorn out of her skirt pocket.

Shuddering, the duchess turned around, waving the hartshorn and the hovering servant away.

Finally Morgan just leaned over and picked the paper up from the carpet. He read the crude block letters: "PREPEAR TO DIE IF YEW DONT LEAVE NOW DUCHISS. YERS TROOLY, A PATRIOTT."

Chapter Four

"Do you have any idea who might have written this?" Morgan asked in the direction of the duchess's rigid back.

Lord Halston came bustling back into the room from the adjoining one into which he'd been banished. "I demand to know what all the commotion was about! What have you done?" His eyes shot pale blue daggers at Morgan.

The duchess, ignoring her uncle, looked over her shoulder at Morgan, her face tight and set. "No, of course I don't know," she said to Morgan.

Morgan held out the note to Lord Halston, then watched the English lord's face as he read it. The man's eyes widened, then bulged. His face went a strange reddish purple and a vein bulged alarmingly in his temple. "This is an outrage!" he announced. "We must notify the authorities!"

If the man was acting, he was damned good at it, Morgan thought, turning back to the duchess.

"Are you sure, Duchess? Sure you don't know anyone who has a bone to pick with you?"

She gave a tremulous smile at the phrase, and murmured, "No, no one…certainly no one who writes like *that*. Whoever it is has a deplorable inability to spell and rather a lack of penmanship, wouldn't you say?" she asked, with an unsuccessful attempt at a laugh.

"You're a duchess. You're rich. You have everything a body could ever need. Are you sure there isn't anyone who wants what you've got, Duchess?" Morgan persisted, glancing casually toward Lord Halston. The man had gone back to glaring at him.

Duchess Sarah blinked once, twice. "I suppose anyone who is poor might be envious, Mr. Calhoun.... Or I suppose it could be some American who's opposed to royalty and titles and all that—I'm aware there are some of your fellow countrymen who still feel that way. Is that what you meant?"

He shook his head, wondering if the duchess was as naive about people as she sounded. She'd told him her uncle would have been duke but for her and her sister back home, after all.

"Your grace, I believe you will now accept my earlier suggestion that we leave at once. You will see it is necessary," Lord Halston said. "You could have been killed at the train station, and now there is this note! You must get home where you can be kept safe."

The noblewoman whirled toward her uncle, eyes flashing. "Run home to England with my tail tucked between my legs, uncle? I think not."

"But Sarah—"

"*No*, my lord," she said, her jaw set firmly, and Morgan was surprised to see that even a beautiful duchess could have a mulish streak. "I have not come thousands of miles to retreat," she went on, "just when I've reached the land I've longed to see all my life. I will understand if you wish to return home, uncle—or you, Donald, or you, Celia," she said, facing each of them in turn.

Everyone was silent for a moment. Then Lord Halston said stiffly, "I trust I know my duty to your grace. As your uncle, it is my duty to guard you, to ensure your comforts, to see that all is properly—''

She silenced him with an upraised hand, while her secretary and her dresser echoed their willingness to remain.

Morgan cleared his throat, no longer so certain that the uncle was the one who intended her harm, but sure of one thing. ''Ma'am, it isn't any of my business, but I think your uncle's right. You ought to go home—maybe with a handful of men hired on to guard you till you get there, but you'd be a damn sight easier to protect in jolly ol' England than here— beggin' your pardon for my language,'' he apologized, after he noticed Celia's indignant face.

''Don't give it a thought,'' Sarah said. ''But Mr. Calhoun, you must think violence toward noblemen never takes place in England. I suppose he hasn't heard of the princes in the Tower, or Henry the Eighth's antics, has he, uncle?''

Morgan was annoyed to feel left out as the duchess and her uncle shared a grim chuckle. ''No, I don't known anythin' much about English history,'' he admitted. ''But it's just so much less civilized out here. And you're plannin' on goin' farther west? Lots of places, there's hardly any law. And there's Indians—and outlaws,'' he added, inwardly amused, since he was one of them, ''and so many places for them to hide. You'd need a small army to protect you. At least a cavalry regiment, and I don't reckon the government'd be willing to provide you with one.''

''No, they're not. I've already made inquiries,'' Lord Halston said, surprising Morgan and, from the duchess's face, the duchess, too. ''Please listen to him, niece. We should leave.''

Morgan watched her square her shoulders and lift her chin. ''I am not leaving, and that is final,'' she told Lord Halston, who looked away and clenched his fists in a frustrated fashion.

She looked at Morgan. ''But I *will* accept your assessment that I need some extra protection here,'' she said. ''Would you be willing to accept a position as my bodyguard, Mr. Calhoun?''

He felt as if he had a noose around his neck and the trap-door had just fallen out from under him. A man whose face was on Wanted posters deliberately placing himself at the side of a rich, famous woman who would be the center of all eyes, wherever she went? Morgan suppressed an ironic laugh. True, he wasn't likely to be notorious up here in Colorado or as far west as she mentioned going, but there were apt to be news-paper reporters talking to her, and writing their articles about the duchess and her entourage. There was no telling how far those newspaper stories might go. Someone might even pub-lish a pen-and-ink drawing of the duchess with him standing by her. No, much as the idea of being in this beautiful woman's presence for weeks appealed to him, as it would to any red-blooded man, he was going to have to pass for his own safety.

''Ma'am, I'm afraid I had other plans—you know, the minin' I mentioned? So I'm gonna have to thank you for your kind offer, but I'll have to say no.''

''But Mr. Calhoun,'' she said, her voice musical and per-suasive as she glided forward to lay a hand on his arm, ''you can see I have a real need for a man who can keep me safe.''

He forced himself to look away from the appeal in those blue eyes. ''Ma'am, I've never had any experience as a body-guard. You need a man with experience—several men, in fact. And I need to be gettin' on up into those mountains, and finding some riches of my own.''

''But you've already shown me you can protect me, Mr. Calhoun. That's worth more to me than all the credentials a man could carry. I don't want to have to hire some stranger or strangers. I want *you*, Mr. Calhoun,'' she said, giving him the full force of her compelling gaze.

His groin tightened as the words echoed in his head. *I want you*. Lord, what he'd give to hear a woman like her saying such words with a more intimate meaning! Maybe she even guessed as much, and was playing him like a bass on a fishing line.

"And you'll be handsomely paid, I do assure you—probably more than you could earn mining, and with none of the backbreaking work."

"No, none of the backbreaking work," he agreed. "I could live real easy, bein' your bodyguard—and get killed with an easy bullet."

Her face paled. "Yes, there is a risk, as you saw this afternoon. But I don't want to die, either, and I'm willing to pay you well to protect me as best you can. Perhaps all it will take to discourage this—this *scoundrel*," she suggested, "is the presence of a strong, intelligent man who is prepared to defend me."

"You don't know me," he told her, locking his gaze to hers. "You don't know anythin' about me, Duchess. Everythin' I've told you could be a lie."

"Well, I can agree with *that*, at any rate," Lord Halston said from behind them. "He's right, your grace, we don't know the first thing about Mr. Calhoun. He has the look of a ruffian, if I ever saw one. That may not even be his real name. It would be ridiculous to consider placing your trust in such a man. How could you trust a man who might steal the very jewelry from your neck, not to mention the valuables of the important people we will encounter? Why, we might all be murdered in our beds."

Even as he suppressed a mighty urge to knock the stuck-up, mouthy nobleman into the middle of next week, Morgan's gaze was involuntarily drawn to the matching, square-cut sapphires at her neck and on one elegant finger. He had to admit the man had a point, even if he didn't suspect how accurate he was. Not that Morgan would ever murder anyone, but stealing just the gems she was wearing right now would probably keep him for a year, if he could sell them for a reasonable price. And if she had more, he might even be able to buy that rancho he was always dreaming about in Mexico.

But the thought died as quickly as it was born. He wouldn't steal from this woman. Not if she had all the riches of England and America combined.

"My lord, that is unforgivably rude to a man who has offered me nothing but kindness," the duchess snapped. "You will apologize."

"I stand by my opinion," Lord Halston retorted. "It is my duty to say it, even if 'tis not what you want to hear, niece."

Morgan pretended to ignore the argument and suddenly took the hand she had laid on his wrist into his own. Maybe he could scare her into abandoning the idea, make her realize she was playing with fire, even though he'd love to hear her defy the pompous fool.

"Listen to your uncle, Duchess," he said, staring down at her with a deliberate, predatory air. He rubbed his thumb over the smooth, soft surface of her palm, lowering his voice so that it seemed they were alone in the room. "He could be right. I might steal all your jewelry…and murder you in your bed."

The last three words seemed to take on a resonance of their own. He saw the pulse beat quicken in her neck, and felt the faint tremor of the cool hand he held.

"I believe you're trying to frighten me, Mr. Calhoun, though I cannot think why," she said. "You already proved you're to be trusted, even at great risk to your own personal safety. My mind is made up. You're the man I want for the job, Mr. Calhoun. I can double the salary I was intending to offer you, if that's all you need to accept."

He heard Lord Halston start to sputter behind them, and then she gripped his hand as tightly as he'd been holding hers.

It would have taken a stronger man than he was to resist that kind of temptation. Maybe he could stay with her for a little while, at least until she got out of Colorado Territory, until whoever was threatening her figured out he'd have to go through a bodyguard to get to the duchess, and got discouraged. And it wasn't too likely anyone looking for him would think he'd dare to be seen at the side of an English noblewoman, even if she was going to be in the public eye much of the time. Even if it was summer, it'd be nice to be off the outlaw trail for a while, to have good food to eat that wasn't cooked over a campfire, to be dry and warm, and not have to sleep on the cold hard ground under the stars.

"You don't have to double my salary, Duchess. I reckon I'll take the job."

Chapter Five

She blinked, and a hectic flush of pink suffused her cheeks, making her look more like an English rose than ever. "Y-you will?" she managed to say at last. "That—that's awfully good of you. Shall we say four thousand pounds, or would you prefer a weekly amount?"

He waved the thought of money aside for a moment. "You haven't heard my conditions yet."

"Conditions?" A trace of hauteur crept back into her voice as she raised an eloquent eyebrow.

"Yeah, conditions, Duchess. You need to hire three other men, too. There should be at least three of us on duty during the day and evening, at least two after you've gone to bed."

She wrinkled her nose in distaste, then shook her head. "That's out of the question, Mr. Calhoun. I have no desire to be surrounded by a trio of armed strangers treading on my skirts. They would make it appear that America terrifies me. That would hardly generate goodwill, would it? I want one man—you. Are you saying you're not up to the job?"

Damn, but the lady was foolhardy—and stubborn, he thought, seeing the challenging glint in her eyes. "No, ma'am, I'm not saying that, but it just stands to reason three or four men could guard you better than just one," he said with all the patience he could muster. "If there were three men guarding you at all times they could cover all the angles—"

She gave a silvery laugh. "Good gracious, it sounds as if we'd be preparing for a red Indian attack," she said lightly. "No, Mr. Calhoun, my mind is quite made up. I shall either have you to safeguard me, or no one. What will it be?"

He'd worked with mules that were less headstrong than this titled Englishwoman. The only smart thing to do was to refuse, but he didn't want to do that. He'd taken the measure of the two men in the duchess's party, and he wouldn't trust Lord Halston or that skinny secretary fellow, Donald, to protect the duchess from so much as a raindrop, let alone a bad man intent on harming her. He could tell she meant what she said—if he didn't agree to guard her, she'd try to survive without a bodyguard. Which meant she wouldn't be alive long.

He tried another approach. Perhaps he could appeal to her pride. "Ma'am, if it's a matter of money that keeps you from hirin' more than one, I'll work cheap. I'm used to not having much money jinglin' in my pockets."

Now she was really amused. The laughter bubbled up from some wellspring within her, and she covered her mouth with a graceful hand as if trying to smother her mirth. "My good Mr. Calhoun, I do assure you I can afford to pay you and a dozen men, if I desired to, but I do not. You will be my sole bodyguard until such time as conditions warrant otherwise. Is that clear, Mr. Calhoun?" She was every inch the titled aristocrat now, and it made him want to look down at his boots to see if they were muddy.

"Yes, ma'am," he said, frowning at her tone. "I just thought you ought to know my opinion."

"And now I do."

She seemed to be waiting for something, but he didn't know what, so he was silent, too. At last she said, with a touch of impatience, "You said you had 'conditions,' Mr. Calhoun? What other concerns did you have?"

He didn't have an ounce of confidence that she'd agree to the second condition if she hadn't to the first, but he had to try. Someone wiser than this English rose had to be in charge.

"I want to know that if I tell you to do somethin' in the middle of a serious situation, Duchess, that you'll do it—right then, without any questions, 'cause there might not be any time to argue about it. It won't be because I like havin' my own way—it'll be because your life depends on doin' what I say as soon as I say it."

Their eyes dueled for an endless moment, and he saw a glimpse of the steely strength of her will. But she looked away first.

"Agreed," Duchess Sarah murmured, "though I'm afraid I'm not very good at taking orders—I've not had much practice with it recently, you see. Now, we must settle upon your salary. As I asked before, how does four thousand pounds sound to you? I can give it to you at one lump sum, at the end of your employment, or in spaced increments, as you prefer."

Morgan hesitated. "I don't know. What is four thousand pounds in American dollars?"

She shrugged. "I'm afraid I haven't the least idea. Donald?" She looked over her shoulder at her secretary, who by now had caught his breath and was less red faced.

Donald stared at the ceiling for a moment, then said, "I believe it's in the vicinity of twenty thousand dollars, your grace."

Morgan whistled through his teeth, an action that had Lord Halston glaring at him all over again. Twenty thousand dollars could take him off the outlaw trail forever. And it would sure make the trials of dealing with a mule-headed foreign woman downright pleasant.

"Okay, you've got a bodyguard, Duchess. When do I

start?'' he asked, wondering if he'd just set his foot to a road that was going to end in disaster.

It was as if the sun had suddenly come out. Duchess Sarah's face was radiant with her smile. "Good. I'm very grateful. Can you present yourself back here tonight, say, at half after seven? I am expected at a reception in the home of Edward McCook, the territorial governor, at eight o'clock, and that should give us ample time to get there. You were carrying a saddle when I first encountered you—do you have a horse here?"

He nodded, his mind still on the reception, but she went on, "Very well, you will want to install it in the hotel's stable. Tell the liveryman you work for me."

"Duchess, you're going to go to some party that half of Denver knows about?" Morgan said dubiously. "I don't think you ought to go—not after that note."

"Mr. Calhoun, I'm not hiring you so that I can stay meekly in my rooms here like a little mouse. I have agreed to be present at this event, and there are many important people who will be expecting to meet me. *I will be there.*"

He shrugged. He hadn't really expected to win that round.

"Oh, and Donald, do give Mr. Calhoun an advance on his salary—say fifty dollars? Mr. Calhoun, you'll need to pick up a suit of ready-made clothes for the sort of formal events you'll be attending with me. Do you suppose Denver has such an establishment?"

"Well, yes, ma'am, I imagine so, but it's probably already goin' on six, and I reckon the stores're all closed."

She looked disappointed, but darted a glance at Lord Halston and said, "All right, you may attend to that in the morning. Perhaps you could wear one of my uncle's suits, just for this evening?"

Morgan was amused to see the Englishman bristle and begin to sputter, "Now, just a moment, niece—"

"No, ma'am, I don't reckon I could. Looks like his lordship's trousers would end at my shins, and I'd probably rip 'em at the shoulders the first time I flexed 'em." He was trying to be tactful, but he felt the Englishman's hostile stare intensify at the words. The duchess's uncle sure spent a lot of his time looking angry. "Reckon I'd better be leavin' if I'm gonna get back here in time for your party, ma'am. Don't worry, I may not look fancy, but I'll try to find somethin' to wear that doesn't disgrace you."

If he left now, he'd just have time to explain to the widow that ran the Mountain View Boardinghouse why he was checking out the same day he'd checked in. And she might have a solution to his clothing problem. She'd mentioned that her late husband had been a tall man like him. With any luck, she'd still have his clothes, and with some of the money that the duchess's secretary was holding out to him, he could induce her to part with something suitable for this evening—at least until he could get something of his own. Then he could get Rio, his pinto stallion, out of the livery down the street from the boardinghouse, ride him over to the Grand Central Hotel's stable and present himself back to the duchess.

Sarah, now wearing her spectacles, watched in the mirror while Celia put the finishing touches to her hair with a curling iron. *If only Thierry were here with me, then I should not be so nervous.* She smiled at the thought of the handsome, tawny-haired Frenchman with his thin, elegant mustache, resplendent in his uniform as an officer of Louis Napoleon's cavalry, escorting her to the reception tonight. She wondered what he was doing right now, back home in England. Perhaps he was attending some ball in London, at the side of his exiled emperor, Louis Napoleon?

Thierry had told her he despised such events because of the fuss dowagers with marriageable daughters made over him, when he had much rather be with her. *Soon, my love,* she had promised. *At the end of my journey we will be man*

*and wife, and then you will be forever out of the reach of the
matchmaking mamas, my poor darling.*

"Your grace is in prime looks tonight," her dresser said
fondly from behind her, meeting her eyes in the mirror.

"Thank you, Celia," Sarah murmured, studying her reflec-
tion critically. The gown of light blue grosgrain, with its van-
dyked bertha, opened in front over a white lace underwaist
confined by a cluster of white satin roses, and showed off
slender white shoulders and a hint of cleavage beneath a necklace of pearls with a rectangular blue topaz pendant. Matching
topaz stones gleamed from her ears.

"Your grace's gems set off your eyes."

"They do, don't they? They've always been my favorite
set of Mama's. Papa said I have her eyes," Sarah said, and
then found herself wondering what Morgan Calhoun would
think of her appearance. The thought of his eyes straying
toward the shadowy hint of cleavage made her pulse quicken.

The thought startled her. Why was she, a woman in love,
thinking that way about a man she had hired to perform a
service?

And what would Thierry say if he knew she had hired a
bodyguard? He should be glad, if he could not be there to
protect her, right? Instinctively, though, she knew that if the
Count of Châtellerault had met Morgan Calhoun, he would
be jealous, not glad.

Thierry de Châtellerault's only fault, really, was his jealousy. Sarah had never been a flirt, had never given him cause
to be insecure about her affections, but she could tell Thierry
wasn't happy whenever a well-favored lord conversed with
Sarah or asked her to dance at a ball. They'd talked about it,
and Thierry had claimed to understand the need for such sub-
terfuge until their surprise marriage was a fait accompli, but
each time, his face looked like a thundercloud.

Morgan Calhoun was just an employee, not a social equal,
but Thierry was a very perceptive man. If Thierry had been

present, he would have sensed that Morgan Calhoun had a certain effect on Sarah—and he would have been on the alert.

Just then, through the door of her bedroom, she heard the muffled knock on the outer door of her suite, and the sound of footsteps as Donald went and let in the knocker.

"Oh, it's you, Calhoun," she heard her uncle say, and her heartbeat quickened. He had come. Morgan Calhoun was here, and now, officially, her bodyguard. "What, you're not dressed yet? Good God, man, we must leave within moments!"

"Now, just hold your horses," she heard Calhoun drawl. "I got a suit of clothes right here on my arm, but I didn't want to wear it ridin' over here, and end up smellin' like my horse, so I brought it in my saddlebags instead. Give me a coupla minutes and a room to change in, and I'll be ready."

Celia's eyes met Sarah's again in the mirror. "Doubtless Mr. Calhoun's clothes will need pressing," she informed her mistress primly. "Unless there's something else your grace would want me to do, perhaps I'd better go put the iron on the fire. I'll summon you, ma'am, when all is finally in readiness for our departure."

"I believe I'm ready as I am," Sarah said. "Yes, do go see if Mr. Calhoun needs assistance."

And so Sarah found herself waiting in her room for a good fifteen minutes, listening to Lord Halston fume that they were going to be late, and what would everyone say if the duchess were late to the reception being given in her honor?

At last Celia opened the door and said that Mr. Calhoun was dressed, and if her grace was ready, they could depart for the reception.

Her mouth was suddenly dry, her pulse pounding. Sarah rose halfway out of her seat, then sank back and reached for her bottle of scent. She applied the moistened stopper to her wrists, the area behind her ears and between her breasts, and smiled slightly at herself when she smelled the rose essence.

Then she arose and started for the door, only to stop stock-still halfway out of the room and step back to the mirror. She'd almost gone out there in front of Calhoun wearing her spectacles—that would never do! Sarah frowned as she removed the gold-rimmed circles of glass and everything farther than six feet from her became blurry.

She supposed she had so many material blessings as the Duchess of Malvern that wishing for perfect eyesight was a little ungrateful of her, but she wished it anyway. Taking as deep a breath as her corset would allow, she stepped into the other room.

Immediately she heard a sharp intake of breath. A dark-clad figure lounging in a chair by the door sprang to attention.

"Duchess, I...I reckon you look pretty as a...well, I don't know what to compare you to, ma'am. You look *beautiful*, and that's a fact."

Sarah felt the blush spreading down from her scalp all the way to her toes as she came close enough to be able to focus on him.

"Her grace's appearance is of no concern to you, Mr. Calhoun," she heard her uncle mutter.

"Don't be tiresome, uncle," she chided. "I could hear you fussing from inside my room. Mr. Calhoun is very nice to compliment me."

Now close enough to be able to see Morgan Calhoun clearly, she could tell the man was transformed. From somewhere he had managed to find a black frock coat and trousers, and a dazzlingly white shirt with a stiffly starched, upstanding collar and wide, red-striped tie knotted at his neck. The coat had been made for a man with narrower shoulders, though it was not as ill-fitting as Uncle Frederick's would have been, but it would do very well until he could have a tailor take his exact measurements and make something especially for him. He looked imposing—and the stark black and white of his clothes made him look formidable, Sarah decided. He did not look like a man to be trifled with.

"Do I pass inspection?" he asked.

She gazed up into green eyes over which the lids drooped halfway, giving him a deceptively sleepy appearance. She was reminded of a dozing leopard—sleek, black and just as deadly.

"Yes, I believe you'll do, Mr. Calhoun," she said, injecting a note of briskness she was far from feeling. "Now, Donald, has the carriage been sent for? Yes? Very good. Then perhaps we had better leave for the reception. Celia, Donald, we'll try not to be too late," she said, waving to her dresser and her secretary. "Come, uncle," she said, and started for the door.

But Morgan was there before her, barring her way.

"Just a moment, Duchess. I reckon we should start bein' careful right now. Just let me check the corridor first, and the stairway down to the front of the hotel, and I'll come back and tell you it's safe to go."

"Yes, very well," she managed to say. She hadn't realized how having a bodyguard would affect her every step, but clearly Calhoun was taking his responsibilities seriously.

He was back moments later, saying it was all right to go, and Sarah, on the arm of Uncle Frederick, descended the stairs, preceded by Calhoun.

The sun was hanging low over the mountains beyond Denver as they stepped outside the hotel and toward the waiting landau.

Morgan stopped without warning, nearly causing Sarah and her uncle to career into him.

"I gave an order for the top to be put back up, but I see your driver didn't do it," he said, gesturing to the folded-down roof of the landau, which was made in two sections to go over the facing seats when desired.

"Her grace's instructions were for the top to be down,"

Ben, her groom, growled back from beside the carriage. He had been doubling as coachman when required during this journey.

"The top's got to be put up, Duchess," Morgan said, his face implacable. "Please just step back inside the hotel until I've fixed it."

Ben wouldn't like the newcomer telling him what to do, Sarah thought, dismayed. "Oh, but is that really necessary?" she asked Morgan, then wished she could call back the words. She sounded like a child being denied a sweet at teatime. Perhaps if she explained… "It's such a pleasant night! I'd fancy feeling the breeze in my hair on the way to the reception."

"Would you?" His face was unreadable in the twilight, but his next words were clear enough. "As long as you leave the top down, that man who tried to shoot you this afternoon might *fancy* getting a clear shot at your head or your heart, Duchess."

She couldn't stifle a gasp at the graphic image.

"Surely it's not necessary to speak so bluntly to a gentle-woman," snapped Frederick.

Morgan looked down at Lord Halston. "Your lordship, I reckon I don't know any other way to speak. You want someone to make big speeches, you hire someone else. But I'm telling the duchess it ain't safe to ride around in an open carriage when someone tried to shoot her just hours ago."

Sarah said crisply, "Uncle, this is the very thing I'm paying Mr. Calhoun to tell me. Ben, I'm sorry, but the top will need to be put back up. Mr. Calhoun, we'll just wait inside as you've suggested until it's done."

Calhoun's nod of approval should not have mattered so.

Chapter Six

The drive to the territorial governor's residence, an imposing brick two-storied building on the northeast corner of Welton and Blake Streets, did not take long and was without incident. Morgan hopped down from his perch beside the truculent coachman, and the curtain over one of the landau's windows was pushed back.

"Goodness, it's going to be a crush," Sarah Challoner said, referring to the people spilling out over the governor's porch and thronging the upstairs balcony.

"Just wait in the carriage a moment, Duchess," Morgan said in a low voice as he looked up and down the street, and scanned the shrubbery and rooftops of the neighboring houses. He could see nothing moving in the rapidly fading light. He didn't like the idea of Sarah Challoner mingling with all those people without his searching them first, but he knew that wasn't possible. "All right, let's go ahead, but I'm sticking right by you."

"Do you suppose you could address your employer properly as 'your grace,' at least in public?" hissed Lord Halston as he emerged from the depths of the carriage.

Two men, dressed in evening black, separated themselves from the milling crowd on the porch and came forward, and

Morgan recognized the taller and thinner of the two as the mayor, who'd greeted the duchess at the train station.

"Your grace, we're happy you're here," John Harper said. "May I present Edward McCook, governor of the Territory of Colorado?"

The other man, whose face was decorated with a heavy mustache, bowed gravely. "Your grace, my apologies for not meeting your train, especially in view of what I'm told took place there. I understand you suffered no injury, madam—is that true?"

"How nice to meet you, sir," Sarah Challoner said, smiling, her face serene. "And yes, I'm perfectly fine. Please don't give that incident another thought. I'd like to present my uncle, Frederick, Lord Halston, the Marquess of Kennington...."

"My lord."

She wasn't going to mention the written threat she had received, Morgan guessed as he kept looking in all directions. He wished they'd hurry up and go into the house. She was too vulnerable out here in the open.

"And this is Mr. Morgan Calhoun, my...bodyguard," she said, nodding over her shoulder to indicate Morgan.

McCook and Harper looked alarmed, but were evidently not about to question a duchess. They nodded to Morgan, but did not extend their hands.

"Your grace, I'd feel better if we got inside," Morgan said in a low voice.

"By all means, your grace," McCook said, offering his arm even as he flashed a disapproving look at Morgan. "We've assembled the cream of Colorado society to greet you, madam. Everyone's quite excited at the prospect of meeting an actual duchess."

"Then let's not keep them waiting further, gentlemen," Sarah said, taking McCook's arm with regal ease.

The crowd on the lantern-lit porch parted to let them through as the governor led them into the house.

"We'll have a receiving line in the ballroom first, your grace, if that's agreeable to you," Morgan heard the governor say as he led the duchess and the rest of them up a long stairway.

They came to a large room with chairs and settees lining the walls, interspersed at intervals with large potted plants. At the far end a woman was playing a huge golden harp, her soft music reminding Morgan of clear green water running over the limestone bed of a Texas river. Here and there paintings hung on the wall, portraits of Washington and Lincoln and one of the Founding Fathers signing the Declaration of Independence.

The room hummed with chatter, and held even more people than had been out on the porch and balcony. Silence fell, however, as the invitees stepped aside to allow the host and his important guests to form a line at the entrance to the room. Morgan observed from the side of the room as they assembled, with the mayor first, followed by the governor, the duchess and finally Lord Halston.

"Mr. Calhoun?" called Sarah Challoner, looking around for him and sounding a bit uncertain.

He crossed over to her and said softly, "I'll be right over there by the door, Duchess." He nodded his head in that direction. "I can keep an eye on who's approaching you from there."

She nodded, apparently reassured, and then the guests began coming through the line. Morgan saw her turn with a brilliant smile to meet the first of them.

He watched as she was introduced to mine owners, bankers, speculators in real estate. Then came half a dozen men in the dress uniform of the U.S. Army.

Morgan nearly jumped out of his skin. He hadn't seen them as they had entered the governor's residence, and the sight of those blue-uniformed officers in their gold-braid-trimmed uniforms made his heart thud beneath the borrowed white shirt. He didn't take his eyes off them as they waited to meet the duchess. If just one of them looked at him a bit too long or pointed at him to one of his fellows, Morgan knew he was going to have to run for it—and though he'd hate himself for abandoning her, the duchess would just have to look out for herself.

None of them seemed to have eyes for anyone but Sarah Challoner, though. It was almost as if Morgan were invisible. If those soldiers only knew that the very man the army wanted for robbing the stage that had carried the troops' payroll was right here in the room with them, they wouldn't be so concerned with bowing over the duchess's hand, he thought grimly. What a difference his shaving and wearing some fancy duds made! They didn't recognize him as the desperado whose face was on all the Wanted posters.

The women at the sides of the men coming through the line were each more gorgeously dressed than the last, in silks and satins, feathers, flowers, ribbons and lace, in a rainbow of colors and accented by a blinding array of jewels.

He smiled at the irony of being in the same room with all those jewels. The ladies wearing them would have been jumpy as cats on ice if they had known how many lovely baubles he'd taken at gunpoint off the necks of wealthy women like themselves.

He wasn't here to rob anyone, though, so he studied the ladies' faces. Some of them were attractive, some merely well-dressed and groomed, but none was as lovely as the duchess. She shone like a gleaming diamond among fool's gold.

He felt a pang of regret as he took in the entire scene. Once, as a Calhoun, descended from one of the original settlers of Texas and owner of the finest ranch for a hundred miles, Morgan had belonged in such a world. He had been dressed as well as any of them, not wearing rented clothes. He'd had a beautiful belle on his arm.

But that was a long time ago, before the war, and now he was a breed apart from those chattering, fancily dressed people. He was an outlaw, no matter what his temporary role was with the Duchess of Malvern.

"Hello," he heard a husky voice say as the last few guests were going through the line, and then he was startled to feel a hand on his wrist.

Morgan looked down to see one of the ladies who had gone through the receiving line, a short brunette whose garnet brooch drew attention to the scandalously low neckline of the dark red gown she was wearing.

"I know it isn't conventional for a lady to introduce herself to a gentleman," she said, "but I kept waiting for you to leave the wall you seemed to be holding up and come through the line, and you haven't moved. So I decided I'd have to be unconventional and introduce myself. I'm Helen Wharton. My brother William over there—" she jerked her head in the direction of a ginger-headed young man talking to a group of businessmen underneath the chandelier "—owns the Double W Mining Company. You've heard of it? I haven't met you at any of these gatherings before, and I thought I knew everyone in our social circle."

Morgan breathed in her perfume, and was aware of a quick flaring of lust as his brain appreciated the musky scent that surrounded the woman like a cloud. At another time or place he'd have enjoyed a dance of seduction with this woman, for her bold eyes told him she'd be more than willing to partner him in that particular waltz.

"Morgan Calhoun, ma'am," he said, inclining his head politely, "and I reckon we haven't met because I'm not exactly in your social circle. I'm just here to guard the duchess." Deliberately he cut his eyes back to the receiving line, expecting the woman to stalk off in search of more prominent prey.

He was wrong, it seemed. She was still there when he looked back down. Excitement flashed in her brown eyes, and she removed her long-nailed hand from his wrist to stroke down his biceps.

"*Ooh,* you're a *bodyguard?*" she breathed. "How very exciting. Why don't we get some punch and step out on the balcony? You can tell me all about your experiences...."

He narrowed his eyes in what he hoped was a discouraging manner, and shook his head. He couldn't afford to let her distract him. "I'm here to keep my eye on the duchess," he said, returning his gaze to Sarah Challoner. "I've got to stay by her."

Helen Wharton pouted for just a moment. "Ah, I can see you're devoted to duty...very commendable, I'm sure. But you're entitled to a little refreshment, aren't you? Why don't I go get us both some punch and bring it back here? You can keep your eye on your duchess, and I'll keep you company."

Morgan gave a wary okay to her offer, then went back to watching the duchess.

The dark-haired Helen was back within moments, somehow managing to bring two cups of punch and a plate full of finger sandwiches through the crowd without mishap.

"Much obliged," Morgan said, taking a grateful sip, and blinking in surprise as he tasted liquor mingled with the fruity liquid. Rum, he guessed.

"This is rather...potent," he said, his eyes leaving the duchess for a moment to rest on Helen Wharton and the cup she was raising to her lips. "I hope there was something a little less...strong for you, ma'am?" He'd better limit himself to one cup, and sip that sparingly, or soon he'd be too blind drunk even to see the duchess, much less protect her.

Helen laughed merrily. "There *is* a punch for the ladies,

but I'm drinking the same thing as you are. I'm afraid I find the other stuff rather insipid. Here, have a sandwich.''

He accepted the morsel from her, then searched and found Sarah Challoner in the crowd. The receiving line finished, she had joined the same group of businessmen that Helen Wharton's brother had been standing among. Just then William Wharton returned, bearing punch and sandwiches, which he offered to the duchess.

''Hospitality seems to run in your family,'' Morgan observed.

''Yes…I ran into my brother at the refreshment table. He's quite taken with your duchess. Says she's the most beautiful woman he's ever seen.''

Morgan sure couldn't disagree with that, so he said nothing, just kept his eye on the duchess as the mining magnate went on chatting with her. His conversation was evidently very stimulating, for Sarah Challoner was animated, her color high, her blue eyes sparkling. Then he saw that something Wharton said had amused her, for she tipped back her head and laughed. The sound was lost in the noisy room, but Morgan fancied he could hear its silvery music.

Lord, he wished he were a rich man so he could stand talking with Sarah Challoner like this, and have her laughing at some clever thing he said.

Then he saw Wharton gesture toward the balcony, and Sarah's narrow-eyed stare in its direction before she nodded.

From here he could see that the balcony was empty of other guests, and someone had blown out the torches that had illuminated it at their arrival. So the rich fellow imagined he was going to lure Sarah Challoner out into the darkness?

''You'll have to excuse me,'' he growled to the woman beside him, handing her his cup without even looking at her and striding forward to intercept the couple heading for the balcony.

''Pardon me, Du—your grace,'' he amended, planting himself in front of the couple. The duchess had her hand on Wharton's arm, a fact that fueled his ire.

The two halted, Wharton blinking at him as if Morgan had two heads. "Mr. Calhoun, is something wrong?" Sarah Challoner asked.

"No, ma'am, but I can't have you…I don't think…that is, you shouldn't go out on the balcony."

"Oh, don't be silly. It's dark out there. No one who'd want to harm me could even see me."

"Harm you? What do you mean?" Wharton asked. Then, when he received no answer, he glared at Morgan, his face reddening, a pulse beating in his temples. "Now, see here, fellow, just who do you think you are to be ordering her grace around?"

Morgan ignored him. "Ma'am, there's a full moon, and your dress is a pale color. A sniper wouldn't need much more."

Sarah Challoner lifted her chin—always a sign of imminent rebellion, he'd discovered—and her lips thinned. "Oh, don't be tiresome, Mr. Calhoun. I'll be fine. Mr. Wharton merely thought I might like some air."

I'll just bet he did, Morgan thought, fixing his piercing gaze on the mining magnate until the other man's eyes fell.

"I'm afraid I'll have to agree with Mr. Calhoun, your grace," said Lord Halston, who had suddenly appeared at Morgan's side in time to hear the last exchange. "It would be most unwise."

"My dear duchess, what on earth are they talking about? Have you been threatened?" Wharton demanded.

Her face smoothed out as she looked at Wharton. "It's nothing, Mr. Wharton. Truly. They're just being cautious. Isn't there some quieter room to which we can go and chat some more? I vow, all this noise is giving me a headache!"

"Certainly, your grace," Wharton said with a genial smile—a smug smile that Morgan wanted to wipe off the man's ginger-cat face with his knuckles. "The governor has a small library downstairs where we may be private, I'm sure. If that's all right with your...guardians," he said with deliberate provocation.

Morgan's fists clenched at his side as he struggled to be polite. Out of the corner of his eye he saw Lord Halston bristling and white-faced. *Good for you, Halston.*

"I reckon that's all right, if I can go with you and check out the room first, and then I'll stand outside the door and make sure no one else comes in," he said.

"Well, it's not all right with me," Sarah Challoner snapped, her eyes blazing with blue fire at Morgan and Lord Halston alike. "You two are smothering me, and I won't have it. There is absolutely nothing amiss in my speaking to Mr. Wharton privately, and if you wish to continue in my employ, Mr. Calhoun, you'll stay upstairs, *is that clear?* Come, Mr. Wharton, show me this library."

Morgan stared at her retreating figure as she left the reception room. Life was too short to put up with a woman so obstinate she wouldn't even accept guidance when she'd asked for it. He could be back at the boardinghouse within the hour and heading for the mountains day after tomorrow, a free man. And the duchess could go to blazes.

Then he felt Lord Halston's hand on his shoulder. "I'd like to apologize for my niece's behavior, Calhoun. I'll speak with her later, get her to see reason. I—I'd take it as a personal favor if you wouldn't quit without giving her another chance."

Morgan couldn't have been more surprised if Lord Halston had suddenly sprouted a halo and wings, and it was the surprise that cooled his anger. "All right," he conceded, "if you'll talk to her, I'll stay. I'm not going to go through this every time she disagrees with me."

"She's very headstrong," the marquess admitted. "A result of her being raised as heiress to a duchy. The late Duke of Malvern treated her as if she were the son he'd never had. Once it was apparent she would be duchess one day, he encouraged her to make decisions on her own just as if she were a man. As her oldest male relative, I've tried to guide her as best I could, but…'' He shrugged. ''Sometimes that strong will leads her into error.''

''I just hope that stubbornness doesn't get her killed,'' Morgan muttered, and stalked away to find a drink—a real one, not just that damn punch.

Crouched in the darkness outside the territorial governor's residence, the assassin waited on the roof of the mansion next door to the governor's. The owners of the mansion, who were present at the reception, didn't know he was there, and since their servants had been lent to McCook for the evening, too, he'd had no difficulty stealing inside and making his way to the roof. He was dressed in black from head to foot. Even the barrel of his Winchester rifle had been rubbed with grease and then coated with soot so as not to give off a betraying gleam.

He'd taken up his position on the roof long before the duchess had arrived. He could have shot her as she strolled into the house with her uncle and that watchdog she'd hired, but he'd decided it was too risky. There were a lot of people outside, and someone might have seen the flash from the muzzle of his rifle when he fired. He'd decided to wait until the duchess took the air out on the balcony or on the porch, but that hadn't taken place yet, either. Maybe her watchdog had warned her against it. But it wouldn't save her. He had a contingency plan already in place.

He pulled a pocket watch out and studied its face by the light of the full moon. Any moment now the duchess would come rushing out the door with her entourage, and their faces would reflect the panic they felt inside. Panicked people were easy targets.

* * *

"Mr. Calhoun, we've got to leave. Immediately!"

The duchess was suddenly standing in front of him, white-faced and trembling. Wharton was standing by her side, looking as if his genial composure had permanently deserted him.

Morgan had been sipping whiskey by a potted aspidistra with Helen Wharton, who had rejoined him, apparently not minding that he had challenged her brother. He had felt his knotted-up gut relax under the influence of her pleasant chatter and the mellow amber liquid.

It took him a few seconds to refocus. "What's wrong, Duchess?"

She was trembling like an aspen in the wind. "Show him, Mr. Wharton."

The other man reached into his waistcoat pocket and produced a folded piece of paper. "This was just delivered by a servant who claims to have been paid by a stranger to deliver it at half after ten."

Morgan unfolded the note, feeling the knot reforming in his gut. It said "HAVIN A GOOD TIME DUCHISS? SOON YOUL BE IN YER GRAVE. A PATRIOTT."

Chapter Seven

"Yeah, we've got to leave, but careful-like," Morgan said, suddenly all business. "Where's Lord Halston?"

Suddenly it seemed as if there was little air in the room. None of the blurry figures standing around the room looked like the familiar figure of her uncle. "I don't know! But we've got to find him, and I must say my farewell to the governor! It would be rude not to thank Mr. McCook—"

"There's no time for those things. We'll send the carriage back for your uncle. I don't want *anyone* else knowin' we're leavin', Duchess," he said in a low voice. "Wharton, go out and find the duchess's driver. He should be standing by a landau with a matched pair of grays. Talk loud—say that the duchess and her party are gonna stay the night, and she wants him to go on back to the hotel. Then whisper that he's to wait about midway down the street behind this one. We'll find our way to him. And don't tell anyone else what we're doing."

Wharton blinked, and Sarah was reminded of an owl. "I will, but wait for me here. I'm coming with you to make sure the duchess is safe."

"Thank you, Mr. Wharton," Sarah breathed. "It's very good of you—"

Morgan interrupted, saying, "Just go do what I told you, Wharton."

As soon as Wharton had disappeared, Morgan's hand was on her elbow, propelling her toward the staircase. "Come on, Duchess, this way," he said.

"But we were going to wait for Mr. Wharton!" she protested as Calhoun pulled her down the carpeted staircase.

"No." They reached the bottom, and he steered her down a darkened hallway that apparently led to the rear of the house. Coming to a door, he opened it and pulled her inside.

It appeared to be a parlor. Letting go of her arm, Morgan crossed the room in three rapid strides, took hold of one of the dark, heavy curtains hanging over the window and gave a yank, pulling it down.

"Here, put this around you like a cloak—over your head, too," he said.

"But..." she began as she pulled the curtain around her.

The dust rising from it made her sneeze.

"We're goin' out the back way. The dark curtain will make you a little harder to spot in the darkness," he explained. "Come on." And then he seemed to notice that she was shaking. "You gotta take hold of yourself, Duchess," he commanded. "Panic is just what this fella is countin' on. Just do what I tell you, and we'll come outa this okay."

She nodded, braced by his certainty, and determined not to appear a frightened mouse in Morgan Calhoun's eyes.

Moments later she was running with him across the darkened back lawn, clutching her makeshift cloak at her neck and holding Calhoun's hand with her other one to keep herself from falling. His hand felt warm and strong. He clutched a pistol in his other hand.

He found the gate into the alley, and pulled her after him into the dark passageway.

"We'll take it slow from here, Duchess," he whispered. "Try and walk quiet."

No matter how quietly she walked, though, Sarah was sure any pursuer could hear her panting like a winded fox. She knew how that fox would feel, hearing the dogs come closer and closer. She'd never ride to hounds again.

He paused when he came to the gate to another yard down the alley. "We'll cut through here."

This yard was more uneven than the governor's, and she stumbled, going down heavily on one knee. She heard the fabric rip, and a stinging pain shot through her knee.

Calhoun pulled her to her feet without comment, and they continued on around the side of a darkened house. There was a tall tree with low-hanging boughs on the front lawn, and he pulled her into the deeper darkness against its broad trunk.

"We'll wait here for your driver," he whispered.

"What if he doesn't come?" she whispered back, straining to see his face in the darkness. Ben might not believe that Wharton had really come from her, and might insist on speaking to her or her uncle personally.

"Then eventually we'll have to walk back to the hotel," he told her. "But I reckon the wild eyes on that jackass Wharton will convince him."

His contemptuous tone ignited her anger, burning away her traces of fear. "How dare you speak of a gentleman like that? And what about you? I saw you standing there all cozy with his bold-eyed tart of a sister when you should have been—"

"Should have been *what*, Duchess?" he demanded. She could barely make out his eyes glittering in the darkness. "You wanted me to leave you alone, remember?"

She was silent, trying to rein in her temper. Her heart felt as if it was pounding in her ears. "I—I just won't have you speaking of Mr. Wharton like that. He—he was very pleasant company, that's all." She could feel him staring at her in the darkness.

"You're the boss."

"Indeed." She wouldn't give him the satisfaction of protesting too much, but pleasant company *was* all Wharton had been. He'd been entertaining and complimentary and clearly awed to be speaking to a duchess. And he was one of the few men she'd met this evening who hadn't been staring down the front of her dress, asking sly questions about her wealth, or offering to be her duke, as if that were possible. She hadn't felt any tug of attraction to Wharton, though she'd agreed when he'd asked to escort her to the theater.

It wasn't as if she were looking for an American man to replace Thierry, she assured herself. And it wasn't like being with Morgan Calhoun, whose very presence seemed to demand much of her. Maybe too much.

Wharton had meant nothing improper when he'd asked her to take the air with him, she was sure of it. But she'd seen the look in Calhoun's eyes when he'd stopped them, and guessed how it had looked to him. Good Lord, what if he'd known she was secretly engaged? Would he have an even worse opinion of her for wanting to go out on the balcony with Wharton then?

By God, she was a duchess, and not about to let a man dictate to her, especially a man whose salary she paid!

Then she heard a soft clip-clopping, which grew louder, stopping just down the street.

Calhoun peered around the broad trunk of the tree. "There's the landau," he said. "Come on." He seized her hand and pulled her into a zigzagging run to the coach. Sarah would have stopped to explain to Ben, but Morgan thrust her almost roughly into the coach and followed her inside, calling out, "Get on back to the hotel! I'll explain once we get the duchess back safe in her room."

Sarah held herself rigidly erect on the way back to the hotel, hoping Calhoun would see that she was furious with him, but he didn't even seem to remember she was there. He kept lifting the curtain and peering out the window. Neither of them spoke.

Back in her suite at the Grand Central, Sarah gave her dresser and her secretary a terse explanation of their early return without Lord Halston, watching out of the corner of her eye while Calhoun checked windows and looked behind curtains and under furniture.

"Well, thank God for Mr. Calhoun, I say," Celia muttered as she knelt before Sarah to examine the dirt-stained rent in the skirt of Sarah's gown. "Better to have ruined a dress than to be shot at again. Isn't that right, Mr. Alconbury?"

But Sarah's secretary, hovering at Sarah's elbow, could only stare at her, white-faced.

"Cheer up, Donald," Sarah said bracingly, patting him on the shoulder. She was touched that her secretary cared so much. "I'm unharmed, as you see. Do you suppose you could sit down with me and help me quickly compose a note for Ben to take to the governor when he goes back to pick up my uncle? I owe the poor man *some* explanation for disappearing from his reception! We shall have to tell him the truth, I suppose. Whatever will he think?"

"Why not tell him you're leavin' Denver tomorrow while you're at it?" Morgan suggested.

"Because I shall not be leaving, Mr. Calhoun," she told him. "Do me the favor of not bringing it up again."

Calhoun sighed and looked away.

Donald managed to pull himself together, and within moments the missive was ready and the secretary was taking it down to Ben, who waited at the landau.

"Now, your grace, why not let me help you out of that ruined thing and into your dressing gown?" Celia said practically. "You can wait in your bedroom for my lord's return. I'll have hot milk sent up from the kitchen."

Calhoun stopped his pacing long enough to growl, "You can go fetch it. I don't want to wonder if it's really a hotel employee knocking on this door."

"Very *well*, Mr. Calhoun," Sarah's dresser fairly snarled

back at him. "*I* will be *happy* to 'fetch' it. But I will assist
her grace first. Come, my lady."

The two women headed for Sarah's bedroom, which lay
directly off the main room, only to have Sarah stop in amazement at the cot that lay in front of its door. "What on
earth—?"

"*He* directed it be put there," Celia informed her archly
with a nod toward Calhoun, who'd begun prowling about the
room again. "He says he's going to sleep there."

"*Is* he? How very medieval," Sarah murmured, then allowed herself to titter. She hoped Calhoun heard it.

The next morning she had Donald escort her down into the
stable through an entrance in the back of the hotel. Her secretary had told her Calhoun had gone there to check on his
horse.

Uncle Frederick had been beside himself when he'd returned last night and received the full report on what had
happened. Once again he'd begged Sarah to leave Denver
immediately, not even waiting till morning. But when Sarah
had once again adamantly refused to go, he'd proceeded to
give her a stern dressing-down for her display of temper at
the reception.

She found Morgan Calhoun in a stall, currying a tall, skewbald horse.

"Mr. Calhoun, if I might have a word?"

Calhoun whirled as if he'd been shot. Clearly he'd been
deep in thought and hadn't heard her approach.

"I'm sorry…I didn't mean to startle you," she said.

"What are you doin' here, Duchess? I thought I told you
not to leave your room without me." His eyes were like green
icicles.

"It's all right, Donald came with me," she said, indicating
her secretary standing behind her. "Donald, why don't you

go and post the letters I dictated? Oh, and don't forget to take the note I wrote my sister—I left it on the tea table.''

She waited, staring down at her feet, feeling his eyes on her, until they were alone. "I—I've come to apologize," she said at last. "I realize, after talking to my uncle, and doing some thinking, that I behaved rather badly last night." She would not tell him that she had tossed and turned last night, and had even contemplated leaving her bedroom in the middle of the night to apologize right then and there. The only thing that had stopped her was the impropriety of waking him. "My attitude at the party, when you were only trying to counsel me for my own safety…and when we returned here…did me no credit," she went on, then darted a glance upward to see how he was receiving her words.

She saw surprise flicker across his face, but nothing more.

"I'm afraid arrogance…and a dislike of being told what to do…are failings of mine. I want you to know that while I may not always agree with you, I shall not be discourteous again. I will cooperate as fully as possible." There. She'd said it.

A trace of a smile made his lips curve the least bit upward. "Well…maybe you're not arrogant, but you do put me in mind of a horse's long-eared relative sometimes," he admitted, mischief dancing in his green eyes. "But I reckon we can start over from here, Duchess."

She was so relieved, she didn't even mind his comparing her to a mule. "Capital, Mr. Calhoun," she said. Then, wanting some kind of confirmation that peace had been achieved, she extended her hand over the stall door. "Pax."

She could tell he didn't know the word. "It means 'peace' in Latin, Mr. Calhoun," she explained as he took her hand and shook it. As before, she found his touch disturbingly powerful.

"The Indians would say we were buryin' the hatchet, I reckon," he said. "And while we're bein' so peaceable, do you think you could call me Morgan? You keep callin' me Mr. Calhoun, and I keep lookin' around for my pa." His grin warmed her soul.

"I *reckon* I could, Morgan," she said, smiling back at him. Of course, she couldn't reciprocate and ask him to call her by her given name, but he didn't seem to expect that.

She was loath to just turn around and leave. "So that's your horse, this skewbald?" she asked, gesturing toward the brown-and-white-splotched horse, who watched her with pricked-forward ears. "He—he's very handsome." *You sound like a giddy schoolgirl, Sarah.*

But Morgan didn't seem to find her remark stupid. "His name is Rio," he said. "And he thinks he's handsome, too— don't ya, boy?" he asked, scratching the horse's ear. The stallion tossed his head as if to agree. "Here in the west, though, we call horses like that *pintos,* or paints."

"I see." It was a moment of perfect harmony. "I—I'd best look in on my mare."

"I'll come with you. I'm done here." He let himself out of the stall. "What're you planning for today, Duchess?" he asked as they strolled down the aisle to where Trafalgar was stalled.

"I've been invited to a luncheon at the home of Mr. and Mrs. John Byers—he owns the newspaper, and apparently he's quite a prominent developer here in Denver, as well. And I'm invited to the mayor's for dinner. Ah, there you are, my beauty," she said when her bay mare poked her well-shaped head over the stall door at the sound of her mistress's voice. "Are they treating you well? But you're bored, aren't you? Yes, I managed to obtain an apple for you," she said, laughing, when Trafalgar butted her hand with her soft black muzzle. She pulled it from her pocket and watched while the thoroughbred lipped it delicately from her hand.

"Beautiful animal," commented Calhoun.

"Thank you. Morgan, do you think we could take our

horses out for a ride? Trafalgar badly needs some exercise, don't you, girl? You're getting fat, with nothing to do but eat your head off.''

Calhoun looked dubious. ''I don't know if that's such a good idea, Duchess. It'd be awful hard to protect you out in the open. I could take the mare out for you, if you like. She's a big one, so she wouldn't have any trouble with a man's weight.''

Sarah quashed the impulse to argue. She didn't want to destroy the progress they'd made. ''Oh, please... We could leave before dawn, before any self-respecting evildoer is awake.''

Her attempt at humor won a smile from him. ''We'll have to see how things go, Duchess, all right? Let me think about it.''

''I thought Mr. Calhoun asked you not to look out the window,'' Celia commented from her seat in the landau as it rolled through the streets of Denver toward her luncheon engagement at the home of Mr. and Mrs. Byers. The servant was accompanying Sarah to the event, since her uncle and her secretary had gone to check on the seating order for the dinner party at the home of the mayor, to make sure it followed protocol.

Sarah, wearing her spectacles, since only Celia was inside with her, shot a guilty smile at her dresser. ''I know, but it's such a gorgeous summer day and Denver's such a pretty new city. Surely it won't hurt if I just take a peek now and then, especially if Mor—if Mr. Calhoun is up on the seat with Ben and doesn't know? It's not fair that I must go from place to place in a dark cage as if I were a vicious lioness.''

Celia looked prim and unconvinced. ''Perhaps not, but you've been threatened twice in less than twenty-four hours, and shot at once,'' she observed, speaking freely with the ease of a valued servant.

"Just once more…" Sarah promised with a sigh, and lifted the curtain again just as the carriage was passing a particularly attractive row of businesses.

A man was standing in front of one of the buildings, staring at the carriage from the doorway of a building. He was blond and tall, with a dashing mustache. Goodness, he reminded her of Thierry, she thought fondly, though of course Thierry would never have been here, dressed as an American civilian. In the next letter she had Celia post secretly, she'd have to tell him he had a double in America!

Just as the carriage was rolling past, the man stroked his mustache, just as Thierry so often did. *Was it Thierry?* Might he have decided to join her here, rather than in Santa Fe, and be out looking for her? She had to see!

"Ben, stop the carriage!" she cried. "Stop it at once, I say! Thierry!"

The vehicle rolled on for a few more yards, and Sarah became frantic, beating at the roof and the window like a caged bird. *"Stop the coach!"*

"Whoaa!" Ben called. Sarah felt the carriage slow just as she pushed on the door handle and got it open.

"Your grace, what are you about?" she heard Celia ask in a mystified voice, but she ignored her, determined to see if the man could actually be de Châtellerault. What a joyous reunion they would have, even if it would be awkward explaining it to Frederick! How much Thierry must love her if he couldn't stay away any longer!

She opened the door just as Calhoun jumped down from the driver's seat to the ground beside her, landing with a thud.

His face was alarmed and he looked her up and down. "Duchess, what're you screamin' about? Are you shot?"

Frantically, she looked past his body to where she had seen Thierry in front of the building. There was now no one there. She tried to force her way past Calhoun, but he caught her wrist. "Let me go!" she cried. "I—I saw someone I know back there!"

"Who?"

"A friend from home—*please!* I have to catch up with him before he goes away! He must not have seen me—he must have gone inside one of those buildings!" Suddenly she succeeded in pulling herself free, and she was off and running back down the street in the direction from which they had come.

With Calhoun's boot heels pounding right behind her, Sarah reached the row of businesses, and peered inside, seeing within only clerks and a few customers—but no one who resembled her handsome French fiancé.

Calhoun caught up with her. "Have you gone loco, Duchess?" he cried. "Get back in the coach!"

She ignored him, dashing into the middle of the business establishment, a men's haberdashery. Calhoun followed.

"Have you seen a fair-haired man in here? A Frenchman?" she asked the astonished haberdasher.

"No, miss…"

Narrowly eluding Calhoun's grasp, she ran back outside and tried the adjoining business, a printing office. The man hadn't gone in there, either.

Calhoun had given up trying to stop her and just silently followed her into the third establishment, a drugstore.

She asked her question again. This time, the proprietor pointed to a back entrance. "A man like you're talking about went out through there."

"Did he have an accent? A French accent?"

The man's brow furrowed. "Don't rightly know, ma'am. He didn't say nothin', just went out our employees' entrance back there without so much as a by-your-leave."

"May I?" she said, indicating the back door. "It—it's very important that I catch up with him."

The man shrugged, and Sarah dashed through the rear entrance with Calhoun at her heels.

The alleyway was empty of everything but ash cans and a stray cat.

"You mind tellin' me what that was all about, Duchess?" Morgan demanded.

"I—I thought...I s-saw someone I knew," she panted, feeling utterly foolish.

"Who?"

She was not about to explain now about her secret fiancé. "Just s-someone from home," she stammered, still out of breath. "B-but I must have been mistaken.... It was too silly of me, wasn't it? I'm sorry to have startled you. Oh, well, I suppose we can go back to the carriage now," she said with an elaborately casual shrug. She dared a glance at him through her lowered lashes, and saw her explanation hadn't mollified her bodyguard. Calhoun was looking all around them, his face set in hard planes.

"'Too silly' doesn't hardly begin to cover it, Duchess," he said. "Did it ever occur to you that you coulda been shot at? Let's get back to the carriage before 'a patriott' notices what you did."

Suddenly she felt exposed and vulnerable in the vacant alley, and a thousand times more stupid than his face told her he thought she was. Wordlessly she obeyed as he indicated she was to retrace her steps back inside the drugstore and back to the carriage.

Once he'd given her his arm and assisted her inside, however, he leaned in and drawled, "Duchess, by the way, since when do you wear spectacles?"

Sarah gasped. She had completely forgotten she still wore them. Her hand whipped out and yanked them off as her face flooded with heat.

"I...well, now you know my secret," she said, embarrassed but glad she could distract him. "I'm afraid I can't see very well without them."

"So why don't you wear them all the time?"

"Vanity, I suppose. Lord, what a foolish creature I must appear to you!"

She couldn't read his suddenly shuttered eyes. "I reckon we'd better be going, or you're going to be late, Duchess."

Chapter Eight

The luncheon was so pleasant that Sarah almost forgot about the anonymous notes she had been receiving. The wives of the ten most prominent businessmen of Denver were genuinely friendly, absorbed with Sarah's tales of the queen and her peers back home, and clearly impressed with the fact that Sarah held the duchy in her own right.

"Why, I wouldn't be *anyone* if I wasn't 'Mrs.' Someone," one of them said. "Just imagine, being your own mistress..."

It was obvious they found Sarah's bodyguard fascinating, too. Even though Morgan withdrew to a corner of the room near the door while the luncheon was going on, Sarah noticed more than one of the ladies closest to her staring at Morgan Calhoun's lean form and handsome visage with expressions that could only be described as longing.

But she was pleased that from what she could see, Morgan seemed totally unaware of the eyelashes being batted in his direction. Every so often he would rise to peer outside the windows, and then, apparently satisfied, he would sit back down and seemingly withdraw to some place inside himself.

On the way back to the hotel Sarah caught no glimpse of the man who looked like Thierry de Châtellerault. Surely the sighting had been merely wishful thinking, she told herself after greeting her uncle and Donald, as she and Celia headed for the privacy of her bedroom so she could change her dress.

She stopped just inside the room, nearly causing Celia to collide with her.

There was no disorder, but nothing was as she had left it. A book she had left on the bedside table to the left of her bed was now on the table on the other side of the bed. The ormolu clock that sat on the mantel now faced the wall. A framed picture of Kathryn, which Sarah always kept on her bedside table, was lying facedown.

Feeling the hair prickling at her nape, she strode forward and peered into the chest of drawers where Celia always laid out her clothing in the precise order Sarah preferred—gloves and handkerchiefs in the top drawer, chemises in the second with her stockings, petticoats in the third, nightgowns in the fourth, corsets and corset covers in the fifth.

Everything had been changed. The gloves were now in the bottom drawer, the corsets in the top. Her chemises were now where her nightgowns should be.

"Celia..." she murmured as she crossed the room to look into the wardrobe where her gowns hung and her shoes were kept. "Did you rearrange things in my drawers while I was taking breakfast this morning?"

Her dresser blinked at her. "Why, no, your grace. I folded your nightdress and dressing gown and left the room."

A glance into her closet confirmed Sarah's expectation. Here, too, garments had been moved around. And Sarah's shoes and boots, always precisely arranged, had been matched up with different mates, so that a kid slipper was now placed next to a riding boot, a brown high-buttoned shoe with a black one.

"Uncle! Donald! Morgan!" she called. "Come in here!"

Morgan led the other two at a run. She explained what she had found. "Uncle, was aught amiss in the other rooms when you and Donald returned?"

Lord Halston, his face grim after Sarah's announcement, shook his head. "Actually, Donald returned ahead of me, didn't you, Donald?"

"Oh?" Morgan, who had been peering into the wardrobe, was suddenly alert. "And why didn't you come back with him, your lordship?"

Lord Halston glared at him. "I remained behind to chat with Jerome Chaffee about possibly investing in one of his mines, *Mister* Calhoun. What on earth are you implying?"

Morgan's gaze was steady. "I'm not accusin' you of anything, your lordship, so don't get your feathers ruffled. Do the hotel maids have access to this room when no one's here?"

"No," came Halston's prompt reply. "The rooms were cleaned under my watchful eye after her grace left this morning, before Mr. Alconbury and I departed."

Morgan looked thoughtful. "And nothing was out of order in your rooms, gentlemen?"

Sarah saw her secretary shake his head. "Nothing, Mr. Calhoun. Everything was just as I had left it."

"Not that I noticed," muttered Halston. "Perhaps I'd better take a second look." He turned on his heel and left the room.

Sarah watched as Morgan went over to her bed and ran his hand over the coverlet, then pulled the coverlet back and felt the pillow. Even from where she stood she heard the crackle of paper. Morgan's hand dived into the pillowcase and came out holding a folded piece of paper.

"Give that to me, please," she said, feeling an icy fist squeezing her heart.

Morgan handed it to her, still folded. Inside was the same nearly illegible, misspelled scrawl she had become all too familiar with: "Ive bin this close, duchiss. Walls and locks cant keep me out. That guard cant save you neither. And it dont matter wher you go. I will git you. A patriott."

Sarah read it through once, then tried to read it again, but her hand was shaking too badly. She gave up and handed it to Morgan.

She raised her eyes to her bodyguard's after he had read it. "Well, so much for the theory that all I had to do was leave Denver to be safe," she said, attempting a wry tone and failing miserably.

"He might be bluffing about that part," he observed.

"But we can't be certain, can we?" she retorted.

"No," he admitted. "We can't be certain."

"In that case it seems to me I might as well go ahead with the social events scheduled," she said, meeting his gaze.

His lips compressed to a thin line, he said, "I reckon I'd better go have a talk with the hotel manager. Lock the door behind me."

Peering through a window in the attic of Mayor John Harper's residence, he watched them arrive. The hired bodyguard rode up front with the coachman, as he had the evening before. This time he had a rifle cradled in his lap. The watcher saw the bodyguard's eyes scan the area thoroughly before he hopped down and went to open the coach.

He knew the bodyguard couldn't see him watching from the darkened room. *No, my would-be white knight, you will not see me aiming my rifle from this window, or from a rooftop, this time. I am not one to keep trying any tactic repeatedly. I am more deadly now because I am even more invisible.*

As he continued to stare at the coach below, the duchess alighted. To look at her, one wouldn't think Sarah Challoner had a care in the world, he thought, much less that she had received several assassination threats. Dressed in a gown of midnight blue, with a low, square-cut neckline edged in lace that was echoed at her wrists, with a matching blue band threaded through her golden curls and pearls around her neck, she was blindingly beautiful, like a goddess come to earth.

Did her American bodyguard think so, too? he wondered. From what he had seen of Calhoun's face, it did not look as if he betrayed his feelings easily.

Just then the watcher saw Sarah Challoner give her bodyguard a dazzling smile and murmur some pleasantry, and he saw the bodyguard's lips curve slightly in response.

The duchess's smile sent a dagger of jealousy straight through the secret witness's vitals.

I knew I could not trust you not to betray me. You will die for that smile—painfully, tonight. Calhoun is but one of many, I am certain, but I will take my revenge on him separately.

"Oh, there you are, Pierre," said a voice. She pronounced it "Pee-air," as if it were two separate words, which irritated him even though it was but an assumed name. "What're ya doin' up here in your room spyin' on the guests when I need ya in the kitchen? You promised t'make me that special sauce to go over the venison."

He smoothed his features before turning around, and when he spoke his voice was bland and deferential. "I am coming now," he said. "I just had to glimpse the beautiful duchess, before I am busy cooking for her, yes? Like a fairy-tale princess, is she not?"

The rotund black woman eyed him stolidly. "I dunno about that, but you better hustle yo' French behind on down to the kitchen, Pi-erre, or ya won't get the chance to cook for no duchess. I bin the mayor's only cook fer a long time and he didn't need no special Frenchie cook before this duchesswoman come, and I don't have time to go lookin' fo' ya every time I need ya."

Muttering a curse in French under his breath at the cook, he followed the servant down the narrow attic steps that led from the servants' quarters. What he would achieve tonight before he suddenly disappeared from the mayor's house would make these minor irritations more than worth tolerating.

* * *

Sarah was more than ready to leave. Her head was throbbing unmercifully and she longed to get out of the tight stays that made eating more than a minimum of the excellent meal an impossibility. There had been numerous and interminable toasts to Anglo-American relations, to future statehood for Colorado Territory, to Lord Halston's investing in the Chaffee Mining Company. Good Lord, there was still the dessert course to endure, and probably after that she would have to go into the drawing room with the mayor's wife and make polite conversation with the other ladies while the gentlemen lingered over port and cigars.

"Delicious, wasn't it, your grace? I was so fortunate to find this Frenchman to cook for us just in time for your visit," John Harper was saying into her right ear. "Of course, my regular cook's nose is thoroughly out of joint because I hired him, but Maisie sure can't make sauces like whatever that was on the venison."

"It was excellent. *Sauce au poivre,* I believe. The entire meal was the best I've had in America, without a doubt," she praised. "Please pass along my compliments." Harper had bored her to death boasting of his French chef.

"Ah, but you haven't tasted dessert yet. Pierre has promised something special, 'fit for a duchess,' as he says."

Sarah forced herself to smile and murmur something polite.

"But I'm sure your grace has sampled the finest French cuisine before," opined the man on her left, a barrel-chested old real estate speculator named Ellis Edwards, who at least offered an alternative to Harper's boasting, even though he was very hard of hearing and called her "your grace" in every sentence he uttered.

She'd never been *your-grace*d so many times in her life. If she ever got done with this interminable evening, she was going to reward herself in the morning with a few hours of horseback riding, and nothing Morgan Calhoun said was going to change her mind. Surely she'd generated enough goodwill with the prominent men of Denver and their wives that she had earned a little pleasure. If Morgan wouldn't go with her, she'd go alone, Sarah thought rebelliously.

She glanced over her shoulder and saw Calhoun still standing between her and the wall, as if he were but another of the liveried waiters hired for the occasion. He'd been there throughout the meal. Without her hated spectacles, she couldn't tell for sure, but she was fairly sure he didn't move a muscle in acknowledgment of her look.

The mayor had offered to seat him at the far end of the table just as if he were a guest, but Morgan had declined—much to Harper's regret, Sarah guessed. John Harper wanted to pretend nothing untoward had happened during the duchess's visit to his city, and would have been happier still if the duchess's bodyguard had consented to eat in the kitchen.

She wondered if Morgan was hungry, standing there watching everyone eat like that. She'd have to make sure the kitchen sent something up for him when they got back to the hotel.

At least William Wharton was sitting just on the other side of Edwards, and she could see and be warmed by the commiserating rolling of his eyes. Sarah wanted to wink back at him, but duchesses did not do such vulgar things, even in the wilds of America, and she settled for smiling down at her plate, knowing he would see and understand.

What a nice man Wharton was, Sarah thought as the waiters cleared the table of the dinner course. She was quite looking forward to their evening at the theater two nights from now.

"And now for the pièce de résistance," the mayor announced, his French accent exaggerated and incorrect as a waiter brought in an elaborate pastry and set the first one in front of Sarah. Behind him other waiters were bringing in more of the pastries and setting them in front of each diner, until finally all of the powerful and influential guests at this dinner in Sarah's honor had been served.

"What is this, some kinda fancy Frenchie cake?" the real estate speculator asked her in a stage whisper, and immediately plunged his fork into his and shoveled an enormous amount into his mouth.

"D'lishus," he mumbled through a mouthful of pastry. "Tashte it, Dushess."

Sarah glanced at Harper and saw that he was speaking to another guest.

"Actually, Mr. Edwards, I find I cannot eat another bite, especially of something so rich looking. You would be doing me quite a service if you ate it for me," she said appealingly, with a meaningful glance at Harper's back.

Edwards chuckled. "I could be your knight in shining armor, huh? No sooner said than done." He winked, and scooped her *éclair à la Martinique* onto his plate, leaving just a bite so it would appear that she had eaten most of it. "Scrumptious," he muttered, jabbing his fork into what he'd taken and eating it with gusto.

Amused, Sarah turned back to the mayor, who, fortunately, had missed this little byplay. "It was so kind of you to have this dinner party in my honor, Mr. Harper. I don't know if you ever plan to visit Britain, but you must visit Malvern Hall if you ever—"

A high-pitched cry from the left cut into her words. It was Edwards, she saw as she whirled around. He was clutching his neck, his face purpling above the tight starched collar. His eyes bulged in terror as he turned them on her, as if imploring her to save him.

"P-p-p…" he managed to sputter, his voice squeaky as if it was forced past spasming vocal cords. Then his eyes rolled up in his head and he fell backward, tipping the chair with a mighty crash.

Chapter Nine

Mayor Harper's new French chef, "Pierre," smiled to himself in the kitchen when he heard the muffled *thud* and the first screams, imagining the sight of Sarah Challoner's limp, lifeless body, still clad in its fancy gown and jewels, collapsed in a heap on the floor. Her uncle would doubtless be slapping the face that was rapidly turning a dusky blue, trying in vain to bring the dead duchess to her senses. Pandemonium would soon break out as they realized she was beyond help.

"Lord Gawd, whuss happenin' out there?" cried the cook as one of the waiters ran into the kitchen.

"One of the guests just keeled over dead, that's what!" shouted the man, his eyes wide with horror. "It was the old man sitting next to the duchess—you should see him, Maisie! His face is purple as a grape!"

"Pierre" jumped to his feet, ignoring the chair he'd just kicked over. "But how is this possible?" he demanded. He'd specifically told this very waiter to place the first serving of his éclair at the duchess's place, not in front of the old sot beside her!

"He ate his, then hers, too—the duchess gave it to him, said she couldn't eat it. It was awful—I was watchin' him when he took sick! He'd eaten about half of it when all at once his eyes got all bulgy an' he just clutched his neck and tried to say somethin', and then fell over backward, dead as a six-card poker hand! Now everyone's all runnin' every which way, and the guests is leavin', and the mayor's apologizin' to them Britishers for Ellis dyin' like that an' spoilin' the party...."

"Merde!" growled "Pierre," but there was no one to hear him, because the cook had followed the waiter out to the dining room to gape at the spectacle. He had thought his idea of a poisoned pastry was foolproof!

Frantic to salvage victory from this debacle, he ran unnoticed up to the attic where the servants had their quarters and grabbed his rifle from its place of concealment under his bed. He shoved open the window through which he had gazed upon the arriving Sarah Challoner and her bodyguard, refusing to worry about how he would escape after the deed, just praying that he would get a second chance to kill her this evening.

"The poor man," Sarah was saying as Morgan hustled her and Lord Halston out of the mayor's house, not through the front door, but via the French doors that led from the dining room into Mrs. Harper's rose garden at the side of the house. From there they made their way to the carriage turnaround at the back, where Ben waited with the landau. "To be taken like that so suddenly...I wonder what he was trying to say?"

"Unfortunately, we'll never know...but I'm certain it was an apoplexy," her uncle said in soothing tones. "Not unexpected in a man of his age. It's just terrible that you had to be a witness to it, niece."

Morgan allowed himself a snort of disgust as they reached the carriage. "Apoplexy, my foot," he said, scrutinizing their surroundings as he assisted the duchess into the carriage. "The man was poisoned—only he wasn't meant to get that dessert, the duchess was!"

He saw Sarah's jaw drop, heard Lord Halston *tut-tutting*.

"Really, my good man, I know she's received threats, and there was that gunshot, but—*poison?* That's too much like a bad stage melodrama, Calhoun!"

He expected no better from Halston, but Morgan was astonished to see a smile of amusement lurking on the duchess's lips as she settled her skirts on the padded cushions. "Really, Mr. Calhoun! I think the Borgias and their ilk have been dead for centuries. It's sad that Mr. Edwards is dead, but I cannot imagine it could be anything but natural causes."

"I don't know who the Borgias are, but you don't think it's suspicious that Harper just happened to hire some foreigner who claims he can cook?"

"Good God, man, you don't mean to accuse Harper—" began Lord Halston.

"No, of course not," Morgan answered without looking at him. "I'm talking about the foreigner."

He saw Sarah begin to chew on her lower lip and uncertainty cloud her eyes.

Morgan shifted his gaze to Lord Halston, but the duchess's uncle's face just looked skeptical. Try as he might, Morgan could see no trace of guilt there, but the man might just be a hell of an actor, as he'd thought before. Damn it, he stood to gain too much if his niece died.

"We'd better get going," Morgan announced, shutting the carriage door and ending the conversation. He wanted to get the duchess safely back to the hotel, and then, by God, he was going to come back and question every one of the mayor's staff.

If none of them acted guilty, then Lord Halston had to be behind the threatening notes and assassination attempts on his own niece. Sure, he'd cooperated, and encouraged the duchess to do so, too, but what better way to look innocent than to go along with the bodyguard?

Hours later, Morgan rode back from the mayor's house to

find a lamp left dimly burning in the main room. The duchess and her entourage had obviously gone to bed. Just as Morgan had suspected when he'd gone back to question the mayor's staff, the new French chef was inexplicably missing, along with all of his belongings.

Morgan had then asked if he could see the remains of the pastry Edwards had been devouring, only to be told it had been thrown out. On a hunch, he'd gone to the trash heap beyond the barn where the cook said they dumped scraps. There he found an already stiffening carcass of a pig who'd been out scavenging, confirmation of his suspicion that the pastry had been poisoned.

It seemed he'd been asleep only moments when he woke to feel someone shaking him awake.

He had his hand on the gun he always left by his right hand and was cocking it even before he managed to get his eyes open. Then, as he was struggling to focus his gaze on whoever was bent over him, his nose identified the scent of roses.

"Lord, Duchess," he muttered, now recognizing the woman who knelt by his bed. "You don't know how close I came to shooting you." He was angry at himself for falling so deeply asleep.

"Sh, Morgan," she whispered, her breath whisper soft on his face. "I don't want to wake the others."

"What's up?" he said, instantly alert. Had she found some proof that her uncle was indeed the man behind the threats? Was she looking to escape?

But no, she was smiling, and even in the dim light of the lamp she'd lit and left with its wick barely showing, he could see the mischief dancing in her blue eyes. She was wearing a dark-colored riding habit, and her golden hair was coiled under one of those charming but useless bits of fabric she called a hat.

"We're going riding, and I don't want the others—especially my uncle, who can be a bit of a worrier, you know—to know till we've gone," she added with a wink. "They'll just come up with all sorts of reasons why we shouldn't go, or why we should wait until my uncle and half a dozen others can join us, and I've no wish for a large party. I just want to go for a gallop on my mare. I've nothing scheduled today, so it won't matter if we're gone for hours! We'll leave a note, of course," she said as Morgan frowned and opened his mouth.

"But Duchess—"

"But nothing. You promised me yesterday, remember? I very much *need* to get out into the fresh air—especially after what happened last night. Besides, the horses are all ready—I told Ben what we'd be doing. And I managed to leave a note yesterday for the kitchen staff without any of my people seeing it, requesting a picnic lunch for two be ready in the stable at dawn. So you see," she said as she sat back on her heels, grinning, "it's all arranged. All you have to do is get dressed."

Morgan started to protest that he hadn't promised her they would go for a ride, he'd said he wanted to *think* about it, but he could see it was about as much use as arguing with a Texas twister. Besides, if he got the duchess off by herself, it would be easier to tell her about the poisoned hog and the French cook's disappearance. And once he got her attention with those facts, maybe he could even persuade the headstrong lady that her uncle was the most logical person behind the threats, and that she needed to get away from him. Lord, he hoped that groom of hers wasn't in on the plot, since she'd taken him into her confidence about the ride. Just to be on the safe side, he'd lie to the crusty old groom about where they were going.

Morgan sat up, rubbing a hand ruefully through his bed-rumpled hair and over his beard-roughened cheeks, all too aware that he was wearing only a union suit beneath the sheet. "I need a shave."

"No, you don't," she insisted. "The horses won't care, and if you start clattering about with your shaving mug and getting water and everything, the others will wake. Besides," she said, running a hand playfully over his chin and pretending to wince when she encountered his bristliness, "you look like a desperado. Surely no one we meet would dream of molesting me with a tough hombre like you along."

If you only knew just what a desperado you're talking to. "You've been readin' too many of those silly novels, Duchess," he said, turning his back to her as he stood so she wouldn't see how her nearness, her touch and the scent of roses that clung to her had affected him physically. "Now, go on back into your room for a few minutes so I can get dressed."

They rode steadily westward out of Denver, away from the rising sun. He'd let the duchess and her bay mare with that ridiculously fancy name have their gallop for a few minutes, keeping pace on Rio until the kinks and the deviltry had been run out of the horses. He didn't know how any woman managed to stay on a galloping horse when riding sidesaddle, but he had to admit Sarah Challoner was an excellent horsewoman. She managed the spirited mare with ease, even when Trafalgar had tried to unseat her mistress with some unexpected crowhops.

Clearly Rio found the leggy thoroughbred mare as entrancing as Morgan secretly found Sarah Challoner, but when the pinto stallion got too friendly, Trafalgar made it clear with a few kicks in his direction that she was not interested. Rio seemed to take his rejection in stride, however, and soon the horses were walking amicably along together, tails swishing in unison.

Though Morgan had said it would be hard to protect her

out in the open, he'd felt his anxiety about the duchess's safety lessening more and more as they got farther away from Denver and any signs of human habitation. Here there was nothing but buffalo grass and the occasional cottonwood tree. They saw rabbits and a couple of groundhogs, and once, a skunk went ambling away from them through the tall grass.

Then, as they reached the beginning of the foothills, the inclining, rock-strewn path into the pines narrowed, and they had to ride single file. Morgan led the way, constantly scrutinizing their surroundings in all directions. He heard the duchess humming, and while he didn't recognize the tune, the melody was in perfect harmony with the sunshine and crisp air.

Finally, when the sun was high in the sky, they reined in their mounts on a level rise, and decided to eat their picnic there. It was a good open spot, where anyone or anything approaching them could be seen a mile away. Dismounting, Morgan could see the town nestled on the plain below, with the silvery ribbon that was the South Platte River winding through the middle of it.

"It looks like a toy village, doesn't it?" he commented, pointing, after the duchess had dismounted. "Hard to imagine anyone down there could want to harm anyone."

She made some noncommittal remark, staring blankly in the direction his finger indicated. For a moment he thought the second thing he'd said had upset her by reminding her of the danger she faced, but then he realized what the problem was. "You can't see what I'm seein', can you, Duchess?"

Slowly she shook her head in chagrin. "No, I'm afraid not. It's just a soft blur."

"Then why don't you put on your spectacles?" he asked, mystified.

She looked away. "Vanity is such a stupid sin, is it not?"

"Duchess, do you mean to tell me you care more about how you look than seeing where you're going? Does this mean you couldn't see all the pretty scenery we passed all the way up here?''

She shook her head at that last question. "Not exactly. Actually, I can see things fairly well if they're within oh, say, six feet or so, like that tall evergreen over there. So I *have* enjoyed the beauty around me—''

"Did you even bring your spectacles with you?''

She nodded, her face wary, but made no move to bring them out.

He made an exasperated sound. "Duchess, don't you even want to know if that fine mare of yours is about to put her hoof in a gopher hole?''

She paled at that. "Oh! You're right, of course,'' she said. "From now on I shall wear them when riding.'' She reached into the breast pocket of her riding habit and put them on, coloring a little as she did so. For a moment she stared silently at the scene below, then she turned to him, the glass slightly accentuating blue eyes that looked suspiciously moist. "I know you don't understand this, Morgan—I know I must seem a vain and silly creature to you, but...I just feel like such a bluestocking, so awkward and ugly when I'm wearing these things!''

He stared at her, hardly able to believe what he was hearing. The gloriously golden, beautiful woman before him thought anything so minor as putting spectacles on could make her *ugly?* "Ma'am, I don't know what a bluestocking is, but no, ma'am, you've got it all wrong, if that's what you think,'' he said, before he could wonder if what he was saying was too forward for a bodyguard to be expressing to his employer. "You're way too pretty for a little bit o' wire an' glass to make you ugly.''

She blinked. "You're...you're very kind, Morgan.''

"I'm just tellin' the truth, Duchess.''

For a long moment they just stared at each other, awareness humming between them. Then she said, "Shall we unpack our luncheon? All this fresh air makes me rather hungry. And what shall I do with Trafalgar, tie her to a tree? I'm afraid she isn't trained as yours is," she added, referring to the fact that Morgan had just dropped the reins over his mount's head when he dismounted, "ground-tying" him.

"I have some hobbles," Morgan said, reaching in his saddlebags for the pair of attached, braided-leather loops that encircled a horse's fetlocks and kept it from straying too far.

After hobbling the mare, he helped spread the large checked cloth out over the grass and then helped the duchess unpack the food. The cook at the Grand Central had sent cold chicken, biscuits, an apple pie, cheese and a corked bottle of wine—though she had apparently forgotten they would need a corkscrew for the wine. Sarah stared at the bottle, crestfallen. "I suppose we can always wash the food down with the water in your canteen...."

"Don't give up yet," Morgan told her with a grin, charmed by the way an errant breeze had loosed several strands of her chignon. Now those golden tendrils caressed her neck—as he'd like his lips to be doing, he realized with an inner groan. He reached inside one of his boots and brought out the knife he always carried with him.

He saw her eyes widen at the sight, then went to work trying to impale the cork on the narrow knife blade.

To his dismay, the best he managed to do was push the cork down into the wine, but she just laughed as she saw the cork bobbing around in it. "Don't worry, it'll taste just fine," she said as she held out her glass. Then she waited, and finally said, "Aren't you going to have some, Morgan?"

"Um...maybe I'd better just drink the water, Duchess," he muttered. Wine was just what he didn't need, out here alone with the most beautiful woman he'd ever seen.

"Don't be silly," she said, shrugging out of her riding jacket and leaning back on her elbows, so that her starched white blouse gleamed in the sun. "Unless you're abstaining for…ah…religious reasons? There's a whole bottle here, and we might as well not let it go to waste. We shan't be able to bring what's left back with us, now that we can't use the cork anymore.''

He had to smile at the idea of himself abstaining for religious reasons. The abstinence pledge he had taken at the Baptist church as a youth seemed a century ago.

"All right, Duchess, I reckon I'll have a little, then." *But you've already gone to my head.*

Chapter Ten

"I vow I cannot eat another morsel!" Sarah said, falling back on her extended elbows in mock exhaustion. Thank God Celia had not been awake to insist she wear a corset! She'd long ago taken her spectacles off, feeling no need to see anything beyond Morgan.

"It's good to see a woman enjoy her food, not just peck at it like a little bird," Morgan countered with a grin.

"Enjoying one's food is one thing, devouring it like a plowman is quite another," she informed him, trying to sound prim and failing utterly. It was too glorious a day, and she was too happy to be out in the fresh air with the sun beating down on her back, alone with this dangerously attractive American man, for her primness to be convincing.

Morgan had relaxed, too, his face losing its expression of constant, wary vigilance. He looked open, approachable, and, despite the night's growth of beard shadowing his cheeks, too damnably appealing to a woman who was supposed to be in love with another man.

Somehow she couldn't manage to condemn herself at the moment, though, for her fascination with Morgan Calhoun. Maybe the wine had exacerbated the feeling. She probably ought not to drink any more of it. But whether she was tipsy or not, right now her "understanding" with Thierry seemed a distant, unreal thing....

"There's more pie," Morgan observed, mischief dancing in his green eyes. He had taken his pistol out of its holster and laid it on a rock within arm's reach, and was lying on his side as he polished off the last chicken leg. All Morgan needed was a laurel wreath on his head and a toga on that long, lean body, and he could pass for a Roman senator reclining at the banquet, she decided, and chuckled at the thought.

"What's so funny?"

She couldn't very well tell him what she had been imagining, so she said, "Oh, nothing...everything. It's just so...*liberating* to be up here so far away from schedules and protocol and Uncle Frederick's nagging." And those threatening messages, she wanted to add, but she didn't want to spoil the pleasant day by mentioning it. Besides, she could see by the shadow that flitted across his eyes that he had the same thought, and she silently blessed him for not saying it either.

"Duchess, you haven't said—where does your tour take us after Denver?" Morgan asked.

She smiled, grateful for his implied promise to continue as her bodyguard for the rest of the tour. "When we leave Denver in three days, I'd planned to take advantage of the new transcontinental railroad to go to California, see the Pacific and San Francisco and so forth, and then travel back through Arizona and New Mexico Territories—I'm particularly eager to see Santa Fe," she said, thinking of her planned rendezvous with Thierry in that city. "Then we'll just travel overland until we can connect with a railroad that will take us into Texas."

He was thoughtful. "Well, Duchess, that last part might be a tad difficult. You have to understand that the War between the States slowed down railroad buildin' in Texas. Maybe it would be best to take the train all the way back east from California, 'cause I don't think there's a railroad connection close enough to New Mexico to do you any good.''

"Oh, but I couldn't leave without seeing Santa Fe! I've heard so much about it—isn't it supposed to be one of the oldest cities in your country? Besides, our plans are all set to sail from Galveston."

He shrugged. "Okay, but you're probably going to have to take a stagecoach clear from California into Texas. That'll sure be a long, uncomfortable trip," he warned her.

"I'd have to hire the entire vehicle, of course, since there are five of us," she mused. "Lord, the thought of traveling in such a confined space with Uncle Frederick for long distances!" She shuddered, then had another thought. "But I needn't stay inside the coach the entire day—I could spend much of it riding alongside the coach on Trafalgar."

His face was skeptical. "You haven't seen the country, Duchess. It's rocky and dry, and frequently hilly. I really don't know if a highbred horse like your mare is up to it...."

"But Trafalgar has wonderful endurance!" she protested, stung at the thought that he was criticizing her beloved thoroughbred. "She's carried me over fences all day when we foxhunt! I'll make sure she's freshly shod, and we'll carry oats for her—she'll be fine, you'll see!"

"This trip isn't a foxhunt," he told her bluntly. "It's wild country, full of Indians and outlaws, as well as four-legged varmints like cougars. Even a train trip isn't without hazards, but if you're determined to leave the rails, I'm going to insist you hire half a dozen other well-armed men—"

"*You're* going to insist?" she repeated coolly, arching a brow in her best haughty-duchess fashion.

He didn't seem the least intimidated by her hauteur. "Yeah, I'm gonna insist," he repeated, "or we'll part company at the train tracks. It'd be plumb foolish to head across such country with only me to protect you and your party.

And if you plan to ride part of the way, you'd be smart to trade that ladylike sidesaddle in on a stock saddle and ride astride.''

"Ride *astride?* Uncle Frederick would be scandalized," she said with a grin, trying to lighten a conversation that had become too deadly serious.

"And you'd be smarter still to stick that pretty yellow hair of yours under a hat," he persisted.

"Oh? And why is that?" Sarah demanded, tiring of the steely authority in his tone. She disliked being the novice in anything.

"Because Indians especially prize yellow hair," he told her plainly. "They'd love to have you as a captive, or maybe they'd just take your scalp."

"I believe you're trying to scare me, Mr. Calhoun," she remarked, keeping her voice light, unwilling to reveal just how much his words truly *had* frightened her.

He surprised her by saying, "Maybe I am, Duchess, but I haven't exaggerated a thing. I want you to realize this isn't gonna be some carefree jaunt across a big park like I think you're picturing."

Then she remembered all the times he had been right about things. This was his country, not hers, after all, and he was bound to know the realities of the terrain better than she. As much as she disliked being told what to do, she reminded herself she was paying him to keep her safe, so it would be wise to heed his advice.

"All right," she said stiffly, looking out over the valley below so she wouldn't have to see the triumph in his green eyes. "When we leave the train, I will be guided by what you say."

"You look a mite riled, Duchess," he said.

"I? Of course I'm not riled, Mr. Calhoun," she insisted, damning those all-seeing green eyes. "I merely dislike playing the ingenue."

He looked puzzled. "If that's the same as bein' a tender-foot, heck, you can't help it. We're all new at something. Why, can you imagine *me* meetin' the queen of England? Reckon I'd look right silly doin' that, 'less someone told me how to go about doin' it proper."

She couldn't suppress an unduchesslike hoot of laughter at the image of Morgan Calhoun, dressed like a Western desperado, being presented to the plump monarch at court. Victoria would faint dead away with shock when Morgan offered her his hand instead of bowing to her—if she hadn't already swooned just from the sight of him!

"There, you see? I'd look like a big ol' fish outa water, wouldn't I?" he said with a grin. Then, as she continued to laugh, he pretended to be offended. "Hey, it's not *that* funny. It's not like I couldn't learn those highfalutin' manners if I *wanted* to."

She covered her mouth with her hand. "Oh, Morgan," she said, "you always know just how to tease me out of taking myself too seriously, don't you? You're such a dear," she said, and before she could give herself time to think, she leaned down across the blanket and kissed him on the cheek.

He looked startled, and his green eyes widened from their usual narrowness for a moment as he propped himself on one elbow and stared at her. She saw him grow pale, then flush with color on his high cheekbones.

She had embarrassed him! "I'm sorry, I'm afraid impulsiveness is one of my biggest faults," she said, reaching out to touch that rough cheek as if to wipe away the kiss.

Morgan's eyes had gone a deeper, darker green, and his smile put her in mind of a great hunting cat who has suddenly spotted his prey. His gaze shifted to her lips. "The only reason to be sorry, Duchess, is if you aren't gonna continue bein' impulsive like that," he said.

Afterward she remembered a split second of fear as she realized how utterly alone she was with this man out here in the wilderness, how completely vulnerable she was to his will. She watched as his mouth came closer, not to her cheek, but to her *lips.*

And then he was kissing her, and the world swam away in a blur, and with it her fear, as she began to return his kiss, allowing him to deepen the pressure as he slanted his mouth across hers. Sarah could feel the hunger in him. As if in a dream, she opened her mouth to him and felt his tongue sweep inside, claiming her mouth as his possession, and instead of alarming her, it only made her want more. She felt a rising of her own hunger, a hunger that until this moment she hadn't known she owned, but she didn't know how to satisfy the heat building inside her. Boldly, as if she were a woman experienced in passion, she allowed her tongue to tangle with his, and was rewarded with a growl of satisfaction from Morgan.

The sound excited her, made her want to get closer still, but it was impossible as long as she was leaning down into his kiss, still propped up one arm. So she put her other arm around his neck and allowed herself to drift downward, still kissing Morgan, until they were lying face-to-face.

"Oh, Duchess," he groaned, and kissed her again. "You taste like champagne."

"It's Sarah—*Sarah*," she whispered between kisses, and then his lips began to nibble at her ear, her neck…. The hand that had splayed out over the small of her back was inching around her rib cage now, but the advance didn't frighten her. It only served to stoke the flames building within her at a frightening pace.

"Sarah," he repeated, the way he said her name a caress in itself. Then his hand closed over her breast, cupping it, and she gasped at the unfamiliar jolt shooting through her, like liquid fire burning its way straight to the center of her being.

"Oh, *Sarah*," he murmured as his thumb found her nipple unerringly through the thick cloth of her bodice and the chemise she wore, and made lazy circles over it that made her moan and clutch at him, wanting she knew not what.

But he knew, it seemed. He unbuttoned the bodice of her riding habit, and then he was suckling her breast right through the thin lawn of her Belgian lace-edged chemise. The feeling of his warm mouth pulling at the exquisitely tender flesh made her want to cry out loud, but she couldn't seem to produce more than a whimper.

With his free hand he pulled her closer against him, and suddenly she felt the hard ridge of flesh straining against the confines of his trousers and the skirt of her riding habit.

"Morgan, *please*," she begged, and didn't know if she was pleading with him to continue or stop the delicious torture.

Again, Morgan knew. He pushed his pelvis against her, all the while continuing to stroke her breast, and then all at once she knew what she wanted, too. This man. Making love to her. Inside her, and as soon as possible.

"Yes, Morgan. Yes, *please*. Oh, please hurry," she moaned.

"Your wish is my command, Duchess," he said, and she giggled and smiled up at him, only to go still as she felt him reach down for the hem of her skirt and begin to inch it upward.

Just then a twig snapped, and one of the horses nickered. Sarah had barely registered the sound before Morgan was rolling away from her, and in one smooth motion grabbing the pistol he had laid on the rock.

"Morgan, what on earth..." Even as she spoke, he was lunging between her and the noise, and at the same time bringing the Colt up to fire.

But he did not shoot. "It's just a damn deer."

As she strained to focus on the brown shape a few yards away, the deer reversed its direction and bounded back down the slope.

Morgan's back sagged and he raked a hand through his dark hair. "Damn it all to hell."

"And what did you think it was?" Sarah, trembling, dazed, asked. Her body was still clamoring for more of him, yet all had changed for him. She could see it in his rigid posture.

He lowered his head, looking everywhere but at her. "I don't know...something dangerous...like maybe the man who's been trying to kill you. My job is to protect you, but here I was, tryin' to..." He seemed unable to finish his sentence.

"Trying to make love to me?" Sarah supplied gently.

"Yeah, damn me for a bastard and a fool."

His words made her sit bolt upright, and she began to hurriedly pull on her chemise, trying to ignore the sensation of the moistened cloth against the breast he'd been suckling only minutes before. "Why, what do you mean, Morgan?" she asked carefully.

"Hellfire, Duchess, I'm your *bodyguard*. If that had been someone gunnin' for you—"

"But it *wasn't*, Morgan," she noted. "Don't be so hard on yourself. It was I who kissed you first, you know." What she said seemed sensible and obvious, even though she was feeling anything but sensible. Her breasts, and the area between her legs, still ached for his renewed touch.

"But it *could* have been, don't you see? You could've been murdered because I forgot what I'm supposed to be there for and instead I was trying to...oh, *hell*."

"Morgan," she said, trying to ignore the chill creeping up her spine at his words, "no harm was done, and you certainly weren't doing anything that I wasn't en—"

He interrupted, "Well, it isn't gonna happen again, Duchess, you hear me? You hired me to protect you and that's just what I'm going to do." He stood up and turned his back as if he couldn't bear the sight of her.

All at once she was aware of how she must look to him—

her face flushed, her lips swollen from his kisses, her bodice still unbuttoned to the waist and her hair falling out of its neat chignon over her shoulders. She had behaved like a wanton, as if she were no more than a tart in Covent Garden!

But she wasn't a tart, she was the Duchess of Malvern! And she was in love with the Count of Châtellerault. She had promised to marry her Frenchman, yet how terrifyingly close she had come to giving herself completely to this American, this comparative *stranger*.

"I expect it was the champagne," she said with chilly casualness as she finished buttoning her bodice and began setting her hair to rights. "I should be used to it, but perhaps at this altitude... What I am trying to say is, the blame is all mine, and I don't hold you in the least responsible. But you're quite right in that it must not happen again."

"It won't, Duchess," he assured her—too quickly.

Sarah found his agreement perversely wounding. She'd be thrice damned before she ever so much as smiled at Morgan Calhoun again.

"Yes. Well...perhaps we should be packing up and riding back. Uncle Frederick will be frantic about my absence, even though I left him a note."

They packed up the remnants of the picnic in silence, and in minutes they were riding back toward Denver.

Chapter Eleven

The assassin peered around the corner of the building just in time to see his quarry and Morgan Calhoun dismount and begin to lead their horses back into the hotel stables. It was about time they returned!

Lord Halston had not been the only one who'd been frantic and furious at the duchess's disappearance this morning. The assassin had been beside himself when his spy told him that the duchess had been missing when the rest of the household had awakened this morning. She'd left a note, saying she was going for a ride.

But what if she hadn't really just gone riding? he'd thought. What if Sarah now suspected the identity of her would-be killer and had decided her only chance of survival lay in de-camping with her thrice-damned bodyguard?

After a few moments of panic, though, cool reasoning had gained control over his panic. He had decided to wait and watch. The odds were that the duchess had only taken one of those early-morning rides of which she was so fond. And now his guess had been proven correct, and his hours of loitering around the outside of the Grand Central Hotel, dressed as a down-on-his-luck prospector complete with a stuck-on beard and a low-brimmed hat, were about to be rewarded.

Quickly he took a glance behind him, saw that the alleyway was still empty of witnesses, then inched forward, feeling for the pistol within his shapeless coat pocket. There would be no escape for her this time, he promised himself with a grim smile. First he'd kill her protector, then her.

He studied the woman he was about to shoot, seeing the tendrils escaping at the nape of her neck, the slightly swollen lips, the way her eyes could not avoid the lean form of her bodyguard, especially when Calhoun was not looking at her. Oh, yes, Sarah had been a naughty duchess, he thought. It was obvious she had been dishonoring the proud name of her family with this American, this *nobody*. Sarah Challoner deserved to die.

Just then Lord Halston stepped from the shadows of the stable into the sunlit stableyard.

"So *there* you are, niece! I am owed an explanation, I think," the marquess announced, advancing on her.

The assassin froze for a moment, keeping his head low so his face could not be seen. It need not matter that Lord Frederick had appeared, he decided; what were three lives taken instead of only two? With the marquess slain, the path to his goal would be even clearer than before.

"Oh? Can you not read, uncle?" Sarah coolly responded. "I left you a note, informing you that I would be riding with Mr. Calhoun this morning. I hope Donald is available to write a message for me? I have just conceived the most delightful plan to invite William Wharton and his charming sister for supper this evening—oh, I know it's short notice, but perhaps they would consent...?"

How very like Sarah Challoner, the assassin thought. Cool and self-possessed, trying to brazen it out, as if she were the master of her own fate, and not a mere woman who should be guided by a man!

"Sarah, you are very cavalier with those who care about

your safety,'' Lord Halston began, his face purpling with obvious frustration.

"Not at all. You knew I had my bodyguard with me. Could you have the hotel send up water for a bath, uncle? It's been so long since I've ridden I believe I'd like to have a long soak before tea...."

Damn her. Damn Sarah for making him imagine the sight of her relaxing in a copper hip bath, her breasts peeking impertinently over the bubbles, her special rosewater scent perfuming the air. A sight he had never seen, but only dreamed of. His hand, gripping his pistol within the coat pocket, trembled.

Now. He should do it now. He should bring his gun out of his pocket and fire.

"Hey, Clem, is that you? When did ya come down from yore claim?'' bellowed a voice behind the assassin, and a heartbeat later he felt a heavy hand clapping him on the back.

He whirled, furious at the interruption, to see another similarly dressed man about to buffet him once again. "I am *not* Clem,'' he growled in a low voice, knowing he couldn't let this interfering blowhard ruin his chance. "I think you mistake me for someone else. *Now, go away.*''

The prospector squinted at him through bleary, red-veined eyes. "Ya look like Clem, though, even if ya sound like some furriner...'' he muttered uncertainly. "Ain't ya afeered of some claim jumper takin' your mine while yore away? Les' go have a whiskey, whaddya say?''

He would cheerfully have blown a hole through the idiot if the shot wouldn't have sent his quarry fleeing. Turning to put his back to the duchess, her bodyguard and Lord Halston in case they should look his way, the assassin hissed, "I am *not* your friend, curse you.'' He brought the muzzle of his pistol just barely out of his pocket and made sure the old sot saw it. "*Now, go away,* or I will allow daylight into your liver, eh?''

The prospector's eyes focused with difficulty on what he could see of the pistol, and he backed away. "Well, okay, but I still say ya look like Clem t'me...."

Merde. He would just kill all of them. He turned back around, but saw that in the brief seconds while the prospector had distracted him, the duchess, her uncle and her bodyguard had all disappeared inside the stable.

It was unbelievable. For a moment he was tempted to murder the old prospector just to punish him for costing him his chance, then thought better of it. The old fool was not worth a bullet. He settled for flinging a lump of manure at the shambling figure.

After turning the horses over to the duchess's groom, Morgan followed Sarah and her uncle up the stairs, trying to keep his eyes off her gently swaying, riding-habit-clad posterior as she ascended.

His head ached with tangled emotions. Damnation, it felt as if there was a four-way dogfight going on in his brain. One of the dogs was lust, for his unsatisfied body still clamored to complete what had been interrupted up in the foothills. It had been stopped by another dog, the dog of decency and common sense, who'd known that he'd had no business taking liberties with the British noblewoman who employed him, even if she'd encouraged him. Then a third dog had shown up, shame, after he'd realized how easily both of them could have paid the price for his lack of vigilance. And now that the duchess was palavering with her uncle about inviting that young tinhorn Wharton and his sister to join her for dinner, a fourth dog had joined the fray: jealousy.

When he'd been kissing Sarah Challoner and running his hands over her beautiful body, her innocent delight had had him thinking she was a virgin, but now he wasn't so sure. He wouldn't be the first man deceived by a woman of experience. Now he was sure her invitation to Wharton was a means of getting revenge for her own unsatisfied passion. Morgan hadn't resumed making love to her, so she was going to show him how easily he could be replaced, wasn't she? And, damn her blue eyes, she was going to go him one better by achieving the revenge with a man closer to her own position in life!

Well, it wasn't as if she could exactly invite the mining magnate to spend the night, not with Wharton's sister along, and her uncle there as chaperon, he reminded himself, but somehow it was little comfort. Perhaps she was just warming up Wharton for the following night, when they were going to the theater? Afterward, would the duchess expect him to stand on guard outside some fancy private room in a restaurant while she and Wharton had a "late supper?"

Once in the duchess's suite, Morgan slammed the door behind him with unnecessary force. That fourth dog was winning the fight. Lord, but he wished he shared this bodyguarding job with some other man so he could go get drunk and find a woman, and not necessarily in that order.

"Good night, dear Helen. So good of you both to come on such short notice. See you tomorrow night, William. Seven o'clock was it, for the theater? And then supper afterward?" With difficulty Sarah suppressed a yawn as she and her uncle stood at the doorway, bidding the guests farewell. Morgan stood just beyond them, on the landing, watching up and down the stairs.

The last-minute supper party had been a delightful way to spend the evening, Sarah thought. These Americans were so flexible, so spontaneous! Back in England she could never have issued an invitation to supper with just hours to spare.

They'd been amusing company, chatty and surprisingly sophisticated in spite of the raw new town they lived in. Through their dinnertime conversation she'd learned more about the mining magnate. Wharton had come out to Colorado Territory in the gold rush days, but instead of frittering his profits away on gambling, whiskey and women, he had saved his money until he could buy a mine, and with the profits of that, bought more mines. He'd brought his sister out from the East when he could afford to build a nice home for them. His wealth had not made him arrogant, though. Sarah thought it a great pity that more of the wealthy peers back home were not so genuinely kind and approachable. She looked forward to going to the theater with him tomorrow night. It would be her last night in Denver, and she meant to enjoy it.

"You'd best go back in, your grace," Morgan said, turning back to her as the Whartons' footsteps died away and Lord Halston left the doorway.

"A word with you first, Morgan," she said. "I know you're angry at me for inviting Wharton to dinner tonight...."

His face darkened. "How could I be angry? I got nothin' to say about it, unless I think where you're goin' or who you're goin' with might be dangerous to you." There was nothing remotely warm in his green eyes, let alone any trace of the heated gleam that had been in them this very morning when he had been touching and kissing her so intimately. Once more he looked the cold, wary desperado.

"It must have felt like a slap in the face after...after what happened this afternoon," she said in a rush, looking away from his set, guarded face. "But don't you see? You were right...about what you said...you know, that we mustn't—"

"Yeah, I was right."

"Well, there you are, then. But...you could have accepted my invitation to take supper with us. I invited William's sister—" She knew she had said the wrong thing even before his eyes blazed green fire at her.

"Oh, you thought since I was right about you and me, you'd throw me a bone in the form of Helen Wharton, was that it?"

"No, you misunderstand," she lied, guiltily aware that he had seen right through her pretense.

"Well, don't do me any more favors, okay, Duchess? Helen Wharton's a pretty lady and all, but if I want a woman, I'll go buy one, you understand?"

"Perfectly." Her face flaming, she turned to go inside.

"Just a minute, Duchess. I don't suppose there's any point in tellin' you I think it's *loco* to be plannin' to go to a big public event like a play when somebody's been tryin' to kill you?"

"None at all. And surely there's safety in numbers in such surroundings."

"It didn't turn out that way for President Lincoln, did it?" he retorted, his face bleak.

Sarah felt her heart lurch. Even in England they had been shocked at hearing of an American president murdered in his box at the theater.

"I'm not taking your concerns lightly, Mr. Calhoun," she said, taking refuge in formality. "I believe you heard me ask Mr. Wharton this evening to take me to the play in the other theater, just in case anyone had heard he had been planning to take me to the Apollo?"

"Yes, I did, and so did everyone in your household," he noted.

She stared at him, dumbstruck for a moment. "Mr. Calhoun, you can't be suspicious of my uncle, can you, after getting to know him? Or maybe you think it's one of my servants?"

"Duchess, I've stayed alive this long because I'm suspicious of everyone," he retorted.

She threw her hands in the air in exasperation, recrossed the threshold into the suite and fled to her own room. There was no getting through to Morgan Calhoun—or getting close to him. He was a lone wolf—wary, cynical, ever on his guard. He might come close to the fire, but he'd never rest easy near it if there were others around. Even a lone wolf needed a mate, she thought, but Morgan hadn't realized it yet.

She and Morgan might as well exist on two separate planets, so different were their lives. Thank God she had not given in fully to passion with such a man when there was no possibility of a future.

She *would* be happy with Thierry. While an exiled French *comte* was not her precise social equal, certainly he understood the obligations and mores of their world. But why did the idea of their secret engagement progressing to marriage no longer fill her with unalloyed joy?

Was it just the months of separation that had turned Thierry into a stranger? She had been away from him for too long, and as it was too difficult to predict her exact arrival dates in certain cities in advance, it was impossible to get letters from him. Perhaps they should have eloped, and spent their honeymoon on this journey! Surely all would be well when Thierry joined her in Santa Fe; she would take one look into his expressive blue eyes and remember why she had fallen in love.

Until then, though, what was she to do about her growing attraction to Morgan Calhoun? Even the hurt she felt at his cross words and cold eyes moments ago couldn't diminish what she felt for him. However unsuitable it was, she could no longer deny to herself that there was a magnetism between them. When he was in the room, she wanted to fill her eyes with Morgan and no one else; it was his drawling, Southern-accented voice, so different from the familiar accents of her fellow Britons, that she wanted to hear, his smile she longed to elicit.

It was merely the attraction of opposites, she told herself, the charm of forbidden fruit. She'd heard of other noble-women conceiving passions for their footmen or other unsuitable men—even conceiving love children with them—and had felt pity and a mild disgust for how they had disgraced themselves.

Now she understood a little better, she thought. Her attraction to Morgan Calhoun was the thrill of the unfamiliar, her intoxication with his aura of danger and the added factor that he was only a temporary figure in her life. It was not as if she would marry him, and then have to face the humiliation of seeing him fumble at a bow to the queen, after all....

Chapter Twelve

The policeman waiting at the side door of the theater nodded to Morgan. "It's all clear, Mr. Calhoun," he said. "I've got one man stationed in the duchess's box, another in the stairwell and I'll be out here. Bring them on in."

Morgan smiled inwardly at the man's professional cordiality, knowing he'd have gotten another reception altogether if the officer had known that Morgan was a wanted outlaw. He strode over and rapped on the landau window. "Everything looks okay, your grace," he called out in a low voice. He'd be a lot happier when this night was over.

"I'm sorry it's only an American play, your grace," William Wharton murmured in his nasal Yankee voice as he helped Sarah Challoner alight from the landau at the side of the Denver Theater. "It's called *Cross of Gold, or, The Maid of Croisay. Richard III* is at the Apollo, but—"

"Oh, but I cut my teeth on the Shakespeare plays, Mr. Wharton!" Sarah said, gracefully picking up her train. She favored her escort with a smile that made the anxious, apologetic expression on the mining magnate's face relax at once. "Seeing something new, something typically American, is much more exciting! And I appreciate your being willing to change our plans as late as last night."

Sarah was dazzling in a gown of some satiny gold material whose stylishly low neckline was only emphasized by the necklace of diamonds and gold topaz that she wore. Glimpsing the shadowy hint of cleavage—and knowing Wharton was able to see it, too—made Morgan want to go howl at the moon that now hung over Denver like a great silver disk.

Wharton, preening, ignored Morgan as he strode past him into the side stairway with the duchess on his arm. "It's William, remember? Oh, but I understand about changing theaters," he said. "I wouldn't want your enjoyment of the evening to be marred by any worries, even though I feel sure this lunatic has given up by now, anyway. But if these precautions help you feel safer…"

Didn't the duchess realize how patronizing Wharton's reassurance sounded? And if Wharton wanted to live to a ripe old age, he'd damned well better take his hand off Sarah's arm. Morgan felt his hand itch to draw the pistol he had tucked out of sight in his waistband, and ground his teeth because he had no right to object to what the man said or did.

"Actually, another of the threatening notes was delivered with my breakfast this very morning," Sarah admitted. "The hotel management was very regretful, and said they had no knowledge of how it got there, of course. But I'm simply not going to worry. Mr. Calhoun is here, and you can see he's arranged for extra constables, so…" She shrugged elegantly and settled herself in the velvet-upholstered chair in the dimly lit box, arranging her skirts about her. "We're here safe and sound, and I intend to thoroughly enjoy my last evening in Denver, Mr. Whar—William. It's just too bad my uncle didn't join us. I know he would have enjoyed it."

"That's the spirit, your grace," Wharton said approvingly, then added, "Perhaps he didn't want to be horning in, eh?" He leaned out and indicated the crowd settling into their seats below. "A big crowd tonight, eh?"

He made it sound as if he had personally summoned them all, Morgan thought sourly.

"Yes, quite."

Morgan was amused at her answer, for he knew that the buzzing throng below was all just a colorful blur to his employer without her spectacles—and she was far too vain to consider being seen in them, either by Wharton or the faceless crowd. She wouldn't be able to see the actors on stage much better, either. She'd have to content herself with listening to them spouting their lines.

"Ah, they've spotted you, your grace," Wharton said with smug satisfaction when the patrons started to point at the inhabitants of the box and whisper behind fans and cupped hands to those they'd come with. "No doubt this will make the society notices in the newspaper."

You damned little banty rooster, if that's all you want, I hope you're happy, Morgan thought contemptuously as he took up his seat closest to the entrance to the box, with Wharton sitting between him and the duchess. He went back to scanning the crowd, alert for any furtive expressions or movements, but he could see nothing but avid curiosity in the faces turned upward to stare at the English duchess.

Yet why did he feel this prickling along his spine, the same sensation that had always preceded danger in the past? Was the man who was trying to kill Sarah in the crowd? Had the policemen let the assassin slip right by them?

In a moment the lights would dim and the play would begin, and he wouldn't be able to see anything. Hellfire, why had he ever let Sarah come here? It was just plumb crazy!

Later, Morgan could not have told anyone what the play had been about if his life had depended on it. He'd been too tense to sit still. Initially he'd taken turns pacing the back of the box and opening the door a crack to assure himself that there was still a guard outside the box. Then, when his fidgeting had earned him an annoyed glare from Wharton and a whispered "Do be *still,* Mr. Calhoun," from Sarah, he'd contented himself with leaning against the side wall and trying to see through the darkness that surrounded the other boxes and the rows of seats below. Once or twice he'd allowed himself quick glances at Sarah, who had sat enthralled with the melodrama unfolding on the stage.

At the intermission the duchess and Wharton had arisen and announced their intention of seeking refreshment. Morgan had shaken his head and told Wharton *he* could go fetch the refreshment if he liked, but Morgan didn't want the duchess mingling with the milling throng below.

The mining magnate's face had clouded over. Evidently he didn't like being told to fetch as if he were a dog, but before he could begin arguing with Morgan, Sarah had spoken up, her cheeks pink. "But Mr. Calhoun, I'm afraid that won't do. I need to—ahem!—stretch my legs, you see." She'd looked him straight in the eye, and Morgan had suddenly realized that even duchesses needed to answer calls of nature once in a while.

Gritting his teeth and praying an assassin wouldn't pick this time to make his move, he had accompanied Sarah to the door of the ladies' retiring room while Wharton went down to obtain refreshments. Morgan suspected the mine owner would have preferred to parade about the lobby with the duchess on his arm for all to see, but too bad.

Wharton had got a revenge of sorts when he'd returned to the box, for he'd been accompanied by a stream of acquaintances clamoring to meet the duchess. But Morgan had insisted on patting each one of the gentlemen down before letting them in.

Now, however, the play and the short farce that had followed were over, and everyone was rising to leave.

"Why don't we go backstage before we leave, your grace? The theater owner told me the actors wanted to meet—"

Morgan cut him off at the pass. "Forget it," he said quickly, ignoring the other man's sputter of indignation. "I want to get the duchess out of here before most of that crowd gets out the door." He didn't mention the fact that he could feel the hairs at the back of his neck standing straight up now. He wanted Sarah safely back at the hotel, and the sooner the better.

"Perhaps that would be best," the duchess murmured, but her eyes revealed her annoyance with her bodyguard for being so abrupt. "In any case, the hotel has a fine late supper waiting for us."

Wharton gave in gracefully and pronounced himself eager to dine with her.

Morgan checked the stairway, found the policemen still at their posts, and shepherded the duchess and Wharton down the stairs.

Ben had the carriage right in the narrow alleyway between the Denver Theater and its neighbor to the north, just as he'd been instructed to, and was already perched on the high driver's seat, ready to go.

Morgan had a brief glimpse of Ben's hand raised in greeting before Wharton stepped in front of him, his arm outstretched as if he intended to open the carriage door.

Damned meddling—

Morgan hadn't even completed the thought when the alleyway exploded with two thunderous reports in quick succession. Wharton collapsed at Sarah's feet, suddenly as boneless as a rag doll, his ginger hair drenched with blood. The policeman who'd been holding the side door open fell over backward, an ugly hole between his eyes. Sarah's scream mingled with the echoing gunshots.

From the landau Ben shouted, "Duchess, get in—" and then another *crack* sounded, and the groom's body sagged on the driver's seat.

The terrified horses reared and bolted, neighing frantically as they plunged down the alleyway, throwing Ben's body off the landau.

The shots had come from above, Morgan realized, even as he thrust Sarah behind him and yanked the Colt from his waistband. The neighboring building had no window—where was the assassin? He fired three shots in rapid succession toward the roof, then grabbed Sarah's hand. He thought for a heartbeat about seeking refuge in the building—

A bullet hit the wall behind them, just to the right of their heads, spattering them with shards of brick. That made Morgan's decision. He wasn't about to go in there with her—it could be a trap.

"Run, Duchess!" he yelled, pulling her in the direction the horses had galloped. Another shot was fired, and Morgan felt it whistle past his neck.

"But...Ben...Wharton...the constable—" she protested, even as she grabbed up her skirts and obeyed.

"They're dead!" he told her as they ran. "We can't help 'em now! Gotta get you...outa this!"

Behind them, pandemonium had erupted. Morgan heard shouts as the policeman who'd been guarding the inside stairway reached the street and found the bodies, and then more shouts and screams as the exiting playgoers reached the side alleyway and saw the corpses. There were no more shots, but was the assassin coming after them? A glance over his shoulder showed no one in pursuit yet.

Coming to a narrow passage between two buildings, he pushed Sarah into it. "Keep running!" he commanded. "I'm right behind you!"

They ran to the next street, then rounded the corner and found another alley. The duchess was surprisingly fleet for a woman running in kid slippers and holding her skirts up with her free hand, but she wouldn't be able to keep up this pace long, Morgan realized. And they were terribly vulnerable as long as they were fleeing through the darkness in an unfamiliar town. He had to find a place for her to hide, and then he'd see about summoning help and going out to hunt down the assassin....

An assassin who'd been hired by Sarah's uncle, if it wasn't Frederick himself. There was no other explanation. Damn, but he'd been a fool to let Sarah's faith in her uncle lull him into trusting Lord Halston!

"Can't...run...much farther," panted Sarah beside him. "Must...stop...a minute...rest..."

"Not yet," he told her. "We don't rest till we get you off the street." But he stopped nonetheless and listened, straining to hear over his own and the duchess's ragged breathing.

There were still no sounds of pursuit, just the distant sounds of confusion back at the theater. But there... Up in the next street Morgan could hear the faint tinkling sounds of a piano. "Come on," he whispered, and pulled her after him, and they ran in the direction of the music.

As they drew closer, the lights blazing through the sheer lace curtains illuminated the discreet sign proclaiming the place Madame Hortense's Parlor House. The windows were all open, for it was a warm night.

Morgan pulled Sarah up onto the steps. "Stay behind me and let me do the talking," he warned her, then knocked.

A ripe-looking madam with an ostrich plume draped over her fading red hair and wearing a gown of spangled red satin answered the door.

"We need a room," Morgan informed the woman, his nod including Sarah.

Madame Hortense blinked at Sarah. "Usually we provide the woman, mister. And where'd all that blood come from?" she added, her eyes narrowing as she extended a beringed finger to touch Morgan's shirtfront.

Morgan looked down, and in the light spilling out from the door he saw the crimson spatters that desecrated the whiteness of the starched shirt. Wharton's blood? The policeman's?

"Morgan? Are you hurt?" Sarah cried, dashing around him and staring at the blood, her blue eyes enormous in a face as pale as his shirt had been. She was in shock and had been running on pure nerve, and now she looked as if she might swoon.

"Naw, honey, that's ol' Eddie's blood," he said, seizing a name from the air and praying she would play along. "A jealous rival," he told the madam with what he hoped was a smug grin, then he winked at her with all the charm he was capable of mustering. "I'm afraid I bloodied his nose when I knocked him out. But he's gonna be plumb hateful when he comes to, and I want to get the little lady out of his way until he cools off, okay?"

Madame Hortense took her hand off her hip and extended it, palm up. "Let's see the color of your money—and I don't take gold dust, mister."

Lord, now they were stuck. The agreement had been that he'd be paid at the end of the trip, and with the duchess providing him with his food and the roof over his head, he'd had no need for money of his own ever since hiring on with her. He knew Sarah didn't carry money—it was always Lord Halston's job to tip the waiters and such.

"Will this buy us a room?" the duchess inquired, and Morgan saw her coolly pulling off the topaz-and-diamond earbobs that matched the magnificent necklace.

Madame Hortense held them up to the light and smiled. "Honey, if you want to throw in the necklace, you can hide out here for the whole month! No? Well, come on in and I'll go roust Natasha outa her room. She won't like it much, but I don't give a damn."

They entered and found themselves in a large, grandly decorated room that obviously served as the reception area for the gentlemen who patronized the house, for half a dozen women in scanty, low-cut dresses in garish hues lounged on the sofas that lined the walls. The piano player, whose tinny plunking had lured them here, stopped playing and swiveled around to join the whores in staring at Morgan and Sarah.

"Hey, mister, if you want a threesome I'll join ya," offered the smirking, blowsy brunette who was closest to them.

Morgan felt Sarah shrink closer to him. "Another time, sweetheart," he told the whore, plastering a silly grin on his face. "Tonight I promised the little lady we'd be all alone."

Moments later a sulky-looking faded blonde who must have once been pretty stomped down the stairs, eyed them and snarled, "It's all yours—last door on the left. I just changed the sheets after my last customer."

The room was small, ill lit with a smoky kerosene lamp, and possessed only a washstand, a mirror, a trunk and a narrow bed. The supposedly fresh bed linens were gray and threadbare, and there was a thin coverlet pulled halfway up. A wide strip of oilcloth covered the foot of the bed.

Sarah watched as Morgan closed and locked the door. She had held her tongue downstairs as he had asked, but now she needed some answers.

"Morgan, we can't stay here!" she cried before he had even turned back around. "We have to get back to the hotel! My uncle must be terribly worried about me...he must have heard what happened by now!"

The face he turned to her was that of the dangerous desperado, all grim, hard lines. "Nope, we're not goin' back to the hotel. It's time to face the facts, Duchess. Your uncle is the one behind this—he has to be! *He's* the one paying the assassin!"

She felt her jaw drop. "That's utter nonsense. You tried to make me think that he could be the one who wanted me dead before, and I didn't believe it then and I don't believe it now."

His eyes narrowed. "I tried trustin' him. But he's the only logical one, Duchess! I know it hurts to think this way, but who stands to gain as much as he does if you're dead?"

"Well, there's Kat—Kathryn," she noted, "my younger sister, who becomes duchess in the event I die without issue. But you're even more insane if you're suggesting she—"

Morgan's eyes softened just a fraction. "No, of course not, but if I'm right, maybe you better be thinkin' about her safety, too."

"What on earth are you saying?" The room started to spin at the thought that Kat could be in any danger.

"If you're out of the way, and she becomes the duchess, she's the only one between the title and dear old Uncle Frederick."

"You're demented, completely and absolutely demented," she told him. "I cannot—*will not*—believe such a crazed idea."

"Am I? Do you want to stake your life on it, and then your sister's, Duchess? Think about it. Who besides your uncle knew you had changed your plans and decided to go to the Denver Theater rather than the Apollo?"

"My secretary and my dresser, of course...and poor Ben..." She had an instant, terrible image of the sight of her groom's lifeless body tumbling from the top of the landau. "Oh, my God, poor Ben..." she said, trembling as the tears began to fall.

"Easy, Duchess," he murmured, placing a hand on her shoulder. "I know it hurts, but you can't think about him right now. Now, back to who betrayed you. I don't think it could have been your dresser or your secretary. If something happened to you, after all, they're out of a job."

She forced herself to stop weeping, to wrench her concentration back to what Morgan was saying. "Yes...Uncle Frederick hardly needs a dresser, and he's never been that fond of Donald Alconbury, unfortunately," she said with a wry quirk of her brows. "And in any case, anyone could have followed the landau."

"Maybe, but those shots came from the roof of the bank

building next door. It gets locked up at five. I arranged for the police to watch the neighboring buildings between closing time and when you were expected, so that no one could break in,'' he told her, stopping in his pacing for a moment. "So someone had to know in advance where you were going, tell the shooter, and he had to get inside the bank building when it was still open and manage to get to the roof or a window that looked into the alley, I'm not sure which.''

"You've thought this through very thoroughly, haven't you?''

Morgan looked surprised. "That's what you were payin' me for, wasn't it? And, Duchess...I know it's hard to face this, but who else but your uncle had anything to gain by your death?''

His voice was insistent, echoing inside her brain. Sarah spread her hands in front of her face. She did not want to imagine it, *could not* imagine her *uncle* plotting her death! Not Frederick, the curmudgeonly but kindly man who had stood solid as Gibraltar for her ever since her father had died. *No, it couldn't be...*

She shook her head, and the tears she had been holding in by sheer force of will started coursing down her cheeks again. "I can't bear the idea that he would want me dead.''

The argumentative light went out of his eyes, and the tension in his jaw relaxed somewhat. "Aw, hell, Duchess, I don't like tellin' you these things,'' he told her, throwing his hands up in the air. "But you hired me to keep you safe. If you go back, though, sooner or later he'll succeed, one way or the other, and even I won't be able to stop it.''

She shivered, suddenly feeling as if she were encased in a sheet of ice. "I'm not saying I believe you about my uncle, Morgan, but what do you propose to do?''

His gaze was steady as he said soberly, "I think we ought to go to the governor, Duchess, and tell him all this, and claim his protection for you while the police arrest your uncle. McCook will order an investigation.''

''But what if there's no proof? What then?'' she demanded, realizing she had just as much as admitted she was beginning to believe Morgan's horrible charge.

Chapter Thirteen

Morgan raked a hand through his hair and looked suddenly weary. "Then he can at least hold him long enough to buy us time. We'll get on a train goin' east, and I'll stay with you till you board the ship for England. The sooner you're back home, Duchess, the safer you'll be."

She shook her head. "I wouldn't trust the governor to protect me from a horsefly, Morgan. Oh, he was pleasant enough when I met him, but I could see McCook as just another one of those men who pats a woman on the head and tells her not to imagine nonsense."

"But you're a duchess!"

She allowed herself a cynical laugh, thinking back over a lifetime of having men rule her existence. "Beneath that title, I'm still just a woman to a man like that, and my lord uncle can be very persuasive. What if Frederick decided to tell him I'd been...ah...subject to delusions, or something of the sort? He'd believe him, I'm sure of it. No, Morgan, I'm not wagering my life on the governor's chivalry. We've got to escape on our own, you and me."

"Escape?" he demanded in the same tone of voice he'd use if she suggested jumping off a cliff. "You mean hide somewhere until we can get on a train east, without the governor's protection? I don't know, Duchess...."

Thierry would be waiting for her in Santa Fe. He would keep her safe once Morgan brought her to him, she thought, wondering why the idea didn't warm her chilled soul. But she'd never confided in Morgan about her secret engagement to the French count, and if she was going to ask him to take her on such a perilous journey, it was only fair that she tell him everything.

But after what had passed between them yesterday, did she dare? Would the feelings that existed between them make him refuse to take her to another man?

"Surely Uncle Frederick would expect me to go east, since the railroads would get me there fastest," she observed. "That's why you have to take me south—to New Mexico, and on into Texas. I can board a ship at Galveston and sail home."

His jaw dropped. "Duchess, like I said before, there's no train that'll take you all the way to the other end of Texas, and there's no way in hell I'd consider takin' you through country like that, just the two of us.... No, you'd be much safer goin' east by train."

She took a deep breath. "Morgan, there's something I haven't told you," she said, her heart pounding as she looked into his eyes. "*Someone* I haven't told you about. I *must* go by way of Santa Fe. I—I'm meeting someone there. The man I'm going to marry."

She watched the color drain from Morgan Calhoun's face.

"The...man you're going to marry?" he repeated, as if he couldn't trust his ears. "You're *engaged*, Duchess?"

Sarah nodded, feeling sick as she saw his jaw tense and the warmth leave his eyes.

"Yes...to Thierry de Châtellerault, a French count on Louis Napoleon's staff. He was also a captain in the French cavalry...before Louis Napoleon was exiled to England. He came over with the emperor,'' she explained.

His gaze impaled her. "How come you never talk about this fellow, if you're promised to him? Don't you love him?'' he demanded.

He wanted to add, *And if you love him, how come you were kissin' me like that yesterday? How come you would have given yourself to me if I hadn't stopped?* But maybe yesterday had nothing to do with love...and maybe duchesses didn't fall in love, anyway. It was too bad fools like him did.

She looked away. "Of course I do.''

Something wasn't right here.

Sarah's laugh sounded brittle, forced. "I—I'm afraid it's a secret betrothal, Morgan. We...we've planned to elope once I meet him in Santa Fe.''

"Why is it secret?''

She shrugged. "In England it's thought that a duchess should only marry her equal, a duke. A mere foreign count is viewed as a bit of a mésalliance—marrying beneath me, you see.''

He didn't see. "Who thinks so?''

"Her Majesty Queen Victoria, for one. She'll be horrified. She wanted me to marry the Duke of Trenton. Uncle Frederick will be scandalized, too,'' she added. Then she shuddered, remembering Uncle Frederick was trying to kill her.

"But you want to marry this Frenchie,'' he said, feeling his heart die within him.

"Yes,'' she said simply. "That's why I need you to take me to Santa Fe, Morgan. Thierry will be there by the time we get there. We can get there on horseback, can't we?''

"No.'' *No, damn it all to hell, I'm not taking you to Santa Fe only to give you away. I'd rather be tortured by Comanches first.*

"No? Do you mean it's impossible, or merely difficult? I'm tougher than I look, Morgan—''

"I mean no, I'm not taking you, Duchess. You're loco if you think you and that horse would survive a trip over the kind of country that lies between here and Santa Fe, let alone here and the coast."

"But *you* could, couldn't you?"

"Well, yeah, I reckon, if some Indian doesn't scalp me on the way, and nothin' happens to Rio, and—"

"Then I can do it, too."

"No, you can't, Duchess. Why don't you understand about the dangers I'm talkin' about? It's hundreds of miles over mountains, through deserts…"

"I'll double your salary."

"No," he said, turning his back so he wouldn't see the pleading blue eyes. *There isn't enough money in the world for me to do what you're asking. Not if I have to see you go to another man when we get there.*

"Very well, I'll more than double it. Nine thousand pounds, Morgan Calhoun, for getting me to Santa Fe, and then escorting us on to Galveston. It's a fortune! Think how you could live if you had that much money!" she pleaded.

Damn you for thinking you can buy me, Duchess. "It doesn't matter how much money it is if we aren't alive to finish the journey," he retorted, turning back to her. He thought he would see her pale, but her luscious mouth just took on a more determined set.

"Name your price, Morgan. I must get to Santa Fe, and you must take me there."

Lord, but she was one determined lady. "Why Santa Fe?" he asked, just out of curiosity. "Why not New York, or California?"

Sarah hesitated and looked away. "Oh, I'm afraid I'm a bit of a romantic," she said with an airy wave of her hand. "Santa Fe sounded so charming with all of its Spanish-American architecture.…"

She must really love this Frenchie, damn it all to hell. But she'd have to back down if she knew the truth about him, wouldn't she?

"Duchess, I reckon I got some confessin' to do, too, and after I do, you'll see why it'd be loco to travel with me, even assumin' we'd survive the trail," he told her.

She waited, her eyes shining with such faith in him that he hated to open his mouth and destroy her hope. But he had to.

"I—I didn't tell you the truth about why I'm here in Colorado Territory, Duchess. Oh, yeah, I plan to go minin' up in the mountains—but that's because I have to get to some place where the law can't get me. I'm an outlaw. My face is on Wanted posters all over the Southwest."

Sarah looked startled, as he'd expected. She turned away and went to stare out the window, though there was little to see in the darkness. He waited while a minute or two went by.

"I think I suspected, the moment I saw you," she told him. "You have…such an air of danger about you…. Is Morgan Calhoun even your real name?" She turned to see him answer.

"Yeah. I still don't know why, but I gave you my real name."

He was astonished to see her smile then. "You couldn't lie to me," she said. "And your being an outlaw—don't you see? That makes you even more suited to the task, Morgan. You've eluded capture this long, so you must be very…ah, adept at escape. I—I need someone with such a talent right now."

Was there no getting through to this woman? "Duchess, I don't think you understand," he said. "I'm a *bandit*. I've robbed people—*I'm a bad man.* You're a duchess…. You can't be riding all over creation with a bad man! What would your Frenchman say if you rode into Santa Fe with a fellow like me?"

"I know you, Morgan, and I know you're not a bad man.

And Thierry will know that I did what I had to do to reach his side.''

There was such a dogged, martial gleam in her eye, he wanted to kiss her—if that light hadn't been there for the sake of another man. He just couldn't do what she was asking, damn it, not and give her up. He decided to play his ace.

"Duchess, you can't go with me. I—I'm wanted for murder." *He* hadn't killed the driver of the stagecoach that was carrying the army payroll, of course, but he'd been accused of it.

The roses left her cheeks. "Did you do it?"

"No."

She closed her eyes and sighed. Then, as he watched, her widened blue eyes simply flooded with tears. "Oh, Morgan, *please*," she said, catching hold of his hand with hers. "I'm begging you. For the love of God, take me to Santa Fe...."

She was *weeping*. Good God, why did she have to go and weep? And all for the sake of another man. She loved this Frenchman enough to sacrifice her pride in front of Morgan, to risk dying, just to reach his side.

He took a deep breath. "Stop cryin', Duchess. I—I'll take you. I reckon I must be the one who's crazy—"

She gave a small cry and launched herself at him, laughing and crying at the same time, and kissed his cheeks.

"Oh, Morgan, I don't care what anyone says—you're wonderful, a *prince* among men! Thank you! Thank you!"

She danced out of his grasp just as he was about to wrap his arms around her and kiss her back in a way that would leave her in no doubt about how he felt about her.

"Now we must make a plan, Morgan. We must find a way to obtain our horses without being seen," she said, suddenly very businesslike.

"Duchess, I've been tryin' to tell you, that thoroughbred of yours isn't suited—"

"But we have to have horses, don't we? And you don't wish to leave your pinto behind, do you?"

No, he didn't want to leave behind the horse he'd ridden since the day he left his home in Texas. He shook his head.

"Then we can get Trafalgar, too. And she'll do fine, Morgan. You'll be surprised at how well she'll travel, I know you will."

Well, at least the mare ought to survive long enough to get her out of Denver. By the time the highbred hayburner dropped over dead, they ought to be far enough from immediate pursuit that the duchess could ride double with him until they could get her another mount, somehow.

"All right, I'll get the damn mare, too. Now, here's what we're going to do...."

Minutes later Morgan tiptoed down the back stairway out of the parlor house, leaving Sarah behind in the room, and stole through the now-quiet streets of Denver back to the Grand Central Hotel. He managed to avoid a pair of lawmen out patrolling the streets, probably looking for some sign of him and the duchess.

Approaching the hotel from the side, he saw the hotel manager nervously pacing up and down in front of the door, pausing every so often to mop his forehead. Poor overwrought fellow. Lord Halston was probably making his life hell. Then, looking up, Morgan saw light still gleaming behind the curtains in the duchess's suite. He wished he could somehow let Celia Harris and Donald Alconbury, Sarah's servants, know that their mistress was all right, but of course there was no way.

It proved easy enough to sneak up behind the lone groom guarding the hotel stable and knock him out with the butt of his gun, then tie him up and gag him so he wouldn't sound the alarm. Quickly and efficiently, Morgan saddled both horses, thanking God he'd left his spare Colt and holster in his saddlebags. Minutes later, Morgan rode away, mounted on his pinto and leading Sarah's saddled thoroughbred.

They left Denver before dawn, riding south.

Chapter Fourteen

"What do you mean, she has disappeared?" the assassin demanded the next morning when he met with his informant in the stable of the Grand Central Hotel, empty now of any other human inhabitants. His head already throbbed from the wine he had drunk last night.

"J-just what I s-said, sir." The informant's eyes bulged with apprehension. "A-after the shooting, the two of them ran off—"

The assassin cut him off. "I *know* they ran off, idiot, I was the one up on the roof shooting at them! But they didn't make their way back here? His lordship has received no communication from them?"

The informant shook his head so vigorously it looked as if it might go flying off at any moment. "No one has found a trace of them, even though the local constables are combing the streets! Lord Frederick sent a message to the governor at dawn, but the duchess was not there, nor had she sought protection with the mayor—"

The assassin made an impatient gesture. "What else do you know?" he snarled.

"Her grace's horse is missing—so is Calhoun's!"

The assassin's pulse quickened. "The horses are gone?"

He looked down the shadowy length of the barn, and sure enough, the stalls that had held her grace's fine bay mare and the Texan's paint were empty. "When was this discovered?"

The informant looked blank for a moment, making the assassin want to scream with impatience. He should never have relied upon this dolt!

"Someone—the police that were lookin' for the duchess, I suppose—heard sounds in the stable in the middle of the night. They rushed in here and found the liveryman tied and gagged, but he wasn't any help—he hadn't seen who knocked him out. When he woke up, those horses were missing."

"Calhoun must have come for them," the assassin concluded.

He had to admit, at least to himself, that he found the Texan's quick thinking and stealth admirable, even though it complicated things mightily for him. Morgan Calhoun was proving a worthy opponent, and Sarah Challoner had surprised him by trusting the man. It was going to be so much harder to find her now, but once he found her, he would still kill her—and her would-be savior. "She must have decided her uncle cannot protect her."

"You have Calhoun to thank for that, I think. I could tell he didn't approve of Lord Halston. He was always watching him out of the corner of his eye," the other man said.

The assassin considered the information. "So Calhoun thinks my lord is the one behind the attempts, eh? He is the obvious one to gain, of course, if one does not consider Lady Kathryn back home...." But of course *he* had considered the duchess's younger sister. "I suppose this means they intend to make a run for it on their own."

"Run? Run where? His lordship has a policeman watching the train station, in case her grace should show up there. He's to stop anyone who could possibly be the duchess—she might be disguised, you know," Alconbury told him importantly.

Sarah was too clever just to go to the train station in Denver, the assassin thought, if she was in fear for her life and trusted no one but the damn Texan. He'd wager all the money he ever hoped to have that his sweet duchess was still planning to go to Santa Fe. But how? Hundreds of miles lay between there and Denver.

And what about Calhoun? Would he help her get there? How would she persuade him? He knew that Sarah never carried much money, if any. She had gone to earth with only the clothes on her back.

On her back... The phrase seemed to reverberate in his mind as he remembered the way Calhoun had looked at the duchess—*his* duchess! The acid filled his already raw stomach. *She'll seduce Calhoun into taking her, she'll smile and bat those myopic blue eyes at him, and open her legs.... Damn her! Killing her will be sweet!*

Morgan reined in once they were clear of the town. He was silent for a moment, obviously listening for any sound of pursuit, but nothing disturbed the chill predawn air.

"The first thing we have to do," he told her, "is get provisions for the trip. We'll find a trading post and—"

"But Morgan, we have no money," she reminded him, "except for about a dollar in coins I had in my reticule— unless you have some, that is?" she added hopefully.

"Not much," he said with a rueful smile. "I have a half eagle left from gettin' that fancy frock coat and shirt made," he said, nodding at the coat he'd insisted she wear over her wrinkled, mud-spattered gown of gold faille. He wore only his union suit and the trousers that matched the coat; he'd stuffed the ruined, crimson-stained shirt in an ash can far from the parlor house.

"A half eagle?"

"Five dollars, Duchess. We have six dollars, all told. So unless you plan to ride all the way to Texas in that fancy gown, with nothin' to eat, you're gonna have to use that necklace to trade. Of course, you won't get near what it's worth, but we can probably get all the things we're going to need.''

She felt her jaw drop. "Sell my necklace? But it's been in the family for a hundred years or more!''

Morgan gave a rueful smile. "Well, I reckon I could hold up a stagecoach, then we could hang on to your bauble a bit longer...."

She swallowed, knowing she had no choice. "No, I...don't think I want to...encourage you to break the law, Morgan. Very well, we'll trade the necklace for supplies.''

They rode on for about an hour, following Cherry Creek as it meandered to the southeast, until they came to a little cabin set a few yards back from the creek. A crudely lettered sign on the porch labeled it the Cherry Creek Trading Post. No one was in evidence outside, but the smoke curling from the chimney proclaimed its inhabitant was awake.

"Hello, the cabin!" he called out.

"But will they even take my necklace?" she asked dubiously as they dismounted. "Surely they have no market for such costly things here—''

"Oh, you'd be surprised what places like this take in trade, Duchess,'' Morgan said as he tethered Trafalgar for her. "I've traded supplies for jewelry at trading posts before,'' he added grimly, then turned and walked toward the cabin.

She started to follow, then stopped dead as she realized what he was telling her. He'd *robbed* people—not just men of their money, but ladies like herself.

He turned around. "Look, I ain't proud of robbing folks, okay, Duchess? But thanks to the damn Yankees, a scalawag robbed me of my land after the war—*my land*—and left me with nothin' but my pistols. I've never taken so much as a penny from anyone but Yankees, and only those who could well afford to lose it, so you don't need to act so snake-bit about it. You weren't that upset a few hours ago when I told you I was an outlaw—you were just thinkin' how you could use my talents to your advantage, remember?'' He started walking again, his long strides taking him onto the porch.

She heard the bitter defensiveness in his voice, and the pain that lay underneath it. ''I—I'm sorry, Morgan,'' she said, hurrying to catch up to him. ''I didn't mean to sound so prud—''

Sarah stopped in midword as the biggest, blackest man she had ever seen opened the door.

''Well, I'll be—Morgan Calhoun, you ol' bastard!'' he cried out, a wide grin splitting his face to reveal gleaming white teeth.

Morgan looked equally astonished and delighted. ''Socrates Smith, as I live and breathe! What the hell—'' he hesitated, evidently remembering Sarah behind him ''—I mean, what're you doin' up here in Colorado Territory, you black reprobate?''

''Women troubles—you know how them womens is,'' he said with a chuckle, and then he caught sight of Sarah. ''Oh, my lands! Beggin' your pardon, ma'am, I didn't mean t'blister your ears—''

''No offense taken, sir,'' she assured the man, determined to leave her prissiness behind. It would not serve her well on this journey. She saw him goggle at her accent.

''Your grace, may I present Socrates Smith,'' Morgan said, as formal as if they were in a drawing room. His eyes held an amused glint. ''Socrates, this here's Sarah Challoner, the Duchess of Malvern.''

''A real live duchess? For real? You ain't foolin' wit' me, is ya, Morgan?''

''I swear on a stack o' Bibles, Socrates,'' Morgan said, grinning. ''She's even met the queen.''

''Mr. Smith, it's a pleasure to meet you,'' Sarah said, giving her best court curtsy.

Socrates Smith got even more goggle-eyed, clearly not knowing what to do. At last, though, he managed a bow. ''It be mah honah, ma'am.'' Then he turned back to Morgan, demanding, "Then what she doin' wit' *you?* Last I saw you, you was half a mile ahead o' the law."

Morgan rubbed his beard-shadowed cheek and looked down at the unpainted planks of the porch beneath his shoes. "The duchess has had a speck o' trouble, Socrates, and I'm tryin' to help her," he said. "We need to make tracks outa the territory, and we're gonna need some provisions. You reckon you could fix us up, in return for that pretty necklace she's wearin', and not tell a soul you saw us?"

Socrates narrowed his eyes at the necklace and came closer. Feeling suddenly very self-conscious to be having the huge man staring at her upper chest—at least, the part that wasn't covered by Morgan's frock coat—she reached back, unfastened the clasp and held the necklace out to him.

"Those are real diamonds and topaz," she said as the man took the necklace with hands that were bigger than some dinner plates she'd seen. Good lord, she sounded like a Billingsgate pickpocket, boasting about her take! She added, "That necklace was in my family since the reign of Queen Anne."

"Yes, ma'am, Miz Duchess. I shorely am sorry y'all are havin' to part wit' it. But I'll get y'all fixed up for your trip, I shorely will—an' I won't tell nobody I seen you, neithah. Come on inside," he said, beckoning.

"Thank you." With Morgan, she entered the small shop, seeing the barrels lined up at one end and shelves packed with dry goods.

"Socrates," Morgan said, looking around him, "we're gonna need a packhorse, plus flour, salt, sugar, coffee, beans, bacon, a Winchester, shells for it and for my pistols, two pair of boots, a coupla pairs of denims and a coupla shirts for each of us, blankets, a hat apiece—"

"Denims and shirts?" she interrupted. "Morgan, are you suggesting I'm to wear *trousers?* But surely Mr. Smith has a less formal dress, or a skirt or two...." She could see a few ready-made garments hanging on hooks on the wall. The ma-

terial was just calico and coarse homespun, but surely it
would be better than wearing *men's trousers....*

"Yes, *trousers,* Duchess. Socrates, we're also gonna need
to trade the sidesaddle on her mare for a stock saddle." He
turned back to Sarah. "Duchess, I know you ain't used
t'wearin' men's clothes, but trousers and shirts'll be warmer,
and there's no use temptin' the rascals out there from a distance. We'll have enough problems with the ones who see
you up close. And we're gonna have to do some hard ridin'
over mountains and plains. If we're unlucky, we might have
to run from Indians. You can't be tryin' to hang on to a
sidesaddle then. Your mare ever been ridden astride?"

"Only when B-Ben exercised her," she said, nearly losing
her composure at the thought of her slain groom.

"Then she'll do all right," he said, his tone brisk and bracing. "Here, go try these on behind that blanket yonder," he
said, handing her a pair of folded trousers and a shirt after
the black man had gotten them down from a shelf. "You'll
have to leave the dress behind. It's only gonna take up room
in your saddlebags."

Sarah looked down at the rumpled gown that had looked
so splendid on her—was it only last evening? She had seen
the admiring look Morgan had tried so hard to conceal when
she'd first appeared in it, and had reveled in the knowledge
that she was beautiful in his eyes.

"No," she heard herself saying. "It won't take up much
room if I roll it up and leave the petticoats behind. But I
might need it. I can't very well show up in Santa Fe wearing
men's trousers, can I?"

His eyes narrowed. "Whatever would Thierry say?" he
said in a mocking drawl, and she was suddenly sorry she'd
wanted to keep the dress. His mouth twisted. "All right, all
right, keep it! Now go put these on, Duchess. We can't be
jawin' here all mornin'. We've got to be hitting the trail."

She started toward the blanket, then turned back and

stepped closer to him. "Um, Morgan," she whispered, "I—
I'm going to need some help to get out of this." She nodded
over her shoulder at the row of tiny buttons that marched
down the back of the dress from between her shoulder blades
to her waist.

Morgan groaned, but followed her as she lifted the tattered
blanket that divided the shop area from Socrates's humble
living quarters. Touching each of the buttons as if it were a
white-hot, glowing coal, he made quick work of unbuttoning
the back of Sarah's dress and left her alone to change into
the rust-colored trousers and shirt.

Moments later Sarah emerged, clad in the unfamiliar garments. It felt distinctly odd to be walking without skirts and
petticoats swishing about her ankles. She had left her chemise
and pantalets on, but the shape of her breasts was ill-
concealed. The trousers, of course, had not been fashioned to
be worn by a woman; they were loose at the waist, then clung
lovingly to her hips.

Morgan took one look, then became very busy looking over
what Socrates had laid out on the counter. "She needs a
belt," he said, growling as if the fit of the trousers was the
black man's fault. "We'll need coats, too."

Within minutes the supplies had been loaded onto a
scrubby brown packhorse Socrates had brought from a lean-
to barn in back of the trading post.

Trafalgar showed the whites of her eyes as the unfamiliar,
heavier saddle was lowered onto her back, and sidled away
when her mistress approached in her strange clothing.

"I know, dear girl, nothing's as it usually is, is it?" Sarah
murmured soothingly. "'Twill be different for me, too, you
know," she reminded her as she swung a leg over the bay
mare's back. "I haven't ridden astride since I was a schoolgirl."

Socrates had gone inside, but he returned and handed Sarah

a leather pouch from which a savory aroma of bacon and biscuits arose.

"Here, ma'am. I reckon that ol' rebel yore ridin' wit' ain't remembered t'feed you nothin' this mawnin'."

"But that's your breakfast," she said, remembering having seen the food sitting on the stove in his living quarters. "We can't take your breakfast, Mr. Smith."

"I'm just Socrates, Miss Duchess, and doan' you worry, I'll just make some more. Y'all be careful, now," Socrates admonished. "Morgan, you take care of this lady. You do right by her."

"I mean to," Morgan replied, and there seemed to be layers of meaning to his words. "You take care of yourself, ol' friend."

Morgan sat by the campfire, listening to the coyotes howl in the distance and watching Sarah sleep.

They had traveled all day, covering miles of rolling land covered mostly by buffalo grass, pausing only to rest the horses. The thoroughbred mare had done surprisingly well, not only adjusting to the unfamiliar saddle but keeping up with Rio, and she had even stopped laying her ears back when the pinto ventured too close. She'd even decided she liked the patient brown gelding packhorse.

Sarah had not uttered a word of complaint the entire day. She hadn't mentioned stopping for the night until Morgan said they should. Morgan had seen her wince when she dismounted, though, and watched her stiffly moving about as she helped him lay out their bedrolls and gather what little firewood there was to be found. But still, she said nothing of how sore she must be. Once the fire was burning well, he'd set her to cooking the beans while he saw to the horses.

He'd come back from the horses only to find her sitting by the fire clutching the spoon, her head sunk on her chest, fast asleep. Fortunately, the beans hadn't boiled dry, but they were just about to. She'd muttered something incomprehensible when he'd picked her up and carried her over to her bedroll, but once he'd laid her down and wrapped her in the coarse woolen blanket Socrates had provided, her regular breathing told him she was deeply asleep.

He shouldn't be surprised. Neither one of them had slept a wink last night, and his eyelids felt as if they were full of sand. But he was used to such things. Many times over the past few years, when he'd been running from a posse or some particularly persistent bounty hunter, he'd gone for two full days without sleep.

Poor little duchess. Too exhausted to stay awake for supper—such as it was, he thought wryly as he rested his tin plate full of beans in his lap and took a sip of the hot black coffee. Sarah hadn't eaten a thing since the breakfast Socrates had provided. She'd be hungry in the morning, for sure.

Finishing his meal, he laid the plate aside, too weary himself to go down to the creek and rinse it.

She had placed his bedroll on the opposite side of the fire from hers. No doubt it would never have occurred to her to do otherwise, for propriety's sake. But as deeply as she was sleeping, she'd never know the difference, so he got up and moved his bedroll until there was a scant foot between his and hers.

He lay wrapped in his blanket, staring at her lovely, unconscious face, until at last sleep claimed him, too.

[faded bleed-through text]

Chapter Fifteen

Sarah was dreaming of hot tea and delicious buttered scones, enjoyed in front of a crackling fire in her sitting room at Malvern Hall. Her sister, Kat, was there, and was smiling instead of pouting, as she had last seen her. Morgan Calhoun sat by Sarah's side. The Texan, oddly enough, was dressed in tweeds as an English lord might be on a country weekend, but he seemed completely at his ease. Amazingly, both Lord Halston—who looked happy to be taking tea with his niece and her bodyguard—and Ben were there, too. She was just wondering where Thierry was, and pondering how weird it was to see the dead groom and the uncle who was trying to kill her—as if nothing were amiss—when the earthquake struck. Surely only an earthquake could be shaking her body so insistently.

"Rise and shine, Duchess," a voice drawled in her ear. "It's time for breakfast."

Morgan's face swam into fuzzy focus as he bent over her, shaking her shoulder. A blurred wedge of moon hung low behind him, and the sky still seemed inky black.

"It's not," Sarah said. "It's the bloody middle of the night." She shut her eyes again, hoping she could go back to her dream.

But Morgan wouldn't allow it. He shook her again, but gently. "It's nearly dawn, Duchess, and you need to wake up and eat some breakfast. It's going to be a long day, so we need to get started."

It seemed he wasn't going to give up, so she muttered, "Perhaps just some coffee." The air around her was chill, and the grass she pushed against in her struggle to sit up was drenched in cold dew. She clutched the blanket about her and struggled to open her eyes.

"Good morning." By the light of the crackling fire—well, at least that had been true enough in her dream—she watched Morgan crouching next to the flames, ladling fried eggs and bacon onto a tin plate. He poured steaming coffee from a pot sitting on a rock in the middle of the fire, dropped a lump of sugar into it from a nearby sack and handed the plate and cup to her.

"No, really, Morgan, just coffee. I'm not nearly awake enough to eat all this." She was more used to a gradual start in the mornings, sipping tea until later, when she was awake enough to nibble on something.

"*Eat it*, Duchess," he insisted as he scooped bacon and eggs onto his own plate and sat down next to her. "You haven't eaten since breakfast in the saddle yesterday, and Lord knows that was little enough. This'll stick to your ribs."

She took a sip of the coffee. The brew was strong, but the bracing warmth spread through her stomach, and suddenly she realized how very hungry she was. She picked up her fork and began to eat, and in no time at all the plate was empty.

"You're not a bad cook," she commented wryly, thinking this breakfast surpassed all the broiled kidneys and kippered herring she'd ever consumed. Perhaps it was the open-air atmosphere. "Want a job in the kitchen at Malvern Hall?"

"Tomorrow it's your turn, Duchess," he retorted. "You know how to make biscuits?"

She had to admit she did not. Her experience at cooking had been limited to scrambling eggs on midnight kitchen raids after Cook was asleep, or making toast and tea for Kat when she'd been ill. And there were no more eggs, and certainly no bread.

"Maybe I'll teach you tonight when we stop," he said. "Soon as you finish, do what you gotta do, 'cause we're breakin' camp and leavin' as soon as the sun's up."

His reference to her taking care of the demands of nature made her blush, but he appeared not to notice. This morning, unshaven and rumpled, he looked even more the desperado than he had before. Putting down his plate and cup, he went to saddle the horses.

It didn't take her long to get ready, since she hadn't undressed the night before. After emerging from behind a clump of bushes, she brushed out her hair and rebraided it, then donned the hat he'd obtained for her at Socrates' store.

"What can I do to help?" she called to Morgan, who was just lifting the heavy saddle onto his stallion's back.

"Take those plates down to the creek yonder and wash 'em out. Rub 'em good with sand," he told her.

Sarah did so, feeling a ridiculous sense of well-being now that she'd eaten and had a good night's sleep. She was pleased that he was treating her as a capable equal on this journey and not as the pampered noblewoman that she was. It must be very akin to the camaraderie men experienced on their hunting trips....

Suddenly she had the sensation she was being watched. Lifting her head from her task, she stared downstream, but all she could see was a blurry figure standing by a horse about a hundred yards away from her on the opposite side of the creek. She couldn't make out what sort of person it was, or the expression on his face, but it seemed he was facing her direction. Friend or foe? Oh, God, was it the assassin—had he caught up with them?

Cursing her nearsightedness, she backed up. "Morgan?" she called, then broke into a run. *"Morgan!"* She ran back over the rise to the camp.

He was beside her in a moment. Evidently her tone had alerted him, for he had drawn his pistol. "What is it, Duchess?"

She pointed downstream. "There's someone standing down by the creek with a horse, down that way."

She watched as he crept down to the creek, using the cover of the cottonwoods to the left of where she had been washing the plates.

He was back in a moment. "It was a Ute Indian," he said. "He saw my gun and decided to take off. I hope to thunder he's by himself. The Utes haven't bothered the whites around here lately, but you never know what they'll do when it's just two of us, especially when they know one of us is a woman. You keep that hair up under your hat today, you hear, Duchess? And where in hell are your spectacles? I want you wearin' 'em every minute the rest of this trip, you understand?"

She opened her mouth to acquiesce, but he never paused.

"Vanity be damned, Duchess—like I told you, this ain't no pleasure jaunt. It'd be nice to see if someone's about to fire an arrow at you, don't you think? Go put your spectacles on right now!"

Had she really just been savoring the feeling of camaraderie between them? Surely she must have been dreaming once again!

"It isn't necessary to harangue me, Mr. Calhoun," she said with icy hauteur, and stalked off to dig the hated spectacles out of her pack. Thank God she'd had them in her reticule at the theater.

He must have realized how harsh he'd sounded, for when she came back, wearing her spectacles, he said, "I'm sorry, Duchess. I reckon I just got scared for you, thinkin' what could've happened just then. Here, I want you to carry one of my pistols in your belt. I don't want you goin' outa my sight without havin' this with you. It ain't enough to *see* the danger, you gotta be able to shoot it, if need be."

Sarah stared at the Colt he was proffering. "But...don't you need a spare?"

"I've got the Winchester. And," he said, tapping his boot, "there's a little derringer in here—had it in my pocket at the theater. It'll do in a pinch. Here, take it," he said, offering her the pistol again.

"I—I've never shot one of these...I've never fired any sort of weapon...." Of course she hadn't. To have participated in the shooting parties that were so much a part of country weekends, and grouse-shooting expeditions to Scotland, she would have had to wear her hated spectacles. She stuck to foxhunting instead, trusting Trafalgar to judge the jumps over fences and fallen logs.

He sighed and stuck the pistol back in his holster. "All right then, for the time bein'. But as soon as we get somewhere safe, maybe tonight, we're gonna start you on target practice, Duchess," he promised grimly. "Even before you learn to make biscuits."

The assassin had spent the previous morning visiting the police, and the mayor's and the governor's residences, posing as a foreign newspaper reporter, but whether their ignorance was real or feigned, the assassin was able to gain no new clue as to where the duchess and her protector had gone. It was as if they had vanished from the face of the earth. He'd even gone to the railroad station, even though he'd doubted earlier that the duchess would use this obvious escape route, but the ticket taker could remember talking to no one with a foreign accent, female *or* male, "except for yourself, of course, sir." Nor had he seen anyone fitting Morgan Calhoun's description.

By noon he'd decided to trust his original guess that the

duchess and her bodyguard had fled southward on horseback, and had spent the afternoon purchasing a horse and provisions for himself. Once done, he pondered starting out that very afternoon and riding till it was too dark to go farther, but decided against it.

The fact that his quarry would have a whole day's head start did not overly dismay him. They wouldn't be able to travel as fast as he would, for Sarah was a lady and unused to hardship, while he had been hardened by his years in the cavalry. And while the sturdy cow pony he'd purchased this morning wasn't his usual choice of a mount, it had stamina Sarah's thoroughbred wouldn't have. In addition, he'd learned much in the way of tracking lore from the scouts he'd worked with, and knew that with just a little luck, he'd find his quarry.

It was going to be an arduous journey, so he decided to treat himself well his last evening in Denver. He bought himself a steak dinner and a bottle of the best red wine that could be had in this benighted corner of the world. When he finished the bottle, he decided it had been too long since he'd had a woman, and inquired of the waiter where he might find a willing whore.

The waiter, assessing him as a refined gentleman, did not send him to the nearest crude crib, but to Madame Hortense's Parlor House, where he was assigned a blond whore with breasts that strained at the bodice of her garish red dress.

"Hey, you're a furriner, ain't you? We had a furriner in here last night, but she was a woman. She was with some man, though—sounded like a Texan, he did—and Hortense kicked me outa my room fer them! Kin you imagine that, bringin' yore own fancy woman to a parlor house fulla them? But the madam give it to them fer the nite, so I had to cool my heels down here in the parlor. I still got a crick in my neck from fallin' asleep on this here sofa," she babbled on, pointing to the couch.

What a happy chance—he'd come to the very brothel in which his quarry had passed the night!

He smiled beatifically down at the whore as he took her arm and started for the stairs with her. "What a coincidence," he purred. "I have been looking for that very woman. I fear she is my long-lost, erring wife, you see. By any stroke of fortune, did you overhear them talk about where they were going this morning, or perhaps see the direction in which they departed?"

The whore blinked, clearly dazzled by the foreigner's charming smile and the lilt of his accent. "Naw, I never did. They was long gone when I woke up and checked my room."

"Never mind," the assassin said, giving the whore his most courtly bow. "We will pass a good time anyway, yes? I need you very much, my dear. It has been long since I have enjoyed...the comforts of a woman...." He winked, and the whore tittered.

He would enjoy her "comforts," all right—and then he would pretend she was Sarah, Duchess of Malvern, and practice how he was going to punish the duchess.

Before dawn he arose and took the coins he'd paid for the whore's services the night before. She wouldn't be needing them anymore, he reasoned as he stole down the back stairway and out into the street.

Luck continued to stay with the assassin that morning.

He'd been about to head out onto the plains, away from the creekside path he'd followed out of Denver, when he encountered a trapper bringing a packhorse full of skins into the city to trade. The trapper hadn't seen anyone fitting the duchess's or the Texan's description, but he did recall seeing a pinto and a bay tied up in front of the Cherry Creek Trading Post yesterday morning. The trading post lay about five miles downstream—"Just keep on follerin' the creek and ya cain't miss it, friend."

He didn't miss it. Socrates, the black man running the store, was a veritable fount of information—he didn't even have to resort to a bribe. Yes, there'd been a foreign woman here. "Just yesterday mornin', one wit' pretty yella hair and the funniest way o' talkin', an' real purdy, too. Yassuh, she was wit' a Texan who give his name as Morgan Calhoun, though wit' these Texans, a body could never tell iffen that was their true handle or not. Where'd they go? Why, suh, they headed up yonder inta th' mountains, goin' straight west, they did. Said they was tryin' t' lose somebody who might be trailin' 'em.''

The assassin deciphered the black man's molasses-thick drawl with difficulty, then decided to ask one more question. It sounded as if Calhoun had spent a fair sum buying provisions here. Just why was Socrates so willing to give away the direction the Texan and the lady had taken, after the man had even admitted they feared pursuit?

"Well, mister," the black man had answered with a grin, "I figger from yer talk, you prob'ly wouldn't understan' it, but I used ta be a slave, an' I belonged to a Texas massah what whupped me all th' time. So I don't owe nothin' to no damn Texans.''

"I see..." the assassin had murmured, grateful for the ill feelings that lingered because of slavery. And how fortunate that he had stopped here instead of heading out onto the vast plains! His instincts were as clever as those of a hunting wolf!

So Calhoun had taken the duchess up into the mountains? The fool! Sarah's horse would break a leg and they'd have to ride double! Then it would be child's play to catch up with them. After all, *he* had campaigned in the Alps! Thanking the smiling black man profusely, he left the trading post and headed west toward the Rockies.

Chapter Sixteen

Late that afternoon they made camp in what Sarah would have described as a narrow gully; Morgan called it a "draw." It had obviously been used as a stopping place before, for a pile of empty whiskey bottles and tin cans lay in a heap under the sparse shade of a pair of cottonwood saplings. On one side of the draw, the bluff overhung the dry, flat ground. They'd put their bedrolls there, Morgan said, for they'd be less visible to wandering Indians or white rascals that way. Sarah guessed he was particularly thinking about the assassin who might be trying to follow them.

Surely all Denver was abuzz with the news of her disappearance, and perhaps the local newspaper had even printed a story about it by now, so her would-be killer would surely be aware that his quarry had flown. *Was* he somewhere behind them, even now? Was he that determined to see her dead? The thought was on Morgan's mind, too, she guessed, for he frequently stopped to look back over his shoulder. Thank God for Morgan's keen vision—he'd be able to see the glint of the sun off a gun barrel or field glasses that would betray the fact of another rider following them. So far, he'd seen no sign of pursuit, but his action caused her to frequently glance over her shoulder, too, even though she couldn't hope to see as well, even with her spectacles.

Sarah, you'll run daft if you imagine yourself the hunted hare all the time, she admonished herself. Vowing to put the thought aside, she looked longingly at the shallow trickle of a stream running through the draw as the horses lowered their heads to drink.

"What's wrong?" he asked, his eyes on her.

"Oh, just wishing the water were deeper," she admitted with a rueful chuckle. She bent over, upstream of the drinking horses, and splashed some water on her face. "You've no idea how I'm longing for a bath, but it's hardly deep enough to get my ankles wet." She blushed at the admission, for a lady did not mention any part of her legs, let alone that she longed to wash her entire body! But a lady did not go fleeing into the wilderness with a man, or wear trousers while she did so, either.

He looked away, but not before she saw his green eyes darken with—what? Could it be desire?

"Oh, I reckon you'd see plenty of water if we were to get a sudden cloudburst. In fact, we'd have to run for high ground—this draw could be full to the rim in nothing flat," he said, pointing in the direction from which the flood would come. "I wouldn't even consider camping here if there was a cloud in the sky, but there's isn't, and I can't smell any rain, either. But we can jaw about the weather later. Soon's I get the horses unsaddled and secured, you got a shootin' lesson to attend, Duchess."

She groaned. "Can't we cook dinner first? I'm famished," she admitted. "I could have my cooking lesson," she added hopefully.

He grinned. "All this fresh air's good for the appetite, isn't it? But no, we'll shoot first, while the sun's still high."

"Impossible man," Sarah grumbled, but it was a good-natured grumble. She was beginning to realize that she enjoyed doing just about anything with Morgan, though she'd never have said so. She helped him unsaddle their mounts, staggering a little with the weight of Trafalgar's stock saddle, then, seeing him picking up his stallion's feet to check for stones, she did likewise with her mare.

"How're you holding up, old girl?" she murmured, pitching her voice so it was low and soothing to distract the mare while she picked up each hind foot. Trafalgar hated having her hooves fussed with, but she suffered Sarah's ministrations with no more than a toss of her proud head. "You miss Ben, don't you? So do I—but he'd be so proud of how well you're doing, I just know it. You're showing that gaudy painted stallion of Morgan's just what a British horse is made of, aren't you? Stiff upper lip and all that." She stroked the mare's back, looking for sore spots and feeling the dampness of the hair where the saddle and blanket had rested all day. Was Trafalgar thinner already? She'd have to see about getting her some oats as soon as they came to a town—the thoroughbred wasn't used to a diet of grass only.

"How's she doing?" Morgan said, right behind her.

How did he manage to move so quietly, as if he were barefoot instead of wearing boots? She hoped he hadn't seen how he'd startled her. "Fine!" Sarah insisted, trying not to sound shocked.

"Since we're going to be shooting nearby, we'd better tie her extra well," he said, slipping a loop of rope around the mare's neck and securing it to one of the young cottonwood trunks. "Don't want her running off down the draw in a panic."

After unbridling the thoroughbred, Morgan, carrying an armful of the empty tin cans from under the mesquite, led her back up onto the plain by the path they'd used to descend into the draw. After lining up the tin cans on rocks, he motioned for her to follow him and strode several yards away from them.

"Here," he said, handing her one of the Colts. "Time to get friendly with this—it just might save your life."

She took it and was amazed at how heavy it was, for he handled it as if it weighed nothing. She ran her fingers over the smooth wood grain of the butt, praying she'd never have to use this against anything human.

"Hold it in both hands—you'll need both hands to steady it," he said, stepping behind her. "Now raise it…and sight down that barrel. That's it, Duchess." His drawling voice was just inches from her right ear, causing her neck to tingle. "Now, cock the hammer—that's this thing up here—and you're ready to shoot. Keep your eye on that tin can yonder, the one in the middle, and just squeeze the trigger…."

She did as he instructed, and the resultant reverberating explosion was so loud in her ear—and the jolt of the pistol against her hands so unexpected—she nearly dropped the Colt in fright. When she managed to open her eyes again, she saw a puff of dust rising from the ground well to the right of the last can, nowhere near the center one she had been aiming for.

"I reckon I forgot to mention about the way she'd kick," Morgan admitted. "Now try again."

Her next effort was even more laughable than the first, though she was more ready for the recoil of the pistol this time.

"Let me help you a little, Duchess," he murmured, coming closer behind her and reaching around her on both sides to wrap his larger hands around hers. This brought his chest and arms in close contact with her back and arms, and his cheek against the side of her head.

She shivered as his beard-rough cheek caught at strands of her hair. He smelled of horse and leather. Couldn't he feel the way her pulse immediately raced into a full gallop? But he seemed oblivious to anything but the lesson as he said,

"Now, keep one eye open, Duchess, and just squee-eeze that trigger...."

That shot was better; at least, they hit the far right can, though she'd still been aiming at the center one. She heard a tinny *clunk* as it rocketed up from the stone it had been sitting on, then fell back against it.

"Don't worry, Duchess, we'll make you a deadeye shot yet. For a Britisher, anyway," he promised into her hair. "Keep trying."

Lord, his nearness made it so she could barely *breathe*, let alone shoot accurately, but the honor of England was at stake, so she fired again and again, until on her sixth shot she finally hit the edge of the can and caused it to jump a couple of inches into the air.

She wanted to jump and whoop like a wild Indian, but he merely said calmly, "That's better, Duchess. Now I have to show you how to reload, 'cause you're outa bullets."

He did, and then he set up the cans again before taking up his position behind her, steadying her hand for another six shots. This time she hit the target three times out of the six, once squarely in the middle of a can, and came close to the other three.

After she reloaded under his supervision, he made no move to come closer, and realizing she was now on her own, she raised the pistol and shot. She hit only one can, but as she turned and saw him give an approving gesture, she felt as triumphant as if she'd been given a trophy.

Just then Morgan took the gun from her and, without a word of explanation, sighted down the barrel and fired at something off to their left, twice as far away as the cans.

"What was that?" she asked, startled. All she had seen was some grass rustling before he fired.

"Jackrabbit," came his laconic explanation. "Now we'll have meat for dinner instead of just beans."

Load. Aim. Fire. Load. Aim. Fire. Her hands and arms

ached, her head throbbed and the ground at her booted feet was littered with empty shells by the time Morgan decided they'd better quit and make dinner, but Sarah hardly noticed her aches as she strode back to camp. She was filled with a new feeling of confidence. *I can do this. I can hold my own, and I will survive.*

She was not allowed to rest on her laurels, however. "You didn't do half bad—for a woman," he teased as he built up the fire in the gathering dusk. She looked away while he gutted and skinned the rabbit, until he had it spitted and roasting over the fire.

"Now let's see how you are at biscuits. That ought to come naturally to any female."

She shot him a rueful grin. "No fair, Morgan. I wasn't allowed in the kitchen at Malvern Hall when I was a little girl, except on rare occasions. But if you ever need to know how to pour tea gracefully or make your curtsy to the queen, I'm an expert."

"I'll keep that in mind. Now you watch how I do this, 'cause you're going to make the breakfast biscuits." The biscuits he made were fluffy and light, and they ate them slathered with the jelly they'd bought at Socrates' store, along with the roasted jackrabbit. She had to admit the rabbit was tasty, though anything was palatable when one was this hungry!

"We'll reach Castle Rock tomorrow, with any luck," he murmured, leaning back against his saddle as the light faded in the draw. "The Denver and Rio Grande railroad stops there, and we ought to be able to ride a fair distance toward the New Mexican border on it. Duchess, I'm going to turn in," he said, covering his mouth to hide a yawn. "If you wanted to go a little ways down the draw and wash, I reckon I'd be close enough to holler awake if you needed anything." He sank back against the saddle and pulled his blanket up over him.

Sarah was a bit nonplussed, for she had looked forward to

talking more. She'd planned to ask Morgan how he thought she could improve her shooting, if he knew how big a town Castle Rock was, what he planned to do with his life after she went back to England.... But now his eyes had drifted shut, so she might as well go have a wash.

Maybe the duchess believed he was asleep, but his body knew better. Morgan could still feel the imprint of her shoulders against his chest, and the softness of her hair as he'd helped her with her aim. He kept savoring the joyful sound of her pleased laughter and the sparkling blue of her eyes behind the lenses of her spectacles as she'd struck her target—first with his help, and then without. He'd gotten hard just watching her delicately pulling the meat off the rabbit leg with her even white teeth surrounded by those kissable lips, and he stayed hard now as he heard the splashing water just a few yards down the draw.

He imagined each step of her washing in excruciating detail, his groin aching. First she'd unbutton her shirt, then pull down her chemise and expose proud breasts surmounted by nipples that were doubtless as rosy and perfect as her lips.... She'd take the cloth and soap and wet them, then work up a lather before rubbing the cloth over her neck and shoulders and the hollow of her throat....

She'd probably dry herself, and put her chemise back on before shedding the trousers that had so perfectly outlined the length of her legs and the curve of her bottom during the day. Then she'd slip off her pantalets, and lather up the cake of soap again....

He groaned and struck the ground with his fist in frustration, causing Rio, tethered a few feet away, to nicker in inquiry. Damnation! That soap wasn't the only thing getting lathered, he thought, feeling beads of sweat break out on his forehead as he heard her humming snatches of some tune.

He wanted nothing better than to throw off that blanket,

get up and walk down the draw and fill his eyes with the sight of her. Then he'd fill his hands with her—and his mouth—before sinking his aching flesh into her sweetness.

He'd get up and go to Sarah right now if he thought she'd welcome his caresses—but she'd made it very clear she was interested only in having him help her join her lover in Santa Fe. A duchess wasn't for the likes of him.

But dear God, how on earth am I going to survive this kind of temptation on a daily basis? How am I going to take Sarah Challoner all the way to Santa Fe without touching her?

It wasn't her fault that it had been weeks—or was it months?—since he'd had a woman. Lately he'd been so busy running from the law that he hadn't given the matter much thought. But once he'd hired on with the duchess—especially now that he was alone with her day and night—he'd thought of little else. Damn him for a randy fool!

He'd better slip away the first chance he got—maybe while they were waiting for the train in Castle Rock—and find himself a whore. Maybe after he'd spent his lust between the legs of a woman who satisfied men for a living he'd be able to be around Sarah without aching for her—at least for a while!

Chapter Seventeen

The biscuits she made the next morning were not, to put it mildly, an outstanding success. Before baking, they had looked oddly gray, but Sarah hoped they'd be better when they had baked. But the finished products had not looked a whole lot more appealing, and Morgan eyed them suspiciously when he came back to the campfire from washing up. He ate one, but after the first bite he put the leftover beans back on to warm up.

The biscuit she bit into tasted like paste and sank to the pit of her stomach like a stone. Her eyes rose to Morgan's, and she saw that he was watching her with some amusement.

"Not very palatable, are they? It's all right, you don't have to spare my feelings," she commented ruefully. "I *did* warn you I hadn't any experience, you know."

"Aw, you'll get better, Duchess. It just takes some practice. Maybe corn bread would be easier. Besides, with any luck we'll be traveling by train for a spell after we get to Castle Rock, and we can eat at the railway cafés."

"That's not much better," she said, rolling her eyes, "if the ones I've been in on the way to Colorado are anything to judge by. The food was so dreadful that after the first couple of days I had Celia obtain a picnic lunch for us at the hotel every morning when we departed for another city. But the train we took from Kansas City to Denver had a restaurant car, so that wasn't too bad.''

"I don't reckon we'll be finding restaurant cars on the Denver and Rio Grande line. It's mainly just for carryin' miners to and from the fields. I'm just not sure how far south they've got the line built. I'm hopin' to go as far as possible by rail, to spare your mare.''

For once, Sarah didn't protest that Trafalgar had as much endurance as Morgan's stallion. After a couple of days on the trail, even a tenderfoot like herself could see that the rangier pinto was better suited to living off the land than her thoroughbred, though Trafalgar had coped very well so far. But she was well aware of her mount's weariness at the end of each day's ride. How long before the sleek flanks became thin, and her gleaming coat dull?

They reached Castle Rock by noon, and found the train station easily enough, for there was not much to the town beyond the train station itself, a livery, a saloon and a small hotel that looked brand-new. But when they inquired about the next train south, they were told that they'd just missed it by an hour, and there wouldn't be another until tomorrow.

Sarah heard Morgan curse under his breath at the news. "Looks like we're going to have t' keep ridin' a ways, then, after we have a bite to eat at the hotel yonder,'' he told her. "We could travel to another station or two down the line before we meet up with the next train. It ain't smart to be stayin' anyplace if we don't have to. Close up, it's obvious you're a woman, Duchess—we'd be easy marks if anyone *is* trailin' us.''

Looking down at her rough shirt and her trousered legs, Sarah smothered an unladylike snort of disbelief. "*I?* Surely you jest, cowboy! I look just like another disreputable—ah, what do you call them?—drifter, at least as long as my braid stays tucked under my hat.''

His eyes raked over her from head to toe, lingering at her mouth, her breasts, her waist and hips. "No, you don't. Not to any man who really looks."

The remark should have made her want to slap him for his impertinence, but after a couple of days of feeling dirty, travel worn and quite unfeminine, his words had the bracing effect of a tonic. She felt herself flushing with pleasure.

"And there's your accent, too, Duchess. Anyone who hears you is going to remember speaking to a blond English-woman."

"I won't say a word if I don't have to," Sarah promised.

She knew it was wise to ride on, but she sighed inwardly at the prospect of more hours in the saddle. For the past two days she'd been sore in places no *lady* should be sore, but she wasn't about to mention it.

"I wish there was some place we could purchase some oats for Trafalgar and the other horses." She felt guilty at the prospect of eating a civilized meal when her mare had only the sparse buffalo grass to crop.

"The livery'd likely sell us some."

After a surprisingly good meal of fried chicken and mashed potatoes at the hotel, Sarah felt almost cheerful about the prospect of an afternoon in the saddle.

When they came out to the hitching post where they had left the horses, however, she noticed Trafalgar stood with her off forefoot canted so it did not fully touch the ground, and when Sarah tried pushing her over, she resisted putting her full weight on that foot.

With a sinking feeling, Sarah stooped and picked up the mare's foot, looking for a lodged stone, but didn't find one. Trafalgar snorted nervously, flinching as her mistress ran her hand assessingly over the mare's slender leg. As Sarah had feared, she found increased warmth in the cannon.

Her heart sinking, Sarah untied the mare and led her in a small circle, watching the mare dipping her head every time the near forefoot hit the ground, then raising it again when the off one struck. The sinking feeling was replaced by the cold chill of guilt. Had she been oblivious to Trafalgar favoring the leg those last few miles into town? Ben would have given her such a tongue-lashing, even though he had only been her groom!

"She's lame, Morgan. We can't go on any farther today," she said, then waited for him to say *I told you so, I told you a highbred beast like that wasn't capable of hard travel.* This was only the third day, and they hadn't even reached the tougher mountain terrain yet.

But Morgan wasn't an I-told-you-so man, it seemed. "Reckon that could happen to any horse," he said. "I recollect a time when Rio pulled up lame once, after we'd had a hard run from a band of Kiowa. I expect we better get rooms in the hotel for the night, and settle the horses at the livery. We can wrap your mare's leg, and maybe she'll be right as rain in the morning. At least she'll be all right to load onto a stock car of the train. This afternoon we can ride double on Rio out of town a ways, and get in some more target practice for you. They'll be callin' you the 'Deadeye Duchess' before the end of this trip, sure 'nough."

Sarah could have kissed him for his easy acceptance of the situation, but knew such an action wouldn't fit with her disguise, so she contented herself with whispering, "Thank you, Morgan."

"As of now, *boy,*" he said with a wry twist of his lips, "you better call me Jake—Jake Faulkner, if you have to talk at all. You never know who knows Morgan Calhoun as an outlaw."

"All right—Jake."

Leaving Rio hitched at the rail, they went to see Sarah's mare and the packhorse safely bestowed at the livery. Then, after giving detailed directions to the liveryman about Trafalgar's care, they returned to the hotel to reserve their rooms.

"Afraid you fellas'll have to bunk together, Faulkner," the grizzled proprietor informed them cheerfully. "Y'see, quite a few gents missed their train like you fellas did. But if you was of a mind to play some poker, they're plannin' on a big game at the saloon after supper tonight, 'bout eight."

Sarah watched as a speculative grin spread over Morgan's face. "Yeah, I'd be interested," he said. "My bespectacled young friend here, he ain't much for cards, but you can catch up on your sleep, eh?" He elbowed Sarah in the ribs, and she nodded, careful not to speak.

"Sorry we couldn't get two rooms, Duchess," he said when they had climbed the stairs and stood inside the small room. "I imagine you're missin' your privacy."

She shrugged. "It's no matter. I suppose I'm getting rather used to having you around. But at least there's a bed...." Her voice trailed off and she stared up at Morgan.

"Don't worry, I'll sleep on the floor," he assured her.

"Oh, Morgan, isn't there a truckle bed under it or something? It doesn't seem right for you to have to sleep on the hard floor...."

"Naw, don't worry about it, Duchess. It can't be any harder than the ground, and I'm used to that. I intend to stay late at that poker game anyway, and I'll probably come back so whiskeyed up I won't know if I'm sleeping on rocks or feathers," he told her with a grin. "Now, let's get to your shooting lesson, Duchess."

"You're certainly going to a lot of trouble just to go play cards," Sarah observed as she watched Morgan shaving. He'd already paid for hot bathwater and a hip bath to be brought up to their room, and gallantly allowed her to use it first while he went to check on the horses.

She was dressed again when he came back, and had pretended great interest in the view of the street from their window while he'd undressed and gotten into the tub, and again when he'd climbed out and dried himself. He'd put his denims back on, but this time with a clean shirt.

His eyes met hers in the mirror for a brief second before he looked back at his cheek while his razor scraped over it, but he made no comment about her probing remark. Instead, he said, "I'll probably be late, but I have the key. You stay right here, and don't you open up the door to anyone knocking, you hear?"

Sarah pulled her spectacles off so she could no longer clearly see his face. "You needn't speak to me as if I'm an infant," she said with a sniff. "I believe I do have *some* common sense."

"Sorry, Duchess, I didn't mean to," he said, unruffled. "You get some sleep, now. It's gonna be a long day tomorrow."

Damn him, she could no longer see his grin, but she could hear it in his voice. "Won't it be a long day for you, too?" she asked. "Perhaps you'd do well to heed your own advice, and not chance losing what little money we have," she retorted. "But as I've no desire to see you stumbling back in here drunk, I'll retire early."

"Don't worry, I reckon I can play poker better than anyone at this particular game." Then he added, his tone carefully neutral, "You know, you're soundin' a mite peevish."

Shrewish was more like it, she thought. She wished she hadn't guessed exactly why he was so damnably cheerful. It wasn't just the prospect of an evening spent over cards with a number of cigar-smoking, whiskey-drinking men. He was going to seek out a woman—and she knew just what kind of woman.

She knew that in a saloon, just as in the pubs back home, there were women who made their living at the world's oldest profession. She'd seen them since coming to America, strolling around in the late afternoons in their garish spangled-and-feather-trimmed dresses, or leaning out of the windows of their rooms above the saloons and beckoning to the men that passed. Morgan had bathed and shaved and changed his shirt because he was expecting to spend some time with one of them, damn him. And he expected her to just go to sleep early, and be blissfully unaware when he returned, stinking of some saloon girl's perfume.

Morgan bade her good-night and left. As soon as the sound of his boot heels no longer echoed up the stairs, she got up and paced as she tried to argue herself out of her jealousy. *Be reasonable, Sarah. You know men have needs. Morgan Calhoun has every right to spend his free time with any sort of creature he likes, and you have no right to feel so possessive. After all, you're betrothed to someone else, and Morgan's only agreed to take you to him, not spend every moment until then with you.*

Think of Thierry, she commanded herself, *think of how handsome he is in evening dress. Why, he would quite put Morgan Calhoun in the shade, would he not?* But she groaned aloud when she could conjure up only a fuzzy picture of her French *comte,* and could not for the life of her remember what he looked like when he smiled. She swore when Morgan's face, grinning as he'd praised her this afternoon for her improved shooting performance, replaced her vision of her fiancé.

Muttering an unladylike swearword, Sarah sank onto the lumpy hotel mattress, loosed her braid and, taking her hairbrush from her saddlebag, began to comb out the golden strands, wavy now from being braided in a plait pinned under her hat all day. She imagined Morgan walking into the saloon, and the soiled doves flocking about him, cooing as if he were the only man on earth.

Unless...

The gold dress would be wrinkled, but she imagined she would look at least as good in it as any of the saloon women looked in their gaudy backwater finery. Before she could contemplate any further what she was about to do, she pulled the curtains shut and began to strip off her clothes.

Life was good. "Gentlemen, I believe I have the winning hand," Morgan said, grinning as he laid down four aces with one hand and began to scoop the pile of gold coins and wadded bills toward him with the other—no easy task, considering the buxom woman perched on his lap.

"You 'bout ready to go upstairs with me for a while, sugar?" the woman purred in his ear, her warm, whiskey-laced breath stirring his loins if not his heart. "These men'll let you stay out for a hand or two, won't you, gentlemen?"

"Shee-it, once you go upstairs with Dixie, we won't see ya again before mornin', Faulkner," someone protested good-naturedly.

"Good, maybe I'll have a chance to win a hand," someone else countered, then muttered, "Lord have mercy, would you look at that...."

Having gathered up his winnings, Morgan had put his hand on Dixie's waist and had been about to rise when he stopped and looked at what had caused the other man's jaw to flop open.

Sarah stood framed in the doorway, her blond tresses twisted into an elegant chignon, dressed in the golden gown she'd last worn to the theater in Denver.

"Who the hell is that fancy piece?" asked another man at the table, his eyes glazing as he also went slack-jawed at the sight of Morgan's duchess. Her eyes were now narrowed as she surveyed the room—searching for him, he realized. But of course she was not wearing her spectacles, and trouble might well find her before she found him.

"Where in tarnation did she come from? I seen all the whores in this one-horse town, and I never seen her before," another man was saying.

"Sorry, Dixie, sugar. We'll have to make it another time,"

he said, pushing the whore gently but quickly off his lap and giving her soft bottom a consoling pat.

"But honey, I thought we was goin' upstairs fer some fun," Dixie whined, her arm still draped around his neck.

"I'm sure there's others who'll be wanting your attention," he said, gently but firmly removing her arm, then turned back toward the table full of salivating men.

"Um, never you mind, gentlemen, the lady's mine," Morgan announced quickly, knowing he was going to have to head this disaster off at the pass. Sarah had no more idea than a newborn kitten would about the kind of danger she was risking by walking into this den of iniquity.

He saw the barkeep approach her, and saw her speak to the man. Evidently she had asked for him, because the barkeep pointed toward his table, and Sarah began strolling with seductively swaying hips toward him.

He was aware of the split second when Sarah was close enough to focus on the whore still hovering around him, for her eyes glinted dangerously for a moment, and then her face cleared and she closed the distance between them.

"Ah, Monsieur Faulkner, there you are," she said, her accent now completely and convincingly French. "It ees not nice that you leeve Fifi alone in our bed, *n'est-ce pas?* Even eef you deed exhaust me weeth your—how shall we say it?— *amour, oui?* Excuse me, *putain,* thees man ees mine," she said to the lingering Dixie, and, pushing none too softly past her, plopped herself down on Morgan's knee as if she sat there every day.

Chapter Eighteen

The piano player had ceased plunking out his tinny tunes. Now someone guffawed in the sudden silence. "Shee-it, Faulkner, what're ya doin' playin' cards with us when ya could be up in yore room rollin' in the sheets with *her?*"

Morgan put his arm possessively around the narrow waist that was snuggled so close against him, and felt Sarah drape an arm around his shoulder. Her position placed the shadowy valley between her breasts, which were pushed up against the low-cut neckline of the bodice, right under his eye.

Damn her. He'd gone instantly and achingly hard, as if the mild reaction he'd had to the other woman's sitting on his lap had been just practice for the real thing. Now that Sarah had joined him, there was no chance he was going to get to use the other woman to relieve the lust he had for the duchess. And Sarah had just stoked that lust into a bonfire.

But he had a worse problem to worry about first, which was how he was going to get both of them out of there safely. These men had never seen a woman like the duchess, and the longer she stayed, the more they were going to want more than a look.

"Hell, gentlemen, a man can't make love all day *and* all night," he said with a wink and a laugh, though merriment was the opposite of what he was feeling. If he was able to get the duchess back to their room without having to shoot somebody, he was going to blister her ears, if not her hide.

"A pretty lady like this deserves baubles, don't she?" he drawled. "I thought I'd just come down and win some money so I can buy her some shiny gewgaws." He gazed into her eyes, apparently the doting lover, but he made sure Sarah could read the warning there.

Gingerly he shifted her from his right leg to his left, so he'd have free access to the Colt he wore at his right hip. Now he had a direct view of most of her right breast, but he tried to avoid the distraction of looking.

"Fifi, sweetheart, iffen he cain't keep up with you, I can," a red-haired cowboy promised. "You wanna come over here and spend some time with me?"

"Yeah, Faulkner. Why not share if yore pecker's worn-out fer a while?" demanded another.

He felt Sarah stiffen, and knew she was realizing the predicament she had just placed them in. These men were not gentlemen playing faro in some fancy London club. All of them were wearing pistols; all of them looked as if they could chew nails for breakfast. More than one of them probably had a price on his head, and had killed a man over something far less important than a woman.

Before he could think of what to say to get them out of there without bloodshed, though, Sarah spoke up. "Ah, I am sorry, for you all appear to be *hommes très gentils,* but Fifi ees a one-man woman," she told them regretfully. "Monsieur Faulkner, he ees my husband, you see. We are just—how do you say?—just married."

"Then where's yore weddin' ring, Fifi?" asked a bald, mustachioed man on her left, picking up her hand and displaying its lack of a ring.

"Well, now, I have a sorry confession to make," Morgan said, thinking fast. He forced his features into a sheepish, hangdog expression. "We had to sell it to buy our train ticket for tomorrow, but I was hopin' to win enough that I could buy her another one when we reach home. So if y'all are ready for another hand, gentlemen, can we get back to playin' poker, so I can win enough to put a ring on my bride's finger again?"

"Hell, Faulkner, you already won that much in the last hand," a man directly across the table from him complained. "But you could earn plenty letting us play *poke-her,* iffen you was of a mind...." He sniggered, and the other men sniggered with him.

Morgan felt his head begin to ache. It sure wasn't looking as if they were going to get out of there without him shooting someone.

"I don't share my wi—" he began, but then Sarah said, "But perhaps, *mon mari,* your friends would like me to sing for them, yes?"

"She can sing, too?" groaned a prospector at another table. "Some fellas have all the luck!"

Morgan started to tell her no, thinking it would be fool-hardy to remain a second longer than they had to, but then he shut his mouth. Refusing to let her sing at this point just might make the other men angrier, and what she was pro-posing just might work. She had a beautiful voice—he'd heard her singing through the door at the hotel in Denver, and she often hummed little songs on the trail.

He took a deep breath. "Fifi, honey, I think that'd be right nice." Lord, he hoped it would work, and not just make this pack of wolves all the more determined to cut him down on his way out the door. He watched warily as she excused her-self with a bashful smile and stepped over to confer with the man at the piano. Then the piano player struck a few opening chords.

"Beautiful dreamer, waken to me..." she sang, and in-stantly every man in the room was entranced. There wasn't another sound in the room but Sarah Challoner's lilting soprano, complete with French accent, until she finished the song, and then there was thunderous applause, and calls for "More!" and "Keep singin'!"

She sang of home and family, and soon the men had forgotten they'd been lusting after her and wanted to worship her instead.

When the clock behind the bar chimed eleven, though, Morgan knew he'd better call a halt. Sarah was looking visibly tired, and her voice had begun to fade, but the smile she gave him as he approached the piano was triumphant.

"Sorry to put an end to a pleasant evenin', fellows," he said, "but my bride is tired, though she's much too nice to say so. And we have to meet that train mighty early in the mornin', don't we, Fifi?"

"*Bonsoir,* gentlemen," she said, bowing gracefully, which gave her smitten audience a tantalizing view of her décolletage.

Morgan heard a collective groan, and hastened his steps to her side.

"I have eenjoyed seenging for you," she said, waving as he put an arm around her waist and propelled her none too gently out the door.

He was silent and did not look at her as they walked through the darkness.

"Morgan, I'm sorry," she said softly as they walked the short distance between the saloon and the hotel. "I didn't realize that I might cause a problem...I just—"

"Shut up, *Fifi,*" he growled. "Don't say another word until we get to our room."

She went rigid, but said nothing until they had climbed the hotel stairs and entered their room.

As soon as the door had shut behind Morgan and he had turned the key in the keyhole, however, she turned on him in a whirl of golden silk, her eyes blazing at him, her entire frame radiating fury.

"How dare you talk to me that way, Mr. Calhoun? I believe you have entirely forgotten yourself," she reprimanded him.

Her anger, in turn, ignited his, and fueled by his sexual frustration and the fear he had felt for her when she'd first strolled into that lion's den, he lashed back.

"I think you're the one who's forgotten herself, and any claim you ever had to common sense, Duchess," he snapped. "We agreed you'd be safer if you were dressed like a boy, an' I left you in this room all safe an' sound. Then here you come sashayin' into that saloon dressed like a box of candy that any man could have a piece of—"

"And I suppose you weren't looking for a piece of candy, as you so delicately put it," she sneered. "I may be near-sighted, but I saw that—that *tart!* She was practically *glued* to you—you lecher! Don't think I don't know what you were about!"

"And what if I was?" he demanded as he advanced on her. "What's it to *you* if I went upstairs with that woman in the saloon? I'm taking you to your French *lover,* damn it! Are you sayin' that I just have to confine myself to worshipin' at your feet until I give you to your precious Frenchman?"

"I never asked you to worship at my feet, damn your eyes!" she seethed back at him. "But I *do* think I have a right to object to your having 'a roll in the sheets,' as they put it, *with what's left of the money you made from selling my necklace!"*

His temper blazed to new heights at the unjust accusation, but he wasn't aware that his forward movement had made her retreat until he saw her back into the wall and saw her eyes widen as she realized she had nowhere else to go. Now his face was just inches from hers, and he placed one hand on either side of her on the wall to keep her there.

"I didn't do that, Duchess. As we agreed, I took twenty dollars out of that amount as stake money. I hadn't lost but about four bits, and just before you came in I made ten times that twenty by having the winning hand. It's all in my pocket, Duchess. It was only gonna cost me a couple of dollars to go upstairs with that woman for an hour or so. You have a problem with my spending a couple of dollars on a woman, Duchess? You can deduct it from my wages!"

The blood had drained from her face, leaving her eyes enormously blue in her ivory face as she stared up at his face that was so close to hers. He could see the pulse beating frantically in her throat.

She opened her mouth, but no sound came out, so she merely shook her head, never taking her eyes off his.

He lowered his gaze to her lips, so lush, so tempting, so close. He had tasted them before. He knew how they would feel against his. But once he lowered his mouth to hers, he doubted he could stop, and so he forced himself to remember his anger.

"You're pretty good at that French accent, Duchess—at least, you sound pretty good to me, but what do I know? I'm just a simple boy from Texas. But do you think I don't know how you got so good at it? It was all that pillow talk with your French lover, wasn't it? I bet you're real used to havin' him whisperin' sweet li'l words into your ears when he makes love to you, aren't you, Duchess?"

Still mute, she shook her head, but he didn't believe her.

"Do you ever stop and think about how hard it is for me, bein' with you like this, Duchess? To sleep by you, and not touch you? A woman who's had a lover would know that sort of thing, I'm thinkin'.... Well, it *is* hard, Duchess—" He leaned into her then, and put his arms around her and pulled her close, close enough that she could feel the dual meaning of his words. "And it's gettin' harder and harder! Goin' upstairs with that woman, Duchess—why, I was just tryin' to protect you from *me*.... But maybe you don't *want* protected?''

''Morgan...'' It was just a whisper, and nothing more, and she just kept looking at him with those enormous blue eyes. He could read no clue in them as to what she wanted—or didn't want.

Damn it, he had to know. And if she wouldn't say, he was going to have to force her hand, so to speak.

Deliberately letting go of her hands, Morgan used his fingers to frame her face, lowering his head to close the distance between her mouth and his own, while his body pressed her more firmly against the wall.

He thrust against her, expecting the next thing he felt would be a stinging slap to his cheek or maybe even his ears being boxed, but it didn't happen. Instead, he heard her moan, and felt her open her mouth to his, and his eyes opened just long enough to see hers shut tight with the passion that was sending rippling shudders through her body and echoing into his own. One of his hands left her face and scooped down into the low neckline of her gown, cupping her bare breast.

He'd never desired a woman so much in his whole life. ''Duchess... *Sarah*,'' he corrected himself. ''I want you... you know that, don't you?''

''Yes...'' she breathed, her eyes still shut, her head lolling back against the wall as if there were suddenly no bones to support the slender column of her neck. ''I want *you*, too, Morgan....''

She was giving him permission to take her, to make love to her. She was giving him the gift of her body—but for how long? She was a woman of the world, a noblewoman who had traveled in sophisticated circles, who had a French lover. Apparently there was no clear division in her world as there was in his, where a woman who gave herself to a man before marriage forfeited the right to respectability. Her body was no stranger to passion.

He wanted her, and she'd come right out and said she felt the same way. He'd be a fool to pass up what she was willing to give him when his body—and his heart and soul—were demanding it.

But he was enough of a fool to want to know something first. Maybe he was loco, but he had to know where the trail led.

"If I make love to you, Sarah, am I still takin' you to Santa Fe?"

There—he'd said it. Now he opened his eyes and raised his head enough that he could look down into her eyes.

Sarah opened her eyes, too, and stared back up at Morgan, her fevered brain fumbling to form an answer. How to tell him all that surged within her heart, without making him feel trapped or obligated to her for more than this moment, this night? She knew now she could never marry Thierry, but knowing that did not mean this man who held her owed her a future with him, whatever kind of future that could be. And Thierry, charming, dashing Thierry, who had made her laugh and thrilled her heart with his seductive smiles and enchanting manners, did not deserve to wait in vain for her in Santa Fe, never knowing why she failed to appear. Not after crossing an ocean to be with her! He deserved to know the truth, and hear her apology.

She hesitated for a moment while she chose her words. "Yes, of course, I'll still want to meet Thierry in Santa Fe. I must—"

But Morgan never allowed her to finish. Suddenly he was releasing her and stepping back, his green eyes glittering with frustrated fury.

"Never mind, Duchess. I reckon I'm good at askin' silly questions. Forget it." He started to back away from her. "I—I'll be back, come mornin'. You lock this door behind me and stay put till I knock, you hear? And be ready to go when

I do.'' Now he had turned around and had his hand on the door, and was turning the knob.

"But wait, Morgan!" she cried, desolate at the idea that he could leave her *now,* and furious, too, because she knew he was going to go ease his frustration on that blowsy whore at the saloon. "Don't go! You *can't* go—you haven't heard what I was going to say."

He gave her a twisted, humorless grin over his shoulder. "Oh, I reckon I have a pretty good idea." And then he was gone.

Sarah stared at the closed door, listening to his retreating footsteps.

She wanted to run after him, to force him to listen to her. She wanted to explain that she only had to see Thierry long enough to tell him that she couldn't marry him because she had realized she loved Morgan. Then she would follow Morgan to the ends of the earth if he would have her, or if he would not, she would board a ship at Galveston and go back to England, and treasure the memory of their passion till the day she died.

But she had her pride, she thought as she heard the sound of the door below open onto the street. And pride would neither let her run to the window to confirm that he was returning to the saloon nor allow her to run down the stairs after him, throwing herself at his feet and begging him to listen while she bared her soul to him. For how could she survive if he refused her then?

Chapter Nineteen

At the same time as Sarah had been giving her impromptu concert to the customers at the Castle Rock Saloon, the assassin was staring into his campfire, his hands curled around a cup of coffee. He'd ridden hard for two days now, after learning the duchess and her bodyguard had ridden into the mountains. He'd used the most likely trail to the Rockies from the trading post, counting on the fact that by riding a fast horse and traveling light, he could easily catch up with Morgan and the duchess. Yet he'd found no trace of Sarah and Calhoun, nor talked to anyone who had seen them. Momentarily he considered they might have taken another, longer mountain trail, but that didn't make sense. The logical conclusion stared him in the face—he'd been given false information.

He cursed himself for ignoring his instincts and listening to the black man. Sarah and her bodyguard must have fled south, just as he had originally guessed. Therefore he would reverse his direction, and ride his horse into the ground, if necessary, to find them.

For a moment he pondered stopping at that trading post and killing Socrates Smith for lying to him, causing him to lose two precious days, but then he thought better of it. He could ill afford the time he'd waste exacting his revenge, and it was always possible that Calhoun and the duchess had lied to the black man about their destination, too.

The assassin was sure the duchess and her protector would board the train as soon as they could south of Denver. But he didn't know the country, or where train stations were situated, so the simplest thing to do was to follow the tracks south out of Denver.

Sarah might well be traveling disguised as a man, but he knew her well enough to know she'd never willingly leave her precious thoroughbred behind somewhere. So he'd ask about the horse—someone around the railroad station was bound to remember the mare, if not the humans with her. It wasn't common to see such a highbred piece of horseflesh in the West.

"Enjoy your dream that you have eluded the hunter, my precious little rabbit," the assassin murmured aloud, picturing Sarah. "Like any dream of the hunted, it will not last forever."

"All aboard!" the conductor cried, precisely at nine in the morning.

"We can sit wherever you want," Morgan said in a gruff voice, gesturing at the rows of bench seats as they entered the passenger car of the Denver and Rio Grande southbound train. He remembered not to call her "Duchess," even though she was once more dressed as a woman rather than a boy.

Morgan had been forced to change his mind about Sarah's disguise when the hotel proprietor had come up to their room that morning.

"Look, I don't know what kind of game you two are playing, arrivin' here with her dressed like a boy, then havin' her showin' up at the saloon all gussied up," he'd said, eyeing Sarah with beetling brows, "but I do try t' run an honest establishment here. A word t' the wise, though, that pack o' men loiterin' outside is expectin' t' see Fifi, not some boy."

The proprietor's information had led to Sarah's hasty purchase of a serviceable calico skirt and white waist from his wife, for the low-cut gold gown was obviously unsuited to travel.

The adoring half-dozen men who had shown up at the hotel for one last glimpse of "Fifi" had escorted Sarah and Morgan all the way down the dusty street to the train station, and were now waving goodbye from the station platform. Fortunately, all of them were headed north, rather than south, so none had followed Sarah and Morgan onto the train.

"You're leaving behind a trail of broken hearts," Morgan growled as he joined Sarah on the seat and saw her waving back to the men. He realized he sounded mean as a javelina with a sore tusk, but he was stiff and sore from sleeping on the hay in an empty stall between Rio and Trafalgar at the livery.

He saw her arch a brow at him as the seats began to fill up around them.

"You're in a rather nasty mood for someone who did what you did last night after you left me," she hissed at him in an undertone. "Isn't that supposed to make a man cheerful?"

Morgan made no comment. He knew she thought he'd gone back to the saloon to avail himself of Dixie's services, and he wasn't about to tell her he hadn't. He couldn't even explain to *himself* why going to seek out the saloon girl to finish what he and Sarah had begun had held no appeal for him. Aching with unsatisfied desire for the woman who now sat next to him, he'd tossed and turned on the hay for hours before falling asleep, only to be tortured by dreams in which he made love to Sarah again and again.

A nattily dressed man carrying a silver-topped cane sat down on the seat across the aisle from them, tipping his hat at Sarah as he did so. As the locomotive whistled and began to pull out of the station, Morgan acknowledged him with a polite nod, then turned back to looking past the duchess out the soot-specked window. He wasn't in the mood to talk to anyone.

"Are you certain one of us shouldn't have ridden back with the horses?" Sarah asked as Castle Rock began to recede into the distance. "I know you said Trafalgar's leg seemed better this morning, and she certainly wasn't limping as badly, but I just feel nervous having her in that open cattle car, with no one there if she becomes frightened."

"Sarah, we've been over this a half-dozen times already, and there's no way I can get into that car while the train's movin' anyway," he said. "She'll be fine, just like she was when she rode to Denver. She's tied right next to the pack-horse and she'll be able to scent Rio in the car ahead of her, so she won't be scared. We can check on her every time the train makes a stop."

Sarah looked as if she might give further argument, but just then the nattily dressed gent on the seat opposite them spoke up.

"Excuse me," he said in an impeccable British accent, leaning into the aisle and looking past Morgan to Sarah, "but I couldn't help hearing that I was traveling with a fellow countryman—ahem!—country*woman*," he corrected himself. "Forgive me for being so bold, madam, but your voice makes me homesick for my native country. Allow me to introduce myself. John Sharpton of London—Southwark, to be exact."

"Mr. Sharpton, I'm pleased to make your acquaintance," Sarah said with a smile before Morgan could quell her friendliness with a meaningful glance. "I am Sarah—" she paused uncertainly for a moment, then went on after a quick glance at Morgan "—Sarah Faulkner, and this is my husband, Jacob Faulkner."

Morgan, relieved that Sarah had remembered to use the alias and had not revealed her true identity as a duchess, gave

Sharpton no more than a perfunctory imitation of a smile, but it didn't discourage the dandy.

"Mr. and Mrs. Faulkner, it's a pleasure indeed," replied Sharpton, leaning on his silver-topped cane. "And where is your home in England, madam, if I may inquire? You are obviously a gentlewoman, but do I detect Herefordshire in your voice?"

"You do indeed, sir," Sarah replied. "The Malvern Hills, actually."

"And what brings a lady of Herefordshire to the wilds of Colorado, if I may continue to be so bold?"

Sarah looked down and smiled demurely, as if slightly embarrassed, then, fluttering her lashes, she favored Morgan with a look so full of adoration that Morgan's heart would have done flip-flops—if he hadn't known she was only acting. "Why, a wife's place is with her husband, is it not, so I suppose one could say *love* brought me to America. We have been in Colorado for a time, and now we are returning to Texas," she said. "And now it is my turn to ask. What brings you from England, Mr. Sharpton?"

"I'm a real estate speculator, my dear madam. I'm returning from Denver, having purchased an acre in what promises to be the premier business district of that up-and-coming city one day. As well, I own property all over Texas, which should be of interest to you, Mr. Faulkner. Are you in the market for some prime land around Austin, sir?"

"No, can't say as I am," Morgan replied, making his voice purposely curt. Sarah could talk to the dandy if she wanted, but the topic of Texas real estate was a sore one with him. He'd had prime ranch land of his own once, the Flying C, and he'd had to leave it behind, knowing that scalawag would take it.

"Ah, then you must already possess your little slice of heaven," Sharpton concluded, "so I won't trouble you, sir. I trust you have no objections, however, to my exchanging reminiscences about England with your missus? It's so rare one finds a fellow countryman—countrywoman—" he corrected himself again with an ingratiating smile, "in this wonderful United States of yours."

"No, I don't mind," Morgan muttered, and even got up and changed places with Sarah so that she could talk to Sharpton without having to talk past him. It wouldn't hurt for Sarah to have something to distract her from the swaying, lurching ride. They might reach the end of the line at Pueblo by midmorning tomorrow if all went well, but it was apt to be a hell of a long day. As for him, he was going to try to get some shut-eye.

The train stopped at Palmer Lake a couple of hours later, and Morgan sent Sarah, accompanied by the loquacious John Sharpton, into the station café to get something to eat while he went to check on the horses.

The thoroughbred mare was still jumpy and wide-eyed from the earsplitting train whistle that had sounded when the locomotive had pulled in to the station, but other than that, it looked as if Trafalgar was surviving the trip as well as his stallion and the packhorse were. He gave Rio a friendly pat before he left, then strode into the café.

The food was just as miserable as he'd feared. Sarah and Sharpton had just been served bowls of a thick, greasy-looking stew, and there was another bowl waiting for him.

"What is it?" he asked as he sat down next to Sarah.

"Chicken stew, I'm told," Sarah said, taking a wary bite with a bent tin spoon.

Morgan figured she'd digest her meal better if he didn't tell her the thin slivers of meat in the broth were probably prairie dog. He washed his first bite down with his coffee and found it as watered-down as the stew was greasy. By some miracle, Sarah had been able to order tea and she gamely pronounced it satisfactory. They were still eating when the train whistle sounded, but no one regretted leaving the sorry meal behind.

When they were once more settled on the train and it was screeching its way out of Palmer Lake, Morgan was surprised to see Sharpton pull out a deck of cards.

"Care for a game to pass the time?" he inquired. "We could probably interest those gents who just got on at our last stop, too, if you're so inclined—with Mrs. Faulkner's kind permission, of course...."

"Why, I have no objections if my husband wishes to pass the time playing cards," Sarah said with suspicious sweetness. Only Morgan saw the warning look she cast him.

"Why, thank you, sweetheart," he drawled, then, turning back to Sharpton, asked, "You play poker?" He imagined he could learn some English game if that was what the Englishman had in mind, but he could empty this tenderfoot's pockets so much faster playing poker. The prospect of fleecing this Englishman at cards—as well as the other fellows who'd gotten on at the last stop—made the rest of the day's journey suddenly tolerable.

"I'm acquainted with that American game, yes," said Sharpton with a genial nod. "Shall we say a dollar a hand?"

"I reckon that'd be fine," Morgan drawled. "Why don't you go ahead and ask those other gents?"

While Sharpton went forward to invite the other men to join them, Morgan flashed a grin at Sarah. "Don't worry, I won't lose against this tenderfoot," he whispered. "And I promise I'll leave your 'fellow countryman' his shirt."

"See that you do," she commanded him in a tart tone. "And remember, 'pride goeth before a fall.'"

"Yes, ma'am." He couldn't wait to show her that his confidence had not been in vain. He didn't know a lot of things, but he did know poker.

Sharpton was beckoning to him to come forward.

"It's all arranged, Mr. Faulkner. These fellows would be pleased to join us."

Morgan rose from his seat, then bent over to Sarah. "A kiss for luck, sweetheart?" Morgan said, knowing the duchess, in her guise as his wife, would not be able to refuse, though giving him a kiss while believing he had spent the night in the arms of a saloon whore would be the last thing she'd want to do.

She closed her eyes and lifted her lips, puckering slightly, and her lips were cool, but he would not let her get by with a perfunctory peck. As soon as his mouth touched hers, he deepened the kiss, caressing her lips slowly and thoughtfully with his, tracing their soft fullness with his tongue. For a moment he forgot all about the card game, or the men waiting to be fleeced, and he sensed by the soft sigh that escaped her she had forgotten her resentment, too.

A hoot from where the other men waited for him brought him back to the present.

"Mr. Faulkner, you didn't tell me you were on your honeymoon," John Sharpton teased as Morgan sat down to join them.

"We're not," Morgan said with perfect honesty, grinning, then added in a tone loud enough to carry to the duchess, "What can I say, gentlemen? I'm a lucky man to have a wife as beautiful as my Sarah, aren't I?" He chuckled as he dared a glance back and caught a glimpse of the duchess's dazed face.

By the time they pulled in to Fountain, a little wide spot in the road past Colorado Springs, Morgan's hopes had more than been fulfilled. He'd let three of the other men win a couple of hands, and then he'd casually suggested raising the stakes to five dollars a hand. Now the pocket in which he kept their money was fatter by fifty dollars than when the game had started, for Sharpton had been no better a poker player than Morgan had guessed he would be, and the other men had been no match for Morgan's skill, either. And to make matters even more agreeable, it looked as if none of them were going to be sore losers, either.

"Mr. Faulkner, I bow to your superior skill," Sharpton said as he arose. "I've enjoyed myself tremendously, but now it is time to bid you and your delightful English rose goodbye."

"You aren't leaving?" Morgan said. He'd assumed the Englishman was traveling on to Pueblo, just as the rest of them were. "Why would you want to stop in a place like this?" he added, gesturing out the window. It didn't look as if there was much to the town of Fountain but the train station itself.

"Ah, but my business partner is meeting me here—he lives in these parts, you see."

"It's been a pleasure, Mr. Sharpton," Morgan said, extending his hand. He'd grown to genuinely like the dapper little Englishman.

Sharpton shook his hand, then, moving into the aisle, murmured, "Mrs. Faulkner, it's been *my* pleasure encountering you and your good husband on the train," before taking her hand in his and kissing it.

While Morgan was enjoying the bemusement playing over the duchess's face at this courtly gesture, Sharpton clapped him on the back with bluff bonhomie. "Mr. Faulkner, you are indeed a lucky man." Then he was moving down the aisle toward the door of the passenger car.

"What a delightful fellow," commented Sarah, who had put on her spectacles and was watching through the window as Sharpton descended the steps onto the station platform.

"A durn good loser, too. Wait'll I tell you how much..."

Morgan's voice trailed off as he saw a bearded, rough-looking man hail Sharpton from the open grassy area next to the train station. The man was mounted on one rangy horse and leading another, already saddled.

"You reckon *that's* his business partner?" Morgan said, pointing at the two. Sharpton had seen the man and, wearing a big smile, had gone forward to him. "He sure wasn't what I was picturing."

"Nor I," agreed Sarah as they watched the little man mount the horse the other held for him, then gather up the reins with surprising agility. "Who'd have thought his 'business partner' would look more the outlaw than you?"

Morgan grinned at the gentle gibe. "Very funny, Duchess, but let me tell you how much I won for us," he said as the Englishman and his odd associate began to trot away from the station. "Thanks to my 'superior skill' at poker, we are now fifty dollars richer," he said proudly, patting the side pocket where he kept the little leather drawstring bag of money—and going cold when he realized it wasn't there anymore.

Chapter Twenty

Sarah saw the blood drain from Morgan's face right along with the cocky pride that had been there. Now apprehension skittered along her spine as he jumped up and, leaning over her, stared out the window.

"Morgan, what's wrong? What happened?"

"Why, that damn bastard," he breathed. "That damn, cheating bastard!" And then he was running for the door.

It was clearly already too late to stop Sharpton, Sarah could see with the aid of her spectacles as she reached Morgan's side. Sharpton and his partner were already out of range, galloping away from the train.

By this time the other passengers were spilling out of the train around them, and the stationmaster had approached.

"Something wrong, mister?"

"The damned English bastard who just left your train picked my pocket, and it wasn't chicken feed he got, either!" Morgan exclaimed. "He saw which pocket I was putting my winnings in—just ask the rest of those fellows who were playing with us, back on the train!"

"Sounds like you've been a victim of ol' English John," the stationmaster commented.

"Yeah, sounds like English John, all right," agreed the

engineer, who had gotten off the train and heard the conversation. "He does this all the time, mister—acts like a green-as-grass tenderfoot, makes friends with some fellers, proposes a game, then as he's leavin' picks the pocket o' whoever wins the most. I throw him off if I spy him gettin' on the train, but I didn't see him this time, and Asa here—" he nodded toward the conductor, who had also joined the group "—is new, so he didn't know him."

The conductor nodded, his expression apologetic.

"I'm right sorry this happened to ya," the engineer added, "but I got a schedule to keep. What's it gonna be—you want your horses so you can go chase that feller, or you gonna get back on the train?"

Sarah watched the conflicting emotions chase one another across the pale, lean features of Morgan Calhoun. He could probably get Rio off-loaded and saddled and still catch the Englishman and his partner, but the train wouldn't wait. And what would become of Sarah if the two thieves got the drop on him?

His shoulders were slumping and his green eyes were dull with impotent fury as he stomped back up the steps and trudged down the aisle to slouch beside her, ignoring the commiserating looks and remarks aimed at him by the other men who'd been in the poker game.

"You might as well shoot me, for all the good *I* am, Sarah," he said. "We don't have much now. After letting me win it for him, that bastard took it all, plus most of the money we had left from buying supplies back at Cherry Creek—and I didn't even feel him do it. Damn me for a fool!"

Sarah's heart was wrenched at the bleak self-reproach she saw in his face. Knowing Morgan, it had to sting all the more that the foreigner who had robbed them looked as if he couldn't survive a strong blast of wind.

She laid a gentle hand on Morgan's wrist. "Don't be so hard on yourself, M—Jake. We'll be all right. You paid for tickets to take us all the way to Pueblo, didn't you? We still have some supplies left, don't we?''

"Yeah, we're set all the way to Pueblo, but those supplies won't last forever. We're gonna need to buy more before long. And the last I looked, you don't have any jewels left to sell,'' he reminded her bitterly, his eyes raking her earlobes, her neckline and ringless fingers.

"I could always put on another concert,'' she observed, then realized there was nothing in that plan to salvage his wounded pride. "I have it! While *I* distract the men as 'The French Nightingale,' *you* can win all their money.''

He gave her a twisted half smile, then said in a soft, wry drawl, "I sure hope your Frenchman knows how much backbone you've got, Duchess.''

Sarah wanted to say she was merely showing the legendary British stiff upper lip, but she couldn't manage a word as she drowned in the admiration-filled green pools of his eyes.

"Sarah, wake up. We're here,'' Morgan said the next morning, rousing the woman who'd been sleeping against his shoulder most of the night.

"Huh? Wha—?'' Blinking like a sleepy owl, she stared up at him as she tried to focus, then sat bolt upright, blushing. "Sorry,'' she muttered, looking away as she tried in vain to set her hair to rights, then started digging into the pockets of her skirt.

"Quite all right, ma'am,'' he said, amused, then handed her her spectacles. "Lookin' for these, were you? I took them off you when you fell asleep, so they wouldn't get bent.'' He hadn't slept much himself. Truth be told, he'd spent a good bit of the night just staring down at her in the pale light furnished by the moon that seemed to be following their railroad car. He'd been wishing she could fall asleep against him every night—but in a bed, lying down, and not wearing all these clothes, either. He didn't tell her that, though.

They decided it was probably best to try to remain in Pueblo that night. Trafalgar was no longer favoring one leg, but it was wiser to rest her for another day. And while they had enough supplies to ride on for a couple of days, what few towns lay between Pueblo and the New Mexican border were even smaller and rougher than Pueblo, certainly not the sort of places he'd want to linger with the duchess—especially not with the duchess playing "Fifi" in that dazzling gold gown.

The owner of the Arkansas River Saloon was more than willing to let "Mam'selle Fifi" sing at his establishment that night, and charge a dollar a customer, provided she and Morgan would split the profits fifty-fifty with him. They agreed, then, buoyed by their success, went on to the hotel.

They had no difficulty in obtaining a room after "Fifi" began batting her eyelashes at the manager and promising him, in thickly French-accented English, a seat up front at her concert that night. They were able to secure box stalls at the livery for the horses the same way, and even managed to get in some target practice before it was time to get ready for the concert.

After replenishing their supplies at the general store, they left Pueblo the next morning.

"Now, Duchess," Morgan began after they'd left the town behind them and trotted over the rolling plains with its dry buffalo grass, "I don't want to alarm you or nothin', but it's possible we'll see some Apaches between here and when we hit the Santa Fe Trail."

"Apaches?" she said, her face alarmed. "You mean… Indians?"

"Yeah, we're in Jicarilla Apache country now," he told her. "I've met some of 'em before and gotten along with them—it didn't hurt that none of us liked 'the Federals,' but there's different bands of Apaches, and you never know. I can speak their lingo, but if I had my druthers, I'd just as soon not meet up with them, since you're along. From here on out, Duchess, you keep those spectacles on, your pistol handy, and don't even think of lettin' that braid out from under your hat, you hear?'' He hated frightening her, but it was better that she know the truth. At least he'd taught her to shoot, but he wished they'd had more time to practice.

After that first flash of apprehension on her face had vanished, though, Sarah appeared unperturbed, giving him a jaunty imitation of a British sailor's salute, saying, ''Aye aye, Captain.''

He chuckled. ''You're in a mighty good mood, Duchess. Still pleased with yourself for havin' every man in that saloon swoonin' at your feet?''

''While *you* took their money at cards? I notice *you* sat and played with your back to the stage,'' Sarah teased.

''Why do you think I did so well?'' he retorted. ''*I* didn't have the distraction.'' He hadn't had any relief, either, from his constant desire for her, but it felt good to laugh with her again, almost as good as it would feel to kiss and hold her— No! He couldn't allow himself to think about that.

''Speaking of moods, Trafalgar's in a strange one this morning,'' she said, just after her mare gave Rio a playful nip and curvetted away from him, then paused to water the ground.

Rio responded with interest, trumpeting at the thoroughbred, and Morgan reined him farther away from Sarah's mare.

''Your mare's comin' into season, Duchess,'' he said, watching as the dawn revealed a blush suffusing her face under the floppy-brimmed hat.

''*Oh!* Of course, how silly of me,'' she murmured, staring down at the mare. ''She does so every fourteen to twenty-one days from late winter through late spring, then less often in the summer, Ben says—*said,*'' she corrected herself with a sad shake of her head, "and she hasn't done so since...oh, Kansas City, I suppose...."

"Sorry, I don't reckon I'm supposed to be talkin' about such things with a lady, especially a duchess," Morgan said, though he loved it when she blushed.

"I think that by proposing this madcap journey, I've lost the right to strict Victorian propriety, don't you?" Sarah commented wryly. "But Morgan, are we going to be able to keep them apart?" she asked as their mounts continued to eye each other and prance, their tails held high.

He shrugged. Of course his pinto stallion must not mate with the prized thoroughbred, any more than he could take the duchess in his arms and make her his. "I'll do my best, Duchess. But it isn't going to be easy, travelin' together." *It isn't going to be any easier than it is keeping my hands off you.*

"Still, it would be a darling foal, though, wouldn't it?" she said musingly. "I wonder if it would be skewbald—that is, pinto—like his sire, or bay like Trafalgar...."

They camped at dusk in another draw, carefully tethering Rio as far away from Trafalgar and the packhorse as they could. This time supper was antelope steaks, for there had been a pair of pronghorns drinking at the thin trickle of a stream in the draw, and Morgan had quickly pulled his Winchester out of its scabbard on his saddle and shot one of them. Sarah had been sad to see the graceful, large-eyed creature lying dead, but she had to admit its meat was delicious.

"Morgan, tell me about the war," Sarah said once their bellies were full and they were lying back against their blanket-padded saddles. She'd wanted to ask him about his time as a soldier for a long while, sensing his experiences in the war had somehow set the stage for the outlaw he had become.

"Well, I was only in the regular Confederate army for the early part of the war," he began, crossing his booted legs at the ankles as he lay back, still chewing on the meat that clung to a leg bone. "I was servin' with Jeb Stuart. Then John Mosby asked me to join his Virginia boys in a partisan raiding group. We stole horses, cattle and wagons from the enemy—whatever our army needed. We captured Yankee soldiers—even a brigadier general once—burned trains, destroyed track...."

"It must have been tremendously dangerous," Sarah commented.

"It was, sometimes, but they never came real close to takin' us. Mosby was too clever."

She could see him smiling at the memory. "You loved it, this guerrilla fighting, didn't you?"

"Yeah...have to admit I did," he said with a sheepish grin, then his face turned serious in the light of the campfire. "We were always on the run, never stayin' in the same place twice...but Mosby's Rangers were the bravest, best men I ever knew."

His answer to the next question would be highly significant, she knew. "Morgan...your experience as a guerrilla fighter...did it make it hard for you to settle down, once you were back in Texas?"

He met her gaze, but she couldn't read his eyes. "You mean, is that why I turned outlaw, because I'd developed a taste for it?"

"No, Morgan, I didn't mean—"

"Yes, you did," he argued, "but it's all right. No, that isn't why. I'd had a good time bein' one of Mosby's Rangers, but I sure was ready to get back to the peaceful life I'd known back in Texas before the war. Only they wouldn't let me."

"'They'?" she echoed softly.

"The Federals, and their carpetbagger friends that descended on Texas like fire ants at a picnic—and the scalawags, the ones who lived in the South but were really Yankee sympathizers. One of them started the whispers—'You say you're missin' some cattle? That Morgan Calhoun over at the Flying C, you know he was one of Mosby's Rangers. I reckon he stole your stock an' ran 'em down to Mexico to sell 'em.' Soon as I'd leave the mercantile, he'd sidle up to the proprietor and whisper that they'd seen me stealin' things off the shelves. 'You know he's used to livin' off the land. Reckon he's still doin' it,' he'd say. He even told the sheriff once he'd been robbed ridin' into town, and the robber looked like me, even though I'd supposedly had a bandanna over most of my face.''

"And people in your town *believed* him?'' she breathed, shocked.

He shook his head and threw the bone into the darkness beyond the campfire.

"Not most of 'em, no, though the girl I'd been sweet on since before the war suddenly wouldn't have anything t'do with me—at least, out in the open. But the rest of 'em, well, they'd known me and the rest of my family all my life, and they weren't about to listen to someone who was a traitor to his own state. But this scalawag wanted my ranch real bad. The Flying C was the best-watered ranch land for a hundred miles, y'see, and when I managed to pay the taxes on it in spite of the way they raised 'em, this fella decided he was gonna have to play rough.''

"What did he do?''

The fire snapped, sending a shower of sparks into the night sky. She saw his mouth tighten and his gaze narrow as he remembered.

"All the rumors didn't run me off, but he saw his chance in 1869, when the army moved its headquarters to Austin. Calhoun Crossing, my town, is about half a day's ride from there. One night the stage bringin' the army payroll was robbed and the driver shot to death. This fella who wanted my land claimed he saw me gallopin' away from the stage on Rio.''

"But it wasn't you," she said with certainty. She knew with the same certainty that she knew her name that it hadn't been him.

"Nope."

"Couldn't you prove it?" she asked.

"Nope."

His eyes had become unreadable in the flickering light. She sensed there was more there that he wasn't telling her, so she took what he had told her and made a stab at guessing.

"You were with a woman, weren't you?"

He said nothing, but he didn't deny it, so she went on. "You said your sweetheart wouldn't be with you openly, but you were with her that night, weren't you?"

She thought he was going to remain silent again, and the idea maddened her. "Morgan, this is not the time to be chivalrous! I'm just trying to understand! Were you with her?"

He looked away. "Yes."

"Then what happened?"

He shrugged. "The Federals came to arrest me, but I managed to get away. I figured as long as they were gonna steal my land and drive me away from home, I might as well *be* an outlaw. So I did some holdups when I had to to survive. But I've never killed anyone, and I've never stolen from my own people, Duchess. Just Yankees, and only the ones who could afford to lose it. Carpetbaggers who had grown fat on what *they'd* stolen, businessmen rich from profiteering during the war. And only when there wasn't any other way. I've mostly kept myself in beans and coffee by playin' poker."

Now she knew what people meant when they said their hearts ached. It was a literal, physical pang. She wanted to reach out and take him into her arms, to hold his head against her breast and comfort him.

"I believe in you, Morgan Calhoun," she said. "You're a good man. I...I want to help you—help you clear your name. I'll hire a solicitor...a lawyer," she corrected herself. "I can pay to get you the best. He'll prove you didn't do that first robbery, and he'll get you your ranch back, too.''

His gaze pierced her. ''Now, Duchess, why would you do that?''

Chapter Twenty-One

"Why? I—I've grown to...to respect you a great deal," she managed at last. "To be absolutely honest with you, Morgan, I even—"

"Careful, Duchess," he interrupted quickly, wanting more than anything to let her finish, and knowing he couldn't, for her own good. She was about to tell him she had feelings for him, and he couldn't let that happen. "I don't reckon your Frenchman would like it too much if you were spending your time and money worryin' over some worthless Texas bandit," he reminded her.

"But you're not worthless!" she exclaimed. "As you said, you've only robbed people when you had no other choice! And as far as what Thierry thinks, I really don't—"

He interrupted her again. "That won't make a difference to your Thierry de-Whatever-His-Name-Is. No, Duchess, don't you worry about me once I've turned you over to him in Santa Fe. I'll be just fine. There ain't a lawman born who can catch me."

He hoped it was true, hoped, too, that Sarah wasn't going to persist and declare her love for him. Because he didn't know if he was strong enough to resist, once she'd admitted it. Oh, he could see the truth of it shining in those beautiful eyes of hers, magnified behind the spectacles she mostly forgot she was wearing these days. The knowledge would have to comfort him in the days and years to come. He could not let the duchess commit herself to a penniless outlaw who might well end his days behind bars, or at the end of a rope.

"But Morgan, please listen to me. I have something to tell you, and I've been holding it inside for a long time—"

"Duchess, whatever it is, maybe we'd better save it for tomorrow," he said, ruthlessly cutting her off. "We've got a lotta ground t'cover, an' it's time we got some shut-eye." He slid his hat down over his eyes to shut out the firelight and the sight of her leaning over him, her face full of naked entreaty.

A nearby scream woke him—how much later, he couldn't say as he grabbed for his Colt. His brain registered the fact that it was just light enough to see a dazed and sleepy-looking Sarah struggling out of her blanket roll, reaching for her spectacles and stumbling to her feet. It hadn't been Sarah that had screamed, then, but who?

"Who…wha—?" she muttered.

"I don't know…"

Then the sound came again from down the draw, and he realized that the scream hadn't been human, but equine. It was Rio, and it wasn't coming from the end of the draw where the stallion had been tethered. And then he heard the thoroughbred's answering whinny from the same direction, and the pounding of hooves.

"It's Rio, Duchess—he's broken loose, and he's going for your mare."

"But he—he c-can't! We can't let this h-happen," she stammered, and then she began to run down the draw in the direction of the horses, and he followed, afraid she would get hurt trying to prevent what was no longer preventable.

Rio trumpeted again, and it was the sound of a fully

aroused stallion announcing his impending conquest of a mare. Trafalgar, still tethered but pawing and stamping, nickered back at the pinto, lifted her tail and arched it proudly, then presented her hindquarters to Rio. The pinto reared up over her, clamping his teeth into her neck as he came down on her. They heard her squeal, saw her tremble as the stallion's hindquarters pumped frantically against her.

It was a raw and primal sight, and yet somehow magnificent in its violence, too. Morgan felt the woman he was holding by the back of her shoulders shuddering beneath his hands.

"I'm sorry, Sarah," he breathed into her hair. "I reckon Rio broke his tether. Normally he's the most biddable stallion I've ever seen, but around a mare in season…"

She turned and buried her face against his shirt just as Rio came off the mare with a thud of his front hooves and a shrill whinny.

"It's all right, Morgan. I suppose…it was meant to be," she breathed, her breath coming in ragged pants. "And it's right, in a way…. Animals don't understand these distinctions we humans place upon them…about breeding, and class…." She gave an unsteady laugh and raised her head to meet his gaze. "Now I understand why Ben would never allow me near the breeding barn when a stallion was servicing a mare. It's a very…ah…unsettling sight, isn't it?"

Out of the corner of his eye he could see Trafalgar standing still, her head down, her flanks and withers still quivering, but he had eyes only for the woman who had turned in his arms so that his former restraint of her now became an embrace.

Yeah, he felt unsettled, all right, and from what he could see, she felt the same. Her eyes were gleaming; her breasts were heaving, creating little jolts of pleasure where they brushed his chest. As he watched, she licked her lips and pushed herself up on her toes, her arms stealing about his neck.

"Morgan," she breathed, "I want you to kiss me...."

Lord, he was going to do it. He was going to lower his lips to hers, and then he was going to pick her up in his arms and carry her back to her bedroll by the campfire and make love to her until she screamed with the pleasure he was going to give her. To hell with her Frenchman and the fact that she was a duchess and he an outlaw...

Crack!

They both heard the gunshot, and hit the dirt simultaneously, even though it sounded as if it came from some distance.

"Are you all right?" they asked each other in unison, passion forgotten as the *crack* sounded again. By now Morgan's ears had located its direction. It was coming from some distance to the right of them beyond the draw.

"What is it? Who's shooting?" she asked. And then the sound came to them on the wind—a muffled, *human* cry of pain.

Of course he didn't know. "You stay right here, Sarah. I'm going to find out."

"But—"

"I said *stay right here.* Don't worry about the horses—Rio will stay right near your mare. And if anything happens to me, you ride back to Pueblo as if the devil himself was at your heels."

Leaving her in the draw with the horses, he crept over the plains until he found the source of the gunshots. He crawled the last few yards in the tall, concealing, dry buffalo grass. He knew that its rustling would alert an Indian, but he had a hunch the men causing the cries were white.

He was right. Two white men stood over an Apache brave staked out on the ground. One of them was holding the reins of a swaybacked buckskin, the other a pistol.

The Indian's face gleamed with sweat and he clenched his teeth in his effort not to cry out. The rising sun revealed a red slash through his scalp, and his arms cratered with scarlet-centered sores—cigar burns, Morgan realized, seeing the half-consumed stogie clamped between the teeth of one of the white captors. The gunshots they had heard had each cost the brave a finger on his right hand. As Morgan watched, pondering the best thing to do, the other man raised his pistol again and aimed, shooting off one of the fingers on the Indian's left hand. Again the Apache was unable to suppress his moan of pain.

"C'mon, now, Injun, tell us where you hid the horse you stole from us," demanded the stogie-smoker, who was obviously the leader. "I'd purely despise havin' to leave you with no fingers a-tall."

The Indian's obsidian eye blazed hatred and defiance, and he gave no answer.

Morgan saw that the other man was about to shoot off another finger. "That'll be enough of that, gents," he said, standing and leveling his Colt at the one aiming the pistol at the Apache.

The two white men whirled to face him. "Mister, where'd you come from?" the one with the stogie asked. "This here red man stole one o' our horses. We was jest…questionin' him."

The Apache was watching him with sullen eyes, probably thinking that he had just gained a third tormentor.

"Well, I reckon I don't like the way you were goin' about it," Morgan responded. "Did it ever occur to you that he might not speak English?" Keeping his gaze fastened on the two white men, Morgan addressed the Indian in rusty Apache.

The Apache brave blinked in surprise, then warily answered.

"He says he doesn't have your horse," Morgan told the other two men. "He said he wouldn't steal your horse if it was the last horse on the plains, because you've beaten it and starved it and its spirit is broken. He says he saw it wandering loose, but he didn't take it. He tells me you creased him with a bullet and knocked him off his horse, otherwise he would not be lying here at the mercy of such dogs as you.''

The two white men growled and bristled. ''You believe the nonsense a red Injun'd spout, mister? He's jes' tryin' to play on yore sympathies, like—until he kin steal yore horse, an' mebbe yore hair, too.''

''Just the same, I'd be obliged if you'd turn him loose— *right now.*'' To prove he was serious he cocked the gun he had leveled at them.

Behind him, a rustling in the grass told him Sarah had disobeyed and crept up behind. A click told him she had brought her pistol and had cocked it, as well. The sound made his blood run cold. He had not been afraid before, but now there was no more room for error. He could not afford to make a mistake, or let the other two men make one, for it might cost her life. He didn't even dare glance back to see if she had tucked her hair back up under her hat so they couldn't tell she was a female.

''So there's two of you,'' the man who did not have a stogie said conversationally. ''Ya must be campin' down in that draw yonder, right? I thought I heard horses over there, an' figured mine mighta found some mustangs, but we were havin' too much fun with the Injun, there.''

''You heard my friend,'' Sarah said in a deep, husky voice that might just fool them into thinking she was a man. ''Let the Indian go.''

''You some kinda furriner?'' the one in charge asked her, and while Morgan was waiting and wondering whether she would answer, he saw the other man raise his pistol.

Morgan shot the man through the arm, causing him to drop the pistol with a yelp, sink to his knees and clutch his bleeding arm with his left hand.

"I'd purely despise havin' to shoot you, too, mister," Morgan mocked. "Why don't you drop the pistol you've got in your belt? That's it, nice and easy in this direction, then you loose that Indian like I told you to. Cover the one on the ground, Challoner."

The man with the cigar threw his Colt so that it landed a few feet from Morgan. Never taking his eyes off the man, he picked up the gun and stuck it in his belt, then motioned toward the Indian.

"You're makin' a mistake, mister," the man protested. "This brave won't be grateful, if that's what you're hopin'. He'll call the rest of them Apaches down on ya and you'll lose yore hair jest the same."

"I reckon that's our lookout, ain't it?" Morgan drawled as the man bent to comply with Morgan's order.

A quick flash of movement from the man on the ground warned Morgan he was going for his boot gun. Morgan shifted his pistol's direction, but Sarah was quicker. She fired, hitting the man in the hand. He screamed, then raised his hands in the air in surrender, one of them dripping with blood.

"See how it feels?" Morgan taunted him. "If this Apache wasn't already hurtin', I'd let him lift your hair if he was so inclined." He saw the leader finish loosing the Indian's bonds, and the Apache warily staggered to his feet, but his color, under the coppery tint of his skin, was ashen. He wasn't going to be able to make it back to his people without some help.

"I'm afraid we're gonna have to relieve you of your other horse, gents," Morgan announced. "Looks like the Apache's gonna be needin' it."

"What about us? We'll die out here on the plains without a horse!" screamed the wounded man.

"You shoulda thought of that before you started torturin' him," Morgan retorted easily. "But you'll make it, if you're careful with your water. Pueblo's back that way just about thirty, forty miles. Oh, one more thing, fellows—you got any whiskey?''

"Yeah, we got some," the leader snarled. "Ya gonna take that, too?"

"Yup," Morgan replied. "Wouldn't want y'all to be gettin' drunk when you should be walkin'." He wasn't thirsty for spirits himself—it was for the Indian. By the looks of him, he was going to need something for the pain, and soon.

"Go ahead, but we'll catch up with you sons of bitches and you're gonna wish you'd never interfered, damn yore hides."

Morgan shrugged. "Challoner, I'll cover you while you help our Indian friend onto that plug they call a horse and find that whiskey in their saddlebags. Then we'll let these fellows be on their way. I don't reckon they're gonna bother us again, but we'll be watchin' for it, won't we?"

"Yeah." Morgan was amused to hear Sarah growl in her best imitation-American-male. "So don't try nothin'. I'd jest as soon kill you as look at you, you ugly galoot." He was going to have to be sure to ask her which sensational novel she'd gotten her lingo from.

By the time Morgan and Sarah were packed and ready to go in the draw, they could see the two men as tiny dots on the horizon, heading due north back toward Pueblo. Even at this distance, Morgan could see that the wounded man was leaning on the other for support. Those two wouldn't be riding after them seeking revenge any time soon.

The Apache's name, Morgan learned, was Naiche, and he'd been on a hunting expedition for his hungry people. When Morgan translated for Sarah's benefit, she immediately walked over to the packhorse, got the remains of their antelope feast and offered the Apache some, but he shook his head.

"He will not eat until the *N'de,* his people, can eat," Morgan told her. "We're going to have to see him back to his village, Sarah. He's in a lot of pain, and he's stayin' conscious out of pride alone.''

''Of course. I wouldn't think of leaving him here alone,'' Sarah replied firmly.

The Apache eyed her, and smiled slightly as he made a comment and then asked Morgan another question.

''He asked what you said,'' Morgan told her. ''After I translated, he said you are a woman of great heart, and asked if you were my woman. So I guess you can quit usin' the deep voice, 'cause he wasn't fooled. I'm goin' to tell him you are my woman, okay? I think it's safer.''

''Go ahead and tell him so, Morgan,'' she said, her voice steady as she looked him in the eye. ''It's true, anyway.''

He stared back at her. ''Duchess, what are you sayin'? Careful now, don't say something you're going to regret—''

''Let's not argue, Morgan,'' she said with serene resolve. ''We'll talk about it later, when we're alone.''

They'd talk about it, all right, Morgan vowed. He had to make her see he couldn't accept her generous offer of herself, no matter how much he wanted to. It wasn't right. *He* wasn't right for her, not for a few nights of passion, and certainly not for the rest of their lives.

''Which way?'' Morgan asked the Apache once they'd bandaged his hands and helped him to mount. The scrubby horse they'd taken from the white men had shied from the smell of blood, but once the Indian was atop him, he didn't seem inclined to buck.

Naiche pointed southwest to the mountains they'd been skirting all along.

''Is it far? My woman's mare was not bred for the mountains,'' Morgan told him.

The Apache eyed Trafalgar admiringly, and said in Apache, ''She is much horse, just as your golden-haired woman is much woman. I would trade all my string of horses for her.''

Morgan wasn't sure whether he meant the thoroughbred or

Sarah, but knew he had to be careful what he said either way. "My woman and the mare's spirits are attached by an invisible, magic cord," Morgan told him, adding, "Each would wither without the other, and I would wither without her."

The answer seemed to satisfy the Apache.

An hour later Morgan spotted a mule deer and shot it, then tied the buck over the packhorse's withers. It wouldn't hurt to have some meat to offer when they met up with Naiche's band of Jicarilla Apaches.

Naiche had tried to remain stoic, but his face got paler with each mile, and finally he consented to drink some of the whiskey Morgan offered. He drank deeply and long, prompting Morgan to urge him to stop. He had to remain alert, Morgan told him, for how would they find his people if Naiche was insensible with firewater?

The Apache just gave a weak grin, and said, "Do not worry if that happens, Texan. Just ride into the mountains, and they will find you." A few minutes later he sagged on his mount and would have fallen off if Morgan hadn't caught him. They stopped and transferred him onto Rio, and Morgan rode from then on with the limp figure of the Indian cradled in his arms.

They rode until the sun was high in the sky. Morgan figured they were in New Mexico by now. He'd planned for them to enter the territory over Raton Pass, and join up with the Santa Fe Trail, but at least this way they wouldn't be charged the toll travelers paid to go that way—four bits each horse, a dollar and fifty cents per wagon.

Just as Naiche had promised, "the People" found them before Morgan and Sarah found the village. One minute they were alone on the narrow mountain trail, the next, four copper-skinned men clad in breechcloths, fringed, tanned-hide shirts and knee-high moccasins had surrounded them, rifles held at the ready.

Chapter Twenty-Two

Sarah froze in the saddle. It was one thing to read tales about wild red men in novels about the West, quite another to confront the real thing.

Silently she stared at the copper-skinned Apache men with their straight, raven black hair held back with wide cloth bands across their foreheads. They stared back at her. The unblinking obsidian intensity of their gazes made Sarah look away first.

One of them, who had gray liberally mixed with the black of his hair, pointed to the limp Indian Morgan held in his arms, and uttered something in Apache. There was no doubt from his tone that it was a question, and more than that, it was a question for which Morgan better have the right answer.

Morgan answered in Apache, nodding toward Naiche's bandaged hands, which had been concealed in his lap. The four men came surging forward, exclaiming.

Their sudden movement caused Trafalgar to rear and whinny in alarm, and Sarah momentarily forgot the Indians as she struggled to keep her seat. Then, once she succeeded in quieting the mare, Sarah saw the gray-haired leader point straight at *her* and heard him ask another question.

Morgan spoke again, pointing to Sarah, then back to himself.

"What's he saying? What have you told him?" she asked.

"I've told him what happened to Naiche, and that we brought him here because we mean well to the Apache. And I said I have told you, my wife, to dress like a man for your safety on our journey," he said.

The leader made a gesture toward her head, and seemed to demand something.

"He wants to see your hair, Sarah," Morgan said. His eyes said, *Trust me. It will be all right.*

Slowly, keeping her gaze locked with Morgan's and trying to keep her hands from shaking, she lifted the hat and allowed the thick blond plait to fall down her back.

A collective gasp—clearly one of admiration—arose from the men. Then Morgan said something else to them, and two of them peeled away from the rest and ran ahead up the path.

"I've told them Naiche needs the medicine man, and that we would be honored to spend the night with them."

Her heart pounded within the man's shirt she wore. "Oh, Morgan, is that really necessary? Surely now that we've brought Naiche back home, our obligation is through. It's early enough that we can find our way back down the mountain, can't we?"

He shook his head. "Hospitality is sacred to the Apache. If we didn't stay the night, they would take it as a grave insult. They might even decide we had something to do with Naiche's injury after all."

She considered his words, then took a deep breath. "Very well," she said. "One night. Only fancy how much fun it will be to tell this story at the palace!"

His expression was approving. "That's the spirit."

The two men who had run ahead had evidently warned the village, if the collection of crude, round huts made of brush and grass could properly be called a village. About two dozen men, women and children came surging down the narrow path to exclaim over their fallen warrior and eye the newcomers with suspicion and naked curiosity.

One of them, skinny, gray-haired and wrinkled, came forward and said something to Morgan, pointing to the hut from which he had just come.

"That's the shaman, the medicine man, Sarah, and he wants me to bring Naiche into his wickiup. You can dismount, but stay right there with your mare and Rio."

As if she would have consented to go anywhere else! As soon as he went into the wickiup, the Indians pressed forward, staring at her from just inches away, some of them even daring enough to reach out and stroke her hair. They were just as inquisitive about Rio and Trafalgar, stroking their necks and flanks. The mare rolled her eyes and tossed her head nervously, but fortunately, she didn't kick.

Just as Morgan came out, a pair of Apache braves thundered past them on spotted ponies, heading down the mountain.

"Where are they going, do you think?" Sarah asked, calm now that Morgan was with her again.

"From the snatches of talk I've heard, I'd guess they were going after the two who tortured Naiche," Morgan told her as a cloud of dust rose in their wake. "I wouldn't want to be those fellows if they're caught between here and Pueblo."

The older brave with the iron gray hair came forward again and spoke to Morgan, pointing at a wickiup set a little distance away from the others.

"That's where we're to spend the night, Duchess," Morgan translated. "They tell me it's normally used by newly married couples in this band."

"Oh?" She felt herself blush.

They were the guests of honor at a feast that evening. They were directed to sit in front of the leader's wickiup, and the warriors, women and children found places on the ground as near to them as possible. The only meat served was the venison they had brought on the packhorse, but a plentiful amount of roasted yucca and agave, woven baskets full of wild onions, berries and piñon nuts were served, first to Morgan and Sarah, then passed to the men, and finally to the women and children. Sarah and Morgan ate sparingly, aware that their Indian hosts had put on the feast not from an abundance of food, but from the gratitude in their hearts.

They were given gourds full of a colorless liquor Morgan called mescal. "Just pretend to drink this," he warned, handing her a gourd, "'cause it'll knock you flat on your back, Duchess."

"I'll be careful," she promised, but took a sip, since the man who had handed it to her was watching closely. The liquid burned all the way down to her stomach, and Sarah resolved to wash her food down with the water she had also been given.

An Apache woman had just laid an intricately woven basket at her feet, filled with pieces of some sort of yellow-and-pink-speckled sweet mixture.

"It's a sort of candy made of preserved yucca fruits mixed with sunflower petals," Morgan told her. "Try it."

It was delicious. But she was equally interested in the basket. "Beautiful," she said to the woman, pointing to the design.

After Morgan translated, the woman beamed and touched Sarah's hair, then the spectacles that she wore.

"She says you are beautiful, too, Woman of Golden Hair and Far-Seeing Eyes," Morgan told her. His eyes added their own praise. Then he told her that the tribal subdivision name, Jicarilla, came from the Spanish word for the baskets the women wove.

Sarah realized she had never felt as welcome in any drawing room or at any country-house party as she did in this village. The court at Whitehall seemed not only an ocean away, but part of another lifetime.

Then the storytelling began. The men of the tribe told of buffalo hunts and raids against other tribes, especially the Comanches, their enemies. Morgan translated each tale for Sarah's benefit, then told a couple of his own, one in which he had successfully outrun a hunting party of Comanches on the Staked Plain, and another in which he had helped a band of Mescalero Apaches steal the cattle bound for a fort on the plains.

The Apache men laughed and clapped Morgan on the back in obvious approval.

Then the older warrior with the iron gray hair, his face turning serious, pointed first to Sarah, and then to Morgan.

"What does he ask, Morgan?"

"He wants to know what we're doing, traveling all alone like this over dangerous country." He addressed the Apache. "I told him we had business in Santa Fe, but we had to come alone because we had enemies back in Denver, and that one of them might be trailing us."

It was a sobering reminder of what lay beyond the night in this encampment.

The stars were twinkling in the velvet sky above by the time Morgan, carrying a burning stick to light their way, led her to their wickiup. Sarah was grateful that it lay at some distance from the rest of the grass-and-brush huts, for she had made up her mind about something, and she turned to face Morgan, who had stooped to light the small pile of sticks in the middle of the round hut.

In a moment tiny flames cast their light across the diameter of the floor. There was a small circular hole at the top, and the smoke began to curl upward, escaping through it.

He'd brought their blanket rolls in here earlier, and they were lying side by side. "If you want, I'll move mine to the other side, Duchess," he said, bending to pick it up without looking at her. "I thought in case someone came in here lookin' while we were at the feast, it'd look more like we were really married if I laid 'em out together."

"No," Sarah said when he would have moved his bedroll. "Don't move it."

He stopped, straightening until his head brushed the round top of the wickiup, staring at her in the dim light.

"Duchess, what are you saying?" he asked.

She let her actions speak for her, removing her spectacles and laying them carefully aside. Then she stood right in front of him and began to unbutton her shirt.

"Sarah, did you drink more mescal when I wasn't lookin'?" Morgan sounded uneasy. "Now stop that," he ordered as she continued to unbutton her shirt.

"No more than a couple of sips," she said, smiling and ignoring his command. "*You* drank a whole cupful, I noticed."

"I'm used to it," he protested. "Sarah, this isn't wise," he added, seeing her pull her shirttail out of the waistband of her pants and lower her hands to the buttons on her fly. He took a step or two backward.

Sarah paused, feeling his eyes on the mounds of her breasts that trembled under her camisole, only partly covered now by the shirt. Her fingers quivered on the buttons of the pants. "I'm tired of being wise, Morgan," she told him, advancing on him. "I've tried to do the sensible thing ever since I succeeded to the duchy, and I'm tired of it. I came to America because I was weary of always doing the safe, sensible thing, and now I want to make love with you, Morgan."

"Sarah," he breathed, his hands coming forward, then sinking to his sides. "Sarah, no. I want you, too, honey, more than I want my next breath, but I can't have you. I agreed to take you to that French fellow, Sarah…and I think that's what I should do. Once we hit the Santa Fe Trail, it won't take long to get there. We—oh, Sarah…"

She had stepped out of the dusty trousers, and let the shirt slide backward off her arms, and was clad only in her pantalets and chemise. Then she raised her arms and pulled the chemise off over her head. As he stared, she loosed her hair from the confining braid and let it fall to her shoulders.

She closed the distance between them, unbuttoning his shirt, knowing there was only bare skin beneath, for he'd been leaving his union suit off because of the heat of the August days.

"*Please,* Morgan," she murmured as she finished unbuttoning it, sliding her hands along his arms until her breasts were almost touching his chest. "As you say, we'll be in Santa Fe soon. Oh, Morgan, I couldn't bear it if you hadn't made love to me—*just this once....*" She injected all the yearning she felt into her voice, knowing if he rejected her now, there was nothing left for her but ashes. Later there would be time to explain to Morgan that she was in love with him, that she no longer loved Thierry and planned to break their betrothal once she arrived in Santa Fe. But for now all she wanted was Morgan.

"Morgan," she whispered, stepping forward so that her bare breasts brushed against his chest, "*make love to me.*"

The sensation of her soft nipples touching his chest, accentuated by every ragged breath she took, was a jolt of lightning that went straight to his heart. He groaned.

"Oh, Duchess—Sarah—are you *sure?* What about—" He couldn't think of the man's name to save his soul. "What about your Frenchman?"

"Forget about him for tonight," she commanded in a whisper. "I don't believe I could live if you don't make love to me now."

Still he hesitated, and she must have read his uncertainty in his eyes, for she said, "Morgan, in my world, affairs of the heart are not unusual. Provided one is discreet, one's heart may be given as one likes."

He understood. She was reminding him she was not a virgin. He'd always figured she and her Frenchman had gone to bed together, but maybe she'd had other lovers, too. And now she desired *him,* Morgan Calhoun, but she had accepted that there would be only tonight for them. She would go to the Frenchman, and back to her own world, when they reached Santa Fe. *God in Heaven, would one night be enough for him?*

Self-control was a thing of the past, though. His arms encircled her, pulling her tightly against him so that her breasts were crushed against the hard planes of his chest. He was sure he'd never felt anything better in his entire life—unless it was the feel of her tiny hands trembling on the buttons of his denims.

He helped her push them down his hips, chuckling as he leaned on her slightly so he could balance on one foot and then the other to pull off his boots and step out of his trousers. And then he was naked, and she was in his arms, and he was pulling her up against his erect manhood, letting her feel how much he wanted her.

She pulled back, and Morgan thought for a heartbeat she had changed her mind, that she'd been too frightened, but she was only stepping away to undo the drawstring tie at her waist so she could pull her pantalets down.

Now she was as naked as he, and he couldn't wait any longer to feel her skin touching his from head to toe. Gently he urged her down until they were both stretched out on his blanket roll, lying on their sides and entwined together.

"Oh, Sarah, if you only knew how long I've wanted to do this," he breathed into her hair as his hand sought and found her breast and cupped it.

"No longer than I have, surely—" she began, and then her voice ended in a moan as his hand was replaced by his mouth. He suckled from her breast until she arched against him.

"That day at the train station..." he said when he could find his breath again.

"Yes, that's when it began for me," she said, her voice unsteady as she added with a laugh, "Mind you, I don't start desiring every chap who knocks me to the ground while bullets fly overhead.... Oh, *Morgan,*" she breathed as his fingers found her.

She was hot and wet and ready for him, he discovered as he parted her curls and stroked her with his fingers, and her breath came in gasps. "Morgan, *please,*" she begged as she writhed against him, and he continued to drive her—and himself—crazy with pleasure.

Still stroking her, he began to thrust against her opening again, too, so that she couldn't tell what was pleasuring her the most, his manhood or his hand, and he wasn't sure himself. He only knew he was about to explode with the effort of holding himself back, but he was determined to give her the ultimate joy before he allowed it to himself.

"Morgan, now! Now, please!" she pleaded, almost sobbing, and he obeyed, parting her legs the rest of the way and thrusting into her—and feeling the resistance as the thin band of tissue around her woman's passage parted to allow him full entrance. He heard her whimper, and raised his head to see Sarah trying to stifle the sound against her knuckles.

He pulled out of her. "You're a *virgin,*" he accused. "Sarah? You said—you implied—"

She opened her eyes and looked up at him. "I know. I wanted you to think I'd...done this before. I'm sorry...I haven't. *I wanted you to be the one, Morgan, the one who made me a woman.* Please, Morgan, the pain's almost gone— I knew it would hurt a little, the first time.... There aren't words for how wonderful you were making me feel before. Please, don't stop...."

She put her hands on his bare buttocks, urging him into her again. Heaven help him, but he couldn't have stopped now if he wanted to. He had taken her innocence, an innocence he had never guessed she had maintained in the glittering world from which she had come, and now he was going to give her something in its place.

Putting his own hands under her buttocks, he lifted her to him, entering her as gently as he could, and began a steady rhythm of thrusting and retreating, slowly at first, then faster and harder until he felt the ripples of her climax and heard her soft scream against his ear. Only then did he release himself in her, feeling the stars burst against his eyes.

Chapter Twenty-Three

They slept little that night. Morgan seemed tacitly determined, since one night was all he would have of her, to make love to her in every way possible. Sarah, for her part, had no wish to refuse him.

Now she lay on her side, still naked and propped up on one elbow, staring down at him as the morning sunlight streamed into the wickiup's entrance. He looked boyish as he slept, the severe planes of his face softened, the tight line of his mouth relaxed. *My desperado,* she thought, smoothing back a lock of dark hair that had fallen over his forehead. She smiled to herself, planning how she was going to tell him, somewhere on the trail, that she had no intention of leaving him to go with Thierry, that she was only meeting "her Frenchman" in order to end their relationship. She would also tell him she was going to abdicate the title in favor of her sister and remain with him.

Morgan would argue, she knew. He'd protest that he wasn't good enough for her, had nothing to give her. But he was going to find out that nothing could be as stubborn as a duchess who knew what she wanted.

A shadow blotted out the sunlight coming from the doorway, and she gasped, grabbing for something to cover herself with. The only thing within reach was his shirt, and she pressed it against her breasts before turning to see who was there.

It was the old shaman, and he said something to her in his guttural-sounding language.

"Wait a moment, sir—I don't understand a word," she muttered, knowing it was useless to say so in English, but he smiled as she reached over to shake Morgan awake.

He came instantly alert, turning to see the old man, who smiled again and said something else.

"I'll just be a minute, Duchess," he said, grabbing for the spare blanket and wrapping it about his middle. He stepped outside the entrance of the wickiup and Sarah could hear them conversing in rapid Apache for several minutes. A few moments later Morgan came back inside, and she could hear other footsteps retreating down the pathway.

"The shaman says Naiche's pain is better this morning, and he has changed the poultice around the stumps of Naiche's fingers. So far the wounds are healing cleanly."

"Thank God," she murmured, guessing he was leading into something.

"He said it will be several days...a week, maybe...before he can ride again, and learn to shoot arrows from his bow because of the missing fingers...."

She nodded. "Does this concern us in some way, Morgan?"

He reached for his denims and began to thread one leg into them. "Only if you're willing for it to, Duchess," he said, pausing before thrusting the other leg in. "The shaman says the Apaches are gonna escort us safely to Santa Fe, and Naiche wants the honor of leading," he told her, his eyes unreadable. "He says it is the only way he can repay what we did for him yesterday."

"What did you say, Morgan?" she said, trying not to show

any sign of the desperate leap of joy his words had engendered.

"I said I would speak to you, but I thought we'd have to say no, for our business in Santa Fe might not wait," he said.

Though she searched his face, he gave her no clue as to what *he* wanted. But hadn't he said Naiche's wishes would concern them if *she* was willing?

"Oh, Morgan," she said, letting him see her smile, "I think it would be churlish to leave now and refuse Naiche that honor...."

"But Sarah," he began, kneeling in front of her, "what about the Fr—"

She put her finger over his lips, stopping him. "My business will wait—*he'll* wait, Morgan. He doesn't know how long it will take me to get there from Denver." The idea of being given another week to be with Morgan, to convince him that she belonged with him, not with some titled Frenchman, was intoxicating.

His lips curved underneath her fingers. "All right, Duchess, I'll tell them we'll stay," he said, starting to rise, but she caught at both sides of his still-unbuttoned trouser fly.

"Don't go, not yet, Morgan...I don't think we've properly said good-morning," she breathed, letting his shirt fall away from her breasts.

He closed his eyes. "But you said...just this one night...."

She rose to her knees, facing him. "We've just been given another week, Morgan. Let's not waste it, shall we? While we're here with the Apaches, let us belong only to each other." Surely a week was long enough to bind him to her forever!

He grinned down at her. "Duchess, your wish is my command," he murmured just before he lowered his mouth to hers.

"What do you mean, she *was* here?" the man demanded of the same hotel manager who'd been dazzled by the French

Nightingale. "Are you saying she is not here anymore?"

"That's right, she's been gone for…l'see, three days now. She was only here for the one night, Mam'selle Fifi was, but she put on quite a show down at the Arkansas River Saloon. You another Frenchie, like her? Ya talk jes' like she does," the manager babbled on inanely, until the man who'd been hunting Sarah Challoner wanted to reach across the polished pine counter and choke him.

"I am her *husband,* that is who I am, you fool, and the man who is with her has stolen my *wife,*" the would-be assassin lied, lacing his voice with righteous indignation. "Would you mind telling me where she and her, ah, paramour went from here?"

The man scratched his chin for a moment, then said, "Naw, I wouldn't mind, since she's yore wife—not iffen I knew, that is. But I don't. They waited for the mercantile to open, then they lit out. Appearances shore can be deceivin', cain't they? Why, she an' her mister—ahem—the man she was with, they *seemed* like right nice folks. I'm shore sorry t'hear ya missed catchin' her, mister."

Not as sorry as *he* was, *certainement!* He'd learned about Sarah's masquerading as "Fifi" when he'd reached Castle Rock early yesterday morning, as well as the fact that her highbred mare had been lame when they'd arrived there. He'd managed to board the nine-o'clock train south just minutes later, hoping that the mare's lameness would keep them here, at the railroad's terminus, long enough for him to catch up.

Ah well, there was no use crying over spilled milk, as the Americans said. He would merely have to keep trailing them. Sooner or later they were bound to make a mistake, and if he did not overtake them on the way to Santa Fe, he would trap them there. He could still make her death look like a random killing by an unknown murderer, as long as he was careful.

As hard as he rode in his effort to catch up, however, he

caught no sight of his quarry. Even when he struck the Santa Fe Trail, where trading traffic was much more frequent, he could find no one who had seen the two, or their distinctive horses. One grizzled old mule skinner even opined that Apaches had probably gotten them.

Perhaps. But how would he know? The assassin did not like loose ends. He wanted to be *certain* that Sarah Challoner was dead before he went home to tell her sister that she had inherited the title.

At last he decided it would be best to go on to Santa Fe and wait for Sarah to appear. If she did not show up within a month, he would write to Malvern Hall and tell Kathryn Challoner he was making inquiries, but that her sister was feared dead from an Indian attack suffered when she eloped into the wild country with her bodyguard.

Santa Fe lay ahead, a city nestled in the foothills of the Sangre de Cristo Mountains. It was time to say goodbye to the four Apache men who had ridden with them all the way from their stronghold in the mountains on the Colorado-New Mexico border.

"Naiche, I don't know how to thank you and these other men enough," Sarah said with a sigh of genuine regret. "You've been so good to us." Their very presence had often deterred trouble, she knew, that might have come from outlaws or other Indians lurking in the rock formations that sometimes flanked the trail. Sometimes, when their scout had reported the approach of parties of "bluecoats" or convoys of freight wagons that might have fired on the Apaches, they would melt into the surrounding countryside, but they always reappeared soon afterward.

Once Morgan had finished telling them what she had said, Sarah was surprised to see Naiche grin, dismount and kiss her hand in a manner that would have done credit to a royal prince.

"Calhoun teaches me this," he said in passable English, and laughed at her expression of delight.

Morgan added in an amused drawl, "He asked me what a warrior in your country would do to say goodbye to you."

Naiche said something else to Morgan, then looked back at Sarah, still grinning.

"He was speaking of the foal that will be born to your tall mare. It will be spotted like Rio, he says, but tall and fleet like Mare-With-Big-Name. He wishes he could see it someday."

Sarah was startled, having scarcely thought about Morgan's stallion mating with Trafalgar since the day it had happened. So Trafalgar was in foal to Rio....

She hesitated, not knowing what to say. Unless things worked out between her and Morgan, there was no way she could make such a promise.

"Tell Naiche," she said to Morgan, "that it would make my heart glad to see him again and show him the foal, but I will be thousands of miles across the ocean, and will have no way to bring that about." Her voice was neutral, giving no clue, she hoped, of the way her heart was breaking. Thus far she had been unable to persuade Morgan he had a future with her, and there would be nothing left for her, once she had met with Thierry in Santa Fe, but to return to England.

"It makes Naiche's heart sad, too, to know that we will be so far away."

"We?" she said, a wild hope humming to life within her breast.

His next words dashed that hope before it was fully formed. "I...I let him believe that I was going also," he said with a shrug. He looked away. "I didn't try to explain the situation, Duchess. It's too complicated, and besides, then we would have to admit we were never married to start with.... He said he is glad that I will be out of the bluecoats' reach," he added with a bitter twist to his mouth.

She looked away, too, feeling tears stinging her eyes. "Tell him we enjoyed their company on the trail, and will count them as friends always."

After Morgan did so, Naiche held a hand upright in farewell. Then he gave a hoarse cry to the other three. The Apaches wheeled their ponies, and soon they were lost in a cloud of dust as they galloped back up the Santa Fe Trail toward the Sangre de Cristo Mountains.

"Well, Duchess?" Morgan prompted after the Apaches were out of sight. He gestured to the city that lay ahead, just visible over a grove of piñon pines. "I reckon we oughta hurry on into Santa Fe and find your dashing Frenchman," he drawled with a lightness he was far from feeling. He felt like a man proposing to hurry his own walk up the stairs to the gallows, where a noose waited just for him.

He and Sarah hadn't made love since leaving the Apache encampment, for there had been no privacy while they traveled. And now the thought of handing Sarah over to this faceless Frenchman, knowing that she would belong to this man, that she would be sharing his bed, receiving his amorous caresses and inevitably, someday, bearing his children, stabbed his heart like a bowie knife. The very thought of what—*who*— he was about to give up was enough to make Morgan want to go off somewhere lonesome and, like a wolf, howl his pain at the moon.

It had to be done, though. He'd gone over it and over it in his mind, worrying the idea like that same wolf chewing the last bone that stood between him and starvation. There was just no way around it. He had to give her up, not because he didn't love her enough, but because he *did* love her, and because he loved her, he had to want what was best for her. And Morgan Calhoun was about the farthest thing from what was best for her that he could possibly imagine.

"Morgan, *please*," Sarah said, reaching out to grasp his wrist as he started to urge Rio onward, her voice one of entreaty that was agonizing to his self-control, "can't we talk about this? How many ways can I tell you that I love you? I can't marry Thierry de Châtellerault now. I don't love him—I didn't know what love *was* until I began to love you!"

He couldn't look at her, couldn't let himself see the love shining in her eyes, so he closed his and rubbed his knuckles wearily over them. "Sarah, it's not unusual for a woman to feel that way...." He hesitated, wanting to find the right words, and there were no right words. "That is, a lady who gives herself to a man...for the first time...well, she usually fancies she's in love with that man...at least for a while. But that doesn't mean he's the man she should marry up with, to spend her life with."

"Morgan! Are you saying *you don't love me?* That what we shared was just...passion? Lust?" Her voice thrummed with disbelief and pain.

The knife twisted deeper into his own heart. He took off his hat and raked his hand through his hair. He knew what he ought to say—*Yeah, Duchess, that's all it was. I'm a normal, healthy man and I wanted you, but don't try to fool yourself that there's any happily-ever-after waiting for us.* But he couldn't say it.

Instead, he turned to her, letting his eyes meet hers. "No, Duchess, I can't lie about it, not to you, not to myself—though you'd be better off if I did. I love you, all right, and that's forever. I'll still love you when I take my last breath. I have nothing to give you, Duchess, *but* love, and it ain't en—"

"Yes, it *is* enough, Morgan!" she cried, her voice breaking at the end. "If we love one another, we'll find a way—"

"*No, we won't, Duchess,* and that's the end of it," he said in a voice that, for all its quiet, brooked no argument. "I won't let you follow me on the outlaw trail, you understand?" Then, hearing her start to sob, he softened his voice and reached across the distance between the two horses to take hold of her hand. "It's *because* I love you and always will that I want you to be safe and happy, Sarah, not on the run with me, with the fear of me bein' caught makin' you old before your time. I won't do that, and that's final."

She jerked her face away from him and was silent for a long moment. "Very well, Morgan, we'll speak no more of it."

Her chill, precise voice was like the drumroll that was played right before they sprang the trapdoor on the gallows, dropping the man into hell.

"Fine," he managed to say. "Now suppose you tell me just what the plans are for meetin' up with your Frenchman."

Chapter Twenty-Four

"When we made the plan to meet in Santa Fe, we didn't know, of course, what hotels were available there," Sarah said as they urged their horses forward. "So Thierry, knowing he would likely arrive before I, hit upon the idea of leaving a message at the local constable's office, a message saying where he was staying. If I arrived and found no message, I was to leave one saying where *I* was staying, you see?"

He saw. "So we need to find the local calaboose. The jail—the sheriff's office," he added when Sarah looked confused at the term.

"Oh, right." She squared her shoulders. "Before we go there, I shall want to secure a pair of rooms—and stabling for the horses. And after we see if Thierry has left a message, I need to visit a telegraph office."

"And look up your Frenchman after that?"

"Oh, no," she said. "Not today, I'm afraid. It's already noon. By the time we have finished our errands, it will be much too late."

He stared at her, suspecting her motives, suspecting the feeling of relief, of reprieve, that had flooded his soul. "Why are you dallyin', Duchess? If it's because you think one more night will make a difference in what I said—"

She uttered a mirthless little laugh. "No, it's nothing like that, I assure you. You've quite convinced me that your mind is made up. Didn't you notice I said *rooms*, not *room*? Naturally, I shall want to bathe away the dust of the road and change my clothes," she said with a gesture toward the dusty, travel-worn masculine attire she still wore. "I shouldn't want to present myself to my *fiancé* dressed like this. I shall wait until morning, when I have been refreshed by a good night's sleep."

"Naturally," he echoed, her casual use of the word *fiancé* eating like acid into his heart. If only his suspicions *had* been right! Instead, she wanted to delay so she would look beautiful for her damned Frenchman. Damn it, if she only knew how beautiful she had looked to *him* on the trail, even dusty and wearing men's clothes! The thought of being with her for another full day was exquisite torture, yet he would not have forgone it at the cost of his salvation.

"Well, if you're determined t' get gussied up for your fancy Frenchman," he drawled, "surely you aren't plannin' on puttin' on that wrinkled gold dress again, or that plain ol' skirt an' blouse? I think we ought t' go shoppin' an' see if we can't pick you up some eye-poppin' ready-made dress to wear. And I reckon you won't have your spectacles on for that meetin', will you?" His mocking words rang in his ears like counterfeit pennies.

She stared at him, and Morgan caught a glimpse of a suspicious brightness in her eyes. "What a fine idea, Morgan," she said in a brittle voice. "Indeed, I think I *would* like a new gown, if you think Santa Fe affords such a luxury."

"What were you sayin' about a telegraph office?"

She looked amused. "Have you forgotten our arrangement, Morgan? You took on this job with the understanding that I owed you four thousand pounds—I forget what that amounted to in dollars—at the end of the journey. I have to arrange a transfer of funds from the bank in New York City, the one I

set up a relationship with when I arrived in the States. We'll
have them send the money to the bank in Santa Fe.''

The idea of being paid such a vast sum, which had pleased
him initially, held no charm for him now. In fact, he hated
the thought of it.

''Naw, forget that, Duchess. I don't want your money.''

She look surprised, even touched. ''But you've earned it,
Morgan Calhoun, and this duchess pays her debts—that's final,'' she said with an ironic quirk to her brow as she repeated
his own words.

He decided to argue no further. He'd just have to find a
way to give her back her money without her knowing about
it.

They threaded their way up the narrow, oxcart-crowded
streets, and he could tell that Sarah was charmed by the quaint
old Spanish-American town. She exclaimed over its adobe
buildings, with their *ristras* of drying peppers hanging from
exposed rafters, and the Indians and Mexicans selling their
wares. She didn't even seem shocked at hearing the colorful
curses the mule skinners leveled at the obstinate beasts pulling
their wagons.

The trail ended in the plaza, at one end of which lay the
long adobe building that was the historic Palace of the Gov-
ernors. The sheriff's office and jail lay diagonally across the
square from it.

''I was here in Santa Fe last spring,'' Morgan told her,
''and I stayed overnight in a little posada, an inn, around the
corner. It had a livery right next to it. You want to stay
there?''

Sarah inclined her head. ''Lead on, Macduff,'' she said
with a sardonic curve to her mouth.

Once they had settled the horses and paid for their rooms,
they returned to the plaza.

''I'll wait over yonder,'' Morgan told her, indicating the
side of the square adjacent to the palace side, but farthest from

the jail, "where the sheriff won't see me. You go ahead on in and inquire," he added, pointing at the jail, barely visible through the low-hanging boughs of shady cottonwoods.

Her mouth formed an O as the realization dawned in her magnified blue eyes. "You think there might be a Wanted poster with your likeness on it in the jail office?"

He nodded. "It's likely, Duchess. But we won't run into any problems if I wait over here."

He waited until she'd gone inside, then went over to where an old Indian sat in the shade of one of the trees. Morgan figured Sarah would be safe enough for a few minutes, especially in the presence of a lawman. The Indian had spread out silver jewelry on a blanket in front of him. Morgan still had some coins jingling in his pocket, and he had a notion about buying something for Sarah. Something to remember him by.

As Calhoun and Sarah stood talking, one of the serape-draped men dozing under the trees raised his sombrero from over his face just enough so that he could see the two, yet not reveal his decidedly un-Latin features.

So they had come. He had been clever to wait here in the plaza, where every traveler to Santa Fe came sooner or later. His fingers tightened around the long-barreled pistol whose bulge in his white cotton trousers was concealed by the colorful serape. For a moment he considered whipping the pistol out and shooting each of them in the back as they walked their separate ways, but only for a moment. He would enjoy watching them fall, dying, the blood drenching the backs of their shirts, and hearing the screams of the others who frequented the plaza in the noonday sun, but it was just too risky to shoot them with the blue-coated soldiers lounging under the overhanging roof of the palace porch nearby.

He had waited this long—he could stand to wait just a little bit longer. It would be enjoyable to just watch and see what happened after Sarah identified herself at the jail. The duchess—now nothing better than a common *putain*—and her Texan lover were about to get a big surprise. Then all he had to do was wait until Sarah sought him out in his hotel room.

He remained in his place, watching surreptitiously as Calhoun strode over to the sleepy-eyed Indian selling jewelry nearby. After a few minutes' perusal and some good-natured haggling, he saw Calhoun purchase a necklace of chased silver with interspersed nuggets of turquoise.

The assassin's lips curved upward as he slid the sombrero back over his face. He wondered if Calhoun would have time to give the present to his whore before the trap was sprung.

"Excuse me," Sarah said, hoping her voice alone would be sufficient to wake the man who sat in the chair behind the cluttered desk, his head tipped back, snoring. Surely he was the man she sought, for he wore a tin star on his tobacco-flecked shirt.

It was not sufficient. The snoring continued unabated, but she did succeed in gaining the attention of another man, who lounged in a chair tipped against the wall, a cigar in one hand, a sheaf of papers in the other.

He sat up with a thump, then stood, narrowing his eyes in the gloom to study her.

"Ma'am? You wantin' the sheriff? You'll have to talk louder'n that—shout, even. Or reach over and shake him a little. Go on, you won't hurt him," he urged.

Sarah stared at the man who had spoken, then back at the man he had called the sheriff. Just then the sheriff snorted in his sleep, startling her. "Oh, no, I couldn't do that," she demurred. "Surely there's some other way to wake him?" Sarah thought the other man seemed to be studying her and listening to her voice with intense concentration, but perhaps it was only the odd combination of a woman wearing men's clothes and speaking in an English accent.

The other man grinned. "Yes, ma'am, there is another way." Stepping up behind the slumbering sheriff, he cupped his hands around one of the man's ears and shouted, *"Andy! There's a lady here to speak to ya!"*

The sheriff came awake with flailing limbs and widened eyes, and in his efforts to regain his balance, fell sideways off his chair, much to the amusement of the man standing in back of him.

She was sure it would only further the sheriff's embarrassment if she shared in the other man's amusement, so she forced the smile from her face and looked around the interior of the jail while the sheriff struggled to his feet.

One side of the square, not overly large room was occupied by cells—three of them in all. The rest of the floor space was taken up by the sheriff's desk and a couple of extra chairs—one of which the other man had been sitting in before she had spoken. A rack of rifles hung on the wall nearest the door. The other wall was plastered with Wanted posters.

Since she was still wearing her spectacles, it took her no time at all to find Morgan's picture among the gallery of assorted rogues and evildoers, for it held pride of place in the center.

The picture was crudely drawn, but Sarah could nevertheless tell who it depicted even without the words written in bold type beneath. "Wanted: Morgan Calhoun," it read, "for Army Payroll Robbery in Texas, and Assorted Robberies of Stagecoaches and Individuals across the Southwest." There was more in smaller type beneath the first sentence, but Sarah would have had to go closer to read it, and she did not want to appear to be interested in any particular poster, especially now that the sheriff had succeeded in standing up and was goggling at her in amazement.

"Kin I help you, ma'am?" he said, his face dubious as he stared at her denim trousers as if he had never seen such a garment before.

"Yes, I hope so," said Sarah, extending her hand and giving him the sort of friendly, open smile that seemed to move mountains in America. "I'm Sarah Challoner, Duchess of Malvern—from England, you see. Please pardon my appearance, but I've been traveling overland, and it seemed more sensible to wear suitable clothes...."

The sheriff blinked, then a light dawned in his red-rimmed eyes. "You're her, the duchess? *Yes, ma'am,* we shorely was expectin' you, wasn't we, Stoner?" He took her hand and shook it with enthusiasm. "M'name's Andrew McElroy, ma'am."

"Pleased to make your acquaintance, Mr. McElroy," Sarah murmured, watching the other man as he stepped forward, too, his hand extended. She had seen irritation flash across the other man's eyes for the briefest of seconds when McElroy had agreed they were expecting her, and then a look was passed between the two men. A frisson of alarm passed down her spine, but then both men were smiling broadly as she shook hands with the second man.

"Jackson Stoner, ma'am." He was also wearing a badge, Sarah noticed, but it seemed slightly different from the sheriff's badge. Perhaps he was a deputy? He said nothing to enlighten her.

"Ah...if you're expecting me, does this mean you have a message for me?" she prompted, eager to get out of the place. "A message from a Frenchman, Comte Thierry de Châtellerault?"

"Yes, ma'am—"

"You call her 'your grace,' Andy," the other man prompted.

"Ahem! *Your grace,* I meant to say!" the sheriff amended. "I shorely do have a message from the count. He—he wrote you a letter," he said, bending over to rummage in the center drawer of his desk, which Sarah could see was cluttered with papers, balls of string and plugs of chewing tobacco. "Here it is," he said triumphantly, holding out a folded sheet of paper. "But he told me where he was stayin'. He says he'll be waitin' for ya in his rooms at the Exchange Hotel, just a short walk from here, yore grace. I understand yore t' be wed?"

Sarah nodded, taking the paper and breaking the blob of sealing wax on the back. She unfolded it and read the words written in Thierry's familiar, ornate script.

My darling, if you are reading this, you have come at last! How happy I will be to greet you, and to kiss you and hold you in my arms as my wife! I have arranged all for our wedding. I hope you have managed to reconcile your uncle, the estimable Lord Frederick, to the match, but no matter if you have not. We shall know a lifetime of bliss, *ma duchesse, ma comtesse*. A thousand kisses until I see you.

> Thierry, Comte de Châtellerault.

Once, his flowery written lovemaking would have thrilled her, but now she only felt sad to know that she was going to have to disappoint this man who had come so far to marry her. She wondered how he would take it. Would Thierry fly into a verbose fit of French despair, or fall into a sullen pout? And she wondered what he would say when she informed him that she suspected her uncle of trying to have her assassinated. Would his sense of chivalry come to the fore, making him insist on escorting her safely back to England? Lord, what an uncomfortable sea voyage *that* would be! But if she were unable to persuade Morgan to give up his foolish sacrifice of their love, what other choice would she have but to go home?

Looking up, she saw that Jackson Stoner was staring at her with narrowed, speculative eyes. She guessed he had been studying her the entire time she had been reading. Wanting to avoid meeting his gaze, she felt her eyes being drawn back to Morgan's Wanted poster, but she dared not look at it.

"Well, ma'am, the Exchange shorely is a fine place," McElroy was saying. "Why, it's been here as long as Santa Fe's been a town, though it's been called other names. Might I offer to escort ya there?"

"Thank you, Sheriff, but no, I do not plan to go there directly. I—I have some business to take care of before I can join the count. But I'll find it, never fear." She tucked the letter in her shirt pocket. "Mr. McElroy, I wonder if you could first direct me to a telegraph office?"

"Why, there's one just about five minutes' walk from here. You just go down this street, make a right and walk straight on until you see the sign."

"That sounds easy enough. Thank you both, gentlemen," she said, turning to go.

"Just a moment, your grace," called Stoner, striding forward. "Forgive my curiosity, but surely you didn't come this far all alone? Surely a lady like yourself—a duchess—has servants with her? Armed men?"

She forced herself to smile. In a moment she would be away from here, away from this man's probing gaze. Should she tell Morgan how nervous he had made her? She'd decide that later. For now she had to frame a suitable reply that would not make Jackson Stoner suspicious.

"Of course I have an entourage, Mr. Stoner," she said, relieved that Morgan had had the foresight to wait where they could not see him. "But I'm afraid I have become very independent in the course of the journey. Most unduchesslike, I know," she said with a flirtatious laugh. "I've sent them to arrange stabling for our horses and a place where I can refresh myself before going to meet my fiancé. You can imagine I would not want to greet him looking like *this,* can you not?"

"I understand, ma'am," Stoner said, apparently satisfied. "My felicitations to you and your fiancé."

Sarah felt his eyes on her all the way out the door. Crossing the plaza, she caught sight of Morgan standing in the shade of a cottonwood tree.

"You find out what you were hopin' to in there, Duchess?" Morgan asked as she drew near.

She nodded. "Thierry is staying at a hotel called the Exchange," she said, forgetting all about Jackson Stoner as she wondered how she was ever going to learn to live without this man standing in front of her. She drank in the sight of his lean, weather-bronzed features. His eyes looked even greener in the hot New Mexican sunlight.

She thought about the night ahead. Once she had bathed, she was going to go to him, still damp and smelling of soap, and make love to him as if her life depended on it. Her happiness did, at any rate. And if she couldn't change his mind, then she would at least have the memory of one more night with Morgan Calhoun to treasure.

"Let's take care of the errands, shall we?" she said. "The sheriff was kind enough to inform me where we might find a telegraph office."

"Okay. But Duchess…I—I bought you somethin' while I was waiting," he said, holding out a closed hand, fingers downward.

Surprised, she held out her hand, too, staring as he opened his fingers and a cool coil of silver and turquoise untwined into her open palm.

"I know you have plenty of jewelry that's worth a lot more," he said, his usual smooth drawl curiously hesitant and shy, "but I hope you like it…an' that your husband-to-be doesn't object t'you havin' a gift from me."

She wanted to cry, wanted to throw her arms around Morgan and kiss him, right here in the middle of the plaza, in spite of all the people strolling around it and lounging in the sun and shade. But she couldn't just now—not after she had let him think her resigned to their parting.

"It's beautiful," she breathed. "Oh, Morgan, thank you! And I don't give a fig what Thierry thinks!" *Because I'm not marrying him,* she wanted to shout. *If I can't have you I shall marry no one.* "Please, help me put it on?"

She turned, and shivered as she felt the cool metal links slide down around her neck as he fastened the clasp in the back.

"And there's something else I think you should have," he said, leaning over and pulling his derringer out of his right boot. "It'll fit in your reticule."

She took the tiny pistol from him, surprised. "But Morgan, why? And what will you do without it?"

He shrugged. "Aw, I can get another some time, Duchess. But now that I taught you how to shoot, you ought to keep in practice. And your Frenchman might not want me escortin' y'all to the coast, so I thought you ought to have it."

"But of course you shall escort us," she said firmly. "Thierry will respect my wishes, I'm sure. But thank you, Morgan," she added as she tucked the derringer into her reticule. "I shall treasure it always, just because it was yours."

They went in the direction McElroy had specified, but just after they turned the corner, they came to a shop called Manuela's Dresses and Alterations. Ah, the very sort of place she had been looking for! She pondered going in now or after they had been to the telegraph office, and decided she wanted to look for a dress first.

"Good day. Do you have anything in the color turquoise?" she asked the little Mexican woman who sat hemming a skirt. "I thought it would be nice to have a dress to go with this necklace," she said, picking up a portion of it from her neck with a finger so that the woman could see it.

"Ah, that is Victorio's work, *sí*? He sells necklaces and rings and hair combs in the plaza?"

Morgan, beside her, nodded in affirmation.

"No, *señora*," the woman said, her large brown eyes sorrowful. "Regretfully, I do not think I have a dress in that color, but I could have one ready in two days' time."

"Oh, I'm afraid that won't do. We expect to be gone by then," Sarah said, disappointed.

"Perhaps I can interest you in something in a different color—ah! But wait!" the proprietress exclaimed, brightening. "I have just thought of a dress I made for a *gringa*—an Anglo lady, you understand—that is the very shade you require. It weel even feet you, with a little sewing...." She glided behind a doorway covered by a Mexican blanket.

"But what of the Anglo lady?" Sarah called after her.

The woman was back in a moment, her brown face creased with smiles as she held out a gown in the very same hue as the turquoise nuggets in Sarah's necklace.

"It ees *perfecto, sí?* And do not worry about the other woman. She ees late to peek it up, you understand? I shall make her another before she comes again."

Sarah reached out and touched the gown, glorying in its rich hue. "I love it!" she cried. "Such a vivid hue! Most unduchesslike," she added, shooting Morgan a mischievous look. "But do you think this will fit me?" she asked the Mexican woman. "It looks a bit large in the bodice."

"Ah, but I can fix that, if you will but try it on first, and then come back in an hour or two. Come this way, *señora*," she said, motioning toward the back room she had gone into a moment ago. "I weel keep your wife but a few minutes, *señor*," she called over her shoulder to Morgan, who was leaning against the door.

"He's not—" Sarah began, then shut her mouth. It was none of the dressmaker's business, after all. "That is...he's very patient—he won't mind waiting."

A half hour later Morgan and Sarah emerged from the shop and continued on their way to the telegraph office, unaware that they were being followed.

Chapter Twenty-Five

Standing next to Morgan in the telegraph office, Sarah handed back the piece of paper the telegrapher had provided, now inscribed with her instructions to the Eastern bank. "I'd like this message sent to this bank in New York, as I've indicated on the top line," she told the telegraph operator.

Sarah heard the door to the street open behind them, and saw the operator look up at the new customer, but she didn't turn. She wanted to make sure he understood the importance of sending the telegram immediately.

"Yes, madam, right away. I—" The telegrapher had paled and was staring at Morgan. *Good lord, had the man recognized him?* Then she looked behind Morgan and saw Jackson Stoner holding a gun at Morgan's back.

"Just raise your hands nice and easy, Calhoun," he murmured. "We wouldn't want any trouble, would we?"

Horrified, Sarah grabbed for the pistol still tucked into her waistband, only to hear another voice coming from the doorway to the back room of the office.

Andrew McElroy stood there, his rifle aimed right at her. "Now, ma'am, don't do nothin' foolish," he urged. He had his rifle aimed right at her. "We really don't want t'have t'shoot Calhoun, especially right in front o' you. Now just lay that pistol right down on the counter, real gentle-like.''

Looking to Morgan for direction, she saw him nod coolly toward the counter, directing her to do as the sheriff ordered.

For a moment she hesitated, remembering the derringer in her reticule. But even if she could retrieve it fast enough, it only bore a single shot. Trembling, she laid the pistol on the counter. The telegrapher took it and leveled it at Calhoun.

"Just what is the meaning of this?" she demanded, sick at heart. "This man is my bodyguard! He's done nothing wrong!"

Stoner ignored her. "Cover me, boys," he said to the other two men as he reached into his pocket with his free hand and brought out a pair of metal handcuffs, then holstered his own pistol. Jackson reached up and pulled down first one, then the other of Morgan's wrists, fastening them efficiently into the handcuffs before taking the Colt from Morgan's holster and sticking it between the Texan's shoulder blades. Then he turned to Sarah.

"Your grace, I might believe you didn't know your bodyguard is an outlaw if I hadn't seen the way you looked at that Wanted poster," he told her grimly, his gray eyes cold. "You know who he is, all right. But I'll be willing to overlook that, *and* the fact that you were going to draw on the sheriff and me, if you don't cause any more trouble. You came to Santa Fe to meet your fiancé, didn't you? With all due respect, Duchess, why don't you go do just that?" he suggested, nodding toward the street.

Filled with shock and despair, she pretended not to hear, and turned to McElroy. "Sheriff, do you always let your *deputy* mastermind the arrests?" she asked in a voice laced with scorn.

"Oh, he ain't no deputy, ma'am," Andrew McElroy told her with a incongruously amiable smile. "He's a U.S. marshal, and he's been waitin' here spe-cifically to arrest Calhoun.''

His words chilled Sarah. "But...but how did anyone know Morgan would be coming to Santa Fe?"

"Lord Halston, your uncle, told us, ma'am—excuse me, yer grace," McElroy explained. "We had a telegram from him in Denver, tellin' us he thought you an' Calhoun might be headed here. Wanted us to be of any assistance to you that was needed. 'Course, I don't figure he knew about Calhoun bein' a desperado an' all, but it just so happens his information came in handy by lettin' us know Calhoun was headin' this way. Marshal Stoner's been after Calhoun for a long time, ain't ya, Stoner?"

"That's a fact."

"But my uncle, Lord Halston, he's the one who's been trying to kill me!" Sarah cried. "I don't suppose he mentioned that? That's why I fled Denver with Mr. Calhoun! Calhoun saved my life, Mr. McElroy! Doesn't that count for something in his favor? As far as I know, I'm still in danger! How do I know my uncle hasn't contrived to follow me here? You can't arrest the very man who was keeping me safe!"

Stoner looked unimpressed, but McElroy's brow furrowed. "Now, ma'am, he *did* mention someone had been tryin' to kill ya while y'all were in Denver, and he sounded real worried about ya. Said you'd disappeared without a word, and he'd been 'sick with apprehension,' I b'lieve he said."

"Oh, I can well believe he said that," Sarah snapped, knowing her irony was lost on McElroy. "But he's not telling you the whole truth—he's only apprehensive because he failed to kill me!"

"Ma'am, I don't know nothin' about that," McElroy said. "All I know is Calhoun's a wanted man, and he's now in custody."

Sarah's shoulders sagged as she realized the futility of arguing with these two lawmen.

Now Morgan spoke for the first time. "Go on, Sarah. Don't worry about me. Something like this was bound to happen sooner or later. You go ahead and find your Frenchman— you'd better go ahead and do it today, so you won't be alone. Don't worry, you're beautiful even in men's pants," he said, and the love, mixed with sadness, in his eyes broke her heart. "Oh, and you go ahead and take Rio with you. I'm givin' him to you," he added. "I know you'll take good care of him."

"But what will happen to Morgan?" she asked Stoner, feeling hot tears spilling down her cheeks.

"He'll spend a few days in the jail here, until I can arrange transportation back to Texas, where he'll stand trial," Stoner told her, but the coldness had vanished from his eyes, and his voice was surprisingly kind.

"I'm going with you when you take him back to Texas," Sarah said.

"Your grace, I don't think I can al—" Stoner began.

"Sarah, now don't be foolish," Morgan interrupted. "There ain't a thing you can do for me, and there's a man who's come all the way from England just for you. He loves you, doesn't he? Go to him, Duchess, and forget you ever heard of me. I mean it. *That's what I want you to do.*"

"Nevertheless, I shall be going with you and the marshal, Morgan," she told him. "I only intended to see Thierry long enough to tell him I could no longer consider marrying him, anyway. As I told you once before, I have the means to hire you the best lawyer in the United States, and that's what I intend to do. There's no use arguing with me, Morgan."

She shifted her gaze to Stoner. "Mr. Calhoun will be in one of those cells I saw? When can I visit him?"

"Any time tomorrow, your grace."

She nodded. "Very well, then, I shall plan to stop by in the morning. I expect him to be treated well, is that clear, Mr. Stoner?"

"Yes, ma'am," Stoner said, touching the brim of his hat with ironic courtesy.

The clock on the wall indicated ten the next morning when Morgan saw Sarah enter the jail.

Gone was the hoyden who'd ridden across the plains, over the mountains and down the Santa Fe Trail with him. In her place was a lady who was every inch the Duchess of Malvern, her golden curls done up in an elegant chignon. She wore the turquoise dress she'd purchased yesterday, and the color brought her sun-kissed features gloriously alive. The necklace he'd given her decorated her neck, emphasizing its slenderness. All she needed was a pair of wings to look like an angel.

He watched through the bars as she sailed by the sheriff and the marshal and glided gracefully to his cell.

"Hello, my love," she said, laying down the reticule she carried and reaching through the bars for his hands.

He couldn't help but give them to her. Lord, it felt good to be touching even that little part of her. She smelled good, too, like roses. She must have found somewhere to buy scent.

"Mornin', Sarah." There were a million questions he wanted to ask her, a million things he wanted to say, but he was all too aware of the sheriff and the marshal sitting within earshot.

"Oh, my poor love, were you able to sleep?" she asked, looking past him into the corner of the cell where his cot with its lumpy mattress covered by dingy, threadbare sheets stood.

"Aw, Duchess, after so many years of sleepin' on the hard ground, I reckon I could sleep anywhere," he said with a grin. "The food ain't bad, either. McElroy missed his callin'—he shoulda been a cook."

Then he realized what *hadn't* changed about her. "You're still wearing your spectacles," he said, surprised. "You leave your vanity behind on the trail somewhere, Duchess?"

"Ah reckon ah did," she said in a teasing rendition of his

drawl. "Actually, Morgan, I found I've gotten rather used to seeing clearly these last few weeks, so you see, you *have* taught me something," she said with a wink. "I started to leave the posada without them, but I was afraid I'd get lost, so…" She shrugged.

"The posada? Why didn't you stay at the Exchange with your Frenchman?"

"I haven't seen Thierry yet," she said. "I decided I still wanted to have a bath and a good night's sleep first, so I went back to the posada. But I'm on my way to see Thierry now, Morgan."

This was the last time he'd see her, then. The fact that she'd taken such pains with her appearance convinced him that no matter what she had said, she was at least considering the folly of her promise yesterday to go back to Texas with him and the marshal. Once she saw her dashing Frenchman again, she'd put her love affair with a Texas outlaw behind her. That was for the best, he told his aching heart.

"Goodbye, Duchess." *I love you, Sarah Challoner.*

"Oh, I'll be back to see you later today, Morgan. I'll want to…after I've told him it's over. Now, don't give me that rubbish about forgetting about you, and your not being good enough for me, and all that rot. I don't want to hear it," she said with forced cheerfulness. "Until then…" she said, blowing him a kiss before she turned and walked out the door. She had already shut it behind her when all at once he felt the prickling at the back of his neck, the same feeling he always got right before something bad happened.

"Sarah! Sarah, come back!" he yelled, but apparently she didn't hear him. It was too late.

"Stoner, call her back. Somethin'…somethin' doesn't feel right," Morgan said, shaking his head as if that would clear it of the troubling notion. "Please, Stoner, for the love of God, bring her back here!"

Stoner, lounging again on the chair tipped against the wall, looked at him curiously.

"What ails you, Calhoun? Haven't you been tryin' to convince the lady she needs to forget you for her own good? It just so happens I highly agree with you on that—she *should* forget she ever met you. So shut up. I'm not gonna help you talk her out of doing the right thing."

The door opened, and she heard a familiar, French-accented voice cry, "Sarah, *ma chère, enfin!* Finally you are here!"

It was a corner room, and the curtains of both windows had been left open, so all she could see was Thierry's form silhouetted against the doorway. Before Sarah could say a word, or her eyes, used to the gloom of the corridor, could adjust, he had pulled her inside and was kissing both her cheeks, and then her mouth.

His lips were warm and persuasive, and she remembered their touch, but she felt…*nothing*. Only an eagerness to get the painful meeting over with as quickly and gracefully as she could.

"Thierry, I— Let me look at you," she said, pulling back slightly, to give her eyes time to focus on him and her brain time to think, to frame the words that would tell him she was not the same woman to whom he had bidden adieu in England.

He was shorter than she remembered, and stockier. She had forgotten what a pale blue his eyes were, and how his elegant blond mustache with the carefully waxed ends emphasized the sensual fullness of his lips.

"Sarah…it has been so long," he said, smiling at her and still holding her hands in his. "You surprise me—you are wearing your spectacles! You look like a…how do you say it? A schoolmistress! And you are brown as a wild Indian," he added. His tone was faintly disapproving. "Where is your uncle? I cannot imagine him letting you ruin your complexion like that."

"Yes…yes it has been a long time," she said, choosing not to respond to his other comments for the time being. She hadn't seen this critical side of him before, and she didn't like it. "Did you…did you have a pleasant sea voyage to America?" She knew she was stalling. But one couldn't just blurt out, "Thierry, I no longer love you and won't marry you," could one?

"It was abominable. But it is over, and now I am here with you."

"Yes… Oh, Thierry, so much has happened, there is so much I must tell you…" she began. Should she tell him first about her uncle's attempts to have her killed, which would lead into how and why her feelings for *him* had changed?

"Yes, my sweet, but first, first there is something I must show you, and tell *you*," he said, stepping away from her and striding around a carved oak secretary until it stood between them.

"All right," she said, relieved that he was no longer in physical contact with her, and because she wouldn't have to dim the pleased excitement in his handsome face just yet.

Reaching down, he pulled open a drawer and handed her a sheet of folded paper.

"This was written by your sister," he murmured.

"Kat sent a letter for me? How wonderful!" she said, taking it. The letter must not contain bad news, Sarah thought, for he was smiling as he handed it across the desk to her. "Oh, I've missed her! What with my traveling around, there was no way I could hope to receive mail from home, but I've been writing her regularly.…" She hesitated. "But I can read it later, Thierry. You said you wanted to tell me something?"

"Read Kathryn's letter, Sarah. It will explain much."

He was still smiling, but something wasn't right. She

looked at him, hoping for some clue, but he only nodded toward the paper, until at last she bent her head to read it.

"My very sweetest darling Thierry," the letter began in her sister's familiar slanting script.

"But this is your letter!" Sarah said, handing it back to him even as she wondered why Kathryn was addressing Thierry in such a fashion. "You must have made a mistake and given me the wrong letter. There must be another in there for me."

"I did not make a mistake, Sarah. That is the letter I want you to see," Thierry told her, still smiling as he returned the sheet of paper to her. "Keep reading, *ma chère*. In fact, why not read it aloud?"

Sarah stared at him for a moment, sure she had misheard him, but he nodded toward the paper. She unfolded the paper.

"'My very sweetest darling Thierry,'" she began again, aloud this time, "'I wish I were there to kiss your lips, and tell you how much I love you, but I am sending this letter along to be of encouragement as you undertake the difficult task of telling my sister that it is *me* you love, and wish to wed, and not her. I am sure it will be painful for you, for my Thierry is not a cruel person, but upon your return I will be yours, body and soul. We shall live in wedded bliss, for you will have done the just and honorable thing by breaking the betrothal with Sarah, whom you do not love, to marry me...'"

At this point Sarah's voice faltered, and she could read no more. "Oh, Thierry," she began in dismay, not looking up at him yet. *How* had her sister gotten the muddleheaded notion that the French count loved *her,* a miss barely out of the schoolroom? Kathryn had always had a vivid imagination, fueled by the Gothic novels she read, but this was too absurd! Thierry had been smiling because he was amused, but she must make him see that learning the truth would be very painful for her younger sister. "Whatever are we going to do about Kat? Poor lamb, she has conceived such a *tendre* for you—''

She heard a click just as she looked up from the paper, and saw that Thierry was holding a gun, and it was aimed directly at her.

Chapter Twenty-Six

Sarah had been gone for perhaps three minutes when the door opened again. Morgan, hoping that Sarah had found a reason to return, propped himself up on his elbow to have a look, but he saw that it was only Benning, the telegraph operator, coming in from the street and handing Jackson Stoner a piece of paper.

"This just came, Sheriff, Marshal," he said, "and I thought I'd better bring it right over. It's addressed to you, Sheriff, but it's about that duchess lady," he added in apologetic explanation as he handed it to Marshal Stoner.

His words brought Morgan up off his cot like a shot. "What is it?" Morgan demanded, clutching the bars with both hands. "What's it say about the duchess? Who's it from?"

Stoner paused in the act of holding the paper up to his eyes and looked at Morgan with amusement. "Hold your horses, Calhoun, it ain't likely to concern you." Nevertheless, he read it out loud.

"'To sheriff of Santa Fe from Frederick, Lord Halston, Marquess of Kennington,'" he read, then added, as if to himself, "Lord, these foreigners have fancy big names, don't they?

"'Trust you received telegram,'" he continued reading, "'saying niece, Duchess of Malvern, arriving Santa Fe, *stop*. Duchess's secretary Alconbury confessed part of assassination plot, *stop*. Thierry, Count of Châtellerault, engaged to marry duchess, to be apprehended immediately, very dangerous, *stop*. Coming to Santa Fe posthaste, *stop*. Signed, Frederick, Lord Halston,' et cetera." He raised his head from the paper and blinked at McElroy. "Now, what is that supposed to mean?"

"It means *he's* the one who's been trying to murder the duchess!" cried Morgan, still clutching the bars of his cell. "Marshal, you've gotta let me outa here! It was that Frenchman who was tryin' to kill her all along, and she's goin' to him right now!"

Now both McElroy and Stoner were staring at him, dumbstruck.

Morgan threw himself against the bars now. "Marshal, listen to me! I thought it was the uncle, but I was wrong! It was the *Frenchman* I was tellin' you about last evenin', the one who was shootin' at us in Denver. For the love of God, Stoner, let me out of here! I swear I'll come right back just as soon as I blow that Frenchman to hell!"

Now Stoner had stood, and was approaching the cell. "Now, hold on, old son. Not so fast. Why on earth should I turn you loose because of a damn telegram? I have no way of knowing if this is the truth," he said, shaking the telegram in Morgan's face. "Just sit tight, and I'll check it out."

Morgan felt a red mist of rage flooding his brain, but he forced himself to be calm. "Marshal, the duchess is on her way to meet that de Châtellerault fella at the Exchange Hotel right this very minute. It ain't far from here to there, so every second counts. Who knows how long before he'll try to murder her, once they're together? It ain't gonna look very good for either of you fellas if it comes out that you had a warnin', but you dallied and the duchess got killed anyway."

The marshal and the sheriff exchanged looks.

"Even if all that's true, Calhoun, why should we let *you* out?" Jackson asked with maddening slowness.

"Because I reckon I can run faster than either of you and shoot better," Morgan said evenly, "and because I love the lady we're talking about. And because if she dies 'cause you were too slow, I'll find a way to kill both of you. Let me out, and I'll come back to the cell, word of a Southern gentleman. *Now open the damn cell door, one of you!*"

Stoner seemed to make up his mind all at once. Nodding to McElroy, he said, "Let him out—and give him his gun back until we see that the duchess is safe. I'm going ahead— you boys catch up." And then he was running to the door, past the bemused telegraph operator.

Dropping the sheet of parchment, Sarah stared into the barrel of the gun, sure she was hallucinating despite the crystal-clear vision afforded by her spectacles. Then she raised her eyes to de Châtellerault.

"Thierry, what are you doing?" she whispered. Her blood had become ice water in her veins.

His face bore a smile, the smile of a predator who has trapped his prey. "Why, Sarah, I am eliminating the barrier to my marriage with your sister."

He *wanted* to marry Kathryn? She couldn't allow such a monster near her sister ever again, but first she had to save her own life.

"But Thierry, you needn't kill me to free yourself," she said, trying to sound calm and logical. "If that's what you want, I'll give you your freedom quite willingly. In fact—"

She had been about to tell him that she was in love with another man when he cut her off. "Ah, but if you're still alive, my sweet, your dear sister Kathryn does not become the Duchess of Malvern. And I had so counted on marrying a duchess," he purred.

"Then why not me?" she inquired curiously, glad he had interrupted her before she could tell him of her feelings for Morgan. "Why not keep to your original plan to marry me? Why would you want to marry a young miss barely out of the schoolroom, when I am nearer your age, have had some experience of the world and know my own mind? Why, Kat's a comparative child!"

"Oh, but my dear Sarah, it is your sophistication that's precisely the problem, don't you see?" he continued in his perfect, French-accented English. "You know your own mind a trifle too well to suit me. You always know what you want to do, for how long and when. You would not have changed when we were man and wife, this I know, and what man wants a wife who will not acknowledge him as her lord, her master? Your sister Kathryn, on the other hand, is willing to be guided by *me*, the man, as is the proper way of things."

He was insane, she could see that now. Tears stung her eyes, tears of fury mixed with fear.

"But why did you pretend to love me? Why not pick some more biddable gentlewoman?"

He shrugged. "I did not see your stubbornness at first, Sarah. But when I did...I was not willing to give up the fortune that the Challoner family possessed. *Eh bien,* if I could not be master with one sister, I could be with the other. Kathryn is young enough to think every word from my lips is the Gospel. She will not mind being duchess, either."

His chuckle only fueled her rage.

"Are you trying to make me believe envy would motivate Kat to go along with *murder—of her own sister?*" she demanded.

"Sarah, Sarah...I had not realized you were so beautiful when you are angry. It almost makes me regret the necessity of shooting you," he said. "But no, I do not entrust a simple *girl* with my plans. Kathryn will never know I was the one who killed you, though I rather thought you would die back in Denver rather than here.''

And suddenly she understood what had been nagging at the back of her brain ever since he'd shown her the letter.

''It was *you* all the time who was trying to kill me, and *not* Uncle Frederick?''

''But of course,'' he said, tut-tutting at her as if she were a silly child. The pistol was lowered slightly. ''I was amused that you thought it was your stuffy uncle, Sarah. Lord Halston has always been sure he should have been the duke, rather than you the duchess, but he is one of those stiffly proper Englishmen who would never do anything so hot-blooded as murder to secure a title!'' He had lowered the gun to his side, though she could see his finger was still on the trigger.

Oh, Uncle Frederick, Sarah thought. *How we wronged you, Morgan and I.* Even if she was going to die, she'd gained a certain measure of peace, knowing it had not been her own uncle who'd wanted her dead. She wished she could somehow at least tell Morgan Uncle Frederick was innocent. Then a new thought struck her. ''Then I *did* see you, on the street in Denver!''

He nodded as if amused. ''I had to be quick to elude you that time. But I succeeded, and you probably convinced yourself your eyes were playing tricks on you, didn't you?''

She nodded, horror-struck. ''Then *you* were the one shooting at me at the railroad? At the theater? *You* killed Ben, my groom, Wharton and that policeman? You—you *monster!*'' she cried, and would have launched herself at him, hands curved into claws, except for the pistol being brought up once again so that it was aimed right at her heart.

''Have a care, Sarah! I should hate to have to kill you before you have satisfied your inquisitive little soul about what has been happening! After all, you will have an eternity to ponder your mistakes that led to your death!'' He seemed to think it a great joke, and laughed hilariously, though he was careful to keep his eyes on her.

"Actually, however," he said, growing serious again, "I regret the necessity of those deaths, and I'm more than a little chagrined at missing my intended targets—you and your bodyguard."

"*Necessity?*" she gasped. "But…who was sending me the threatening notes?"

"Notes?" he said, looking uncertain now. "I sent a pair of notes, only. I delivered them with the help of your secretary, Alconbury."

"Are you saying *Donald* was your accomplice? No, I cannot believe it!" Each new fact he told her compounded a scheme so diabolical she could hardly comprehend all its ramifications.

"Yes, he was promised a share of my expectations as the master of the Challoner wealth in exchange for delivering the note I wrote in the style of an American—how do they say it?—yokel. I thought you would panic and leave Denver by the next train east, and I would follow you to the station and kill you. However, you did not panic, but dug in your heels and stayed. You see, Sarah, what I mean about your stubbornness? But you say you received other such notes?"

Sarah nodded. "Several of them, and I'm afraid I don't understand why you continued to warn me, so that I became more cautious. I would think it would have been much more advantageous to lull me into thinking the threat had disappeared," she observed. He seemed eager to discuss all the details of the plot, and as long as he was talking, he wasn't pulling the trigger. She was still trying to think of a way she could wrest the gun from him, or get to the derringer Morgan had insisted on giving her yesterday, which even now weighed down her reticule.

He looked thoughtful, and then angry. "Alconbury must have sent them, secretly hoping you could still be persuaded to take flight out of my reach. I suspected from the first he had not the stomach for this plan.''

"But why didn't he just come right out and tell me the truth?'' Sarah wondered aloud.

"He knew I would kill him for betraying me,'' Thierry said, so casually that Sarah was chilled all over again.

"You followed us all the way to Santa Fe?'' she said, still temporizing. Now she knew why she had had that sense of a shadow haunting her. "But how is it that you didn't catch up to us? It had to be easier for one man traveling alone to ride faster than we could with a thoroughbred and a packhorse to consider,'' she taunted daringly, hoping to make him angry so that the hand holding the pistol would shake.

His dark eyes narrowed, showing her jab had struck home. His shrug was nevertheless philosophical. "It should have been easy, *bien sûr,* but thanks to some intentional misdirection from that black trader, I lost valuable time. After that, I seemed always to be just behind you—until I lost you in those Apache-ridden mountains. I decided to come ahead to Santa Fe, knowing you would seek me out here, sooner or later. But I could have killed you yesterday, after Calhoun was arrested and you were alone.''

"Why didn't you?'' she asked. "It would have been easy.''

He gave a Gallic shrug. "I decided I would enjoy this one last meeting.'' His grip had never relaxed on the pistol aimed at her. He walked around the desk, coming closer to her. "Sarah, even if I did not have to kill you so that Kathryn could be Duchess of Malvern, I would have to kill you for what you have done,'' he informed her.

"What *I* have done? What on earth are you talking about, Thierry?''

His grin bared his teeth now. "As I indicated when we spoke of Donald Alconbury, I do not take betrayal lightly. *And you have betrayed me, have you not?*''

"Thierry…''

"Oh, yes, you betrayed me!" he said, his voice sounding strained. A crazed red light shone in his eyes now. His grip on the pistol had tightened until the hand clutching it looked bloodless. "You spread your legs for that crude Texan, did you not? You whored for him, didn't you? You were a virgin, and I knew it. I had not besmirched your honor, though I could have many times."

"You're about to take my *life,* and you're boasting that you didn't take my *honor?*" she asked, fighting the urge to laugh hysterically. "Forgive me, Thierry, but if that's the case, I'm glad I have known the love of a man before I died— a man *worth* loving," she added, not caring for that brief moment if they were her last words.

To her satisfaction, the pistol he held began to shake. "You must be done with questions," he growled, "if you are lowering yourself to insults, Sarah. Prepare to die."

Her will to live had flickered only for a moment. Now it was a strong flame again. "You won't get away with this, you know," she told him, praying she could make him believe it. Thierry was insane, but he hadn't lost his self-interest. "The hotel is full of guests, from what I saw. If you shoot me, a crowd will come running at the sound, and you will be trapped before you reach the stairway. You don't want to hang, Thierry."

"Hang? Oh, I won't hang. True, the stairway is far from this room. But there is always the balcony window, and below it, another balcony," he said, pointing to it with his free hand. "We are but three stories from the ground. I can reach the side street before anyone ever reaches this room—and you, my dear, will be lying here quite dead. They will never catch me, for I am a master of disguise. You didn't see me among the Mexicans lounging in the plaza yesterday, did you? But I was there, my sweet. And there are Frenchmen—old cavalry comrades of mine—who are prepared to swear I have been on holiday in Italy with them these few months."

There was a silence while each stared into the other's eyes.

"Very well," she said, forcing herself to shrug as if resigned to her fate. "But even a man facing a firing squad is allowed to have a cloth tied over his eyes, Thierry. Surely you have a handkerchief that I could use? For chivalry's sake?" she added wryly.

He appeared flustered, and his eyes darted around the room. "No, I—let me think, Sarah. Perhaps one of the pillowcases, torn to fit…"

Only Thierry would pride himself on his chivalry when he was about to kill a woman, she thought. She might just succeed, if she was quick.

Sarah made a negligent gesture. "Oh, don't trouble yourself. I had as soon get this over with. I have a handkerchief right here in my reticule, if you will permit me?"

Beads of moisture had begun to spring out on Thierry's high, noble forehead. "Yes, yes, of course. Go ahead," he said, nodding toward the reticule she still held.

"Th-thank you, T-Thierry…" she said, letting her voice tremble while she steeled her heart. Hoping she looked like a woman resigned to dying, she locked her gaze with his and, holding her reticule with her left hand, reached in with her right. She muttered, "Now, where has that thing gone?" as she pretended to dig around for it, until Thierry was visibly fidgeting.

"Forget the handkerchief, Sarah. Just shut your eyes!"

"No, wait, I have it here," she said. Then Sarah removed her hand from inside the reticule, and she was holding Morgan's single-shot derringer, the one he had called his "boot gun." She had a split second to see Thierry's eyes widen, and then she fired.

Once freed, Morgan, who had paused only to demand directions of the dazed Sheriff McElroy, had easily passed the marshal as he ran through the streets of Santa Fe toward the

Exchange Hotel. Even so, he was still only running up the entrance steps when he heard a muffled shot from somewhere on the upper floors. Oh, God, was he too late?

When Morgan thundered into the Spanish-style lobby with McElroy and Stoner pounding at his heels, he found the desk clerk staring up at the ceiling, along with several other inhabitants of the lobby.

"The Frenchman!" Morgan yelled as he ran up to him. "What room?"

The desk clerk blinked owlishly at him, then consulted his ledger, flinching as Morgan pounded the desk again.

"What room, damn you!"

"Three-o-eight! Down at the end of the hall," he added, but Morgan was already dashing to the stairs, flanked by the two lawmen.

Chapter Twenty-Seven

Morgan had just reached the third floor when he heard the second shot. Lord God, was he already too late? If he opened the door and found Sarah lying lifeless on the floor, he wouldn't need the gun McElroy had returned to him—he'd kill the damned Frenchman with his bare hands!

Later he couldn't remember running the last few yards from the stairway to the room at the end of the corridor, or throwing himself against the door until at last it gave way before him. He could only remember seeing Sarah, wonderfully, miraculously *alive* in the cloud of gunsmoke, standing there holding a gun on a man who could only be Thierry de Châtellerault.

"S-Sarah!" he gasped. "Are you—are you all r-right? We heard shots—"

"*Morgan!* Oh, thank God you're here, Morgan! He was going to kill me!" she cried. She backed rapidly toward Morgan, still holding the gun on Thierry, until Morgan could put an arm around her trembling shoulders and pull her against him. He raised the pistol Stoner had given him until it was aimed at the Frenchman's head. Behind him, Stoner and McElroy stumbled into the room, their guns drawn, and for a moment the only sound was the winded breathing of the three men.

"It's—it's okay, honey, I've got him," Morgan said into her hair, and she allowed the hand with the pistol to fall to her side as she collapsed in tears against his chest.

Holding her, Morgan was finally able to study the man who'd been trying to kill Sarah Challoner. Though shorter and a bit stockier than himself, de Châtellerault was nevertheless handsome enough to attract any woman, with his trim soldier's figure, his fair hair and curving mustachios—or at least he probably would have been when his lips weren't curled in a snarl and his dark eyes weren't snapping with hatred. He was pale as bleached buffalo bones, however, and when Morgan looked more carefully, he saw why.

The Frenchman was clutching his bloody right wrist with his left hand, and even from where he stood, Morgan could see the crimson hole.

"She is a monster, this woman!" Thierry growled to no one in particular.

"I shot him, Morgan, with the derringer you gave me yesterday," Sarah said against his chest. "I had to…he was going to kill me."

"But the derringer only holds one shot. I heard two. And I've never seen the pistol you're holding," he said, staring at the ornate carved ivory butt of the gun.

"It's—it's Thierry's," she managed to say through her tears. "My shot knocked his pistol from his hand, but he started to dive after it with his other hand. I—I got to it first, and fired a warning shot with it. I told him if he made another move I'd shoot him right in the heart. I—I meant it! But oh, Morgan, it was awful. I've never shot a man before!" she cried, breaking into fresh sobs.

"Easy, honey," he said, running his free hand through her hair in an effort to soothe her. "You did just right. All that practice—and wearin' your spectacles—paid off when it counted, didn't it?'' His heart was too full of thankfulness that Sarah was alive to be more than minimally aware of McElroy informing the Frenchman he was under arrest, then handcuffing him and leading him out of the room. Stoner remained.

"But…but how did you—all of you—" she gestured toward the marshal "—know about Thierry?" she asked in a bewildered fashion.

Stoner then explained about the telegram, and added that her uncle was on the way from Denver to Santa Fe.

Sarah smiled through her tears. "That was the one good thing I heard out of all the shocking things Thierry told me—that my uncle wasn't the one who wanted me dead. I confess I'm rather eager to see him again, now that I know that. But how did you happen to be with the sheriff and the marshal, Morgan? Have you…? *Oh, Morgan! Have the charges been dropped?*"

He hated having to shake his head and watch the joy die from the blue eyes behind the ovals of glass.

"No, I'm afraid I'm still in custody, Duchess. I just…well, convinced the two lawmen to let me help. I—I reckon it's time to give this back, though," he said, holding his pistol butt-first toward the marshal. Seeing that Sarah was about to protest, he added, "I have to, honey. I gave my word as a Southern gentleman. Besides, it's time to stop running and face the music."

Stoner took it solemnly, with the dignity of a general accepting an enemy officer's sword.

"I'm real glad your uncle's coming, Duchess," Morgan told her. "Why don't you wait for him to get to Santa Fe, and let him take you on home?"

She raised her chin and set her jaw, always a warning that duchess-style stubbornness was about to follow.

"If he gets here before you and the marshal leave for Austin, fine, he can come along if he wants. I'm going with you, Morgan, my love, so you may as well save your breath and stop trying to convince me that I should go home!"

Chapter Twenty-Eight

"We ought to reach Austin by noon, your lordship," Jackson Stoner announced, leaning down from his horse to speak to Sarah's uncle while the stagecoach team was being changed at Round Rock.

"Thank God for small favors!" exclaimed Lord Halston, fanning himself vigorously enough that the breeze fluttered some of the few strands of gray hair left on his head. "When God made hell, he certainly must have had in mind the heat of Texas."

Celia, looking decidedly wilted, heartily agreed.

"Oh, this is what a Texan would call a mild October day, sir," Morgan, who had just led his pinto and Sarah's mare away from the watering trough, remarked in an amused tone. "I reckon you wouldn't want to be here in August, then."

"Indeed I would not, Mr. Calhoun," Lord Halston retorted with asperity. "I believe at this moment I would sell my soul to see the cool green of England."

"Careful, uncle, the devil might be listening," Sarah teased, but her look was sympathetic. Poor dear man, the journey had been hard on him, sitting in the lurching, jolting Concord coach for the nine-hundred-mile journey between

Santa Fe and Austin. But he *had* been bound and determined to accompany her, she reminded herself.

Lord Halston and Celia, her dresser, had arrived in Santa Fe three weeks after the arrest of de Châtellerault, just the day before Sarah was due to leave for Texas with Morgan, the marshal and their cavalry escort.

After hugging his niece with an uncharacteristic emotionalism, he'd repeated, "Thank God you are safe! I've been so worried!" for five minutes straight. He'd told her how Alconbury, her erstwhile secretary, had disappeared shortly after confessing to Lord Halston all about the conspiracy, including his part in keeping Thierry informed about her movements. Alconbury had fled to avoid arrest as an accomplice, naturally, but her uncle had hired detectives and they were presently searching for him.

"I'd never have suspected Donald," Sarah had commented. "He never seemed capable of so much as swatting a fly. Apparently he minded being a penniless younger son more than we realized."

Uncle Frederick had then listened grimly as Sarah told him about the capture of de Châtellerault. She downplayed her own part in it, of course. Uncle Frederick had aged visibly since she had last seen him, and she wasn't sure his heart was up to hearing that Morgan had taught her how to shoot a pistol during the course of their overland trek from Denver, let alone that she had shot her would-be murderer in the wrist.

Judging by the terrible expression on Lord Halston's face when the full extent of the French count's treachery had been discussed, Sarah thought it was fortunate for Thierry that he'd already left town, in the company of another marshal and a pair of deputies, to stand trial in Denver for the murders he had committed there.

"But where is your stalwart Texan? I'd like to thank him personally," Uncle Frederick had remarked then, and Sarah had had to tell him about Morgan's arrest, and the fact that she was going to Texas with him to help him clear his name.

His face had gone pale, then purple.

As she had expected, he'd informed her in no uncertain terms that she must forget such a ridiculous idea. He was taking her straight home to England so that she could put this unfortunate affair behind her and get on with her duties to her duchy.

She had, of course, refused. He'd been appalled when she had explained that she loved Morgan Calhoun, and that if they succeeded in winning his freedom, she wanted to marry him—if she could only persuade him to accept her.

But after Lord Halston had blustered and pleaded with his niece for hours without changing her mind, he'd finally informed her that if she was insistent about accompanying Morgan and his escort to his trial in Texas, he would, of necessity, come with her, as would Celia, her dresser. The Duchess of Malvern could not travel alone with such men as her outlaw, the marshal and the cavalry escort! And she'd see the sense of returning to England with him after Calhoun was convicted, he told her. After all, there was her sister to think of.

"We shall have to see what happens, uncle," Sarah had said.

She would have to go back to England at some point, she knew, if only just to judge for herself whether her sister had been truly innocent.

Whenever she thought of Kathryn, Sarah's heart grew heavy. While she had been relieved to hear Thierry admit that Kat had not actually *known* he intended to murder Sarah, it hurt, nevertheless, to think that Kathryn had been harboring such envy of her. By not realizing the extent of that envy before, Sarah felt she had failed her younger sister in some vital way. But was Kathryn free of other major character flaws? Sarah knew she could abdicate her title in favor of Kathryn only if Kat was worthy of being duchess. And would

Kathryn's becoming the Duchess of Malvern be enough to bridge the gulf that yawned between the two sisters?

First things first, Sarah thought, preparing to remount Trafalgar for the last leg of the journey to Austin. First she must do everything in her power to see that Morgan's name was cleared and he became a free man once more. Then she had to convince him that despite her aristocratic upbringing, she and he belonged together as husband and wife. Then she— and, she hoped, Morgan—could return to England and deal with Kat.

"Niece, I think perhaps it would be best if you rode in the coach for the remainder of the trip," Uncle Frederick said. "It wouldn't do for the Duchess of Malvern to be seen riding *astride.*"

Before leaving Santa Fe, Sarah had made a concession to her uncle's sense of propriety by purchasing a divided skirt so she could ride without showing too much of her limbs, but *this* was too much to ask. "Oh, no, uncle, I have no intention of getting into that swaying monstrosity today," she said. She'd ridden in the stagecoach some of the time, just to keep her uncle company, or once or twice at Morgan's insistence when a thunderstorm threatened, but she'd spent most of the miles on the old Butterfield stagecoach route on horseback.

The hours she'd spent in the saddle, sometimes on Trafalgar, sometimes on one of the soldiers' remounts to spare her thoroughbred, had been arduous, of course, but she could at least spend them riding next to Morgan. Morgan had given the marshal his promise not to attempt to escape while he rode unshackled, and so she could almost pretend he was not on his way to a trial that might result in the loss of his freedom for years, if not forever.

"Your grace, maybe you'd better listen to your uncle," Jackson Stoner said. "The less people see of you as you arrive, the more your reputation can be protected during the trial."

Stoner had been decent and fair to Morgan throughout the long journey, and now she realized he was tactfully trying to suggest something in her best interest. But she'd never cared overmuch about what people thought of her, and now she cared even less. She might not have forever to ride by Morgan's side, so every moment was precious.

"I'll be riding next to Morgan, Mr. Stoner," she said, and the cheeky grin Morgan shot at her was reward enough.

Stoner shrugged. "Have it your way, Duchess." Then he turned to Morgan. "Sorry, Calhoun, but I'm going to have to cuff you and lead your horse the rest of the way."

"I figured you would," Morgan said quietly.

"Why?" Sarah cried, outraged by the sight of the handcuffs.

"Morgan hasn't given you a moment's trouble all the way from Santa Fe! He's been a man of his word! Why should you shackle him now? Is it just to humiliate him? You're not some Roman general parading a captive in ancient Rome!"

Stoner looked distinctly uncomfortable. "I don't know anything about generals or ancient Rome, your grace, but—"

Morgan's voice cut in. "He's just doin' his job, Duchess. It doesn't matter to me."

Sarah shut her mouth. But it made her heart ache to see Morgan hold his wrists out.

The metallic rattling of keys woke Calhoun one afternoon three days later, just as he finished what passed for a prisoner's dinner in the Camp Austin brig.

"Visitors, Calhoun," the soldier on duty announced, pushing open the cell door. Sarah glided in, followed by a man he'd never seen before.

"Hello, Morgan," she said. "How was your luncheon? Never mind, I'll bring you a wonderful supper. This is Matthew Quinn. He's been good enough to agree to be your attorney."

"With your consent, Mr. Calhoun," the other man said quickly, with a trace of nervousness.

The nasal New England accent automatically set Morgan's teeth on edge, but he forced himself to smile. "Oh, I reckon I'm agreeable, all right, if the duchess vouches for you," he drawled, "even if you are a Yankee."

The other man's gaze never wavered. "Yes, from Maine. But I think we can still work together for your benefit, don't you?"

Morgan shrugged. "I reckon, as long as you believe in lost causes. But where'd she find you? From what I've heard, being my lawyer isn't all that popular a job." The judge had refused to allow Sarah the extended time she needed to get him a certain prominent attorney from New York.

"I—I met Mr. Quinn at a reception the governor of Texas gave for us at his residence the second night we were here," Sarah explained. "It seems the local gentlefolk are eager to entertain a duchess and a marquess, even if the duchess has been consorting with a desperado," she added with a mischievous gleam in her blue eyes. "I wasn't exactly in a mood to be entertained, but I figured I didn't have any other way of meeting someone who could help us, so I went, and was delighted when I learned Mr. Quinn was an attorney."

"So what's a Yankee like you doin' in Texas, Quinn?"

"I, uh, had to move here for my wife's health," Quinn said, still looking as if he was afraid Morgan might shoot him if he ventured any closer. "Libby has a rather weak constitution, and she suffered so from the harsh northern winters. She's felt much better here," he added cheerfully.

"Well, that's real nice. I'd hate to hear you came because you were just another carpetbagger." Morgan was aware he sounded surly, but he didn't think this nervous greenhorn could defend him from a horsefly, let alone the United States government. In an effort to sound more pleasant, he added, "Duchess, why don't you and Mr. Quinn sit down?" He stood and smoothed the blanket over his bed. It was the only place to sit in the cell.

"No, I won't be staying, for I think you and Mr. Quinn will get a better start alone," Sarah told him. "Goodbye until this evening, then," she said, coming over and very unself-consciously giving Morgan a brief kiss on the lips. "Oh, Morgan," she said just as she reached the cell door again, "which direction is Calhoun Crossing from here, and where is the Flying C Ranch in relation to the town?"

"But the ranch isn't mine anymore, remember? Why do you want to know, Duchess?"

"Oh, I thought I might like to see it."

The thought of her riding onto his land had him crossing the space between them in two quick strides.

"Duchess, it's too long a ride from here," he said, taking her by the arms, "and I don't want you crossin' paths with Carl Tackett, the rattlesnake who stole the Flying C. He's a scoundrel, Sarah, and he can't be trusted around a lady."

"Oh, don't worry, Morgan, I won't go alone," she promised. "I'll take Uncle Frederick with me. I think he's getting a bit tired of fending off reporters who'd like to interview nobility, anyway."

"But I don't want you tanglin' with Tackett, hear me, Duchess?" he said, pinning her gaze with his.

Sarah smiled and held up her hands in surrender. "All right, all right! I'd be happy just to see it from the fence, if that's your wish, Morgan. I just want to go and see the land you grew up on...." She looked so wistful, he didn't have the heart to argue anymore. These days of waiting for the trial to begin had been as hard on Sarah as it had been on him, he thought, even though she wasn't behind bars as he was. But how would he pass the hours while she was gone?

She smiled again. "Morgan, that ranch *will* be yours again some day, I promise you."

He sighed. "I wish I had your faith, honey." Lord, what

had he done to deserve the love of a woman like this? Her belief in his future, even in the face of impossible odds, humbled him.

She turned back again at the door of his cell. "Oh, Morgan, what was the name of the lady you were with that night—the night the payroll was robbed?" He saw her blush to mention such an indelicate subject, but her eyes never left his.

He shook his head. "Sarah, you go ahead and ride down to Calhoun Crossing tomorrow, if you want. It's a pretty road, and it'll give you something to do. But there just ain't any point in telling you her name," he added. "She's probably not livin' there anymore, anyway. But if she is, it'd be a waste of your breath. She wouldn't say anything the next morning when they came for me, so why should she ruin her good name for me now? Not every woman, Duchess, is as good and honest and true as you."

He watched as Sarah gave him a wan smile and left. She'd been on the verge of tears, he suspected. The violet shadows under her eyes made him think she'd spent a lot of sleepless nights lately. She hadn't mentioned the sensational newspaper articles shredding *her* good name, of course. In the press the two of them had been tagged "the Duchess and the Desperado." One article had even speculated that she was carrying her bandit-lover's child. He didn't figure *that* was true, of course; it had been six weeks since they'd made love in the Apache encampment, and he hadn't seen any of the signs a woman showed when she was *enceinte. Lord, what I wouldn't give, though, to have a baby girl with her mama's golden curls...or a boy with her blue eyes....*

"Mr. Calhoun, perhaps we'd better get started?" Quinn suggested.

Chapter Twenty-Nine

"It's beautiful, isn't it?" Sarah murmured as she dismounted from Trafalgar and gazed at the vast expanse of rolling ranch land stretching in front of her. In the distance, perhaps a quarter of a mile distant, she could see a freestone house nestled at the foot of a trio of hills. Next to the house she caught the gleam of a creek flanked by cottonwoods. "No wonder Morgan loves it so." Indeed, she could see him here, with a pasture full of sleek horses—a few of them pintos like his stallion. She could picture her beloved mare there, too, cropping the lush grass down by the creek, her half thoroughbred, half pinto foal frolicking at its mother's side.

"Yeah, it is right pretty," said Jackson Stoner, still on his horse. Without telling him why, she'd asked him to accompany her and her uncle to Calhoun Crossing, and had been surprised when he had been willing to do so without an explanation.

"Well, I suppose it's all right, if one likes cactus and scrubby little mesquite trees," Lord Halston said, getting out of the carriage he had insisted on riding in. "Personally, I prefer the majestic oaks and beeches of an English forest."

Sarah hid a smile of amusement. Uncle Frederick was an

Englishman through and through, and wouldn't be happy until he was home again.

The four of them—for Celia had been adamant about coming with Sarah to see to her needs—had had no difficulty following Morgan's directions to the ranch that had once been known as the Flying C. Now the name Tackett arched over the gate in black wrought iron.

Trafalgar nickered, and then Sarah noticed the rider galloping in their direction from the barn at the side of the house.

"Here comes the welcoming committee," she remarked, wondering if the rider was Carl Tackett himself, the man who had schemed to take Morgan's land, finally succeeding when Morgan was accused of murder and the army payroll robbery.

Lord Halston harrumphed. "I cannot imagine why I allowed you to talk me into this wild-goose chase just to see this place Calhoun once owned. It's not as if he has much hope of ever possessing it again, niece, even in the unlikely event that he *is* declared innocent of the murder and the payroll robbery. There are all those other robberies you say he did admit to, aren't there?"

Sarah was silent, aware that Stoner was listening intently, no doubt hoping to get a clue about why he'd been asked to accompany them. It *was* important to her to see the land Morgan had grown up on, but she hoped for so much more. She desperately needed this trip to turn out to be more than a wild-goose chase! And she just couldn't spend another day in Austin, fruitlessly counting the hours between visits to Morgan at his jail cell in Camp Austin, and the days until the trial would start. She just had to *do* something, and some instinct had prompted her to come here, to the place the man she loved had called home.

"Afternoon, folks." The man, who wore the simple, rough garb of a cowboy, greeted them from the back of his mount when he reined in just inside the gate. "Are you lost? This here's Tackett land, and he don't encourage visitors."

Sarah, disappointed that the man wasn't Tackett, put on her most charming smile. "Yes, and we wouldn't dream of entering without permission," she told him. "Actually, I was hoping your employer might allow me to visit him and see a typical Texas ranch house."

"And who might you be, ma'am?" the cowboy asked. His voice wasn't encouraging.

"I am the Duchess of Malvern, and this is my uncle, the Marquess of Kennington," she said, gesturing in Uncle Frederick's direction.

The cowboy didn't look the least impressed. "The boss don't like no visitors," he repeated, and began to rein his horse around as if that was his final word on the subject.

"But wait!" Sarah cried. "Surely, after we've come so far, you'd at least tell him we're here? I—I have a business proposition for him," she said, thinking fast. What would Tackett say if she offered to buy the ranch from him? Wouldn't that give Morgan a much-needed infusion of hope, knowing she was keeping it for him?

The cowboy pushed his hat back off his forehead and said, "Listen, Lady Whoever-you-are, the boss hears what goes on in Austin. He told me if you showed up I was to tell you he knows all about the trial and about Calhoun's fancy English mistress. His wife is dyin', an' he's got more important things to do than jaw with you."

Sarah felt her face flame at the cowboy's rudeness, and out of the corner of her eye she saw Stoner bristle, his hand drifting down toward his gun.

"Now just one moment, my good man…" she heard her uncle sputtering behind her.

She held up a hand behind her, hoping it would signal Uncle Frederick to subside. "Please convey my respects to your employer," she said in a voice that sounded miraculously even-tempered to her ears. "I had no idea his wife was ill. And please tell him we will be staying overnight at the hotel in town, should he wish to change his mind and come see me.''

The cowboy said nothing more, just nodded and spurred his horse into a gallop.

She was aware of the surprise on Stoner's face, but he said nothing, waiting.

"Sarah, what on earth are you thinking of?" growled her uncle. "I have no desire to pass the night in that barbarous wide spot in the road they call a town, and in any case, it's obvious Tackett has no wish to meet you."

"No, it didn't sound as if he did, uncle," she said, hating the fact that her uncle had heard her called Morgan's "fancy English mistress." "But the woman who can testify that Morgan was with her the entire night of the payroll robbery may still be living in that town, and if she is, I'm going to find her. You may return to Austin if you'd be more comfortable, uncle. I shall be all right with Celia to help me," she said, nodding in the direction of the carriage, where her servant was still sitting.

Frederick, Lord Halston, rolled his eyes heavenward. "I trust I know my duty, Sarah, even if *you* seem to have forgotten yours. As the oldest member of your family, I shall stay with you and watch over you, of course."

"Fine, uncle. Perhaps we'd better be going, then, since Mr. Tackett won't see us. And it's just as well we aren't going back to Austin today," she said, pointing to the clouds gathering to the northwest. "It looks like they're in for some rain."

"So that's what you're up to, Duchess," Stoner murmured. "Trying to find an alibi for your outlaw for that one night. But even if you do, there's all those other robberies, just like your uncle said."

"Of course you're right, Mr. Stoner," Sarah said, "but one must make a start, mustn't one?"

Sending her uncle and Celia to secure a pair of rooms in

the shabby-looking Calhoun Crossing Hotel, Sarah, accompanied by a bemused Stoner, began going door-to-door to the businesses and residences on the town's main street, interviewing anyone who would admit to ever knowing Morgan Calhoun. Everyone, it seemed, remembered Morgan Calhoun with a fondness tempered by a fascinated awe that he was now such a notorious outlaw. They wished Morgan well, they told her—they hoped he was cleared of the murder, at least, so he wouldn't have to stay in prison too many years. But no one seemed to know who the woman was that Morgan had been with when the army payroll stage was robbed—or at least, no one would admit it if they knew.

Discouraged, Sarah returned with Stoner to the hotel, which was little more than a glorified boardinghouse, just in time to eat the supper of stringy roast beef that was all that was available in the hotel dining room. By now the rainstorm had reached the town, and the rain pounding at the fly-specked windows and the accompanying rumbles of thunder seemed a fitting background for the despair that etched her heart. She had accomplished nothing today, nothing to help Morgan.

Later that evening Sarah was in her room, sitting in her chemise and pantalets while Celia brushed out Sarah's abundant blond hair and clucked over her suntanned face.

"We'll have to bathe your face with cream and lemon every day if we ever hope to restore your complexion—"

Just then they heard footsteps, followed by a knocking at her door. Thinking it was her uncle come to bid her goodnight and groan once more over the discomforts of his room, Sarah flung her dressing gown around her shoulders and bid Celia to let Lord Halston in.

To her surprise, however, it was a black woman, rather than Uncle Frederick, standing at the door.

"You the duchess?" the woman asked her without preamble. At Sarah's startled nod, she added, "I'm Daisy, Miz

Tackett's maid. She's downstairs, and she wants to talk to you."

Before a surprised Sarah could say anything, Celia spoke up behind her. "Show your mistress upstairs," she said with the arrogance of one servant to another. "Her grace was just preparing for bed, as you can see."

The black woman frowned at Celia, then said to Sarah, "Miz Tackett, she cain't climb no stairs. You want to see her, you have to come down, Miz Duchess."

"It's all right, Daisy, I'll see her," Sarah interrupted. "Just give me a moment." She was intrigued. Tackett's wife was supposedly dying.... Why had she come to see her?

Five minutes later Sarah, accompanied by Celia, who was clutching a lighted kerosene lamp, descended the rickety stairs into the darkness of the lower floor. The sight of a light flickering in the parlor led them there, and they found Daisy standing guard over a shawl-swathed figure sitting hunched over in a wheeled chair.

Sarah immediately went over to the figure. "Mrs. Tackett, I'm Sarah Challoner. It's very good of you to call on me," she said, holding out her hand.

Just then Celia succeeded in lighting the other lamp in the room, and with the increased illumination chasing the shadows from the dark room, Sarah could see that the cowboy had not exaggerated the situation. Mrs. Tackett was indeed dying. Her pearly-pale flesh was stretched tautly over protruding bones, and her eyes looked like the only part of her that still lived. It was impossible to tell whether she'd once been a beauty or not. But the hand that took Sarah's, while cool and faintly clammy, had a surprisingly strong grip.

"Call me Nora," the woman said, her voice rasping in between labored breaths. "I...I overheard...one of my husband's ranch hands...telling him you'd come today. I...I know he didn't let you in. I—I'm sorry."

"It's all right, Nora," Sarah said gently, kneeling beside

the chair so that the woman didn't have to try to speak any louder. "He said you were...you were ill, and I can well understand not wanting to meet strangers—"

"Oh, I'm ill, all right," the woman said, with a flutter of her hand indicating her shrunken frame. "It's a cancer, the doctor tells me. But Carl...that's my husband...he wouldn't have wanted me to...talk to you anyhow."

"Oh?" Sarah said, hoping to encourage her to get right to the point. It didn't look as if the woman had too much breath to spare.

Nora Tackett nodded. "I had to wait...until Carl passed out from his drinking...like he always does...of an evening. Then I had Daisy sneak me out of the house."

"Why, Nora? Why, when you're so sick?"

The woman managed a wan smile. "I'm not just sick— I'm dyin'. I might have a few days left...I can't eat nothin' now. Even Daisy's chicken broth won't stay down...." She shrugged. "I heard what happened to Morgan, how he got jailed in Austin...about the trial.... I reckon I just wanted to set things right before I go an' meet my Maker."

Behind her, Daisy moaned. "Now, don't you go talkin' that way, Miz Nora. You the finest woman—"

"Hush, Daisy." She paused, and she seemed to gather strength, for her voice was no longer whispery and hesitant. "But a few years back I could've spoken up and told the men who came to arrest Morgan that he'd been with me in my bed all night, so he couldn't have been the one who robbed the stage. It was the truth, I swear it—as God is about to be my judge."

Sarah sat back on her heels, rocked by the revelation that Tackett's wife was the very woman who had been Morgan's sweetheart, the very woman who could have given Morgan an alibi for the night the army payroll was stolen.

Behind her, the black woman began to weep.

"But I didn't tell," Nora Tackett continued, "because I

knew if I did, everyone in town would know I wasn't the innocent girl I pretended to be. Oh, I wanted Morgan Calhoun, all right—I'd even been engaged to him once—but when he came back from the war people started talkin' about how he'd been raiding with Mosby during the war, and how wild he'd been and probably still was. I—I could see it was only a matter of time before he was accused of something, and I was...afraid. I knew Carl Tackett wanted to marry me, and I wanted to be the wife of a man with land. And once Morgan fled town, it wasn't long till Carl owned the Flying C,'' Nora Tackett continued.

"But...if Morgan didn't steal the payroll and kill the stage driver, who did?'' asked Sarah.

"I don't know for sure...but I suspect it was Carl,'' Nora told her. "He and Morgan are about the same height, and both have dark hair. With a mask on, it'd be hard to tell who it was. He was the one who told the soldiers that he thought Morgan did it, while I...kept quiet, to my shame. I've paid for the wrong I did Morgan every day of my life, Sarah Challoner.... Carl Tackett is a cruel, penny-pinching man, you see, and I think he guessed I was with Morgan that night, so he's made my life hell....'' She paused, clearly out of breath.

"Mrs. Tackett, you're very good to tell me this,'' Sarah said. "But...are you—*can* you possibly testify to this, in court?'' Even as she asked the question, her eyes told her that what she was asking was impossible.

Nora Tackett shook her head, and a tear trickled down the faded cheek. "I'm sorry...I don't think I'd live through the journey. I'm in such pain...the laudanum doesn't even keep the pain down now.''

Sarah tried not to let her crushing disappointment show. To have come so close... "Then how can what you've told me—''

Nora Tackett interrupted. "I can't go testify, but I can still sign my name if you wanted to take down what I said, Duchess. Wouldn't that be almost as good?''

Sarah rubbed her hands together. "But we'd need a witness—two would be better. It can't be me, naturally, since I'm known to be...a friend of Morgan's," she added, stumbling over what to call herself to this woman who had also known Morgan intimately, so many years before.

"Go wake Marshal Stoner, Celia, and the woman that owns this place," Sarah instructed her servant. "Two will suffice as witnesses to the document."

"So that's why you asked the marshal along on this jaunt, niece," said a familiar voice behind her, startling Sarah, for she hadn't heard Uncle Frederick enter the room.

An hour and a half later, the statement providing Morgan's alibi on the night of the army payroll robbery had been signed in Nora Tackett's wavering hand and witnessed by the sleepy-eyed marshal and the proprietress of the Calhoun Crossing Hotel.

"Thank you, Mrs. Tackett," Sarah said, bending over to kiss the pale cheek. "And God bless you for what you've done. Should you even go home? Why not stay in town, so that the doctor will be nearby?" She couldn't bear to think of this woman going home to Carl Tackett, who might enact some savage reprisal if he learned what his wife had done.

Nora Tackett looked exhausted, but she managed one more smile. "You're welcome, Duchess. But don't you worry about me. Carl'll still be sleepin' off his drunk by the time I get home. Daisy won't tell him what I've done tonight—" she looked at the black woman, who nodded in staunch agreement "—and by the time he finds out, I'll likely be beyond his reach, anyway. I—I can tell you'll be good to my—to Morgan. Give him a kiss for me, would you?"

"I will," promised Sarah, touched.

"And you marry him and give him lots of pretty babies,

okay? I could have done that, you know, if I hadn't thought more of my pride than of Morgan's life.''

Now Sarah's heart was wrenched with pity. What she said was true—so much would have been different if the ill woman sitting before her had not prized her reputation and the security of her future so much. But at least she had done the right thing now, before it was too late. If only Nora Tackett's letter could be enough to clear Morgan Calhoun's name of the other charges, too!

Chapter Thirty

Three days after Sarah's journey to Calhoun Crossing the trial began, and it was now into its second day. So far, the judge had appeared unmoved as Morgan, under oath, had described how the rumors had begun upon his return to his hometown after the war, rumors that implied he had not left behind the raiding, thieving ways he had learned as one of Mosby's Rangers, rumors that over the next three years steadily discredited him as an honest man.

Army officers and the journalists who had come from as far away as St. Louis were already speculating about how soon Morgan Calhoun would hang when Matthew Quinn, his lawyer, recalled his client to the stand.

"Mr. Calhoun, did you know a lady named Miss Nora Lane?"

Just as Quinn uttered the name, a commotion erupted in the spectators' rows in the back of the courtroom. Sarah, who sat in the front of those rows with her uncle and Celia, turned in her seat and saw that a man had jumped to his feet, his face furious.

"Your Honor, I object! That was my late wife's maiden name, and I object to it being sullied by this—this outlaw!"

So poor Nora Tackett was now at peace, Sarah mused. *God*

rest her soul. And this red-faced fool was Carl Tackett, her husband. Tackett may once have resembled Morgan in his height and general build, but no more. The intervening years—and too much nightly drinking—had made him paunchy and sallow-faced. But Sarah guessed that his eyes had always been small and mean.

The district federal judge lifted his head and stared at Tackett with bored eyes. "Who are you?"

"Carl Tackett, Your Honor. Nora Lane Tackett was my wife."

"Well, Mr. Tackett, you're not an attorney, so you can't object. While I'm sympathetic to you in the loss of your wife, I'd suggest you not repeat such an outburst."

Sarah watched Tackett sit down, his face sullen.

"Mr. Quinn, you may continue," the judge said in his sonorous monotone.

"Mr. Calhoun, how was the late Nora Tackett, née Nora Lane, significant in your life when you were living in Calhoun Crossing?"

Sarah watched conflicting emotions streak across Morgan's face as he sat on the stand. He'd been astonished when she'd returned to Austin and shown him the letter, and sad, too, when he'd heard that the woman he had once loved was dying.

"Before the war she was my sweetheart," Morgan said, his voice steady and clear. "We were engaged for a time. We planned to marry after the war. Then after I came back, and the rumors started that I was rustlin' cattle and so forth, she…she came to me and broke our engagement."

"How did you feel about her then?"

Morgan kept his eye on Quinn as he answered, "I—I still loved her, but I understood. With all the whisperin' about me, with every rustled horse and missin' cow bein' blamed on me, she was afraid of bein' married to a man who'd end up behind bars—or even bein' hanged."

"But eventually the lady let you know, in no uncertain terms, that she still had a certain, um, *passion* for you, did she not?"

Once again Sarah saw Tackett leap to his feet, wild-eyed with rage. "Your Honor!" he cried.

"Mr. Tackett, sit down and shut up!" the judge shouted.

Quelled, Tackett sat again, but he continued to focus a hateful glare on Morgan.

Morgan looked down and was silent. Sarah ached for him, knowing he was torn between uttering the truth that could help him and keeping silent to avoid sullying a dead woman's reputation.

"Mr. Calhoun, I would remind you, you are under oath," Quinn said gently.

"Yes, she did," Morgan said at last.

"Objection!" cried the prosecuting attorney. "Calls for a conclusion by the witness as to the state of mind of a deceased lady, one who is obviously now unable to defend herself!"

Matthew Quinn looked unruffled. "I'll withdraw the question, and ask instead what the lady, then Miss Nora Lane, *did.* Is it true that on the night of August 8, 1869, she came to you at your house on the Flying C Ranch and offered herself to you?"

A buzz of conversation like the hum of a million wasps ensued, and the judge had to pound his gavel and shout, "Order! *Order!* Quiet, or I'll clear the courtroom!"

When silence had been restored, Morgan finally said, "Yes, she did," but he was clearly uncomfortable at the admission.

"And did you take her to your bed, where both of you stayed until morning?"

"Yes." Then Sarah saw that Morgan was looking right into her eyes, and she tried to project all the love she felt for him into hers. *It's all right, love. That's all in the past, and we're going to win this, you'll see.*

"No more questions, Your Honor," Quinn said.

Morgan was then cross-examined, but the prosecutor failed to find any holes in his story, and said in a disgusted voice as he dismissed Morgan from the stand, "As the late Mrs. Tackett's husband has expressed, it's very convenient for your case that the lady is dead."

Quinn seemed to have been waiting for that moment. He pulled out a folded piece of paper.

"Your Honor, I'd like to have this statement admitted into evidence. It was dictated by the lady herself, just a few days before her untimely death from cancer—"

At this point Tackett launched himself from his seat and ran at Quinn, his hands outstretched as if he meant to choke the Yankee defense attorney. He might have succeeded, too, if several blue-coated officers hadn't managed to catch up to him first.

"Mr. Tackett, you are now under arrest for contempt of court," the judge announced. "Take him down to the brig and let him cool off," he directed the officers who were holding the struggling Tackett.

"Your Honor, might I suggest letting him stay, though under guard, of course?" Quinn suggested. "I have a reason for my suggestion, of course, which will become apparent."

"Very well," the judge agreed, eyeing Quinn with some surprise. Tackett was forced back into his seat, but he was now flanked by soldiers, and an armed sergeant stood watching him from the nearby aisle.

Quinn now handed the paper to the judge, who put on spectacles and read it, then gave it back to the attorney.

"Mr. Quinn, why don't you just read the letter aloud?"

"I'll do that, Your Honor," Quinn said, apparently unable to resist shooting a grin at Sarah. She smiled encouragingly back.

"To whom it may concern: I, Nora Lane Tackett, aware that my death is imminent, and desiring to go to my

Maker with a clean conscience, do hereby set down an account of what happened on the night of August 8, 1869.

"On that night I went to the Flying C Ranch, and went into the ranch house, where I found its owner, Morgan Calhoun. He seemed surprised to see me, but when I informed him I had missed him, he made me welcome. I asked him to embrace me, and he obliged. As God is my witness, Morgan Calhoun had always behaved in a gentlemanly fashion toward me, even when I broke our engagement, but I went there that night with the intent of seducing him into making love to me, and that is exactly what happened. During the night Morgan Calhoun never left his house, nor did I. In fact, I was still there when the sun rose the next morning, though I departed soon after, and managed to steal back into my widowed mother's house so quietly that she never knew of my night of illicit passion.

"It was not until later that I heard of Morgan Calhoun being arrested for the murder of the stage driver and the army payroll robbery that had taken place that night, but I can swear that he could not possibly have done either crime, because he was with me the entire time. It is my decided opinion—though I cannot prove it—that the man whom I later married, Carl Tackett, was the man who robbed the stage carrying the army payroll and killed the driver, for after Morgan fled town Carl had the money to buy the ranch, which had been seized by the government, and he had never had much money before.

"In this statement I would like to apologize to Morgan Calhoun for my cowardice, which resulted in him being accused of a crime he never committed, which I believe forced him into a path he would never otherwise have taken.

"Signed with my hand this seventeenth day of October, 1872, Nora Tackett.

Witnesses present: Jackson Stoner, U.S. marshal, and Flora Wilcox, owner of the Calhoun Crossing Hotel."

There was silence for the space of several seconds as the judge and the rest of the court absorbed the impact of the written statement, and then pandemonium reigned.

Once more, the judge shouted and pounded his gavel until the court was quiet enough for Matthew Quinn to announce that he was calling Marshal Jackson Stoner to the stand.

In quick succession Quinn questioned the marshal and Flora Wilcox, and both confirmed that Nora Tackett had dictated that very statement in their presence. The prosecutor was unable to bully them into saying the statement had been made under any sort of duress, or motivated by monetary persuasion by anyone, such as Morgan Calhoun's English friend, Sarah Challoner, the Duchess of Malvern, who had been writing down the ill woman's statement as she dictated it.

Then Carl Tackett made a desperate, unsuccessful attempt to break loose from his captors. The judge pounded and shouted for five minutes on end, trying to subdue the courtroom, until at last he motioned one of the soldiers to the front of the room, and whispered into his ear. The soldier then fired his pistol once into the ceiling.

No one spoke again as plaster dust drifted lazily downward and the echo of the pistol died away. Sarah saw Morgan's lips curve upward into a grin—the first one she'd seen in days—as he gazed up at the one-inch hole in the ceiling.

"Mr. Calhoun, after hearing that…er…what I would have to call a posthumous statement from Nora Tackett, I believe I have no choice but to dismiss the case against you."

Sarah let out a most unduchesslike cheer, which earned her another grin from Morgan. Her uncle merely rolled his eyes.

"And Mr. Tackett," the judge said heavily, raising his gaze

to where Nora Tackett's husband sat, his face now livid, in the back of the courtroom, "you may now consider yourself under arrest."

Tackett exploded out of his seat in spite of the guards that flanked him.

"But, judge, you can't arrest me based on a dead woman's *opinion!*" he shouted.

The judge raised a bushy eyebrow. "Just a few minutes ago you were demanding respect for that dead woman, Tackett. Now mind you, I don't know at this point if we'll be able to prove you committed murder and robbery, but we'll see, Tackett, we'll see. Take him away, boys."

Sarah saw Tackett glare at Morgan and then herself before he was pushed out of the courtroom by the soldiers. Then the prosecutor was rising, his face indignant.

"Your Honor, may I remind the court there are several other robbery charges pending against Morgan Calhoun, charges from localities all over the West, from as near as Houston and as far away as western New Mexico Territory? I believe we are obligated to hold Mr. Calhoun until these other entities can press charges, charges that Calhoun will not so easily wriggle out of."

Sarah had known such a reminder was coming. When she had returned from Calhoun Crossing, Morgan had warned her not to be too jubilant at obtaining Nora's statement. He'd reminded her that while he had not murdered or taken the army payroll, he *had* robbed a few other stagecoaches and a handful of individuals. He appreciated Sarah's generous offer to reimburse anyone who could prove that Morgan had stolen a specific amount from him, he'd said, but no judge in the United States would be willing to dismiss robbery charges simply because of that.

"But wouldn't your heroic protection of a foreign dignitary—me, of course, and at great peril to yourself—move a

court to be lenient?'' she had asked Morgan, determined to
give him a reason for hope.

"Lenient enough to make him give me nineteen years in
prison rather than twenty,'' Morgan had retorted, his shoulders slumping. "Face it, Duchess, even if we win this first
case, I'm going to be an old man when I'm out from behind
bars. Forget me, and go back to England where you belong.''

Sarah made a desperate gesture to gain Quinn's attention,
and when she had it, she pointed to the clock on the wall,
praying he would understand.

He did, apparently, for he arose and said, "Your Honor,
as the hour is late on a Friday afternoon, may we request a
recess until the following Monday morning?''

"I'll grant that, Mr. Quinn, but your client will continue
to be held until we can communicate with the other localities
in which Mr. Calhoun has allegedly pulled robberies.''

"I understand, Your Honor.''

"Sarah, what do you have up your sleeve?'' Morgan asked
warily when she managed to reach his side at the front of the
court.

"I can't tell you, darling. At least, not yet—I don't know
if it will work,'' Sarah said. "But I've got to try, Morgan!
I've got to try!''

Chapter Thirty-One

"I'll come to visit this evening, sweetheart," she whispered as she embraced Morgan, heedless of the hundreds of curious eyes that watched the whole time. "Don't forget I love you."

"I love you, too, Sarah," he said in a voice so low only she could hear. "I just wish I knew what you were plannin', honey. It isn't anythin' illegal, is it? I'm already in enough trouble, and there ain't no use draggin' you down with me."

She laughed. "No, did you think I was going to stage a jailbreak?"

"Duchess, you've been readin' those dime novels again, haven't you?"

"No, cross my heart," she said, smiling up at him. "And don't worry, it's nothing against the law. And I can't swear that it will work. But take courage, love—I'm betting it will."

He looked as if he wanted to demand an explanation from her, but just then a pair of soldiers approached and announced that it was time for him to go back to his cell.

"All right, Sarah, what *do* you have up your sleeve?" Lord Halston, unknowingly echoing Morgan's question, asked her once Morgan had been led away.

"Wait until we may be private, uncle," Sarah said, indicating the curious spectators that surrounded them as they waded their way through the throng at the back of the court-room.

Once they were shut in the landau Lord Halston had rented for their stay in the Texas capital, though, Sarah turned eagerly to her uncle.

"Uncle, we need to stop at the telegraph office before we return to the hotel. I need to send a telegram."

"Oh?" There was a world of suspicion in Lord Halston's voice. "To whom?"

"To Queen Victoria," Sarah said, and laughed at the look of utter astonishment on her uncle's face.

"But—"

"Yes, uncle. To Her Majesty. The transatlantic cable's been in place for six years now, and I think it's time I used it," she said. "I intend to throw myself on Her Majesty's mercy and see if I can get her to help us work a miracle."

By Monday, neither Sarah nor the judge had received a telegram. A nervous Matthew Quinn was able to persuade him, though, to call another recess until Tuesday. Sarah haunted the hotel lobby, watching for the arrival of the message, heedless of the reporters trying to interview her.

By evening she was frantic. Was Victoria going to remain silent because of her subject's earlier rebelliousness?

She was still pacing the floor of her hotel room when Monday turned into Tuesday and the telegram from Queen Victoria was delivered.

"Wake my lord Halston, please," she instructed Celia.

"But...your grace, he retired hours ago," her dresser protested.

"Don't worry, Celia. I rather think he won't mind being awakened for this."

Lord Halston looked sleep-rumpled even in his brocade dressing gown.

"What is it, Sarah? You'd better have a wonderful reason to have me awakened at midnight."

"Oh, I do, uncle, I do!" she cried, handing the royal message to him and struggling against her urge to dance around the room.

He held the paper at arm's length and read.

"How did you accomplish this, niece?" he asked a moment later.

Sarah grinned as she clutched her shawl around her shoulders. "In *my* telegram, uncle, I promised to marry the Duke of Trenton if he were still available," she said. "How fortunate that he's apparently wed some other young heiress in my absence!"

"Yes…" He continued to eye her with suspicion. "You minx, you knew he intended to, didn't you?"

"Why no, actually I didn't," Sarah admitted. "It was a calculated gamble."

"Sarah, Sarah," murmured her uncle, beginning to smile in spite of himself. "You'll make an old man of me yet."

Bright and early Tuesday morning Morgan watched as Sarah seated herself at the front of the spectators' rows. Dressed in the turquoise gown he hadn't seen her wear since they left Santa Fe, Sarah Challoner was more beautiful than he had ever seen her. But it wasn't the gown, or the turquoise-and-silver necklace she wore around her neck, or even the glow of her golden hair that made the duchess lovely. It was the radiant glow on her face, the glow of a woman in love, a woman who had reason to hope that happiness was within her grasp. And there was something more, too, that only a man who loved such a woman would notice—there was a gleam of secret triumph in those eyes that were blue as a Texas sky. What did Sarah Challoner know that everyone else was about to find out?

Just then the judge entered, and all rose while he strode to his bench and settled himself, putting on his spectacles and pulling out a folded piece of paper.

"Last night something truly extraordinary happened," he began, looking out at the sea of faces over the half ovals of his lenses. "I am about to read to you a telegram, which I received from no less than the president of the United States. It concerns the fate of Morgan Calhoun." He turned so he was looking directly at Morgan then, but his face gave no clue as to the content of the message.

Morgan felt every nerve tense. Ulysses S. Grant had sent a telegram *about him?* Had he ordered him to be hanged at sunrise? Put in prison for the rest of his natural life? He looked to Sarah for a clue.

The judge's announcement had not seemed to discomfit her, though; on the contrary, her lips were beginning to curve upward to match the secret joy in her eyes.

Morgan turned back to the judge, willing him to put an end to his agony of suspense, but the judge was enjoying the drama he had created and seemed in no hurry to end it.

Finally, however, he bent his head, cleared his throat and said in a sonorous voice that had lost its bored, monotonic quality, "Ladies and gentlemen in the courtroom, I'd appreciate your silence while I read this message aloud. I'm going to leave out the word *stop* that one finds in place of periods at the end of each sentence."

His request for silence had hardly been necessary. Ever since he'd said the message was from the president it had been so quiet in the courtroom that all Morgan could hear was the pounding of his heart.

The judge opened his mouth again. "The president writes, 'I am in receipt of a telegram from none other than Her Majesty, Victoria of England, requesting that I issue a presidential pardon for the robberies committed by one Morgan Calhoun of Texas. She cites the outstanding and unselfish heroism exhibited by Mr. Calhoun in his extraordinary efforts to protect

294 The Duchess and the Desperado

the life of Her Grace the Duchess of Malvern from the determined efforts of a would-be European assassin when she was visiting our American West. As I had the pleasure of meeting her grace when she and her uncle Lord Halston attended a reception in Washington, I am doubly grateful for Mr. Calhoun's heroic actions, and am granting the pardon as requested. Judge Hanson, it is my wish that upon receipt of this telegram, you would restore Morgan Calhoun to the freedom he has so heroically earned. I would further add that Queen Victoria wishes to thank Mr. Calhoun personally, and requests that he accompany the Duchess of Malvern back to England, where he will be granted an audience with the queen at their mutual convenience.' Signed, Ulysses S. Grant, president of the United States."

The ensuing uproar was loud enough to be heard all the way back to Washington. While Morgan was still staring at the judge, certain this was only a dream and he'd wake to find he was still behind bars in the army headquarters, Sarah had run to the front of the courtroom. Now she was in his arms, laughing and crying and kissing him all at once.

"Order! *Order!*" the judge shouted, banging his gavel. *"I have not dismissed this court yet, damn it!"*

The prosecuting attorney, his face aghast, had run to the front of the courtroom, too. "But, Your Honor!" Morgan was able to hear him say. "Are we certain this telegram is indeed from the president? What if it's a hoax perpetrated by this outlaw and his—" he turned to glare at Morgan and the duchess "—and his influential foreign friends?"

"Mr. Prendergast," the judge said heavily, leaning on the desk before him with arms stiffened to support his massive bulk, and favoring the earnest young man before him with a basilisk stare, "I'm not sure why you should assume I was born yesterday. I have already sent a telegram to the president asking for confirmation, and have received it. In addition, Mr. Quinn has informed me that the Duchess of Malvern has received a telegram from Her Majesty, Queen Victoria of England, stating her royal intent to make this very request of the president. So I think you can indeed trust that this presidential pardon is the genuine article, son.''

Soundly put in his place, the red-faced prosecutor slunk back to his desk and began gathering his papers.

The uproar had died down only minimally. A cordon of soldiers held back the throng who wanted to rush to the front as Sarah had. After catching a brief glimpse of Sarah's uncle arguing with the sergeant, Morgan became aware that the judge was calling his name.

"Mr. Calhoun, it doesn't seem as if it's going to get quiet in here any time soon, and I'm loath to put another hole in the plaster to make it so. Consider yourself free, sir, but let me warn you, this pardon will not save you should you return to your former larcenous ways."

Morgan felt himself grinning. "I have no intention of that, Your Honor."

"Then get out of here, Calhoun. I believe you and the lady have things to talk about."

Morgan turned to Sarah. "I believe he's right, Duchess."

It seemed an eternity before they managed to wade through the throng of well-wishers and return to the hotel, another eternity before Sarah was able to persuade both her uncle and her servant that she needed both of them to leave her alone with Morgan.

Finally, though, Lord Halston bowed to his niece and announced his intention to seek some luncheon for himself and Celia Harris. Perhaps his niece could live on love, he said with a twinkle in his eye, but he and her servant could not.

Sarah had never felt less hungry. Her stomach, it seemed, was full of waltzing butterflies as she turned to Morgan.

"You are under no obligation to go to England, you know,

in response to Her Majesty's summons. You're an American citizen. It's up to you.''

He stood there, his face lit by the noonday sun streaming in the hotel window. His eyes had never looked so green, or so unreadable, though a small smile played about his lips.

"I know that, Duchess."

Her fingers clenched into fists at her sides. Damn the man, he wasn't going to make this easy for her, was he? Nervously she pulled her spectacles off and laid them on a nearby table. Maybe she could steel herself to say what had to be said if she couldn't see him clearly.

But she was still close enough to see the amused gleam in his eyes that told her he knew very well why she was taking them off. So she turned, pretending an inordinate interest in the view from the window she was closest to, though of course all she could see was a blur of color.

"I shall, of course, have to return to England myself. I have matters to settle with my sister. You know she had the mistaken notion that Th—that the Frenchman," she corrected herself, not wanting to say the name aloud, "was coming to America simply to meet with me and break our engagement so he was free to marry her. I can forgive her for falling under Thierry's spell, I think—Lord knows I was bedazzled by his charm myself, so much so that I wasn't really aware of what sort of young woman my sister was becoming. I need to get to know her again, before..." She couldn't finish that sentence, and allowed her voice to trail off, gripping her hands together in front of her so tightly that they hurt. *Morgan, say something! Tell me you love me! Tell me you don't want me to leave!*

He was silent.

She whirled around, determined to make an end to the uncertainty that yawned before her, as wide as a Western canyon.

"I want you to know that no matter what happens between

you and me—or what does not—''she began with a lightness she didn't feel, ''that, assuming my sister and I are able to achieve an understanding, it is my intention to renounce my title in favor of her. Kathryn will be the duchess.''

''And then what will you do, Duchess?'' he asked, his voice quiet as he came closer, his gaze locked on hers.

She shrugged. ''Then I intend to return to the United States—to Texas, to be precise—and reclaim my mare.''

He was now so close that she could not have fully extended her arm without touching him. Sarah felt her heart begin to pound as the look in those green eyes grew intense and focused.

''Reclaim your mare?'' he questioned.

''Of course. One wouldn't risk an ocean voyage for a valuable thoroughbred who's in foal,'' she said as he took another step closer. ''I shall have to find someone trustworthy to care for her while I am across the Atlantic.''

The air seemed to be sucked from the room as he put a hand on both shoulders.

''And then what are you going to do, Duchess?'' He was smiling openly now. *Damn the man!*

She closed her eyes so she could no longer see his impudent face. ''And then I am going to find the finest piece of land Texas affords, and raise the best thoroughbreds and thoroughbred-pinto crossbreds anyone has ever seen, Morgan Calhoun.''

''All by yourself, Duchess?''

She could feel his warm breath on her face, and his hands tightening on her shoulders. Opening her eyes just wide enough to see, she found his lips were but inches from hers.

''No, of course not,'' she said, opening her eyes the rest of the way. ''If you're not available, I shall just have to scour the countryside until I find another desperado knowledgeable enough about horseflesh to take on as a partner.''

He grinned down at her. ''But I *am* available, Duchess,

and I wouldn't dream of letting my wife return to England without me...."

"Your wife?" she managed to say. "But—"

"I wouldn't mind seein' the queen, either. But mainly I'm goin' with you to keep you out of trouble and wearin' your spectacles, Duchess. I love you, you know that. I can't seem to make you see that you deserve more than a cowboy who's a former rebel and outlaw, so will you marry me, Duchess?"

But she wasn't about to let him get by so easily. "Mind you, I can't pull presidential pardons out of my hat every week or so, but perhaps you'd *better* come to England with me, so I can keep you out of trouble. Even a *former* duchess's husband should be above reproach, you know."

He just grinned. "Duchess, whatever did you say in that telegram you sent to the queen? I've always heard your Victoria is kind of a starchy lady—how on earth did you convince her to intercede on behalf of a man like me?"

She allowed herself a Mona Lisa smile. Morgan didn't have to know that she had offered to marry the Duke of Trenton if Victoria required it in return for helping Morgan. And only Sarah would know how relieved the prim and proper Victoria would be that her unconventional duchess was giving up her title.

"Why, Morgan, a lady must have *some* secrets, you know." He kissed her then, a kiss so long and sweet he had to brace her to keep her upright. "We'll keep *each other* out of trouble, then," he said when he raised his head at last. "Of course, we'll be so busy raisin' kids and horses we won't have time to get into trouble, will we?"

Sarah just shook her head.

"And you'll sing only for me and those kids? Oh, and maybe a solo now and then at church?"

She nodded. "No more Fifi, the French Nightingale," she

promised. ''Kiss me again to seal the bargain, won't you? I—
I can't seem to get enough of them, now that you're free.''
He did.

* * * * *

Heat up your summer this July with

Summer Lovers

This July, bestselling authors Barbara Delinsky,
Elizabeth Lowell and Anne Stuart present three
couples with pasts that threaten their future happiness.
Can they play with fire without being burned?

FIRST, BEST AND ONLY
by Barbara Delinsky

GRANITE MAN
by Elizabeth Lowell

CHAIN OF LOVE
by Anne Stuart

Available wherever Harlequin and Silhouette books
are sold.

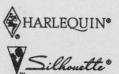

MEN at WORK

All work and no play?
Not these men!

July 1998

MACKENZIE'S LADY by Dallas Schulze

Undercover agent Mackenzie Donahue's
lazy smile and deep blue eyes were his best
weapons. But after rescuing—and kissing!—
damsel in distress Holly Reynolds, how could
he betray her by spying on her brother?

August 1998

MISS LIZ'S PASSION by Sherryl Woods

Todd Lewis could put up a building with ease,
but quailed at the sight of a classroom! Still,
Liz Gentry, his son's teacher, was no battle-ax,
and soon Todd started planning some
extracurricular activities of his own....

September 1998

A CLASSIC ENCOUNTER
by Emilie Richards

Doctor Chris Matthews was intelligent, sexy
and *very* good with his hands—which made
him all the more dangerous to single mom
Lizette St. Hilaire. So how long could she
resist Chris's special brand of TLC?

Available at your favorite retail outlet!

MEN AT WORK™

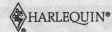 

Happy Birthday, Harlequin Historicals!

Now, after a decade of giving you the best in historical romance,
LET US TAKE YOU BACK...

to a time when damsels gave their warriors something to fight for...ladies wooed dashing dukes from behind their fans...and cowgirls lassoed the hearts of rugged ranchers!

With novels from such talented authors as

Suzanne Barclay	Margaret Moore
Cheryl Reavis	Ruth Langan
Deborah Simmons	Cheryl St.John
Susan Spencer Paul	Theresa Michaels
Merline Lovelace	Gayle Wilson

Available at your favorite retail outlet.

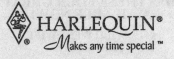

HARLEQUIN®
Makes any time special ™

Look us up on-line at: http://www.romance.net   HH10ANN

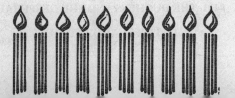

COMING NEXT MONTH FROM
HARLEQUIN HISTORICALS

- **THE TIGER'S BRIDE**
  by **Merline Lovelace,** *USA Today* bestselling author of over
  twenty-five novels
  A missionary's daughter finds adventure and romance with a
  rogue of a sea captain.
  HH #423 ISBN# 29023-3 $4.99 U.S./$5.99 CAN.

- **STORMING PARADISE**
  by **Mary McBride,** author of QUICKSILVER'S CATCH
  To keep her family's ranch, a spoiled "princess" is forced to
  marry the rugged ranch foreman, and together they find a
  special love.
  HH #424 ISBN# 29024-1 $4.99 U.S./$5.99 CAN.

- **THE COURTSHIP OF IZZY MCCREE**
  by **Ruth Langan,** author of RUBY
  After years of self-imposed seclusion, a lonely man must learn
  to put the past behind and open his heart again when a mail-
  order bride appears, courtesy of his fourteen-year-old son.
  HH #425 ISBN# 29025-X $4.99 U.S./$5.99 CAN.

- **FIRE SONG**
  by **Catherine Archer,** author of LORD SIN
  Strong feelings of passion and power ignite the hearts of many
  when a beautiful lady marries the dashing baron of a feuding
  family in place of her sister.
  HH #426 ISBN# 29026-8 $4.99 U.S./$5.99 CAN.

DON'T MISS THESE FOUR GREAT TITLES AVAILABLE NOW!

#419 WILD WEST WIFE
Susan Mallery

#420 A WARRIOR'S HONOR
Margaret Moore

#421 THE DUCHESS AND THE DESPERADO
Laurie Grant

#422 THE SHADOWED HEART
Nina Beaumont